THE
MASTER
PLAN

A Novel by

DAVID M. BROOKS

For Michael Anthony

With Love

Part One

1

Before we begin, I have a question for you.

Do you want to know when you are going to die? If I could give you a date, a day that some greater power has predetermined to be your last, assuming such a power existed, would you want to know what that date is?

Birth and Death.

These are the only two experiences that every human being will share in their existence, one of which cannot be remembered and the other of which cannot be described.

We don't choose life. Whether on purpose or by accident, it is given to us by our parents (or as many believe, "…by some greater power…"). Nor do we pick when we will die (excepting suicide, which is NOT an option for most of us). It happens when it happens, and it happens to us all sooner or later.

This is, in fact, life's only absolute guarantee. If you are born, you will someday die.

Consequently, the two most important events of our existence, our conception and our demise, are ones in which we have no say. We don't pick the family we are born into. We don't pick the year. We don't pick the country, the race, or even what sex we are to be. We just *are*. No choices. No options. Welcome to the world.

I wish I could remember the contentment of my mother's womb. I wonder what it was like taking my first breath of air as I ventured into the new world. How excited was I? How scared or confused was I? What was my first thought? We've all been there, yet none of us can answer these questions, just as none of us can describe what it will be like to die. Or if anything comes afterwards.

The only thing we fully understand about death is that it is the end of life. We do not look forward to death. We do not desire death. In fact, we fear death. We do everything in our power to delay it, push it back, or even deny it. But in the end, there is no denying death.

Out of this fear of death, as is my belief, mankind created religion. Something to take the edge off that looming threat that hangs over us from the day we are born. Religion is a genius design serving many, many purposes and objectives, not the least important of which is its promise of a life *after* death. But of course, in order to achieve this life after death, your life before death must be worthy. In other words, assuming religion is the design of early genius philosophers, its other main function is providing the masses with extra incentive and reason to use common sense and common courtesies in hopes of better maintaining civil order.

Of course, the majority of the world's population disagrees with me. Religion comes in as many different varieties as there are colors in the Ultra Deluxe Crayola box with the crayon sharpener built into the back. Yet each and every one of them subscribe to the belief of "a greater power." And in each religion, there is a promised land, a Heaven of one kind or another, an afterlife guaranteed to all who believe in its existence and abide by its laws. (And I have a bridge in Brooklyn for sale you might be interested in, too!)

At any rate, although I have never believed in any religion, per se, I have always believed that religion is the glue that holds society together. I believe the conception of religion was indeed the work of some great thinkers that were ahead of their time.

In my mind, religion is simply a man-made distraction from the inevitable death that awaits us all.

I'm not afraid of death. Maybe that's why I have never bought into the religion thing. I have always accepted the fact that I am one day going to die, and it will probably be sooner than I would have chosen if I had any say in the matter…but I don't. It will happen when it happens. I am also fine with the idea that my "life," by definition, is no more or less significant than that of a dog or a horse, or even a mosquito or a tree. We live and then we die. A speck of time; a mere split second's worth of existence compared to the billions and billions of years that time itself has existed. We don't matter one iota in the Grand Scheme of things.

I can live with that.

But back to my original question.

Would you want to know?

2

It was just a few months ago that I took a sharp corner too fast down the freeway of life and this story began, but I will need to go back a little earlier than that to properly relate to you what has happened ever *since* it began.

I have always been your average Joe, except my name is John. I describe myself as "good at everything and great at nothing." I've always felt like I was wandering through life just a little off course and slightly lost, unnoticed, unmissed, never quite finding my niche, just blending in with society and trying to keep up as best I could.

I have always been borderline reclusive. I was an only child. My parents died in a car accident three months after I graduated from high school. I live alone. I like to work alone. I like to relax alone. I have a few friends, none close…but that is what makes me comfortable. No ties. No obligations. Responsible for no one but myself. Answering to no one but myself.

I am average height, just a hair under six feet. Average weight for my size at 170. Sandy-brownish-blondish hair at collar length and parted down the right side. Brown eyes, clean shaven (I couldn't grow a beard if I tried…which I have a time or two…unsuccessfully.) I am now 33 years old, 32 when this…whatever it is (I'll let you decide) started. I've never married, though I was once engaged for a couple of years. It just never happened. We weren't ready. We eventually went our separate ways, or I guess I should say, she went her way. I never really went anywhere.

DAVID M. BROOKS

Born and raised in the Twin Cities of Minneapolis/St. Paul, never having traveled much farther than the Wisconsin Dells (about 4 hours away) in all my 32 years, I know the Twin Cities like the back of my hand and for the past five years I have been using that talent as a courier driver. I drive about 300 miles a day all over the Metro area in my little forest green Dodge Neon, picking up and delivering packages and envelopes for banks and lawyers as quickly as I possibly can without pissing off any cops. Usually, the items I am delivering are on an 'urgent-direct' or 'one-hour' service request. And of course, with a job like this, being paid a percentage of each delivery, the faster one makes one's deliveries, the more deliveries one makes, consequently, the more money one makes. I am not one that lives for money, but it does take money to live so I try to make as much as I can.

Now don't get me wrong, I am generally a very fine and courteous driver who shares the road and respects its rules. Like everything else, I am a good driver, but of course not a great one. I am a courier, after all. I've got my Mountain Dew in one hand with a forgotten Winston burning down to the filter at my knuckles while I read the newest order on my NexTel phone laying in my lap and writing down the new info in my log book with the other hand while passing semis on the Interstates at 70 miles per hour (the speed limit would be 60 at that point) and steering with my left knee. All my meals are received through little drive-thru windows and I am usually trying to figure out if they got the order right at the same time that I am deciding if I should merge ahead of or behind the car pulling a boat twice its size.

Like I said, I am not great, but despite all my multi-tasking while I drive, I do stay alert and am always aware of my surroundings. I have avoided countless potential accidents that were almost caused by even less attentive drivers than myself over the miles and years. It's my job…and I am pretty good at it.

Of course, to endure five years of driving the cities the way I do, you *must* respect the rules of the road and be very capable of forcing yourself to be patient at times when you would rather not. If you were to get caught up in the little road rage battles I witness on a daily basis, you'd drive yourself to insanity, literally.

Every day as I work, I listen to the traffic reports on the radio so that I can avoid the bumper-to-bumper chaos caused by the many rush-hour accidents that never seem to cease. I had never been involved in an accident myself…until a few months ago.

But let me ask you a few more questions first. (Have you decided on an answer for the first one yet?) Do you believe in coincidence and luck, or that everything happens for a reason? Do you believe in fate? How about Karma and "what goes around comes around?" Or do you believe that God has an agenda in mind for each of us? Many people believe that God is constantly watching over us all and judging us. And some say He lives in our hearts or maybe in our *souls* (wherever that is) and plays a hand in, helps out, or even dictates for us, the events of our lives and the decisions we make.

Or maybe you subscribe to my personal favorite, the *Domino Theory*, wherein all the experiences and trials and tribulations we live through, both good times and bad, are the direct result of a long, endless chain of events, a domino effect that began on the day of our conception. Everything we do or think or say or decide is based on things we have done and heard and said and experienced in the past. Our future is then based entirely on our past. What happens next is because of what happened before.

Or is everything pure and simple random luck?

A man is driving home from work as a little girl runs in front of his car chasing a stray cat. The man alertly veers out of the way barely missing the little girl but sideswipes a parked car on the opposite side of the street. The young woman watching it all from her window is the little girl's neighbor and the owner of the car the man just damaged. She runs outside to tell the man that he is not responsible for the damage because she had seen that he had no other choice. He helped pay for the repairs anyway and a few years later they were married and had three children of their own, the eldest of which grew up to become the medical researcher that discovers the cure to a new highly contagious and deadly influenza spreading rapidly throughout the world's population. So, in a nutshell, millions of lives were ultimately saved because a stray cat had run in front of a curious five-year-old girl 58 years earlier.

Just lucky? Pure coincidence? Or is it as many very level-headed and well-respected people would believe, "God's Will," or part of His plan?

The day started like any other. I usually wake up at 5:30 am, shower, dress, eat a bowl of Honey Combs cereal with a banana sliced up and mixed into it, and brush my teeth. At 6:00 am, I sit out in the garage with the door open and smoke my first of too many Winstons for the day while I soak in the day's weather and work on the Star Tribune's daily crossword puzzle. I like to start each day out nice and slow and relaxed, at peace with each new day, so to speak. Then I try to carry that attitude with me as I join the masses on our frantic freeway system.

By 7:00 am, I am in my car, engine running, logged onto my NexTel phone and awaiting my first order.

Again, this particular day started out as usual. I remember when my parents had been killed in an accident. I had just seen them that morning. We had breakfast, chatted about something unimportant, and went on with our day as we always did. They didn't tell me that I would never see them again. No one said "good-bye." There was no warning. They were five minutes into their fifteen-minute routine drive to the shop when a trucker who was just finishing an all-night push to make it to the Twin Cities by morning nodded off again for a quick second. But this particular second came as he plowed through a red light. This exact moment also coincided with the moment my parents were crossing the intersection on their green light. I spent a month after the accident trying to figure out what I could have done…no, what I *should* have done that morning to delay their leaving even if only for thirty seconds. A longer hug, a simple question, anything, a *million* things could have changed what had happened and they would still be alive.

A few seconds here or a few seconds there and the entire world would be a completely different place.

Now some people would say it was "their time," that it was part of God's plan. I was told countless times by relatives and concerned acquaintances that my parents were in Heaven now with God, watching over me, still helping to guide their teenage son through life. I never believed it for a second but didn't argue the point with any of them. Dead is dead. My parents didn't deserve what happened to them. They were good people. They were healthy people. They were happy people. They were in the wrong place at the wrong time. They were at the end of a long chain of events, happenstances coming together at a really, really bad time.

Pure bad luck.

My accident was not *pure* bad luck. There was plenty of bad luck that led up to my being in that place at that time, but the accident itself did not need to happen.

I had picked up a one-hour package going south out of downtown Minneapolis to Bloomington, normally a fifteen minute straight shot down I-35W. As I started up the car, on the radio, since it happened to be precisely four minutes past the hour, I heard a traffic update claiming I-35W, which I was two blocks away from and about to head for, was clogged up and not moving due to an accident. A semi-trailer had flipped over and was blocking three out of four lanes of the south bound highway. I quickly changed plans, as any good courier would, and headed for the west exit out of downtown on I-394. It would take a few more minutes to get out of the downtown mess and the trip would be a few miles longer but the time saved by going around the jam would make it all worth it.

Ten minutes later, 11:15 AM, I was finally breaking free from downtown, opening up my window, lapping in the breeze on a hot day, smiling, no traffic, no pedestrians, rapidly accelerating my little Neon towards fifty-five or sixty miles per hour and feeling pretty smart for avoiding the jam.

To my right, a Mayflower moving truck was joining me on the long ramp to I-394 from the second on-ramp out of downtown. There is a third on-ramp and then a car-pool lane off-ramp before our two lanes merge left into one lane ¾ of a mile ahead as it joins the last tributary that forms I-394 out of downtown.

The slower moving, 60-ton truck that was joining the highway slightly ahead of me put on his left blinker and proceeded to cross two lanes at once landing himself directly in front of me. No big deal. I'm a professional. This happens all the time. Every day. I know this street like the back of my hand. I move to the right-hand lane and proceed to resume my acceleration past the truck. It was at this point, as I came alongside the rear of the 70-foot semi, I noticed he was beginning to stray back into the right-hand lane, the one I was using to go around him since he had decided to commandeer the lane I had originally been in. I speed up a little more. He moves more into my lane. Now I am going sixty-five miles per hour, on the shoulder, screaming at the top of my lungs at the object that appears to be about to smash me into the side of the concrete bridge/ramp wall. And then in the next moment I am in front of the truck. A slight jerk of the steering wheel, a small, quick fishtail on loose gravel at the shoulder's edge, the wall fell away to my right and the truck was in my rear-view mirror.

Now generally, I try not to stereotype people, but I did already hold an understandable bias against truck drivers. Believe me. If a clown had killed both your parents, you would probably carry with you a personal bias against *all* clowns. Anyway, had I just hit the accelerator and put the truck driver out of my mind, I wouldn't be telling this story right now. There would be nothing to tell. But I was not able put that trucker out of my mind. In fact, he was temporarily consuming my mind.

Why?! Was he falling asleep at the wheel as the one that killed my parents had? No. I knew he wasn't falling asleep. Whether he was truly maliciously out to get little green Neons or just trying to scare the hell out of me for the fun of it, I didn't know, but I held no doubts that he had done it on purpose.

I was furious, still screaming at my rearview mirror. I don't recall exactly what I was screaming, I just remember that I did not go through the ordeal silently. Nor had I yet accelerated away from the truck. I cannot explain why I made the next decision that I made. I was not thinking clearly. Quite instantly, I said out loud to the truck in my mirror, "Don't you get it?! How would you like it if someone just pulls in front of you to deliberately slow you down?! Sure, you can dish it out, but can you take it?!"

I never hit my brakes, but I centered myself in front of the truck and took my foot off the accelerator. I started to coast, my speed dropping rapidly even without applying the brakes. I took my eyes off the truck in my rear-view mirror only for an instant to determine how much distance I had before the two lanes merged into one. There was plenty of space available for another vehicle that comes along to go around us both…good. Back to the rear-view mirror and the task at hand, slowing down a 60-ton truck with my 1-ton Neon.

As I returned my gaze to my mirror, only a second or two from the previous look, I noticed that the truck driver was *not* noticing me. I only had time to *think* about going for the accelerator again as I watched the truck's grill coming through the back of my car. I was lurched forward, now laying flat on my back still in the driver's seat.

Out of the corner of my eye, I saw the truck roll slowly past me on my left. Then I noticed the street light pole outside my other widow was not moving so I knew that my car had stopped rolling. Still on my back, I felt my way to the gear shift and slid it into park. I couldn't tell if I was hurt or not. I didn't feel hurt, but at the same time, in the instant that I saw the truck's grill tattooing the rear of my car through my mirror, I had already accepted the fact that I was probably going to be hurt, if not killed.

I closed my eyes and concentrated on my breathing. I *was* breathing and that had to be a good thing. It was hard to think, but at least I could breathe. I figured the police would be along pretty soon. I didn't know if the truck was still there or not, but I was fairly certain that *I* was still there…somehow. For now, that was good enough. Leaving my eyes closed, not wanting to move until necessary, I tried to empty my mind, and I waited.

THE MASTER PLAN

Let's go back in time again for just a moment. Two years ago, more than a year and a half before the accident, the little Honda I used to scoot around town with was pushing 250,000 miles on the odometer and was no longer reliable. I need reliable transportation in my line of work so I went car shopping. I custom ordered a new Neon with as many luxuries as I could fit into the thing, cheap but loaded. I spend almost as many hours in my car every day as I do at my home so it was worth the three-week wait to receive my special factory order.

I got a call two and a half weeks later saying my car was ready which was a good thing. My Honda was definitely on its last legs. I sputtered into the dealership to complete the transaction, to trade in my old workhorse for my brand-new steed only to discover they had made one very serious mistake with my order. My car was a five-speed stick. I had ordered an automatic. I already drive with three hands as is. Add a stick to the mix and I would need a fourth. I didn't have a fourth.

In the end, my very apologetic salesman had set me up in another Neon they had on the lot that was pretty close to what I had ordered. Someone else had ordered this one and then lost his job and decided not to buy it. It was green instead of blue and didn't have the CD player I had ordered or the rear windshield wiper. And it had a trailer hitch attached to it. I got another thousand bucks knocked off for the inconvenience and rolled away thinking tapes were cheaper than CD's anyway. No biggie.

Now leap ahead again to a few months ago and imagine what happens to a little Dodge Neon traveling about thirty-five miles per hour when a 60-ton truck traveling about sixty miles per hour runs right up its back not even aware that it is there. Normally, the results of a meeting of this ilk would be a flattened mass of metal beneath a relatively undamaged truck. (I really, REALLY have no idea what the hell I thought I was doing when deciding to slow down that truck!)

I got lucky. But I didn't get lucky at that point. It was incredibly *un*lucky for me that the trucker who had just tried to run me off the road for kicks was busy looking at his wife in the passenger seat "…he be thinkin' twice 'fore he try go 'round *me* nex' time…" and had no idea I was still directly in front of him. But rather, I got lucky sixteen months earlier when Dodge screwed up my order. I got lucky that some other poor soul got fired from his job and couldn't pay for his new car. I got incredibly lucky that this guy had a small boat he had wanted to tow with his new Neon that he never bought. Ultimately, it was that hitch that saved my life more than a year and a half later.

The car was totaled. The rear end was in my back seat next to my head where I lay waiting for the Highway Patrol to arrive on the scene. The steel hitch with ball and bar had soaked up the initial impact and deflected the truck's hit. Despite the fact that my car was now four feet shorter than it had been that morning, I had *bounced* off the truck instead of just crumpling beneath it. I didn't know it then as I lay there with my eyes closed, perfectly content at the moment with the feeling of air flowing into my lungs, but it had been the hitch that made that feeling possible.

Just lucky? Or is it all part of a plan?

We're getting to that.

I'm not sure how long it was, I would have guessed just a few minutes, but it had obviously been longer than that. There were people in all my windows around the car. They were all looking at me. The sun was bright on my eyes, too bright. I tasted blood on my lips. I squinted against the sun. I heard someone call out, "They're here!" and a woman leaned in over me through my open window. She spoke softly, almost in a whisper, but I could hear her just fine.

"Don't move," she said. "Help is here." Her deep blue eyes were inches from my own. They looked caring and calming. I was willing to do whatever she told me, so I remained still and tried to focus on her soporific eyes. I could have gone swimming in those eyes. Cool, deep, beautiful, blue eyes. I smiled and she smiled back. I felt her hand run down my left cheek as I gazed into her depth and a thought *(84:32)* more like a memory raced through my mind.

I knew I had been in an accident. I was still a bit fuzzy on the details, but I knew that I was in my car and that it had just been hit by a truck because I had made a really stupid decision. I was in no pain but could tell something wasn't right. *(84:32)* flashed in my mind again like a memory, as though I was supposed to know what it meant, but I didn't, and I ignored it. The woman was backing out of the car window now and that concerned me more than the meaning of some random numbers at that point.

"Don't move," she repeated as she pulled her soft, warm hand away from my cheek and backed out of the window.

For an instant, as her face disappeared from my peripheral vision, I attempted to recall the memory that had just unsuccessfully tried to steal my attention from the comfort of the woman's eyes, but it had escaped me. My brain still felt fuzzy. Thinking at all was still difficult. Two new faces were now leaning in my window. One of them repeated the instruction the woman had given me, "Don't move." I just blinked at him in response. I didn't feel like trying to talk yet. I felt no reason not to do as he said, but I had liked looking into the woman's eyes more than his. *At least he doesn't have to give me mouth to mouth,* I remember thinking.

Then the new guy with the boring business-like eyes pulled out a huge needle and tested it. I hate needles. He must have seen a little panic in my eyes because he signaled to the other guy who leaned in farther and held me still with two large, incredibly soft hands, one pressing hard on my chest, the other with his palm firmly against my forehead. When the second guy leaned in and placed his hands on me, his face was in front of mine as the woman's had been moments before, blocking my view of the guy with the needle. I braced myself for the prick but could only think (56:6).

Just as I was trying to figure out what the hell 56:6 meant, I felt the prick in my left arm. The man's hands relaxed against my chest and forehead and his eyes suddenly started to actually swim on his face. I may have tried to ask him how he did that with his eyes but I knew the prick in my left arm was probably why the guy's face was melting and ultimately, I decided to simply shut my eyes and go with the flow. I didn't want to have to think. It was far too difficult to think.

A moment later, the morphine took hold and I was out.

3

The surgeon who removed the thin metal rod from my head said I had been very "lucky." I am required to carry safety triangles in my car, along with a fire extinguisher and first aid kit since I drive professionally. The impact of the truck shattered the safety triangles along with just about everything else in my trunk. As my driver's seat broke on impact and fell backwards, a small metal rod, part of the safety triangles, no thicker than a wire hanger in your closet, broke free and shot forward. It pierced straight through the head rest of my seat, and then through the base of my skull at the back of my neck. The rod is twelve inches long. One end was still buried in the head rest. Two inches of the other end had been protruding from my head, just above and in front of my right ear. This is why all the people had been staring at me when I awoke at the scene. I had probably looked like one of those insects pinned through the side of the head to a collection board.

I don't know how the paramedics managed to get me free from the car and to the hospital. I'm not sure I want to know. I never asked. The morphine worked, and then they did their job well… that was always good enough for me. What I do know is that I was indeed very "lucky," for lack of a better word. The force of the collision had fired the rod cleanly through the base of my neck aiming north and had pierced, rather than shattered, my skull as it exited. It had pressed up against, but not damaged, the Cerebellum located at the bottom rear of the brain. Had that been damaged, according to my doctor, I might have lost movement capabilities in random parts of my body temporarily or permanently. He said that the rod had missed vital areas of the brain, as far as he could tell, and it appeared to have mostly traveled through the Periaqueductal Gray, the gray matter that surrounds the Cerebral Aqueduct.

I didn't understand most of what he told me, except the part about my returning to a normal life.

But of course, that never happened.

In simple terms, once in the operation room, they went in and repaired damaged brain tissue as best they could, scanned the brain for skull slivers, cleaned up fluid leakage and sewed it all back up. As long as my skull had not fractured, they seemed to think it was okay that there was still a small hole in it. They assured me that my head would heal up and nothing could seep into the hole. I was not real comfortable with the idea of a hole in my skull, but he explained that it doesn't surround the entire brain anyway, it is only protection for the brain and my skull still supplied my brain with quite sufficient protection.

He also warned that I might experience a few "brain farts." My use of the phrase, not his. I don't remember what he called it exactly, but he said I might temporarily forget things like how to add or spell or where I live. Or I might experience occasional spasmodic sensations or tics. He told me to let him know if anything like that did occur, that they were still learning what specific parts of the brain controlled.

I assured him I would, though I knew I would not unless I felt it was something that required his attention. I just wanted out. The fact is, I was already experiencing some weird "brain farts" but they weren't anything I couldn't handle. Plus, I was still a little pissed that he had left the hole up there in the first place. I mean, if you're already in there, why not patch it up? But I guess they know best. Certainly more than I do about such things.

I just wanted to go home to the house I had lived in my entire life. My only injury had been the rod through the head and they had apparently done all they were going to do about that, so I talked him into releasing me to my home for the remainder of my recovery period. I promised him that my "best friend" would pick me up and move in with me until I could handle everything myself.

The doctor agreed, instructed me to schedule a follow-up with the nurse on my way out for sometime in the next three to five days, wrote out a prescription for pain and shook my hand.

(*63:137*) came to mind, but I thanked him instead and called my old boss to order a pick up and delivery…on a direct service. I was told it would be no charge and a driver I had never seen before showed up twenty minutes later at the hospital's emergency entrance and I was on my way home. I told the driver when he dropped me off to make sure he thanks Al for me for the ride and to let him know that I was done.

"You quitting just 'cause of the car?" he asked "Insurance will buy you a new one, man. You can probably get whatever you want. Wish someone would rear end this piece of shit. Man, I could use a new car."

"Just tell him I'm done," I said. I thanked him again for the ride and closed the door before he could make any more suggestions. I fully intended to get a new car out of the deal. No question about that. But I was done driving for a living. I didn't know what I was going to do next, and I wasn't harboring any new found fears of driving, maybe a more intense hatred for truck drivers, but I just felt it was time for a change.

I unlocked the front door to my house and instantly felt better as I stepped over the threshold. These were the walls that I had grown up with. These were the rooms that had comforted me when my parents had met with their untimely deaths. Here was the furniture that would get me through this ordeal, and the familiar sheets and personally shaped and molded pillows looked like the perfect place to start. Sleep came quickly.

I had left the hospital about a week before my doctor's original estimated departure time but I was already pretty well able to handle the daily necessities myself. The first sleep in my own bed upon returning from the hospital was a long and restful one. I awoke feeling much stronger and ready to start thinking about what comes next.

Money was not an issue for me but only because I had always kept working. My parents had owned a little pizzeria inside the Southdale Mall in Edina. They usually had only three or four part-time employees to help them through the lunch rush and on weekends, but for the most part, Dad made the pizzas and Mom took the orders and filled the drinks. The pizza was served by the slice on paper plates shaped in a wedge with paper napkins and plastic knives and forks available. The customers took their order to a shared eating area of the Mall's Food Court. There were no tables to clear and no dishes and silverware to collect and wash. Mall employees roamed the eating area throwing away the trash left behind by the inconsiderate patrons and wiping the tables of the messy ones. A simple operation, nothing more than needed to provide a basic, yet desired service. Business had dropped quite measurably a few years earlier after the world-famous Mall of America moved in just six miles down the road in Bloomington, but they still had enough business to keep themselves from ever getting bored. It wasn't making them rich, but their bills were paid, they owned their home outright, they enjoyed their work as well as each other, and they had no complaints in life whatsoever.

It had always been assumed, and with no argument from me, that Pizza Time Pizzeria would one day be mine. I had been helping out in the shop since I was old enough to walk. Once out of high school, I had already begun to take on more and more responsibility and had been working full-time with my parents. I took Tuesdays and Wednesdays off. It had been on a Wednesday that they had died.

I lost the desire to run the family business once the family was so abruptly disrupted and sold the place to the first offer. That and a small cash sum my parents had saved for the retirement they never reached created a decent sized nest egg for myself for emergencies. Not enough to live on for too long by itself, but as long as I had an income of any kind, it was enough that money should never be a problem. The house was paid for, a small, cozy, two-bedroom, one story with attached garage, so I had no rent to pay. I knew I would need to find a new job, but I was in no real hurry. I'd always thought being a blackjack dealer at the casino would be kind of cool. They make you pay for a class for a few weeks before you can start the job, but like I said, I was in no hurry. I decided that once I was sure I was fully recovered from the accident, I'd run down to Mystic Lake and inquire about their career opportunities as a dealer.

I had already come to this conclusion even before rolling out of bed that first morning home after the accident and was pleased that a decision had come so easily. I moved into the bathroom, again taking great pleasure in the usually taken-for-granted comfort and familiarity of this room compared to the generic, overly white and impersonal hospital bathroom, and became momentarily lost when I looked at the *un*familiar face in the mirror.

It had been three and a half weeks since the hospital barber had prepped my head for surgery and with the exception of the two small sterile pads covering the surgeon's handiwork, it was still as smooth as a baby's butt. My chin, on the other hand, was sprouting thick dark stubble all over my lower face. I couldn't remember the last time I had shaved so I opened up a new disposable razor and smoothed out that area too.

It didn't help much. I still didn't look like the me that I remembered with hair. I decided I couldn't go job hunting anyway until I had some of my hair back. It wasn't a vanity issue; I just didn't want to have to explain it. And besides, a little vacation between careers would probably be a good thing. I could wait. I had scheduled my return to the hospital for the check-up and bandage dressing for four days away. Until then, I just needed to relax and regain all my strength.

The next morning, after rolling out of bed and into the bathroom for my morning rituals, I again noticed a rather thick growth of stubble on my chin, and I had sideburns. I had never had sideburns before. Nor had I ever shaved two days in a row. The sideburn on the right side seemed to be growing where the scar from the surgeon's fiddling about had occurred. I decided to leave it be for now. See what happens. Wait for my hair.

Friday morning, the time I had scheduled for my check-up, had arrived, but so far, my old hair had not. I was also now sporting the beginnings of the first beard of my life. It was still noticeably in the early stages of growth, but that would be one or two stages farther than I had ever achieved before the accident. It was growing in darker than my old head of hair had been, too. It was at that moment, as I looked at the reflection of the stranger staring back at me from my mirror, I understood that my old hair was not going to be coming back. The stranger in my mirror was the *new* me…for my *new* life. But the look was so different, it was hard to get used to. Had I understood then how much different my life was about to become, I might have thought my strange new look to be more appropriate. But one couldn't possibly know that…

…could they?

4

It's healing up very nicely," Dr. Getz told me.

"How much longer do I need these band-aids on my head and neck?" I asked him.

"Keep replacing them each day for just a little longer. I want to look at you again in three days and I'd bet we can leave them off after that visit."

He moved around from my side where he had been examining his work to face me. "Any concerns? Problems? Anything feeling slightly off or unusual since the accident?" he asked.

"Nope," I replied a little too quickly. So I was growing hair where I couldn't before and couldn't where I could before. It was obviously because of something accident related, probably even brain damage related, but I wasn't about to become their guinea pig to find out. "Thought I'd stick with the bald look for a while though," I said, noticing he appeared to be focusing on my bald head. (But what else would he be looking at. That *is* what he had been working on.)

I don't know if he sensed I was lying or was looking for the razor marks or just further admiring his handiwork but he reached up and rubbed his finger along my head just above the old hairline. I watched his face, hoping he would be satisfied with my explanation. (*63:137*) came to mind just as plain as the nose on my face, you know, just out of sight but you still know it is there.

"Well," he said, pulling his hand back away from my head, "make the appointment with Katelynn on your way out and I'll see you again in three days."

"Yes, sir. Thank you," I said and turned to walk out.

63:137. Another brain fart, I thought as I left the room and headed for the counter in the waiting room. I hadn't wanted to tell the doctor about my hair, and I *really* didn't want to tell him about this. It was nothing anyway. Random numbers entering my head like freshly remembered names of old forgotten friends. I didn't need them probing around my brain to figure out why. I didn't even need to know what the numbers meant. If this was going to be the worst of the aftershocks from the accident, a hair reversal and random numbers floating around my head, I could live with that.

I stepped up to the nurses' reception desk to make my appointment with Katelynn as instructed. I liked Katelynn. She was very pretty, always smiling. Long dark hair, mysterious, bright eyes. She had come in to change the bandages on my head a few times before I had left the hospital. I always had to make a point of looking anywhere but into her eyes as she would wrap up my head. I was afraid I would get a hard-on if I were to look into those deep blue eyes while she gently caressed my crown. That would have been embarrassing.

"Do we need to set you up for another?" Katelynn asked as I approached.

"Just one more, I think," I said.

"I like the bald look on you," she said. "It's really you. You planning on keeping the chrome dome?"

I didn't know if she was just being nice or if she meant it, but either way it sounded good coming from her. "Thanks," I responded. "Yeah. I thought I'd keep it clean for a while, anyway. See if I can get used to it. You really think it looks okay?"

"It does," she said with a smile. "When does he want you back?"

"Oh, um, he said…three days," I stuttered. My mind was still back on the "it does" part of her reply. If such a pretty woman right around my own age truly thought I looked okay bald, then I figured I could get used to the face that looked back at me in the mirror eventually.

I watched her long, nimble fingers pluck off an appointment card from a stack of cards and write down the date three days away.

"How's eight-thirty AM on the eighteenth?" she asked, looking up at me again.

"That'll work."

She wrote down the time and held out the card. "We'll see you at eight-thirty then."

I took the card from her hand and said, "29:29...I mean… yes…see you then," and quickly turned away towards the door.

What the hell was that? I thought as I left. *Just another brain fart, I guess.* But this time the thought had actually made it to my lips before I had known I was thinking it. It made no more or less sense than the other seemingly random numbers that had infiltrated my thoughts at various times. It was totally and completely meaningless to me. In fact, before today, I hadn't even experienced any of these weird numbered thoughts for a few days and had almost all but forgotten the few times it had happened. It was the hair phenomenon that had stolen my attention.

I left the hospital and hailed a cab for the ride home. I hadn't been car shopping yet, but then I didn't need to go out too much. It could wait until I was ready to start looking for a new job. I got into the cab and gave the driver my address. I told him it would take us twenty minutes to get there and then instructed him of the route I expected him to take. He leered at me a bit in the mirror and that was fine. I knew we wouldn't have to chit-chat now for twenty minutes.

I leaned back and settled into my thoughts for the ride home. *29:29. And what was the other one again? 63:137? I think that was it. 29:29. 63:137. Nothing.* For the life of me (just a figure of speech) I couldn't imagine what the numbers stood for or meant, or why they were popping into my head for no apparent reason. I decided I'd rather think of Katelynn's eyes again and they, along with her long dark hair and sweet smile, got me the rest of the way home, seventeen and a half minutes after we had left the hospital. I tipped the silent, compliant cabbie an extra ten spot and went inside.

The rest of that day and the next two were once again eventless. I spent the days as anyone would recovering from major surgery--played a lot of solitaire, did a lot of crossword puzzles, and I stared a lot at the new face in the mirror. In spite of Katelynn's kind words, it still didn't look like me. But it was obvious that my hair had chosen to abandon the mountain top and settle in the valley. There was still not a stubble, not even a single strand of hair peaking out of my smooth dome up top. Yet I was trimming my new beard and sideburns on a daily basis.

I had practiced my answers and even shaved my head a couple of times for effect, just in case. I really didn't want Dr. Getz probing around my brain. I didn't actually think they would open up my head again if I let them in on this current phenomenon, but they would still want to do tests and who knows what else. While some people might thrive on that kind of attention, I am not one of them. I have always just wanted to do my time as quietly and comfortably as possible. Live and let live.

I woke up and showered on the morning of what I figured to be my final return to the hospital. I didn't bother replacing the band-aids this time. I was sure Dr. Getz would concur. I spread shaving cream over my head but then just washed it off. It was the smell that I was after. I called for a cab and was told it would be about 45 minutes before one could get to me at that time of the morning. I told the dispatcher that would be perfect and took the morning's Star Tribune crossword puzzle out to the garage to wait.

"Are you okay?"

It was just after eight. My appointment was for eight-thirty. I had called the cab a little before seven knowing they'd be busy with the morning commuters, trying to make sure I wouldn't be late.

"I was just trying to call you," Katelynn said. Her eyes were red and teary. She sniffled as she spoke. It was very obvious well before I approached her counter that she had been crying. "We will need to reschedule you to see Dr. James."

That meant I probably wouldn't need to pull out my rehearsed responses, but obviously the cause for this switch was not going to be good news.

"Are you okay?" I repeated. I have a real soft spot for tears, especially ones falling from such a pretty face. "What's happened? Is Dr. Getz okay?"

"We just found out that Dr. Getz died of a heart attack this morning shortly after waking up. He was just getting ready for work in his bathroom. His wife called for the ambulance but he had died before they even arrived." She paused, sniffed, and trying to remain professional, she asked, "When would you like to reschedule for?"

"Oh, no." I said, ignoring her question. "I'm so sorry." What can you say? So, I asked Katelynn for the third time, not yet getting a direct answer to the question, "Are you going to be okay?"

"Yes," she said with a deep breath. "I'm fine. It's just so sudden…and his wife…I feel so badly for her."

"I don't think I really need to reschedule." I looked left and pointed to the area now hidden deeply in sideburn action along the right side of my head. "I think he was just going to say we were done anyway."

"Well," Katelynn sniffed, "you should still probably have Dr. James confirm that. But under the circumstances …" She stood and stepped around the counter getting a closer look at the rear of my head where the rod had entered. Only a red scar remained. "…you're probably right. It does look practically healed to me." She smiled. Such a pretty, sad smile.

"Well, then, um, I guess I should go," I said reluctantly. I hated to leave her here in her tears, but I mean really, what could I do? She was going to be having a tough enough time repeating the sad news to all his patients as she tried to reschedule the day's appointments. She didn't need me hanging around. She was still standing next to me and I instinctively reached out my hand as I said, "I'm really sorry for the news."

I don't know if Katelynn thought I was holding out my hand for an invitation or if she just really needed a hug after receiving the news but she ignored the gesture to shake hands and stepped closer, into my arms, wrapping her own tightly around my back. I returned the hug and after a very long few seconds she stepped back and looked at me through eyes newly filled with fresh tears.

Our hands were clasped in front of us. She smiled bashfully. "Thanks," she said. "I needed that." She took a deep breath. "Okay," she let go of my hands, "back to work. Thank you, John."

"Yeah," I said, ignoring the thought that was actually pushing its way to the front of my mind. *(29:29)* "Take care, Katelynn. Give my best wishes to his wife for me."

I turned and left the building.

5

I didn't call for a cab. Something was eating away at the edges of my brain. I felt like I was being asked a simple question and I couldn't come up with the simple answer, nor could I decipher the question. But there it was, whatever it was, tugging at the corners of my mind.

I left the hospital and started walking south, the general direction towards home. It's nine or ten miles from the hospital in St. Louis Park to Bloomington and I hadn't actually planned to hike the entire journey home. I just kept putting one foot in front of the other, head bent down, watching the hypnotic repetition of my steps, thinking about Dr. Getz, Katelynn, 29:29, 63:137, hair, hole in skull, goddamn truck drivers…and when I looked up again, I was turning down my street, the property line to my home just a few more paces away.

Sanctuary.

I didn't come to any conclusions during my hypnotic trek home. I entered the house just as baffled by everything as I had been when I turned away from Katelynn at the hospital some four and a half hours earlier. *It just doesn't matter*, I tried to convince myself. But I knew different. *I really, truly couldn't care less how or why these numbers are floating to the surface of my mind. Nor do I care what the numbers mean.* But I knew that they did mean something. And the fact that I knew they meant something, meant I also knew, deep inside, that I would not be able to fully let it go until I understood what these mystery numbers actually meant.

When will I ever learn to leave well enough alone?

.Curiosity killed the cat, I reminded myself. *Ignorance is bliss*, I tried to convince myself. *But knowledge is power*, I scolded back.

The battle within the brain was on. Did I care? Could I not? I knew the answer to these questions but fought them anyway. I didn't want to care but I did and I couldn't not. It's how I'm wired. I couldn't ignore the nagging questions my seemingly independent mind was hurling at me ninety miles per hour any better than a mosquito can resist that heavenly blue light beckoning it to come pay it a visit. I didn't know if I would be able to discover the answers I was seeking, but I knew I would never feel right again until I tried.

The battle didn't take long. I could easily understand why the cat died. I didn't know where to look for the answers, and I wasn't even sure exactly what the questions were, but I knew there was no turning away from them.

I've always hated cats.

First thing I did was try to think of a number.
Any number.
Pick a number.
Nothing came to mind so I tried to recall all the numbers I had once thought of. There had been the two recent ones at the hospital, of course, 29:29 and 63:137. I had to think hard to recall any others. I hadn't been going out much. There were a couple of other times while in the hospital. My aunt had visited

a few times. One time when she was there, I had thought of a pair, 98:1, I think it was. And there was that other nurse that changed my bandages, not Katelynn, but the older one. I think her number was 79:308, or something like that.

All thoughts suddenly came to a screeching halt. *Her* number. That was what I had called it. This was the first time I had associated the numbers directly with the person I was with at the time and I thought about this new revelation for a moment. I was just beginning to think that maybe I only thought of the numbers when at the hospital for some unexplainable reason, but then I remembered the accident itself. That had been the first time I had experienced these "brain farts." It wasn't the hospital. It was definitely the people. I would have rather it to have been the hospital. I could avoid hospitals if I had to. Avoiding people, even though that was already almost considered a hobby of mine, was still quite a bit harder, not to mention not exactly desirable even despite my reclusive tendencies. I don't hate people. I'm just not a big fan, so to speak. No. I wouldn't be trying to avoid people altogether. That would never do.

So now the question was why? And of course, why sometimes not? Why not the cab driver? Why the older nurse but not Katelynn in my hospital room? Why Katelynn in the reception room and not the other patients in the waiting room? Was it even Katelynn's number? Yes. The second time, this morning, there had been no waiting patients. We had been alone in the room. 29:29 belonged to Katelynn. 63:137 belonged to Dr. Getz. Maybe the cab driver didn't have a number. Maybe only some people have numbers. I went to the mirror and looked for my own number and although the face I studied was still that of a stranger's to me, no numbers came to mind.

I decided I needed more Mountain Dew and a carton of cigarettes if I was going to try to follow my mind down the road it was preparing to traverse and headed for the Kwik Trip convenience store a couple of blocks down the street. I also grabbed a carton of milk and a banana for tomorrow's breakfast and went to the counter to pay for my goods.

"That'll be fifty-six fifty-three. Did you want a bag?"

"No, thank you. I can manage this." I held out three twenties for the teen-aged cashier. She took the bills from my hand and I began to study her, searching for her number, if she had one. But again, as at home, nothing new was coming to mind. I was just about to start getting early frustration pangs in my gut when she turned toward me and placed the change in the palm of my outstretched hand. (*88:8*) knocked me in the side of the head like a freight train. Right out of nowhere. Bam! Plain as day. I stood there staring at her with my hand still held out, the change sitting unnoticed in my palm.

"It's all there," she said a little hesitantly. "You okay?"

"Yes, sorry," I said, reeling back in my arm. "Do the numbers 88:8 mean anything to you, by any chance?"

Jill, who was also a trainee apparently going solo, according to her name tag, seemed to relax a little and smiled bashfully, "No. Should they?"

"You're sure?" I asked.

She assured me she was sure she had no idea what 88:8 was supposed to mean. I didn't tell her it was apparently her own personal set of numbers. She didn't ask why I wanted to know, not that I would have told her if she had. I thanked her and turned towards home.

It only took one block of the walk home for me to figure out that it had been Jill's touch that had inspired her number.

I had been watching her from the moment I had stepped up to the counter. She hadn't touched my hand when I gave her the twenties, but she did touch me when laying the bills and coins into my palm giving me change. It was at that moment, the very instant she had touched me, that her numbers entered my mind.

Okay. Now we're getting somewhere. Now I have something to work with. I could avoid touching people. I could wear gloves. I could silence the brain farts. Now *this* was exciting. *But what do the numbers mean?* I don't care what the numbers mean. *But what could they possibly mean?* What does it matter? It doesn't matter. *What could it hurt to know what they mean before you say good-bye forever to the feel of another human being's skin?* It doesn't matter. *You want to know, John.* No, I do NOT want to know anything. I just want to become a blackjack dealer and silently watch the entertaining people lose all their money. Nobody is even allowed to touch the dealer. Perfect job for me. *But what do they mean?*

Have I told you how much I hate cats?

I opened up the garage door, took a seat in my favorite chair to sit and think in, and lit up a Winston. The day was a perfect, sunny, summer day. I don't like perfect days. Nothing to look at. Nothing to lose your thoughts in. No rhythmic sounds from nature to help with the hypnotic thoughtful trances I am so susceptible to, and enjoy. I picked up the morning's crossword puzzle I had left on the tool counter when the cab had arrived. It had been fairly easy that morning and I only had two squares left unfilled. Something, or someone inside me, (that would be that other me, you know, the cat-like curious one) was not allowing me to concentrate on the final clues. I was reading, "Oriental nurse maid" with my eyes, but could only think, *Who gets a number?*

At that moment, the mail truck pulled up along the row of mailboxes on the street in front of the house. Without hesitation or forethought, I raced down to the street as he inched forward to my box. "Howdy," I called out as I trotted up next to his truck. "Got anything for me today?"

It was a silly question. I get mail everyday. 80% of it is tossed without ever being opened, but I get mail every day. Today proved no exception. I reached for the mail he was offering me and somewhat clumsily on purpose grabbed half his outstretched hand along with the mail and braced myself.

Nada.

"Can I have my hand back?" the mailman politely asked.

I was still looking at his hand in mine. I looked up at his face. I couldn't see his eyes. It was a bright day. He had on a pair of mirrored sunglasses. All I could see was the distorted face of some weird-looking bald guy starring back at me out of each lens. I let go of his hand. "Sorry," I said. "Thank you. Have a good day." A conditioned response to customers I did business with from my days behind a pizza counter that still hung with me years later.

It had only been for a second or two, but still long enough for the mailman to probably begin to question my sexual preference. He would likely get my mail into my box first when he pulls up to the row in front of the house from now on. Oh well.

But why had he been numberless? Or maybe some people's numbers I couldn't read. Or maybe…maybe…

…it was his sunglasses.

A light bulb went on inside my head. A voice from inside me called out, *BINGO*! I had avoided Katelynn's eyes in the hospital room, but hadn't felt the need to avoid the other nurse's eyes. The cabbie took his money over the car seat, he hadn't been facing me when our hands had briefly touched. And the mailman had been wearing mirrored sunglasses.

I needed another test subject. I closed the garage door and headed back down the street to Kwik Trip. There was an endless stream of people flowing in and out of that place. It would work fine as my temporary lab.

Ten minutes later, I had the next piece of the puzzle falling neatly into place. It was the eyes. AND the touch. If my skin came in contact with someone else's skin *and* I was able to look into their eyes at the moment of the contact, a number came to mind. Without the eye contact, no number. Without the skin contact, no number. But with both, without fail, a number did indeed surface each and every time.

One had been an old man who pulled up next to the gas pumps and appeared to struggle a bit to get out of his car. I walked over to him and offered a hand. He took it gratefully enough, "Thank you, son. These legs just can't lift the weight the way they used to."

I pulled him out of the driver's seat and he stood next to me as I continued to hold his hand.

"Thank you," he said again, forcibly pulling his hand free of mine.

"You're welcome, sir," I responded. And then asked, "Do the numbers 82:123 mean anything to you?"

"Well," the old man chuckled, "not unless you count the fact that I am 82 years old and would love to live to be 123. But I don't think that's what you mean."

"I'm not sure what I mean," I said to the man. "But thanks."

I walked back into the store and looked again at the teen-aged cashier. She noticed me coming back into the shop for the third time now in fifteen minutes and that I was once again looking her way. I think my continued presence was making her a little nervous. Her number had been the first time, and still was the second time when I bought the 3 Musketeers candy bar a few minutes ago, 88:8. One thing I knew for sure, however, she was a long way from 88 years old and well past 8 years old. But that would still have only explained one of the two numbers. It was always two numbers. They were together, I could tell, but I could not yet explain why.

I pounced on several other people as politely as possible before going home and allowing the young cashier to relax. I touched a couple while looking into their eyes and a couple while not looking. The results of the experiment were in and undeniable. There were two contact points, touch and the eyes. Together they created a thought that only I was aware of, a pair of numbers that only I knew existed.

Wonderful.

Walking home after leaving Kwik Trip with my new found revelations running amok inside my head, I took a detour to the Walgreen's drug store, a block out of the way. I picked up a box of disposable rubber gloves and a pair of thick, furry winter gloves at a great summertime discount. I pretended to be interested in the Sports Illustrated magazine cover at the counter as the cashier was preparing to give me my change. After a moment of slight rudeness on my part for ignoring her outstretched hand, she placed the change on the counter for me to grab whenever I was ready. I thanked her right away and swept up the change, grabbed my purchase off the counter and headed next door to the sporting goods store. I picked up two pairs of thin batting gloves there. I managed to find exact change and placed it on the counter.

By morning, I had pretty much convinced myself that I was simply done touching people. I wouldn't even need to wear the gloves all the time, just when I thought I might come in physical contact with another human being, you know, whenever I go out of the house. I'd be known as that nice but somewhat eccentric bald guy that never removes his gloves. I can live with that. I thought the overly curious part of me had finally been silenced with the discovery and the purchase of the gloves. I thought I had finally persuaded my bothersome side not to bother.

I was wrong.

I set myself up in the garage with the newspaper after breakfast. I had no problem concentrating on the clues. The puzzle was completed in fifteen minutes. I decided it was probably about time to start thinking about my next career. I hadn't heard a peep of protest with this thought from inside anywhere so I began flipping through the paper towards the used cars for sale in the classifieds. As I passed through the obituary section, I paused and found the one belonging to Dr. Getz. I told myself I was reading it just to pay him my last respects. I'm still not actually sure if I was lying to myself or not.

Getz---Dr. Donald David Getz died suddenly
at his home on Aug. 18th of a heart attack

at the age of 63. Born April 3, 1940, he is survived by his wife, Elizabeth. Funeral Services will be Tuesday, 11:00am at Washburn-McReavy in Bloomington.

I calmly laid down the newspaper next to my morning Dew on the workbench that doubled as an end table for my den in the garage. I opened up a fresh pack of smokes and, while briefly wondering what it would cost to set myself up for life on some deserted island somewhere with a favorable year-round climate, I slowly lit up another Winston. I watched the tree in the front yard as its leaves and branches danced in the morning wind and realized when I shut my eyes, how closely the sound resembled that of the waves breaking on the beachy shoreline of my deserted paradise. A light rain started to pitter-patter against the blacktop of the driveway, adding a wet sound to the windy waves, further enhancing the depth of the Eden I had created in my head. I could go back to the Kwik Trip and buy a lottery ticket and if I won, I could even have my house moved with me to my island.

Opening my eyes again, the vast empty ocean quickly receded, revealing my familiar driveway and then the mailboxes, the street, the house across the way and the crowded world beyond. I took a deep, long drag off my cigarette. I knew what I was going to do next even though I really didn't want to do it. Also, in that very same instant, while I watched a small mouse scurry across the driveway looking for cover as the rain's rhythm quickened its beat almost in unison with that of my own heart, I knew what I was going to discover after doing what I was about to do, and I really, *really* didn't want to discover it…but I no longer felt as though I was piloting my body as it went inside the house to pull the calendar off the refrigerator door. That curious, bothersome, cat-like me had suddenly assumed full control.

I went to yesterday's date, August 18th, and started counting backwards…to 137. I already knew before I got there what date I was going to land on. I counted a second time just to make sure, but with the same result.

April 3rd.

Damn.

6

I asked you at the beginning of this journey if you would want to know in advance when you are going to die. Now let me rephrase that question. Would you want to know when *everybody else* is going to die? Although I would have to give the first question a lot of serious thought to come up with an honest answer, this new question is a no-brainer. No! Absolutely not. I do *not* want to know when everyone I meet is going to die. I would have also added, given the structure of my belief system, that such information would be completely and totally impossible to come by.

Wrong again.

I now possessed said information. I could now walk right up to a perfect stranger, "Hi, how ya doing. Glad to meet you. By the way, I hope you have your affairs in order because you only have until the 5th day of your 36th year to live." Or, "Why yes, that's an adorable little child. Too bad she isn't going to live to see her adulthood."

Or worse. My relatives and acquaintances. They all have eyes and skin, too.

I told myself that one test subject does not make a proper experiment. It could have been an incredible coincidence. But I wasn't convincing myself. Actually, I held no doubts whatsoever in my mind about the true meaning of the numbers anymore. I made the call. The call was right on the money, or rather, right on the date, in this case.

I knew.

Obviously, discovering what I felt to be the truth behind the numbers was not a triumphant moment. It did, however, finally silence my curious side. I heard no argument from within as I vowed to myself never to touch another human being ever again. Both sides of me, the passive, reclusive side and the naturally curious side, seemed to agree that this was simply too much information for any one soul to possess. It had to be silenced and ignored and, if at all possible, totally forgotten altogether with the help of the gloves that I had now decided to be wearing every time I set foot outside the house.

But something was still not sitting well inside me. The matter was done, resolved. I knew the mechanics of the anomaly---through contact with eyes and skin. I knew most likely why---because of the accident and maybe that hole they decided to leave in my skull. And I knew what the numbers stood for---death.

But how *could* I know? Was I seeing the future somehow? That too, based on my old belief system, was simply not possible. I assumed there had to be another explanation but even my more curious side seemed willing to forego the answer to that question in exchange for never experiencing the phenomenon again.

But there was still something eating at me. There was still a question left unanswered that I needed to explain to myself before I tried to put it all behind me. I just couldn't quite put my finger on exactly what that question could be.

I walked back out to the garage. The light rain of only moments ago had turned into a steady downpour. I took my seat next to the work bench and listened intently to one of my favorite sounds that nature has to offers us, the rhythmic pattern of the raindrops slapping the leaves in the trees and the pavement on the driveway. I lit up another Winston. I lifted my hand and smoothed out my bald head as if pushing aside some phantom hair that I sometimes felt was still there. Something was definitely wrong, I mean, other than the fact that I could now foresee the deaths of all the people I came in contact with. I briefly wondered if this new infliction of mine also worked on animals, but I knew that wasn't the question that I was seeking and quickly shoved the thought aside. I was fine with my new conclusions. I could accept my punishment of forever wearing gloves outside the house for the poor decision I had made that caused the accident. I didn't need to know how it was possible for me to be acquiring this privileged and undesired information, especially since I was not going to be experiencing it ever again. But something...something *else*...was still very wrong.

I tried to force myself to shove the whole matter behind me and out of my mind, to think of something more pleasant. I thought of Katelynn's comforting, beautiful eyes. Then it hit me. My pleasant thought suddenly turning sour before I had a chance to use it for the purpose it had been retrieved. Katelynn. 29:29. That was the problem. Here the question was found. This was why I could not yet let go.

So, here's another question for you. How do you approach someone who appears to be in the prime of their life and warn them that they might be dying soon…very soon? How do you tell a young, vibrant, gorgeous woman that she will not live to see her 30th birthday? And then there's the moral question. Do I even tell her at all? Should I tell her? The doctors always tell you when they discover you are going to die soon. But I am no doctor and I've never even played one on TV.

I didn't know the answers to these questions or the others at war inside my brain. The battle was raging full bloom. *Yes, tell her.*

No, she probably wouldn't want to know. You don't have the right to tell her. *But she does have the right to know.* She won't believe me anyway. I wouldn't believe me. No one wants to get that kind of news. There was no reason to tell her. Live and let live, or in this case, live and let die. Why ruin the last days she has left to live with worry and fear? Maybe she already knows she is dying. Maybe it's some disease she already knows about that is calling in its hand.

It was almost settled…almost. There was still one question that wouldn't go away. One thought that stubbornly wouldn't budge and seemed to single handedly shove away all other concerns. One deciding question.

What if she doesn't have to die?

I decided the first thing I had to do was to find out how old Katelynn was. If I found out that she was 30 already, then it would prove that I had came to the wrong conclusion, and not for the first time in my life. I could live with that. And more importantly, so could Katelynn.

If I discovered that she was under 30, however---well, one step at a time. I didn't exactly have a plan. I'd never had to do this before. I just needed to know how old she was.

I called the hospital to see if Katelynn was in. She answered the phone herself. I recognized her voice and hung up. I didn't know what to say. I couldn't do this over the phone. She had already been through a tough couple of days with Dr. Getz dying and all. I had no desire to make it worse. Yet, still, I had to know. What if she had just turned 29 a couple of weeks ago? But the jury was still out on whether or not I would, or could, to say nothing of whether or not I should, let her in on this knowledge I had stumbled onto.

If Katelynn was still working her normal shift, the same one she had when I had been a resident for two and a half weeks there, she would be getting off work at five PM. I called the cab company and was told I could easily be there before five.

$$7$$

"ey there."

"Hi, John. If I didn't know better, I'd say you were waiting for me," Katelynn said as she walked towards me. "Do I know better?"

"No need to know any better," I said with a smile. "I am indeed here to see you." The rain had all but stopped. A light drizzle mixed with an occasional fat drop still lingered. The air had a fresh clean smell to it that only nature can occasionally provide a big metropolis with. I had been sitting on the stone wall beside the entrance to the employee parking lot waiting for her, hoping she drove her own car as opposed to riding the bus or carpooling. When I saw her approaching, I hopped down off the wall and stood to face her. "I wanted to make sure you were okay. I know you've had it kinda rough just lately."

"Yes, but not as rough as some others have had it. I'll be fine," she assured me with a weak smile. "But I can't believe you came all the way down here just to see how I was doing."

Oh, how I hoped she was 31, okay, albeit a young looking 31. Her shiny brown bangs fell over her brow stopping just short of her eyes which had returned to their original whites, accentuating her midnight blues. She had pulled out the tie that holds her hair back while working and it flowed gently over the shoulders of her white uniform. I had already noted the absence of a diamond around her finger while staying at the hospital. I knew she might just be taking it off for work. It was hard to imagine a young woman as pretty as she without a proud, loving husband to go home to. But for the purpose of my fantasies while she had been at my service, she had been single. I thought briefly for the first time, if she were married, how much her husband would hate me if I let her know what I know and all came to fruition. *All the more reason* not *to tell her,* I thought.

I still had no idea where this road was leading or how far down it I was prepared to travel when I responded to her presumption.

"Well," I said carefully, "I had been thinking about you today. But yes, there is another reason for my coming to see you."

"Is your head feeling okay?" she asked. "Did you decide you want to make an appointment with…" She paused and put on a quizzical look. "No, that's not it or you'd have come inside."

"Correct again, Sherlock," I said, trying to smile. This was not going to be easy. We were still walking slowly as we talked, presumably towards her car. She stopped in the middle of the lot and turned to face me, expecting full disclosure of my presence then and there. Obviously, I wasn't ready for full disclosure.

"Can I buy you a coffee or something? Do you have time to talk a minute? I need a little advice," I finally spit out. Assuming she had the time, I had at least just thought of an approach. I could ask her opinion on something without letting her know it was her I was actually concerned for…or something like that. Not the best plan but the best I could come up with on the fly.

"I don't have long," she said. "I need to pick up my daughter at day care by six, but I have a half an hour or so. There's a coffee shop across the street. You buying?"

I smiled. I couldn't help it. Her voice was as comfortable to my ears as her appearance was to my eyes. The smile quickly vanished however, as I remembered why I was there and the word "daughter" registered at the front desk in my brain. It didn't destroy any of the old fantasies I had held for her, but it meant there was even more at stake here than just her life. This was not going to be fun.

"Certainly," I said. "On me."

"So how old is your daughter?" I asked after testing my hot chocolate. Katelynn had chosen a vanilla cappuccino.

"Five, just turned. How's your hot chocolate? As good as I advertised for them?"

"Yes, it is. Thank you." Quickly doing the math in my head, thirty minus five is twenty-five. A couple more for the wedding and honeymoon. Plus a year of dating, probably during med school days. It was possible. "So you are married then, I take it?"

"Widowed." Katelynn said, looking down. "My husband died of cancer a year after Faith was born. It took him quickly, thank God."

"I'm sorry," I said. That is, after all, the expected programmed response to that statement whenever it gets laid out there on the table and catches you off guard.

Death is much harder on the living than it is on the dead.

"It's okay," Katelynn said looking back up at me. "It seems like a lifetime ago and I am sure God had His reasons for taking him. Faith and I are doing well. So, tell me what brought you all the way down here to wait for me in the rain?"

Damn. The more I learned, the worse things seemed to be getting. Not only was she a mother, but a single mother who had already been touched by Death's cruel hand. Again, the moral questions of my right to inform her and her right to know clashed loudly inside my head. I took another sip of my hot chocolate, stalling, trying to figure out how to get the information my needy side needed without tipping my hand.

"How old are you?" I blurted out. No way to get the answer without asking, right? Every courier knows that the shortest distance between two points is a straight line, so I naturally took the most direct route.

Katelynn put down her cappuccino and studied me a moment before answering. I think she was trying to decide if this was still the casual conversation portion of the visit or if we had suddenly transitioned towards its purpose. I must not have succeeded in sounding as casual as I had hoped.

"You know," she finally said, after a short pause, "that hug yesterday morning was much needed and very nice of you to allow, but I hope I didn't give you the wrong impression. I really don't have time for any new relationships in my life right now. And with that said, I am twenty-eight."

I wanted to leave. Just stand up, thank her for her time, apologize for calling up any unwanted memories, drop a few bucks on the table, and go home. But I couldn't leave. I couldn't move. I couldn't think. Nor could I speak. I didn't have a clue what to say, but I couldn't leave. She might be in trouble and not know it. She's 28. She's not 30. She will never be 30. Her daughter will have lost both her parents in the first five years of her young life. She doesn't know. I shouldn't know. I can't possibly know.

But I did know.

"Did I burst any bubbles there? Are you okay?" Katelynn asked, only half sarcastically.

"When's your birthday?" I heard myself ask her. I was on auto-pilot.

"Tomorrow. Why?"

I think my face must have suddenly gone pale. She's a nurse. She notices these things.

"John, are you feeling okay? You look faint."

"I need to go." I said as I finally found the strength to stand up, and in doing so too quickly, shoved my chair into the empty table behind me. "I'm sorry," I said, trying to speak through the whirlwind of thoughts spinning wildly in my head. "I shouldn't even be here. Um…thanks for your time…um…I might need to talk to you later…I mean…soon…I mean…no…I shouldn't…I…I need to go…I'm sorry."

I heard my name once as I walked quickly out the door, forgetting to drop a few dollars onto the table before I left. It had sounded more in the form of a question, I think. Didn't matter. She probably now thought I was tip-toeing down that fine line of sanity, probably due to the accident. And she probably wouldn't have been that far off, either.

I walked the entire way home…again.

8

Needless to say, I didn't rest very well that night. I realize of course, that I have been asking you all these questions as I go here, and even to this point in time, I don't have all the answers myself yet, but I had even fewer at that time. I was pretty much alone, at the mercy of my own imagination gone mad. Reality as I knew it, and had always known it, was crumbling at my feet. Okay, maybe that's actually a bit over dramatic, at least at that point in time. Suffice it to say that once again, hostilities had broken out from within my newly bald head. And the combat was fierce with no room for a compromise in sight.

The main issue on the table was obvious even though the answer was not. *To tell or not to tell.* That was indeed the question. But it had a hundred spin-off questions like, *How* is she to die? *Why* is she to die? And of course, the million-dollar question of the day; Does she really *have* to die at all?

It wasn't until morning that I finally decided that a proper decision can never be made without all the facts. I needed to know more. I needed to know if she was healthy. I needed to know why this young woman only had thirty days left to live. I needed to know if I could somehow postpone her departure from this world.

By six in the morning, the battle had finally grown sluggish enough for me to get some much-needed sleep. I set the alarm for three PM. I figured I would have about a half an hour to repair any damage done by yesterday's performance and try to learn a few more facts. I know I dreamt of Katelynn. I remembered a little after

my alarm suddenly stepped in to pull me from my own deep well--
and it hadn't all been pleasant.

"For some unexplainable reason, I didn't think I had seen the
last of you yet. But I must admit," Katelynn said, as she approached
me a bit apprehensively, "I didn't think it would be quite *this* soon."

"I'm really sorry for yesterday," I said sheepishly, pulling my
hand out from around my back. I held out my peace offering of a
single rose I had picked up at the Kwik Trip before I left. "Happy
birthday," I said. "I hope you didn't have any trouble covering the
tab. I totally forgot when I bailed out on you. I wanted to try to make
that much right at least, if I could."

"They know me there. I have a tab," she said, looking a little
longingly at the flower.

"Ah. Good." I felt very awkward being here so soon myself,
but need had intervened, so here I was. I held out the rose and she
accepted it graciously.

"Thank you for the flower," she said, as she touched the tip of
her nose with its petals. "But I guess you should know that this is
my last birthday," she added with a smile.

Hold on! Stop the press! What was that? She does know? I felt
my heart skip a beat or two and then try to catch up again. "What do
you mean?" I asked, trying to sound more shocked by her statement
than I actually was.

"You know," she half giggled. "There are more twenty-nine-
year-old women in the world than any other age."

Oh. Yeah. A joke. My heart tried to slow back down, though I
didn't know which was worse--for her to already know about some
irreversible, tragic fate waiting to claim her life in the very near

future, or for her not to have a clue that her daughter will be an orphan by this time next month.

"I have that same half hour available if you want to try again," she said when I didn't respond quite right to her joke. "Just don't get mad if I am the one that gets up and walks out first this time. Okay?"

I forced a smile. "Deal."

We walked in silence across the street, at least I don't think she could hear the loud argument going on inside my head on how to proceed. I got another hot chocolate. She got coffee. Black.

"You look better today than you did when you left yesterday," she finally said, breaking the ice, but not yet cracking the smile.

I didn't feel any better, just a little more under control. "Yeah," I said.

"Half an hour," Katelynn repeated as she brought her coffee towards her lips. "Clock's a tickin'."

"Thanks," I said sincerely. I'd take anything I could get at that point. "I'm not really sure where to begin."

"With the accident?" she intuitively suggested.

No. Not yet.

Katelynn put down her coffee. "You said you needed some advice."

Yes. But not yet.

"You know, I can't read your mind, John."

"Yes. Sorry. I know." I took a long sip of the steaming, creamy hot chocolate and burned the back of my throat. "Let's take you, for example," I said, deciding to go fishing. "You are a healthy young woman, right?"

"Yes."

Good…I think.

I took another long sip of my hot chocolate, collecting as many seconds of thought as I felt I could get away with and winced from the pain at the mouth of my throat. But there simply weren't going to be enough. *If what I know is right, she has a right to know*, I finally conceded to myself. *If I am wrong, what's the worst that can happen? She'd be still alive in thirty days.* "I guess the truth is always best," I said out loud, though I was probably still talking to myself…and then I sarcastically added in a half mutter, "not that she is going to believe me." Then looking back up at Katelynn, "I know some things I am not supposed to know," I said. "I am probably the only one in the world that does know. I am not sure what I am supposed to do with this information." I paused to see if she was still with me.

"So why are you coming to me? Does this mysterious knowledge somehow involve me?" she asked.

"Yes," I said simply, abandoning my original plan.

"Okay. Enough. Spit it out," Katelynn said, trying to sound impatient. And understandably so, I had to admit.

"First of all," I said slowly, locking her eyes to mine from across the table. This above all else I hoped she understood and remembered. "I am only here right now because if I can, and I don't know if I can or not, but if I can, I want to help you. I am your friend, though you might not think so in a minute. Just try to remember that much, please."

"And why do I need your help?" she asked, nonchalantly picking her coffee back up.

"Because I have reason to believe that you only have twenty-nine days left to live."

Katelynn put her coffee back on the table in front of her, stood without looking in my direction and turned towards the door.

I didn't try to stop her. A deal is a deal. And I figured I still had twenty-nine more days--actually 28 and counting after my latest failure of a few moments ago.

I left the rose on the table for the waitress along with a ten spot.

"We have got to stop meeting like this," Katelynn said without a trace of humor in her voice.

"I didn't want you hating me for the wrong reasons," I said, hopping down from my new daily perch atop the four-foot stone wall. I stood where I landed, taking no steps towards her. "If you still hate me after I have had the chance to explain, then so be it."

"I could call the police," she said matter-of-factly, stopping just short of the entrance to the parking lot. "I'm sure this is beginning to border on a few stalking laws."

"I am not the enemy here," I said calmly. "And before you ask, I haven't a clue who, or what, is."

"So," Katelynn said. She crossed her arms and settled into her left hip. She was not looking directly at me as she spoke. But at least for the moment, I held her curiosity. "According to you, is the whole world doomed in twenty-eight days and you are out to inform us one by one? Or is this a more personal problem you think I have?"

I started with the accident, the woman in my window and the medic. I finished with Dr. Getz and the calendar on my refrigerator door. Twenty-five minutes after I had begun, Katelynn hopped down from the stone wall where she had sat patiently and silently listening to my story and stood for a moment saying nothing, looking off in the distance at nothing.

When she finally spoke again, her voice cracked a bit on the first word from dryness. She stood in front of me, took a deep breath, and asked, "You gonna be here tomorrow?"

"If you want me to be," I said.

"I think you are wrong. I think there must be another explanation,." she said soberly, looking at the thin white-silver watch on her wrist. "But I'm going to be late for Faith if I don't go right now. I don't have time to think about all this right now." She looked back up at me, more at my bald head than my face, I think. "Yes. I want you to be here."

"I'll be here."

9

I didn't feel like going home but I had no where else to go and my legs were far too stiff to even think about walking home a third time. Part of me felt like I should stay with her, watch her, protect her...but from who or what I had no idea. Besides, I may not have known the who, what, where or how of the portentous matter at hand, but I did know the when. In twenty-eight days.

I settled for the cab company. On the ride home, two blocks before getting there, I saw a motorcycle on the street corner in the grass with a for sale sign on it. It hadn't been there yesterday when I had walked home. It had to be fate. Not that I actually believed in anything as controlling and supernatural as fate, mind you, but sometimes certain beliefs are useful when they suit your own personal agenda.

I had the cabbie drop me off by the bike.

When I arrived at 4:20 the next day with the daily crossword puzzle tucked into my shirt so that the wind from the ride wouldn't blow it away, I noticed the perch I habitually waited on was already occupied.

"You're off early," I said, as I cut the engine and rolled my new black Honda Shadow to a stop a few feet in front of her.

"I have the day off," Katelynn said, sliding down off the wall. "Just got here myself a few minutes ago. New wheels?"

"Yeah. Cabs were getting expensive."

I had already figured out what she had in mind. She had just gotten done telling me she had the day off and had even only just arrived herself. Yet here she was with her hair tied back, wearing a cute, all-white, high neck number that came down to just below the knees. I had always thought she wore her uniform very well.

"So, did you forget you took the day off?" I asked. "Or are those the only clothes you own? You know, I heard that Einstein's complete wardrobe was ten of the exact same suits so that he never had to waste a single thought on what he was going to wear each day."

"No," she said, mostly ignoring my Einstein comment. "I've thought about your story…"

"…and you need more proof," I finished for her.

"I want a second opinion. I want you to tell Dr. James. And yes," she added. "I would like more proof. I know you believe what you told me, but…"

"How am I to provide more proof?" I interrupted. Though I was pretty sure what her answer was going to be, I was still hoping I might be wrong.

"First, we have to talk to Dr. James, John. Then if he agrees, if he allows it, I would like for you to meet some people."

I looked down at my gloved hands. I had bought a new pair of sleek looking black leather riding gloves from a motorcycle shop the day before, after purchasing the bike. I had also picked up a helmet and some sunglasses but had only put the latter to use so far. The helmet was more for passengers and rainy days. This was the fourth motorcycle I had owned since getting my driver's license the day I turned sixteen. It had been a dirt bike on that day. After beating that bike up for a couple years, I had taken my fair share of spills, enough to not want to take any more, anyway. Now, three more motorcycles and sixteen years later, I was just as over-confident a biker as I was a driver, certainly a little more focused behind the handlebars than the wheel, but my brain still allowed the operation of motorized vehicles to take a back seat to the more pressing concerns of the day. I knew who she wanted me to meet. The old folks. The ones that are dying. Preferably the ones that will be dying soon. I would shake their hands and say hello-glad-to-meet-you and then walk away. I would then confirm the dying persons age through my own mysterious sources and we would wait. We would wait for the early predictions to die. Then she would have her proof. It was the only way. I knew it had to be done. I wasn't looking forward to it.

"Okay," I said submissively. What else could I say?

We had to wait until five. Katelynn had already set up the appointment, hoping in advance that I would agree, though she had not told Dr. James what the meeting was to be about. We worked on the crossword puzzle together across the street while sipping hot chocolates and waiting for five to roll around on the clock behind the counter. We didn't speak a word of yesterday's conversation.

Dr. James looked to be in his early forties, comparatively younger than most of the doctors I had seen here. He had well groomed, short, jet-black hair with eyebrows that matched and almost met in the middle above his long slender nose. His eyes appeared just as dark behind his dark, thick plastic framed glasses. He was a fit man; tall, dark and growing more handsome with age;

a touch of gray beginning to highlight his short, distinguishing sideburns, the small lines of wisdom just beginning to appear where they will permanently etch themselves into his face, adding to the aura of authority and confidence that already surrounded him. He immediately captured one's trust. His handshake felt firm and confident even through the gloves I wore. He was easy to talk to, to confide in, and appeared to be genuinely attentive and concerned as I related to him the same unbelievable story that I had unfolded for Katelynn the previous afternoon. While walking back to the hospital from the Coffee Shoppe, Katelynn had mentioned how she had only met Dr. James a handful of times before yesterday, but he had been the first one she had thought of when trying to figure out who might listen to this incredible story with an open mind, to say nothing of consenting to the ensuing experiment she had in mind.

Dr. James said nothing as a heavy silence filled the room at the completion of my story. It had only taken fifteen minutes for me to tell this time. I was already getting a feel for which of the details were important and which ones weren't. He got the straight-to-the-point version, though still just as hard to believe. His facial expression remained unchanged as though I were still talking. He sat motionless behind his antique looking dark, oak desk in a black leather executive's chair, hands neatly folded in his lap. Katelynn and I awaited his opinion in matching red high backs at each corner of the desk across from him. Katelynn was also noticeably anxious, waiting out the silence as patiently as she could, allowing the story to settle like a lone ripple in a still pond.

Then finally, "The human brain is a miraculous organ and we know so little about it."

Both Katelynn and I were holding our breath and hanging on to his every word.

"We only know how to use a very small portion of it," he continued. "Who knows what the rest is capable of. One thing we do know is that the brain can do some amazing types of processing and calculating all on its own. The brain stores and remembers everything we have ever experienced. We don't always know where to retrieve it from, but it is in there. The brain can do calculations as fast and as accurately as any computer, keep time as precisely as any clock and dates as well as any calendar. It can reason, make adjustments, and most importantly, it learns. But we, as an ever-evolving species, still have no idea what 90% of that miraculous organ is even capable of."

Dr. James' gaze left the far wall and turned towards me for the first time since I had begun my story.

"The brain is the central office, the head quarters. It regulates and monitors every inch of our body from head to toe, inside and out. It tells us when something gets hurt, when we are hungry, when we need to go to the bathroom, when we are sick. It also works on healing and repairing. It creates its own armies of antibodies to fight off attacking viruses. It seals its own wounds, generates new cells, sheds old skin. If one knew how, I am sure one could even stop his own heart by using his own brain to do it. Maybe in a few thousand more years we will evolve and survive as a society long enough to someday discover the full capacity of our own brain. Maybe by then, as a society, we will be ready."

He was looking back and forth between Katelynn and I now as he spoke. He spoke slowly and deliberately, pronouncing each word clearly, making eye contact, softly yet firmly commanding our attention.

"I have a theory, John," he said, turning his full attention back to me, "but it is just a theory. I don't have any idea how the actual information is entering your mind. You may have jarred awake some part of the brain that the rest of us have not learned to use yet. Maybe a mild form of ESP. Unlike most of my colleagues and those of the scientific fields, my own personal belief in unproven phenomenon like ESP, UFO's and such, is simply if 99.9% of all the millions of reports of these phenomena are made up or false, that still leaves .1% that must be true. And if one is real, then the phenomenon is real. Although I am a man of science at heart, I still try to keep an open mind on just about everything because of that fact alone.

"Let's first accept the fact that you are retrieving the information and it is what you think it is because I certainly believe that you believe it to be true and as I just said, anything is possible. Then the question is, how could the numbers exist at all."

"Yeah!" I chimed in exuberantly. I had asked myself that exact question a million times over. "I've been wondering the same thing. That would be like telling the future and I have a serious problem believing that is possible."

"I have my doubts as to whether or not the future can be seen too, John. But it *could* possibly be predicted. Even Nostradamus claimed that his future 'visions' were merely predictions and that man could change the gruesome outcomes of these 'visions,' but that he himself did not have the faith in mankind to alter what he had *seen*, or if you prefer, *predicted*.

"The brain, once again, is monitoring every organ in your body. It is perfectly aware of the condition of every blood vessel, which pores are blocked, how well the lungs are working, how hard the heart is pumping, the liver, intestines, all the moving parts. The brain, it only stands to reason then, could make calculations with the information we have input into it through the years, such as the definition and calibration of time, our chosen habitual diets and exercise and the chemicals we are adding to our bodies in whatever fashion, coupled with the input it is retrieving itself, the body's over all condition and health. The result of this calculation would then be a prediction of how long each of these organs is going to last or when they are going to stop working or, if you will, when you are going to die. Therefore, it could be possible, if we knew how to do it and/or where to retrieve it from within the brain, that each of us could accurately predict the day we, ourselves, are going to die and probably even why. These numbers may also be susceptible to constant change as things in our life change and our habits or diets change, and then so would the calculation's result. Also, with this knowledge ahead of time, that would allow people like me to fix things before they go bad and end up extending the average life span of the human race by who knows how much. But then again, I have to wonder if we are ready for something like that as a society?

"My theory, John, is that this calculation may exist in all of us and the accident, the rod through your brain, somehow opened a doorway allowing your brain to retrieve just that information from other people's brains through their eyes. Possibly a form of partial ESP or even something we haven't named yet scientifically. We may never know, but it brings us down to one final question, one I feel we should try to figure out the answer to"

"What is that?" Katelynn and I both blurted out at the same time.

"By whatever means the brain is producing these numbers or predictions you believe you are retrieving, John, for our purposes, doesn't really matter yet. The only thing that matters right now is, for Katelynn's sake, plain and simply, 'Is this phenomenon of yours for real or not?'"

10

nce again, I didn't sleep well that night after the interview with Dr. James. Even though I kept waking up throughout the night, I kept falling back into the same dream theme. I must have had a hundred dreams that night. Katelynn was in everyone of them and I witnessed her death a hundred times over in a hundred different fashions. I woke up exhausted, feeling as though I had already put in a full day's work and wanted to just go back to sleep but I had no desire to watch reruns of Katelynn dying over and over and over again. I got up and tried to sere away the sleepiness in a steaming hot shower and came to realize that the reality of the day ahead looked no more promising than the nightmares I had just left behind. More death.

I didn't know exactly how Dr. James was going to decide on conducting his experiment, but the method was not my biggest concern. It was the mere *idea* of the experiment that bothered me.

At 2PM, I was to meet Dr. James and Katelynn at his office in the hospital. Then I would briefly be introduced to some pre-selected group of presumably dying elderly people under some false pretense invented by Dr. James, and report my findings. The whole idea made me feel dirty, like a peeping tom or a thief; like I was trespassing in someone's very personal space and stealing vital information not intended to be shared.

As we had completed that initial meeting, just to confirm its consistency, Dr. James had politely asked if either one of us minded if I were to remove my gloves and repeat the process with Katelynn since her numbers had already been exposed. I looked at Katelynn before I answered. I was willing, but it wasn't my death I was predicting. Her intense blue eyes were already locked with mine as she slowly nodded her assent to Dr. James' request.

I hated doing it. I could see in her eyes that she was hoping beyond hope that the numbers would for some reason be different this time, proving that I had been wrong about the meaning of the numbers all along. Maybe Dr. Getz's numbers and death were just a crazy coincidence. But I knew they wouldn't have changed. I think she knew, too, deep down. She had only agreed so that Dr. James could witness the phenomenon first hand before testing it out on some unsuspecting patients.

I rose out of my chair, stepped towards Katelynn and removed the glove from my right hand. Katelynn remained seated, her eyes never leaving my own and extended her left hand towards mine. For a quick moment before our hands clasped, I too, allowed myself to hope that her numbers would have changed. But even sent together, our wishes were ignored and left unfulfilled by whomever was running the wish-granting department that day. The instant her soft, gentle hand crept timidly into mine, *(29:29)* took its place at the front of my mind. She read it in my eyes before I was able to pass along the information to Dr. James and broke our gaze, looking resignedly at the floor, but her hand remained in mine until I spoke.

"It hasn't changed," I said, and felt Katelynn's warm hand slide slowly from my loose grip. "But I am not convinced that means it has to happen."

I felt like such a schmuck for blurting that out right then at that moment. I had no idea what I was talking about. I didn't have a clue what we were up against here. But I carelessly let my wish fly past my lips and watched Katelynn's eyes return to my own with a renewed hope in them that I had just falsely implanted with my remark. Truth was, I was not at all sure that there was anything that could be done. I just knew if there was, I was going to try to find it.

I arrived at the employee parking lot at 1:45. Katelynn was waiting for me atop our stone wall and hopped down when she saw me angle in towards the lot. Once again, even though she had been granted a few days off by Dr. James after yesterday's meeting, she was dressed in a freshly cleaned, pressed and disinfected uniform. She obviously planned on accompanying Dr. James and I on my tour of the terminal wing.

"Thank you for agreeing to this," Katelynn said, as I dropped the kick stand to my bike and turned towards her. "I know this isn't easy for you."

She seemed a little stronger today than she had when I had said good-bye to her from that very spot the day before. I think we were both still holding on to a sliver of hope that I would be unable to properly predetermine the final day of the terminal, therefore dismissing my original conclusions right then and there.

"It certainly isn't my idea of a good time," I said, "but I also understand that it must be done. I am more worried about how you are handling all this right now than I am about me."

"I'll let you know in a little while," she said, forcing a timid smile.

We walked through the hospital's main entrance and took the elevator to the third floor where Dr. James' office was, silently lost in our own individual thoughts and hopes. I was still hoping like Katelynn that the test would be a failure, but I was also trying to prepare myself for what would happen next when we discovered otherwise. There was no way I could have possibly been prepared for what actually happened.

"I want to involve as few people here as possible," Dr James said, after seating us in our prospective chairs. "I had to first deal with the ethics of what we are doing here. I don't think it is right to approach people under false pretense and try to steal information from them," he said, intuitively voicing one of my biggest objections right out of the box. "But at the same time, I don't want to tell them the truth either." He paused, allowing this moral dilemma to sink in before unveiling his solution.

"To appease the moral ethics involved here," he continued, "we are going to have to tell our subjects the truth. In order to do that, we need to change what is the truth."

At this point he had me thoroughly confused.

"I asked three patients if they would agree to take part in a test and they all agreed. I told them I had a visitor coming today that claimed he could tell people how old they were by shaking their hand. And this is what I want you to do. Just shake their hand and let us know what the first number is in your mind. Keep the second number to yourself. If the first number turns out to be right, you can write down the second number after we leave the room and we will seal them up until they are needed to keep the integrity of the experiment in tact. Only you will know what that number is that you wrote down. You with me so far?"

Katelynn and I both nodded.

"Good. I chose these particular people because, I am sorry to say, I do not expect them to live more than a couple of weeks, possibly less. Needless to say, in order for the test to prove that this phenomenon is undeniably real, you must be right on all accounts. Even one wrong answer, on their ages or on the numbers you write down, and it means you could just as easily be wrong about Katelynn.

"Is this acceptable to you, John?" he finished with.

"Yes," I answered. I was actually very relieved that we weren't going in under completely false pretenses. I was still going to be stealing some personal information out of their minds for my own purpose, as noble as that purpose may be, but at least we were being upfront about the fact that I was indeed trying to get inside their minds. It made me feel at least a little less criminal.

"How about you, Katelynn?" he said turning his attention to her. "How are you handling all this?"

"I'm doing okay," she said. Then she surprised me by adding, "I thought a lot about all this last night. I knelt down to pray before bed. I meant to ask God to make this experiment fail today but then I realized, whatever happens is His will. God has his reasons. We don't always understand them but He is good and I will accept what He wills. I know if I must die, He will watch over Faith and take care of her. If she must grow up without her parents, then God must have a good reason for that."

She said all this with her head bowed towards the floor, as if still in prayer. I think it took Dr. James a little off guard too and Katelynn looked up almost a little embarrassed when only silence followed her confession.

She broke the silence herself. "Shall we?"

"Good afternoon, Mrs. Ikatsu," Dr. James said, as Katelynn and I followed him into the first room of his three pre-selected subjects.

The name registered even before the sight of subject #1 had been established. Dr. James was certainly going to make this as difficult as possible. Ikatsu is Japanese. The Japanese always look a decade or two younger than they are, at least compared to us westerners. Dr. James released her hand and stepped aside and I got my first visual.

She was definitely old. If I were to have to guess without using this new, unwanted supernatural ability of mine, I would have said 125. Well, 100 at least. Any gene the Japanese have to keep their skin smooth and young looking had long since grown dormant in Mrs. Ikatsu. Even laying in bed with the sheets covering up most of her tiny torso, I knew she probably wasn't more than four and a half feet tall. Her skin, however, appeared to have once belonged to someone closer to my own size. The multiple bags under each of her eyes drooped to the lower level of what had once been probably a cute and dainty nose. Her cheeks folded down over themselves, appearing out of place on such a tiny face. Even the ridges in her forehead seemed to be drooping towards the gravitational pull. But her eyes smiled. It was easy to imagine that there had once been a beautiful face surrounding those eyes.

That was the worst part of all this for me. In order for this to work, I had to be looking into their eyes; sad, lonely eyes; knowing their time is so short, so near, so precious. I didn't even hear Dr. James going through his introduction of Katelynn and myself. I knew Mrs. Ikatsu would not be long of this world without having to touch her hand. Despite the still evident smile in her eyes, their color had faded to paler shades of pale, making their original color indeterminable. Once I registered that Dr. James wasn't talking anymore and that everyone was looking at me, I applied a friendly feeling smile to my face and extended my hand out to Mrs. Ikatsu.

She managed with noticeable effort to raise her right arm a couple of inches off the bed and I reached out and gently grabbed it before she had to try to move it any farther.

"Hello, Mrs. Ikatsu," I said as I helped her lower her hand back down onto the bed. "I am happy to meet you."

"You know age now?" she asked in a squeaky, high pitched, heavy eastern accent.

(92:166) had indeed surfaced the instant our hands had met. She was 92 years old. She had until the 166th day of her 92nd year.

"I believe you are 92 years old, ma'am."

Her eyes doubled in size telling me I was correct. "How you know?" Mrs. Ikatsu demanded, making the question sound like one long word.

"You told me with your mind when our hands touched," I said, glad I didn't have to make up any stories.

Her eyes immediately narrowed back down to normal size and beyond. "What else I tell you?" Mrs. Ikatsu asked, surprising me almost speechless.

"Nothing else," I lied. "It's just a weird thing I can do. I can guess someone's age when we touch."

"Bah," she spat out, looking unimpressed. "I, 92," she confirmed.

"Well, thank you very much for your help, Mrs. Ikatsu," Dr. James said, stepping in and taking back the control in this still ongoing experiment. He could tell this was rather awkward for me. Katelynn and I were already back out in the hallway before Dr. James had finished whatever his closing spiel to Mrs. Ikatsu had been. I just wanted to get this over with.

Katelynn silently handed me one of the three envelopes she had been carrying with her. Each envelope contained a name on the outside and a blank scrap of paper on the inside. She was handing me Mrs. Ikatsu's previously assigned envelope. I removed the scrap of paper and took the pen out of Katelynn's other extended hand and wrote '92:166' on it. Folding it once, I returned it to the envelope and licked the gummy flap, sealing inside my prediction of when Mrs. Ikatsu will die. I did not know when her birthday was so I didn't know how long she had to live yet. Dr. James knew her birthday, but not the number in the envelope. We would not be sharing information. The envelope would not be opened again until her passing. All these steps were necessary, according to Dr. James, to keep the experiment honest and uncontaminated. I handed the pen back to Katelynn and the sealed envelope to Dr. James just as he was joining us in the hallway, closing the door behind him. He calmly tucked it into the outer pocket of his white jacket and started left down the hall.

"Mr. Crawley is just two doors down here," Dr. James said, continuing to walk. "Are you ready or do you need any time, John? I take it you wrote a number down on the paper in the envelope you handed me?"

I think he was possibly getting a little excited after witnessing success with his first test. I think, even as open minded as Dr. James had claimed to be, he had never for an instant truly believed that he wouldn't be able to prove me wrong. He might have even thought he had played his strongest chance to do so right out of the gate, for Katelynn's sake.

"Yes," I replied, glancing at Katelynn. "To both questions. I just want to get this over with."

I could already tell, looking into Katelynn's eyes, she understood as I did. We were both now doing this simply for Dr. James' need to remain scientific. She knew as I did, that all three envelopes would soon be sealed with their own folded up scrap of paper with a number written on it. And it really didn't matter what those secret numbers were on those folded up scraps of paper inside those sealed envelopes because all of a sudden, in the last 5 minutes, another clarity of comprehension had just slammed home for her...when she lays down to bed tonight, she has but twenty-five days left to watch her daughter grow.

"If I am right on this one," I said to Dr. James, who was already waiting at Mr. Crawley's closed door for us to catch up, "do you still think it necessary we see all three?"

"It certainly eliminates the possibility of doubt if you get all three correct," he answered. Then he too, for the first time, noticed the effect the last few minutes had had on Katelynn. The first tear was half way down her right cheek though she looked determined not to allow the escape of another. "Why don't you hand me the envelopes, Katelynn," he continued, taking his hand away from the door knob and extending it towards her. "We can handle it from here. Why don't you head on back down to my office and have yourself a cup of coffee. We'll be along rather shortly here, I am sure, and we can catch you up with the results then. Okay?"

"Okay," Katelynn quickly consented. "I could use a cup right about now," she said, but I think she was actually concentrating hard on holding in the flood of escapee-wannabes lined up just behind the corners of each eye.

Katelynn handed Dr. James the remaining two envelopes. Our eyes met once again as she walked back toward me. I wanted to hold my arms out and take her in, tell her I wouldn't let anything happen to her, assure her that everything was going to turn out right and perfect and as it should be. But I could not. I had no words of comfort to offer. I had brought all this into her life. A few days ago, she had been planning her summer vacation with her daughter. They were planning on spending a week out on the farm she had grown up on. She was going to teach her daughter to swim this year in the same pond at the edge of their property line where she herself had learned to swim when she had been five years old. There was so much she still had to teach her daughter to prepare her for life and all that it hurls at us. But now she needed to forget about vacations and lessons and creating memories. Memories were over. There would be no more. Now was time to start planning on who was going to be raising her daughter for her after next month. I was probably the last person in the world she wanted to have hugging her or trying to console her at that moment. This was all my fault.

In spite of my fears of her hatred towards me for bringing all this doom and gloom into her life, her gaze was not malicious or accusatory in any way. Beneath the brave facade she was trying to convey, her moist eyes revealed her sad acceptance of the truth as we both now understood it. And for the second time, she stepped right up in front of me and wrapped her arms around my back, pressing her eyes into my shoulder. As I returned the hug, noticing how natural she felt in my arms, I whispered into her ear, "Don't give up yet, okay?"

She pulled her head off my shoulder and faced me, our eyes inches apart. My hands still clasped one another in the small of her back. 29:29 had the decency to remain silent for the moment. There were a couple of fresh escapees running down each cheek now. She said nothing. A half smile formed as she nodded in response to my request. I saw a few more tears released as she stepped back and continued past me towards Dr. James' office.

11

Mr. Crawley's visit was gratefully equally as brief as the first one had been. Meeting these people, looking into their eyes and reaching into their minds as they lay there in front of me rapidly deteriorating and dying...let's just say it made me hope I never live as long.

Mr. Crawley looked as though he had already passed on...fifteen years ago. His white skin reminded me of a bed sheet draped over furniture to keep the dust from accumulating. His eyes seemed to have shriveled back into his skull. He was breathing through an apparatus implanted into his throat. Yet, the second he laid his vacant eyes on me, his left hand shot up remarkably quickly to his throat and covered something there. The sound of his breath changed and a robot-like monotone voice said with surprising strength, "So you are the one who reads years. Have you ever been wrong?"

"Not that I know of," I answered. "But that's why we are testing it out. I've only recently discovered this ability after I was in an accident."

His right hand suddenly rose with another amazing small burst of energy that didn't seem possible from this skeletal looking form before me. "Go ahead and do me," the metallic voice said. "But prepare for your first failure."

Keeping my eyes focused on the sunken eyes of Mr. Crawley, I accepted his frail hand in mine and *(48:1)* instantly came to mind. But *that* couldn't be right. He had to be at least eighty, maybe older. Maybe he had been purposely trying to send me the wrong number, knowing I was going to try to read his mind. I had no idea what Dr. James had actually told these people as to how I came about my guess for their age. Maybe Katelynn is fine? Maybe...

All these thoughts and more went swooping through my mind in the instant after the numbers had assumed center stage. During my brief-but-still-too-long hesitation due to my logical confusion of this illogical situation, Mr. Crawley snapped his hand back and the robot-voice said, "Told you I would be tough. So, what is my age."

Above the sound of the voice, a smile spread across the lips which had somewhat eerily not yet even moved during this brief exchange.

I was just about to go ahead and state 48 as his age, that had after all been the first number, and that had been the instructions Dr. James had given me. "...let us know the first number, keep the second one to yourself." That was what he had said. The first number was 48, as remarkable as that seemed in itself since Mr. Crawley looked to be at least 80. It was the second number that was the key.

'1'.

If I was right about what was going on with me, if I did actually own the rights to this unwanted talent, if Katelynn was indeed supposed to die in twenty-five days, then Mr. Crawley was only an unbelievable 47 years old unless today or yesterday was his 48th birthday. So my guess was 47. But I couldn't say 47 because that would contaminate the test. That was not the number that came to mind. I was to report the first number that came to mind and keep the second number to myself. This was a scientific experiment and I can't change the rules without altering the result. Either way, 47, 48, Mr. Crawley was certainly older than that.

"48," I finally said, staying faithful in the name of science. And as the monotone voice tried unsuccessfully to express glee in my failure by repeating "47" three times and "you are wrong" twice, the frown on my face was not because I had been wrong, but because all of a sudden, I knew I had been right. As if to confirm this, Mr. Crawley finished chanting '47' and suddenly added...

"Knew I would be tough. My birthday is tomorrow."

In the hallway, Dr. James didn't have to be told that my answer had been correct even though it had been wrong. Maybe Mr. Crawley's upcoming birthday had even been one of his wild cards for testing my validity. The fact that he looked 40 years older than he was certainly weighed heavily in his choice. Then it struck me how difficult it must be at that moment for Dr. James as he handed me Mr. Crawley's envelope and watched me pen down the day of Mr. Crawley's death. Only I knew that he was going to die in two days. Maybe Mr. Crawley knew. But looking at Dr. James, I could tell that he *wanted* to know as he slowly slid the sealed envelope into his pocket with Mrs. Ikatsu's. He wanted to know and then he wanted to do something about it. Wherein after our visit to Mrs. Ikatsu, Dr. James had appeared almost anxious and giddy with the results, this time he seemed seriously concerned and had drawn his dark eyebrows in closer towards each other. If he were to open that envelope up early and find out when, he could be waiting, ready to dive in at the right time with life support to keep Mr. Crawley alive for even one more day. 48:2. He wanted to look. But I believe his high standards of ethics and science would not allow him to look.

Almost as though he had just traveled the same train of thought as I, coming to the same resolve at about the same time, he patted the outside of his pocket that contained the two sealed envelopes and relaxed the muscles that had tensed in his face.

"We've got a two for one deal in the last room here, John," he said, as we began to walk in that direction. "But I want to let you know what's going on here before we go in." He stopped walking and stepped out of the flow of traffic and closer to the wall. I followed suit.

"This is the room of Benny Randall," he explained to me. "He is dying soon just as the other two are. He knows it, but won't admit it. He likes to be called Benny and is much more affable. When I came in to see him this morning and mentioned this test, he was delighted to participate. A couple of hours later, I was checking in on him again and he informed me that he had told his old buddy about what you were going to do and invited him down to take part in it too."

Dr. James looked clearly agitated here. I think he was still trying to make a decision on something and couldn't finalize it until he heard himself state it out loud.

"I met his old buddy just before you and Katelynn arrived," he continued. "His name is Harry. Just Harry. Harry is all excited about meeting you and having you guess his age. He was practically hopping up and down in his chair with anticipation. He said his mom used to read palms back when she was alive. I could hardly turn him away. The point being, John," he paused. I waited. "... after the first two, I believe you. I'm not sure how and I hope you are willing to work with me more on this, but right now there is no doubt in my mind that the numbers you wrote down for Mrs. Ikatsu and Mr. Crawley are correct. I know I shouldn't believe that yet before the fact, but I do."

Again, in the pause, I think he was just then, as he stated it out loud to me, accepting this fact within himself. I waited.

"Give us the number that comes to mind for Benny just as you have, John," he said looking serious again. "But make a wild guess for Harry if you want to. You don't need to write down a number on him or reveal how old he will be when he dies. We don't need him for the test and his numbers can't help Katelynn out. Who knows, maybe you can nail it on a wild guess and no one will be the wiser. You will get Benny's right. Unlike Mr. Crowley, his birthday is not for a while yet. Do him first. For the test." A slight pause. "Then my advice would be to take a wild guess with Harry and forget the numbers that actually come to mind."

His logic made sense. I agreed. He knocked on the door. We walked in.

Benny Randall was indeed a jovial soul. The instant we walked in the room, having just left two that felt every bit as near death as their occupants, this room was filled with life. The lighting was a little brighter. A radio in the corner was softly playing golden oldies in big band style. There were colorful flowers in a tall vase on a table and an assortment of pictures of family and friends displayed on the white dresser as well as the small ledge of the window well. And there were two rather large grown men, both as bald as I was, one white and one black, and each with a grin that stretched from ear to ear. I smiled back. Couldn't not.

Dr. James introduced me and I said hi without yet shaking their hands. Below the mile of smiles, both men had their arms crossed over their chests, hiding their hands in their armpits. Their postures were that of stubborn children refusing to be cooperative. Their faces were lit like their first trip to Disney World.

"John," Benny said, after the round of verbal greetings, "...you want to put a little wager on this here age guessing talent of yours?"

The question sounded perfectly natural stated in the Texas drawl that came from Big Benny. A bettin' man to the day he dies. Probably still wearing his boots down under the covers. A big white Stetson wouldn't be far away. But you couldn't help but to like him. His eyes were honest and friendly. His smile was contagious.

"I'm actually too new at this to start betting on it," I replied. "We're still in the testing stage."

"When you get done testin', I want to be your manager," he chuckled. "Yes sir, I could make you a rich young man."

"Stop teasin' the poor boy, Benny," Harry chimed in, with an accent from a farther eastern deep south. "Don' pay him no mind now, son. You just go right on an' do what ya need to do. Go on an' shake Mr. John's hand now, Benny. Let 'im guess your age for ya."

Still grinning, Benny pulled his right hand out from his left arm pit and I stepped towards his bed. His handshake was firm and practiced, comfortable. *(79:348)* equally comfortably settled into my mind as if it belonged.

"You are 79 years old," I said.

Still holding firmly to my hand, Benny's smile broke for the first time. "Well, I'll be damned!" He exclaimed excitedly. "I'll be goddamned! He got it right, Harry. Harry, get me one of my cards out of the closet and give it to the boy. I'll be damned!" He finally released my hand. "I mean it boy. You take my card. You give me a call when I get outta here, you hear? I'll be..."

"Calm down, Benny," Harry was saying. He was still seated in the chair he had pulled away from the wall to sit next to Benny on the other side of the bed, making no move to the closet to retrieve Benny's card. "He still gotta get me right."

Harry's smile had never left his face. He had not looked all that surprised when I had gotten Benny's age right. I had of course been looking into Benny's eyes at the time I revealed his age but I had thought I could see Harry slowly nodding his head in approval in my peripheral vision, the grin remaining unchanged. Now he stood up to come around the bed to take his turn at shaking my hand.

The chair he had been seated in had not done him justice. He was a small mountain of a man. You wouldn't want to run into these two in a dark alley, at least not until you got to know them. His black dome was as shiny and smooth as a polished bowling ball, his shoulders, though aged and with a slight lean to the right, still looked broad enough to cause him to turn sideways to get through narrow doorways. He only stood about 6'2", probably even a little shorter than Big Benny when back-to-back, but his bulk easily supplied him with ownership of as much space around him as he wanted to lay claim to.

I quickly prejudged him to be in his late seventies. The tilt in his posture, the mixture of knowledge and understanding from a lifetime of experiences already evident in his eyes as he approached, I settled on 77. I wanted to pick a number to guess first before being influenced by knowing how old he will be when he dies. And I really wanted to be lucky and get it right. That would have been sweet. We take a bow and take our leave. I wanted to get back to Katelynn and see how she was doing. Today had not gone the way we had hoped, but I guess it had gone the way we had expected. I just wanted to get this test done with so we could start figuring out what we are going to do about Katelynn's future. He was obviously still strong for an old man. At the last second, I changed my guess to 75.

He stepped in front of me, I had to look up at a slight angle to meet his eyes, and his hand took mine in as I might a ten-year old child's.

(..."4 days...6pm...14 crimson lane minnetonka...tell no one john...bring a dessert...see you then")

I yanked my hand free of Harry's and took two quick steps backwards, still reading amusement in his eyes while feeling shock and confusion emitting from mine.

(...)"4 days...6pm...14 crimson lane minnetonka...tell no one john...bring a dessert...see you then") still sat in the front of my mind just the way all the numbers always had. Yet it took me longer to think through those words sitting there in the front of my brain, to say nothing of understanding their meaning yet, than the handshake had lasted.

"Well?" Harry was asking, still the smile never losing its strength or its appeal. "How old am I?"

I didn't answer immediately. I had totally forgotten what number I had decided on before he had...had what? I didn't have time to think about that right now. They awaited an answer. I didn't have one.

(72)

"72" I blurted out.

Harry raised one hand up and slapped his own bald head pretty hard causing a loud 'SMACK!' He could have been mocking surprise. It might have been genuine. I couldn't tell. It hadn't even occurred to me yet that I had gotten his age correct. "On the money!" he exclaimed, much to Benny's delight, who had started up on his demands for a card out of the closet again.

Dr. James was watching me like a lab scientist watching his favorite test rat. He remained uninfected by the pair of contagious grins and the ensuing hoopla. He knew my reaction to Harry's touch had been different from the previous three, and like any good scientist, made a mental note of the difference. His curiosity more than anything was probably why he came to my aid so quickly, I am sure.

"Okay, gentleman," he began, having to raise his voice a little trying to calm them down. "Thank you for your participation in our test. Benny, if John decides to take his act on the road, I'll make sure he knows how to reach you. Right now, for your own sake, you need to settle down and maybe get some rest. Visiting hours might need to be cut a little short if you exert yourself too much there. Harry, you make sure your friend here slows that old heart down a bit and then you might want to say good night until tomorrow yourself. I'll come back and look in on you in a little while. Got it, Benny?"

"Got it, Doc," Benny said. I didn't know how far along into his 79th year he already was, but I hoped it wasn't far. He was still smiling as I thanked them again and made my escape.

12

Out in the hallway, Dr. James didn't speak as I wrote a pair of numbers on a scrap of paper and sealed it into Benny's envelope. He looked to be a long way away, traversing deep within the winding mass of tissue that provides his conscious and subconscious with thought. He remained silent as we headed towards his office and Katelynn, but his eyes were asking a million questions as I caught him sneaking sideways glances at me every minute or two. Finally, a handful of steps before we got back to his office door, he stopped, willing me to do likewise and face him.

"What happened with Harry back there, John?" he asked in a discreetly quiet voice, but getting straight to the point.

"I don't know," I honestly replied.

"You looked like you had been hit with an electrical shock the moment you two touched."

"Well, it was a little different," I admitted. I had already been busted on that much. "There was nothing," I lied. Anticipating the next question (...*tell no one john...*) I knew I had to give him more than that. "It was like he was blocking it," I said, thinking quickly. "He said his Mom used to read palms. I don't know. But it surprised me and I jumped a bit, I guess."

"But you got his age right," Dr. James stated, still making me feel like I was under his microscope. I don't know, do doctor's have microscopes? Well even if they usually don't, I am sure Dr. James did.

"I had already picked an age to use before we had touched," I said, truthfully enough. But it had been the wrong age and at the last second, I think, Harry (*...tell no one john...*) told me with his mind that he was 72. "It was a lucky guess," was what I said instead.

Dr. James continued to cross-examine me with his dark eyes but remained silent as if waiting for me to finish my story. I had nothing to add.

"I would like to see how Katelynn is doing," I said, gratefully conceding the stare-down contest to the curious doctor and taking a step towards his office. Dr. James hesitated, I held my breath hoping not to hear my name and be forced to turn and try to further explain, but I heard him fall in behind me before I had taken my third step and by my fourth, I was once again fully focused on Katelynn.

Katelynn was standing in front of the third-floor window staring out over the sunlit parking lot sipping a coffee from a plastic Dixie cup. Holding the cup near her lips with one hand while she gently blew on it, her other arm was wrapped in a tight hug around her stomach as though she were freezing cold. I couldn't imagine what was going through her mind. She turned and looked towards us as we entered the room. She didn't look as though she had been crying, but I knew that she had. And there was something missing in her now dry and recomposed eyes. As she took a couple slow steps towards the red high back chair on the near corner of the desk, I saw that it was hope that was missing. Something else had taken its place. Acceptance, depression, panic...I couldn't yet tell. But hope was visibly gone.

I silently took my prospective seat in front of the massive desk and waited for Dr. James to get settled on his side. The Grandfather clock next to the coat closet read 2:30. It had been a very long thirty minutes. A lot had changed.

Katelynn had changed. A light had vanished from her eyes. Her gaze remained steady but her focus looked unsteady. I didn't think she should be left alone for a while.

Dr. James had changed. He had transitioned from professional to childlike to concerned father figure to doctor-on-the-verge-of-a-major-breakthrough-in-the-advancement-of-our-knowledge-of-the-human-brain all in the last thirty minutes.

And in the last six or seven minutes, I had changed. I had gotten Harry's age right. Harry had told me his age with his mind at the last second. I hadn't been touching his hand when he had sent *(72)* into my mind. And when I *had* touched his hand, it wasn't the usual pair of numbers I had received. I hadn't tried to make sense of the words yet that had replaced the numbers, but I knew I wasn't going to forget them. I don't think there was a single second of that previous thirty minutes that I will ever forget. It had seemed to take five times that long. I wanted to get out of there. I wanted to get Katelynn out too. She didn't look well. Everything had changed. I was sorry I had ever agreed to the experiment.

And now there was Dr. James to worry about as well. Not his mental stability, as was looking the case in Katelynn's corner, but his need for mental stimulation. He wanted answers. He was already aware of enough for a guaranteed top three article in the table of contents for the next Medical Monthly but I wanted to make sure that was as far as it went. The only way I saw this happening would be if, after I get his help trying to save Katelynn from some premature death, I pretend the phenomenon has vanished just as quickly as it came. Maybe I could convince him that it had actually stopped with Harry. Benny had been the last. With Harry, the talent had short-circuited and that was why I had not received a number. I had no idea if I could pull it off.

"How are you feeling?" Dr. James asked Katelynn.

"Confused," she said solemnly, not looking up.

"Well, obviously we really don't know much of anything for sure yet until we can open the envelopes. I don't suspect we will have to wait too long for one or two of them." Dr. James leaned forward a bit over his desk on his elbows. "John, why don't you fill in Katelynn on what happened because I am not really quite sure myself."

I didn't like the scientist in Dr. James much. I didn't want to be telling Katelynn what I told Dr. James. If she thought there was a flaw in my new talent, I would only once again be giving her false hope. I knew the scientist in Dr. James selfishly just wanted to hear me try to describe what happened in my own words again.

"I pretty much got all three of them right except there was a fourth one who is not a patient here," I said. "I think he blocked me." And then I quickly added, just to try it on for size, "Or maybe I just suddenly lost the touch. I don't know. But I drew a blank on him."

"But still happened to guess his correct age," Dr. James added, raising his left eyebrow ever so slightly.

"It was a lucky guess," I explained.

"Well maybe we need to just let everything sink in a little bit right now," Dr. James suggested, probably sensing he wasn't going to get much more out of me today. Leaning back into his chair, possibly trying to think of a good title for his upcoming article, he said, "I will of course let you know if we need to open any envelopes over the next few days. John, I don't know why you drew a blank with Harry, but I don't think it is because the phenomenon has simply ceased to exist."

That idea didn't fly far.

"Why don't you leave me with your number, John, and let me give you a call in a couple of days. I want to collect my thoughts and I am sure we can start figuring out a few things just talking them out. Katelynn, if you feel up to it, I would like to have your input as well at that time."

Katelynn nodded. I followed suit with a nod and wrote down my phone number on a blank prescription form Dr. James ripped off a pad and pushed it across the desk for him. We said our good-bye's and thank you's. I stood and faced Katelynn. Without saying a word, she stood and took a place by my side just as naturally as though we had been a couple for years. She laced her arm around mine and walked with her head down, step for step with me all the way to the employee parking lot.

"I don't want you to be alone right now," I said. "Do you want to go get a coffee? Get something to eat? Do you have some time before needing to get Faith?"

"Faith is with her Grandma and Grandpa," Katelynn flatly said. "They drove down and picked her up last night. They only live a couple of hours away. I was thinking about taking my vacation there despite all this. If I am going to die, I would rather be there. It's where I was born."

Once again, her eyes welled up, tears flowed out unrestrained, and I found her wrapped in my arms softly trembling and pressing her eyes into my shoulder.

We found a Denny's a couple blocks away and I pulled her car into an open slot. Speaking a minimal number of words to get the job done back at the employee lot, we had established at least some coffee with an option for food would be good, and that I would drive. We still sat in silence as the first coffee was drank and then the runny, scrambled eggs and the burnt toast and the greasy hash browns were eaten and the second cup of coffee had been poured.

"So, it doesn't look too good, does it?" she finally said.

"I don't know," I replied. I was still working on some pancakes accompanied with chocolate milk. But I had been lost in thought myself when she had spoken. *(...4 days...6pm...14 crimson lane minnetonka...tell no one john...bring a dessert...see you then...)* was the particular thought I had been lost in.

My first instinct was to tell her everything, just the way it had happened. Tell her about Harry, about communicating with him without touching, about this weird message he had presumably implanted. I really, really wanted to tell her. But I didn't want to falsely raise her hopes again. I didn't know what this new twist meant, but it didn't look like it had anything to do with Katelynn's numbers and the numbers still meant, as far as I could tell, what they had always meant...that Katelynn would be dying soon. And then there was the ominous message itself (*...tell no one john...*). But the first reason was the one that held the weight. I couldn't tell her.

"How long is Faith going to be at you mother's place," I asked, trying to change the subject.

"I guess forever," she replied cynically. Then raised her head up and added, "I'm sorry, John. I don't mean to be like that. I'm feeling sorry for myself right now."

"It's okay," I said.

"On the one hand, I believe you. I know you are right. But on the other, I can't figure out why you *would* be right. Am I going to be killed in some freak accident? Should I be locking myself up in a cell? How can you see the future? How can I possibly be believing you? How can any of this be real? It is all so absurd! I am perfectly healthy. And I am angry at myself for being so gullible."

I sat quietly, fork laying idle on my last maple syrup-soaked pancake, allowing her to get this all off her chest, hoping it would do some good. But not only am I not a doctor, as I alluded to earlier, I am no shrink either and I was clearly out of my league here. All I could do was listen.

She swallowed down some more caffeine. "I think I am going to spend a few days straightening up the house and getting things in order. Then I will go join my parents and my daughter until..." she paused, not knowing how to finish that sentence.

"Come home with me tonight," I finally found the courage to say. "I have a spare room you can stay in. I don't want you to be alone tonight. We can stop by your place and pick up anything you need. I won't hound you about talking or anything. I just don't want you by yourself. What do ya say?"

"Okay," she said, though I hadn't expected her to agree. "What about your motorcycle?"

"We'll go back for it tomorrow," I said. "After a good night's rest."

13

And a good night's rest was exactly what we got. We got to my place a little after six. We had picked up her over night necessities along the way, not overlooking the coffee maker and plenty of ammunition for it when I shocked her by stating that I owned neither. I think I barely passed the ensuing onslaught of questions involving my domesticity and she decided she could probably get by without also packing the rest of her pantry along with the coffee. I made popcorn, one of the items which she had quizzed me about in the car, and along with the milk, the Double-Cream Oreo cookies, the coffee, and the giant slices of cold pepperoni and cheese, we watched a couple of Steve Martin movies to take our minds off things.

Walking into the kitchen upon our arrival, she noticed I still had my gloves on. "You don't need to wear those on my account," she said, nodding at my hands.

"I suppose," I said, looking down at my hands. "But I would just as soon not have any numbers pressing their way forward for now."

"I'll close my eyes if I think I am going to touch you," she said. "Go ahead. Take 'em off. Make yourself at home."

"But this *is* my home."

"All the more reason," she had replied with her back to me, randomly opening up cupboard doors as though it were as much her home as it was mine. "Now where's all this popcorn you lured me here with."

It took a few wisecracks from Steve before Katelynn was able to find her laugh again. It started with a guilty sounding, slightly restrained chuckle as he went prancing around the gas station's lot with the phonebook in his hands, screaming, "I'm somebody! I'm somebody!" The chuckle grew stronger with each release until she could openly laugh again by the time his rags had gone to riches to rags and back to riches.

The second Martin flick, something about a highway weather sign that could read the future and give advise, had a more romantic spin on it. Half way through it, with the popcorn gone, the last pepperoni slices looking sweaty and plastic, the coffee pushed forward on the coffee table, Katelynn moved the empty popcorn bowl from the couch between us and slid over next to me. While Steve was asking the highway weather sign for a sign telling him what to do next to win the heart of a woman, Katelynn curled up next to me. I raised my left arm and once she had settled in, I brought it down over her protectively.

When the movie had finished and Steve Martin and his new ladyfriend had thanked the alien weather sign for its caring concern and help while it played the bag pipes in their honor, Katelynn was asleep. I could hear the rhythm of her steady breathing and felt the beating of her strong heart against my ribs. I realized I was holding my breath and let it out slowly so as not to disturb her while I carefully reached for the remote control with my right hand. I hit the power button and the screen immediately shriveled to a white dot that hung for a moment in the center of the screen before disappearing with a small "pop." The room got darker, the only light now filtering in from the kitchen.

Katelynn stirred.

"Is it over?" she asked, groggily lifting herself upright in her seat and rubbing an eye.

"Yes, it is. I still need to get your bed made up." I said, and stood to do so.

"No. Don't." She said, stopping me, yawning, stretching, looking prettier than anyone dying in twenty-five days has a right to. "Let's just go to bed. I don't even want to open my eyes. Just lead me to your bed, lay me down, cover me up in the sheet and then curl up next to me and hold me tonight. Can you do that?" she asked. Her arms were held out blindly, her eyes were still held shut.

I said nothing. I took her hand, felt nothing but her warm hand, thought of nothing but her warm hand. I lifted her from the couch, lead her into my bedroom and tucked her snuggly between the sheets as she had requested. Still fully clothed, sans shoes, I slipped beneath the covers myself, wrapped my arms around her as she rolled her head onto my chest, and proceeded to sleep for nine wonderful dreamless hours.

Katelynn was already up when I awoke. The light in her eyes had found its way home again sometime during the night. That was good, I thought. It meant she hadn't given up completely. At least that was what I was hoping it meant, because I knew one thing for damn sure, *I* certainly wasn't giving up.

Feeling the rhythm of her strong heart sing me to sleep that night only made me surer that there could be no reason for this kind, loving, beautiful, young mother to be facing a premature death. I was sure that Dr. James was already trying to work a complete physical for her into his schedule. At least if he wasn't, that was going to be the first suggestion I made when he called us back into his office. The call would be coming sometime tomorrow. Mr. Crawley was not going to be allowing us any more time than that.

Katelynn was pouring herself a cup of coffee from her coffee maker, into her customary tall morning mug that she had also brought along. Her hair was still wet and hanging out over a white towel draped over the shoulders of her white cotton robe which flowed out enough for just a moment as she turned for me to notice the white silk gown underneath. You'd think she'd get enough of white at work, but I had to admit, she did look good in white. Some people like blue. I'm partial to green. She must like white.

"I take it you found everything you needed," I asked, making my way to the fridge.

"Yes, thank you," she said, with a smile I thought I could get used to should the opportunity miraculously ever arise. "I love your shower. It has that massage option in the nozzle. I've always wanted one of those."

"Did you sleep okay last night?" I asked.

"Yes," she said, with a soft smile. "You were just what the doctor ordered. Thank you." She turned towards the kitchen table and took a seat. When I pulled my head out of the refrigerator with some strawberries and milk, she was silently watching as she sipped her coffee. I moved across the kitchen to the pantry and pulled out a box of Honey Combs. I turned. She was still watching.

"Was there something else on your mind?" I asked. I wasn't used to being stared at while getting my breakfast ready and it was making me and my reclusive nature feel a bit uneasy and crowded.

"Sorry," she said, but I could still feel her eyes on me as I pulled a bowl from the cupboard and filled it to the rim with cereal. She was still watching as I sliced my strawberries up and dropped them into the bowl on top of the honey combs. Finally, when I had moved towards the table with my bowl in one hand and a gallon of milk and a spoon in the other, she looked back into her coffee cup for the answers to the questions she had been silently asking.

"What's on your mind?" I rephrased as I sat down.

"I don't know. Nothing. Everything." She looked back up at me. Anger was back in her eye. Not dominate. Not fiery and boiling over pissed. But it was in there mixing with a whirlwind of other emotions and I was happy to see it. "I was thinking about how hard this must be on you," she continued, "to know when everyone you meet is going to die. How lonely and helpless you must feel."

"I'm sure between the two of us, I have the easier role in all this," I said, using the transporting of the sugar from the sugar bowl to the cereal bowl without leaving a trail on the table for ants to discover later as a mild distraction rather than looking into her soulful eyes. I could have simply moved the sugar bowl closer to the cereal bowl. "Don't worry about me," I said.

"And others are going to die today, having it even worse than we do. But once they die, once I die, it is over. I can move on. I will be in the company of God and gain understanding and contentment. You will have to live through it again. And then again. And again. For you the death never stops." She looked away again, back into the black abyss warming her hands. "I'm not sure which is worse," she said softly, before taking a slow, long sip.

In spite of our difference in opinion about who had the worst end of the bargain here, we came to a couple of conclusions during breakfast. The first of which was, we agreed that it would be a good idea that she spend some time with her daughter out at her parents' farm. She wasn't sick. She didn't need treatment to prevent whatever her fate was to be on the 29th day of her 29th year. Then I had added, "But I think it would be a good idea if you had reserved yourself a room at the hospital beginning the eve of September

17th, the 28th day of your 29th year." This is where we had another difference of opinion.

"I am going to stay there, John. Like I told you and Dr. James yesterday, if this is God's plan for me and my daughter, then so be it." Again, stated with the bowed head. I wondered who she was trying to convince. Her eyes were no where near as empty as they had been when returning to Dr. James' office yesterday afternoon, but I didn't like the acceptance that had moved in and over powered the anger as she repeated the shortened version of the confession. "I want to be with the ones I love in a place where I am comfortable when it happens, *if* it happens, John."

Well at least she added the *'if.'* At least there was still a little bit of room to work with, a handhold of hope at the bottom of the rope where sanity dangled treacherously loose above the unknown and insane world that seemed to be unfolding itself a little at a time.

I had to think of some way to change her thinking. She was giving up, but she didn't see it that way. She was falling back on God. That was fine with her, but not with me. As far as I was concerned, though I would never have been so inconsiderate to say so to her face, if you remember my stated views on such subjects at the open of this story, her faith in God was no different than every child's faith in Santa Clause's ability to know just the right toy to bring you for Christmas. We are told of a number of creature's that no one has ever actually met, that creep around through the night and meddle in our lives, especially the lives of the children. The Easter Bunny hides his eggs. Santa Claus brings his gifts. The Tooth Fairy even enters into your room as you sleep and is allowed to mess around beneath your pillow. And of course, there is God, who is allowed into our hearts and our souls.

One by one, as we grow older, we begin to discover that all these "Superheroes" our trusted, wise and certainly honest parents told us were real, are in fact not. One by one---except one. God. No one has ever actually met him, at least in the most common sense of the word. No one even knows for sure what He looks like, where He lives, what He eats for breakfast or who His favorite girl-band is. He is but a myth. A desperate wish. He is an adult version of the Santa Clause no one wants to believe could possibly not be real because He delivers to us all (at least all of us who worship His existence and abide by His laws) the ultimate gift, the most precious present of all---a life after death. No. God must be real. Even if Ol' St. Nick and Peter Cottontail and Tinkerbell and The Train That Thought He Could all have to turn out to be the candy coating for an otherwise bitter tasting world, surely God is true.

Anyway, she saw it as putting her faith in God. I saw it as giving up. I was desperate for something to say. How do you go up against God himself? I mean, I am just your garden variety mortal human being with no special belief, no roots to grab onto, no Holy Book to prove my faith, no 3000-year-old history to empower my words of loyalty to the belief in my heart. How can I compete?

Steve Martin's comic voice, probably only because I had just listened to it trying to make me forget and to laugh for almost four hours the previous night, suddenly said inside my head, "If you can't beat 'em, join 'em."

And that's what I did...sort of. I dropped a heaping spoonful of Honey Combs capped with a strawberry slice back into my bowl uneaten and locked eyes with my debate opponent, at least that's how I viewed her at that moment on this particular subject. I hesitated, telling her in my silence that what I was about to say was important.

Holding her gaze, I started slowly, "Okay. Think about this a minute." Pause. My eyes said, *Don't look away. Listen. Pay attention.* I consciously held back the small smile that sat at the corners of my lips. It was only to be a small battle won. The war was no where near over. I remained stern. I still needed her attention to win this battle.

"I come into your life after miraculously surviving what by all rights should have been a fatal meeting of the metals with a semi truck and inform you that you are going to die. And you believe me. I want to try to save you, maybe try to prevent this tragic and seemingly needless event from occurring. And then you tell me that if this is what God wants, for you to give your life for some unknown cause, then it is a good thing and you will do as He wills. Does that sound like an accurate summary to you?"

She nodded, only slightly, hesitantly, unsure of where I was going with this, but enough to ensure me that she was listening. I paused again.

"Okay," Now I allowed myself to smile, just a little, to let her know what I was about to say was a good thing. I knew I was trying to do exactly what I had not wanted to do the day before, to give hope where none lay. I still didn't have a clue what, if anything, could be done to prevent the scientifically proven phenomenon from continuing its unbeaten streak. True, that was a streak of only one at that point in time, but I was sure that it would be two by the next day. Three not long after that. With the punch line I was so anxious to deliver here, I would also be trying to deliver hope, in a place where I still didn't know if it could exist. Once stated, I knew there was no turning back. If I am to convince this woman, whom I only met in the past few weeks, to have faith in me over the God that she has been faithful to her whole life, then I must come through for her. After winning her trust with the help of Steve Martin and my next carefully crafted made-up version of truth, as I knew I was about to do, it would be hard to live with myself if I failed. To steal someone's afterlife from them during the final days or their life as we know it, well, if there is a penalty more severe than capital punishment, I might have just applied for it if I let her down now. The small smile I had allowed to surface at the corners of my mouth as I spoke was not genuine, it was part of the sales pitch.

"If it is God's will for you to die, why send me to warn you?" I asked her, going in for the kill. "If He has good reason for your death, why send me here to make you miserable during your final days. You know I don't believe in God," I said cautiously. I don't think she did know that until just then by the look on her face when I said that. But again, I had her attention. Good. I continued before she had time to hold the last fact against me.

"Okay, maybe you didn't know that yet. But that's not the point. Let's say you are right. He exists. He is good. Why would He send me? I ask you...are you sure...how do you know that God didn't send me here Himself. How do you know that He didn't send me this ability so that I could warn you about it? I doubt He sent me here to tease you with it. You can't be at your folks' house in twenty-four days. You need to be here, checked into the hospital, with a crew of capable doctors a moment's notice away and me by your side. And logic dictates that you need to do this because this is what I want you to do. And you must do what I want you to do because it is only logical that if your God does exist, and he is indeed good, then He sent me here to warn and to protect, not to harm and taunt. I need you to believe in me, Katelynn. I need you to trust me. And I need you to believe in yourself. You have reason to exist, to go on. No God would take that all away from you. There can be no good reason for this. He sent *me*, Katelynn. Trust *me*. Help *me* help you."

I already knew I had won her over as I asked for her help. Once again, I had been responsible for the tiny liquid droplets silently trekking down the curve of her smooth cheek and a pang of guilt settled somewhere in my heart as the victory bell sounded in my head. Now I was surely damned to Hell if I was wrong about everything, including the existence of Hell.

14

After the breakfast dishes had been picked up and the few tears had dried up, we talked about a plan. The plan was, for now, to wait. Since we had no plans to go back to the hospital before Mr. Crawley left it, I told Katelynn when his due date was, knowing the leaking of the information could not contaminate the test results. We would then get a call, sometime tomorrow, according to our plan, to go have a visit with Dr. James, providing of course that Dr. James could wait that long. This is when we would get a complete physical scheduled for Katelynn, hopefully about a week away. Katelynn would be able to take the next week or so off and spend it at home with her family on the farm. She would then return for the physical, and then back to the farm.

After another relaxing and carefree week or so of frolicking with family out at the farm, at least as relaxed and carefree as one waiting to die in a few days can be, Katelynn would then return home, with one of her parents coming along to stay with her, the other remaining on the farm with Faith, for a few days until the 17th when she will check into a room on the third floor of the luxurious Park Nicollet Hospital. There, after the stroke of midnight, nurses and doctors and millions of dollars of emergency medical equipment will be standing by if needed, not to mention myself and probably her Dad on either side of her bed.

At least, that was the plan. It didn't take long to come up with. I was simply quite relieved that she had agreed to make use of the accommodations at Hotel Hospital for the 18th. Most people may not have been able to talk their way into such a nice place on the eve of their foretold premature death with the intention of preventing it. Most people would be turned away, some even laughed at, a few maybe given a business card for "someone to talk to." But Katelynn had connections. She had Dr. James. We should have no problem booking a suite for the day. Check out time for Katelynn would (hopefully) be 12:01 a.m. on the 19th.

Having agreed on the plan, we stood from the couch and I went after a pair of gloves while she gathered up the items she had brought for the night's visit. When I walked back out to the entry hallway by the front door where Katelynn was already waiting for me, she suddenly turned and asked, "If you are so sure Mr. Crawley is going to die tomorrow, what makes you think there is any hope for me?"

I knew she was at least feeling a little stronger. The question was not asked with the edge of desperateness or the tainting of depression, but rather quizzically or as an afterthought. It showed that she was still thinking...she wasn't giving up. Of course, I had also been asking myself the same question and I told her the best answer I had come up with so far.

"Mr. Crawley," I explained, "is dying of natural causes, well, of some disease that is eating away his living cells and preventing the regeneration of new ones and leaving him defenseless even to all the most common viruses, but he is expected to die. Just looking at him, you know it is going to be soon. Even if a team of specialists were standing by to help sustain his life for another few hours or another day, it would only be for that many more moments of misery for him. But if Dr. James' theory is even in the ball park, I am hoping the physical will show us something in you that wouldn't have otherwise been found in time and we can get it fixed and all live happily ever after."

Too much hope was flowing into her eyes as she came around to my way of thinking. I did believe all that I was telling her, but just as much of me was already grieving Faith's losses and cursing the world's largest, invisible, evil domino for falling this direction. Yet morally right or wrong on my part to build up her hopes against a predestined tragic fate, it was what she needed if she was to even stand a chance at dressing her daughter for Halloween this year. Hope.

"And," I continued, "even if they can't find anything with a physical and some tests, and you do have to check in on the 17th feeling healthy and scared, they are there if anything happens. To save Mr. Crawley would only be for hours or a day or two at best. To save you would be saving a lifetime yet to come. It would be saving Faith, too."

Another tear. Damn. I'm always making her cry.

"Look," I said, pulling her gently closer to me with a gloved hand, "I really don't know any more than you do. I wish I could tell you that there's nothing to worry about, but I can't do that. You need to be a little worried. But until we know why your numbers are what they are, I can't believe that it has to happen. There's got to be a reason. We're going to find out that reason and then change the fact. Until I know that we can't do that, I think we can."

I could feel her trembling slightly as she pressed her eyes once again into my shoulder. I gave her a squeeze and received one in return that I thought for a moment was going to snap my spine.

Thirty-five minutes later, (she had obviously never been a courier or a cab driver) Katelynn dropped me off by my bike and promised to call me after she got done straightening the house so we could go out and get something to eat together. I didn't want to hound her, but I didn't want her alone either. She was already handling all this better than I probably would have had the roles been reversed. I don't know. I guess that's another question to ask ourselves here, how we would handle knowing that for reason's unknown, we were supposed to die in just a few weeks. Like I said, I don't know what kind of mental state I would be in. I thought she was handling it all remarkably well, but there was no way I could tell how thin the wall was for her between handling it well and coming apart at the seams.

There was another benefit to this plan that I had reluctantly not told Katelynn about. I wanted her to be with someone for the most part, certainly in the evenings and nights when things naturally look darker and bleaker than they do in the morning sunshine. If not me, then family. Our plan had her already with family in four...now three days. I was planning on being somewhere in Minnetonka. I had no idea how long I would have to be there, but I guessed it would be at least through dessert. I was glad she would already be sleeping under rural stars by then.

The rest of the day was much like the calm before the storm, at least in retrospect. While Katelynn busied herself with moving furniture and vacuuming walls and reorganizing a variety of drawers and cupboards around her house, I sat at home and watched the phone. I tried doing the crossword puzzle that hadn't been looked at yet since I had slept in for a change but lost interest before I had even read the entire list of clues once through. I hadn't gotten the answers to too many of the ones I had read, either. I couldn't sit in the garage much longer than half a cigarette for fear that the phone would ring and I would miss it.

I tried cleaning. My heart wasn't in it.

I finished the Oreos, wanted to go buy some more but didn't want to leave the phone. Thought about getting a mobile phone. Hadn't seen the need before now. Tried to sleep, next to the phone. Couldn't. And when it finally did ring, I had been looking at it at the precise second it sounded off and I jumped backwards a moment from shock before recovering in time to answer it, still before its second ring. Katelynn was telling me how clean her house now looked while my heart slowed back to its normal pace. Like I said, she was handling herself a lot better than I think I could have.

At dinner, all you can eat riblets at Applebee's, we talked about many things, none of which had anything to do with death or fate or God. We talked about Faith and how she was adjusting to leaving the nest and going to school. We talked about why she was a nurse and why I wasn't. We talked about movies and actors, of tsunamis and hurricanes, of Dr. Seuss vs. Captain Kangaroo. We allowed Mr. Crawley's final night to be as lonely as most of the rest of his nights had been in his comparatively short life. No one was by his side on this eve of his parting. In fact, no one ever spoke to Mr. Crawley again. As Katelynn and I debated which was more frightening, a giant yellow talking bird or a miniature purple singing dinosaur, Mr. Crawley electronically lowered his bed and closed his eyes for the final time. He didn't die right away. He was well rested for his departure from life as we know it. He had died in his sleep. It was 4am when his overworked heart had simply called it quits. I called Katelynn at 7am, shortly after talking to Dr. James. He didn't sound excited. He was more professional than that. But even through the phone line, I thought his casual sounding voice sounded a bit too casual, like a practiced casual. Even through the phone line, I could hear him trying too hard not to sound excited.

Katelynn was waiting as I rode into her driveway. I parked on the little sidewalk winding its way past the bushes to the front door and climbed into the passenger seat of her idling car. It was the first time I had ever seen her not dressed in white. She wore her long hair unrestrained, flowing over her shoulders, covering the straps to the light blue sleeveless blouse tucked into her dark blue jeans. The Nikes were white, just like the white hospital issued shoes I had always seen her wearing, but the difference in her appearance with the addition of color made it at first difficult to read her mood. She didn't say good morning as I shut the door and put on my seatbelt. I didn't think her rude not to. She already had, of course, when I had called her thirty minutes earlier, but this was not a good morning, if truth be told. This morning my streak had officially increased to two. I was hoping it wouldn't get to three until after she was out of town.

Everything went for the most part as planned as far as the meeting with Dr. James was concerned, giving me a false sense of control over the situation. Dr. James, remarkably enough, had *not* thought of giving Katelynn a physical until I made the suggestion. He had been too focused on what he thought he might have discovered in me to give Katelynn much thought at all to this point. Up until the meeting, where he quickly understood that his oversight was my sole concern, Katelynn's predicament hadn't yet truly hit home with him the way it obviously had with us. Not five minutes into the meeting, his priorities had been put into proper order as I laid out our plans for him.

When Katelynn and I had walked into his office, loosely linked at the arms, the envelope with Mr. Crawley's name on it, still sealed, sat alone on his desk. Everything else had been cleared off the desk as though the letter might suddenly explode and damage anything left within its destructive range. Dr. James was already picking up the sealed envelope before our bodies had completely lowered to their prospective seats.

"It says today," I said as I sat, hoping to spoil any dramatic climax he was playing out in his head. All he had said during his phone call that morning had been that Mr. Crawley had died during the night and he was wondering how soon Katelynn and I could get there. I told him that I would call Katelynn and that I suspected we could probably be there in an hour, hour and a half, or something close. He didn't actually say "Hurry up," as we hung up, but it was in his voice and I had purposely gone out to the garage to smoke a cigarette and greet the new morning in proper fashion before going back in to wake Katelynn with the news.

Dr. James, though without the smile, reminded me of Johnny Carson on The Late Show, sitting at his desk, a swami hat poised slightly askew on his head, Ed McMahon seated on his right. Carson lifts up the sealed envelope, holds it out in front of his face, his other hand at his temple simulating deep concentration, "The answer is..."

"48:1" Dr. James said, as he went ahead and quickly broke the seal and pulled out the scrap of paper with Mr. Crawley's foretold death date written on it, ignoring my spoiler, or maybe just so rapt in the moment he hadn't even heard it.

His displaced and almost morbid thrill exhibited with this confirmation found in the envelope was being unsuccessfully restrained and I knew right away that he needed to get his priorities straight.

"We knew it would be," I said. "So that isn't even important at this point. What is important is what we are going to do for Katelynn."

"But do you realize what this means?" he asked, remaining under perfect professional control despite the very perfectly unprofessional wild look in his dark eyes.

"What it means," I said firmly, "is that we have less than three weeks to figure out how to change Katelynn's numbers."

From there, with out giving up the floor, I rolled out the plans Katelynn and I had put together the previous morning. I spoke with a confidence that I had rarely, if ever, previously displayed in my life. Certainly out of character for me over the last fifteen years or so. Maybe it was the new look, the older looking chrome dome, the dark, more distinguishing facial hair I had to keep tame each morning. Maybe it was a sense of responsibility to Katelynn, or even out of guilt for injecting all this doom and gloom into her life. Or maybe I saw it as a chance for some redemption, a chance to change something where once before I had failed to do so. Maybe I was looking to relieve some of the still lingering guilt for not having changed my own parents' fate, for failing to prevent their pointless deaths.

For whatever the reason, I spoke with the same sense of authority Dr. James had empowered over Katelynn and I at our first meeting. Before even allowing Dr. James a chance to agree or disagree to the plans, as though there was already no room for discussion on the matter, I said, "Then after we have safely delivered Katelynn to the thirtieth day of her twenty-ninth year, you and I can sit down and discuss what we might be able to do to *cease* this new talent of mine. I do not want it and I am not going to become yours or anyone else's subject for the advancement of medical science. I want to make that perfectly clear right here and now. If you won't help us, and then me, I will find someone who will. That is what the scrap of paper you hold in your hand means. That and nothing else."

I don't think Dr. James agreed with everything I had just spewed out at him, but to his humanitarian credit, he could at least see the importance in putting medical science second to the safety of Katelynn. He had agreed to the physical, the timing, and the "waiting room" if still needed at the hospital, where he too will also remain on call all night and the following day, starting on the eve of Katelynn's d-day, the 17th. He had even suggested a small variety of other tests at the time of the complete physical that Katelynn subsequently agreed to. But he never actually verbally agreed to the rest of the demands surrounding the plan. I figured I had gotten what I needed for now. I could deal with the rest, if need be, when the time came. If I could have read his mind, I would have probably discovered him already plotting to expose my talent once we got past Katelynn's date, regardless of the date's outcome, making it harder for me to hide from the world of medicine than just from himself. If he could have read mine, he would have discovered me making plans to disappear, preferably to my own personal island, the moment I knew Katelynn was safe.

The meeting only lasted twenty minutes. Dr. James, at least through the 18th of next month, was on our team. Until then, he was a friend and an ally. After then, he would most certainly become the enemy.

We returned to Katelynn's home after the meeting. As I headed for my motorcycle, she asked me if I wanted to come in for some breakfast. I had already eaten my traditional bowl of cereal before leaving to meet her that morning, but I didn't tell her that. Any excuse to hang around a little longer was fine with me, and it wasn't only due to concern over her mental health and stability with her life hanging in limbo. In fact, she looked stronger than I would have predicted from her silence before we had met Dr. James. Hearing me almost scolding Dr. James and getting him to see things our way, I think may have instilled yet another small layer of strength and hope inside her. She smiled, bashfully looking down at her food several times when I caught her glancing at me over the omelets she had made. I could only bashfully smile in return and try to concentrate on my food. A task requiring more effort than I could ever remember.

After breakfast, after filling in every single square in the Tribune's morning crossword puzzle together, and after each of us had won a game of scrabble (a rubber game wasn't necessary since she had beaten me in the first game by 150 points...I won the second by only 2) I made a couple of heaping sandwiches with whatever I found available in her refrigerator and we again traded bashful smiles while looking around the room and at our plates as we chewed our food.

After lunch, we walked to the park three blocks away and sat on a bench watching the preschoolers play in a fenced-in outside play area across the street. We sat there until all the kids had gone inside and another bouncy, energetic, noisy gaggle of grandchildren had flocked outside for some playful exercise. When their young spirits had flown back into the red brick building, we stood to slowly stroll back towards her home.

I think that was when the plan began to almost sway off track a bit.

Katelynn again wrapped both her arms around my right arm as we headed back in the direction we had come. She felt so natural there, so comfortable. There were no clumsy steps as our feet got tangled growing accustomed to each others' space. It was as though we had walked together in this fashion for years. At first, I had assumed we were walking so slowly simply because we were in no hurry, had no plans, maybe just enjoying a pleasant late August day. But as we neared her home, with two and a half blocks down and half a block to go, I realized how much I didn't want this walk to end. Katelynn felt so good, so perfect, so right. I was feeling a little guilty for even allowing such thoughts to have any weight at all at this point in time. I was on a mission here. To save Katelynn. I couldn't afford to be taken in by her beauty, and I still hadn't actually decided which of her beauties shone brighter yet, the inner or the outer one. I raised my left arm and, reaching across my chest, a little beyond my right shoulder, the fingers of my left hand sunk into thick dark hair and stroked downward. It hadn't come from forethought. It came instinctively. *Hell*, I thought, *I don't even know what her last name is yet*. But I wasn't about to spoil the mood by asking at that point. My hand returned to her head after traveling the length of her hair once and lightly pressed against her scalp.

Two houses to go. Our pace, together, in unison, slowed a little bit more. I realized that she too would probably just as soon walk right on past her house right now, just keep walking, slowly, to anywhere, to nowhere, just don't let go. Keep holding me. Never let go. Keep walking.

One house to go. She raised her head and met my eyes as we walked but said nothing. No numbers come to mind. I was wearing my riding gloves despite the seventy-eight-degree summer afternoon and I wondered if I had already been sweating before that look or only since. I wasn't sure.

We turned into her driveway, towards her house, never skipping a beat with our synchronized steps, the key to unlock our eyes temporarily discarded. Up two steps, over the threshold, where we stopped. The screen door banged shut on its own behind us. Katelynn let go of my arm, took two steps forward while I remained still by the front door recovering from the loss of the warmth she had been enveloping my entire right side with.

She turned to me and said almost in a whisper. "Take off your gloves."

I did.

Katelynn didn't move. She silently watched me remove my gloves and lay them on a small table next to the entry. Our eyes found each other again. She paused, slowly letting her eyes fall closed, and said, "Now come touch me, John, please."

15

The next morning (Tuesday, Aug. 26th-23 days until d-day) after Katelynn and I had shared in the cooking and then feasting of an absurdly large breakfast, we cleared the table and washed the dishes together. Though she and I both appeared rested, energetic and in great spirits this morning, as well as famished, we now apparently had two subjects we were going to ignore as long as we dared.

The first subject was of course, Dr. James, Mr. Crawley, Mrs. Ikatsu, Benny, Harry and anything related to foretelling death. The plans were set, the worried parents awaited their daughter's arrival, the physical and various tests had been scheduled. No need to discuss any of this business until she returned for her physical. Lord knows her parents are going to certainly want to talk about it every evening after Faith is put to bed. No need to talk about it now.

The second subject, one that had *not* been in anyone's plans, was what had happened yesterday afternoon and then through the evening and the entire night. Fact was, there was no way in hell either one of us should feel as energetic as we did after watching the sunrise together before finally napping for a couple of hours until our growling, voracious stomachs had wakened us for breakfast. But I felt as strong and ready to take on the world if need be as I ever had.

Katelynn, too, was smiling as though 23 days was a lifetime away, no different than the 50 plus more years I was hoping to last. We both knew that she was still going to her folks' farm later that day. We both knew that we would see each other again when she returned for the physical and then most likely one more time when she returns to check in at the hospital. We both understood that there was still a good chance, in fact a better chance than not if my success record was thrown into the equation, that she would be packing up and moving on from this life to whatever awaits in the afterworld in just a matter of a few weeks. *I* knew that I had no intentions of hanging around in this *hemisphere* as soon as September 19th rolled around no matter what happened on the 18th. And of course, we were both very much aware that we were in no shape mentally, that it was absolutely without a doubt the worst timing in the world right then to even think about getting anything romantic started because the odds of it ending in heartbreak were off the charts.

Yet with all that said, all that knowledge, common sense and wisdom between us readily available should we decide to retrieve it, those particular files or voices in our brains had remained closed or silent, at least throughout the night. For we also both knew that yesterday afternoon, evening and night was the perfect culmination to a wonderful day that had now spanned from one breakfast to another breakfast during a time when there may not be too many more breakfasts left for one of the parties partaking in the making of the perfect day. Death had been put on hold. Fate was ignored. God had business elsewhere. From the timid smiles behind the omelets, to the giggles while shoulders were pressed snuggly together on the carpeted floor doing a crossword puzzle and playing games; to the green park and the playful, laughing children; to the romantic summer afternoon walk, the looks into each others' eyes growing more and more frequent, more bold, more revealing; to the butterflies traveling in rampant swarms through our stomachs; what happened next only made all the rest of those simple pleasures the day had delivered us after returning from the hospital seem all the more special and unique. Every moment permanently engrained in a memory to be kept fresh for the rest of our days, no matter how many or few those days may number. We allowed ourselves for one night to drown in a passion that each of us possessed but had been keeping locked up and tucked away for different reasons for many years gathering dust while we waited perhaps for old memories and heartbreaks to fade away. We both knew that this particular variety of passion would once again need to be held in check and locked up, pretty much as soon as breakfast was over. It didn't need to be discussed. We both knew that we were each aware of what had happened and why, and that it needed to be left where it was, for what it was.

If for no other reason, our mutual understanding of this was obvious in our mutual willingness not to bring it up and analyze it. We didn't pretend it didn't happen. Our glowing faces would have betrayed that lie to even a stranger. But at least for now, at least for the next twenty-three or four days, this is neither a subject that will be brought up between us, nor an experience that will be repeated. We each knew this and accepted it as we knew we must. Yet it is a memory that each of us will treasure for the rest of this life and hopefully carry with us even into the next if that is at all possible.

After we had cleaned up the last crumb of evidence that we had just eaten a breakfast fit for six, ignoring the pair of numbers at the front of my mind, keeping them to a dull roar as best I could, we playfully dried our hands on each other's shirts and then joined our dried, dishwater pruned hands and faced one another, our eyes no longer meeting under the guise of bashfulness. Without the use of words but instead through a method of communication used only by lovers who have genuinely experienced what we shared over the past twenty-four hours, we consummated a silently made, yet mutually understood vow between us with a kiss born of the previous day's passion. However, it bore the signature of a last kiss, a few salty tears spilling back into the Sea of Passion as the tide must inevitably recede, at least for now, pulling our found spirits apart again. We knew it could be no other way, as our final passionate kiss emphasized our only hope...*at least for now.*

It was just after nine in the morning as her slightly trembling lips pulled away from mine and we both silently acknowledged the possibility that it might also be our final kiss. As she took a step back, the seemingly unconditional bliss that had appeared in both our glowing faces only moments ago, faded away just as quickly as did the welcome warmth her body had delivered to mine while pressed against me. The unconditional bliss had just been reminded of a condition that we couldn't ignore.

Reality.

As wonderful a world as it had been that we had lived in for the past twenty-four hours, it hadn't been the Real World. As much as we both wanted to tell the Real World to take its business elsewhere, that we had found a better world to live in, a better life to live; as much as we wanted to just pack up the kinfolk and get the hell out of Dodge, we knew the Real World would find us.

Katelynn looked down at the kitchen floor between us as though it were the Grand Canyon. A sadness for what might have been mixed with a helplessness towards what may come to be, had replaced the shine in her eyes with a look not all that dissimilar to resignation.

"Thank you," she said, still looking into the abyss beyond the floor. "You have no idea how much yesterday meant to me. I'm just sorry..."

She choked on her words, unable, or unwilling to finish the sentence. Again, the tears. Again, I step towards her to hold her, to comfort her, to protect and to love her...but she held up both hands before I finished the first step and raised her head to face me.

"No," she said. Her eyes met mine and with a moment of effort to establish control from somewhere within, she managed to shut the doorway on the tears. "Any more will transform the love to torture." She dropped her hands, but not her eyes which were now pleading, "Oh, John, I just want this to be over with, whatever happens. I just want it over."

"Maybe it will be over sooner than you think," I said, wondering who in fact *I* was trying to convince. "Dr. James might very well discover something when you return next Tuesday for the tests. And even if he doesn't, I still can't accept your presumed fate as fact. And besides," I added, "who's to say that Dr. Getz might not still be alive if he had been at the hospital when he had his heart attack instead of in his bathroom? Who's to say Dr. James *couldn't* have prolonged Mr. Crawley's life a day or two had he opened the envelope early and been ready? Your envelope has already been opened."

This last new thought, trying to induce Reason and Logic, the gods of anything resembling a religion in my life to that point, was spilling into my head almost simultaneously with its escape past my lips. I had already convinced myself. I was hoping Katelynn would be likewise convinced in a moment. "We are going to be ready. You are not dying like Mr. Crawley was and you don't have a weak heart like Dr. Getz did. You are young and strong. There is no reason for you to die. Dr. James and a full medical staff *will* be ready for anything that comes along on the eighteenth. I will be there with you, too, Katelynn. We *will* get you through this. *We* will be ready."

Okay, so it hadn't been our final kiss after all. This time it was Katelynn that ventured to cross the Grand Canyon but she met no resistance from my side of the gorge.

"You better be right," she said a moment later, retreating once again to her side of the canyon after our second final kiss. Though said with a sarcastic tone and a waggle of the finger in my direction, her voice softened dramatically and her hand moved to her heart as she said, "I believe in you, John. I..."

Now I was the one that held my hand up stopping her even though she wasn't attempting to move into my territory. Actually, I held up my hand to stop her because she was getting far too dangerously close to my territory. If I had let her finish what she was going to say, it might have changed everything. I knew she felt it. She knew I knew it. She knew I felt the same way about her. I had let her know it in every way possible with the *exception* of words over the last twenty-four hours. And she had replied many times over in the same wordless fashions. It was hard enough to let her go off to the farm, even though I knew that was the best thing for her. It was hard enough knowing how I felt, how she felt, even if she didn't buy the farm, I was planning on high-tailing it as fast and far away and as I possibly could the moment the victor, Katelynn or Fate, was officially announced. More precisely, I did plan on meeting with Dr. James on the morning of the 19th, long enough to set up a meeting with him later in the week. By the time he was missing me at that meeting, I was hoping to be permanently out of his microscope's range. But to hear Katelynn, or even myself, voice out loud this mutual sentiment that we were both only too aware of already, to hear those three words spoken with the passion that spawned the emotion itself...that would change everything.

"Faith and your parents will be here in an hour," I said, hoping she would understand. "Is there anything I can do to help you get ready to go?"

"You've already done more than I could have ever asked of you, John. Thank you so much." This time a gentle smile did spread across her face, reminding me of the morning sun rising on a field, touching each flower with its nurturing warmth as its light spreads out to embrace all beneath its reign. Her smile spilled that same warmth into me, spreading over my skin, sinking in through my pores, entering my blood system and warming my heart.

Three words emerged from the warmth enveloping my heart that her smile had caused and began to work their way towards my lips but I managed to swallow them down once again before they could make it up past my Adam's apple.

"Call me when you get back," I said instead. "I would like to meet you here instead of the hospital."

"I can do better than that," she replied, her warm smile now approaching high noon. "I'll call you on the way so you will already be here waiting for me when I get back."

I left before Katelynn's family arrived to pick her up. No need to confuse them further with my presence. Despite reality crashing our brief visit to Eden, there was still an inappropriate fresh glow in our faces that would not escape the scrutiny of already very concerned parents. Plus, I still wasn't comfortable with my role in all this as the bearer of bad news. And since the news I had to bear in this case happened to be the death of their daughter, I guess that made me kind of like a close relative to the Grim Reaper. Katelynn's parents had enough to worry about. They didn't need to add to that the fact that their daughter had fallen for a second cousin of Mr. Reaper.

Katelynn went off to the farm to try to cram a lifetime of fun and memories with her daughter into a week and I went home to wait. After about a half an hour of sitting in my garage waiting for the week to go by, I suddenly remembered I had something else to wait for first that was only little more than a day away...and I still needed to get a dessert.

Being said possessor of reclusive tendencies for the past fourteen years, I was not particularly looking forward to my trip out to Minnetonka, a fairly wealthy community built around about a thousand of Minnesota's ten thousand lakes. The west side suburb of Minneapolis wasn't too far from my south side, more preppy suburb, about forty minutes, but I had absolutely no idea what I was going to find when I got to 14 Crimson Lane. I had actually planned on taking a slow ride on my bike by the address a time or two after returning from the hospital and get a peek at it, but of course, I didn't get the chance. Then when I did leave Katelynn's home the next morning, 14 Crimson Lane had been the furthest thing from my mind.

Once back home, while settled into my thinking chair, smoking one of my thinking sticks, thinking about things I shouldn't have been thinking about, was when the memory of 6pm somehow snuck in and chased away the futile thoughts. Suddenly a throng of new concerns and questions flooded through from wherever they originate, giving cause for lighting-up a worry stick immediately after snubbing out the thinking stick.

...4 days...6pm...14 crimson lane minnetonka...tell no one john... bring a dessert...see you then...

I remembered every word just as though it had been spoken aloud to me only moments ago. *Four days*. That was tomorrow. It was obviously an invitation to a dinner party, but how big was the party and more importantly, why was Harry inviting *me*? I didn't think this was going to be Harry's home. Harry reeked southern from head to toe. So had Benny, and he would still be in the hospital. And there was the *"tell no one john"* part, the part I *didn't* want to think about. But that was also the part that had made me so curious. It was the part that had convinced me to go against my instincts and accept the invitation.

There was no way that I could think of to figure out what was going to happen before it happened, so I decided to ignore the new onslaught of debate topics and try to concentrate on my instructed contribution to the upcoming dinner party and produce a dessert. I didn't know if it was formal or casual, if I was expected to bake something or just go out and buy something. I am terrible at this kind of stuff under the best circumstances, which these were not. I compromised. I went out and bought twenty packages of Grandma's soft chocolate chip cookies at the Kwik Trip, cleaning out their supply and giving Jill, who was still proudly wearing her trainee title on her name tag, one more reason to think that I wasn't playing with a full deck. I opened up all the packages, two cookies per, and fanned them around and about on my largest platter. Next, I drew a couple of sheets of aluminum foil and wrapped cookies and platter to maintain Grandma's freshness. Voila. Dessert is ready...and with twenty-nine hours to spare.

16

Driving by 14 Crimson Lane would have proven a waste of time. By lake, the three-level Castle was noticed and admired by boaters young and old, rich and poor, drunk and sober, as they sailed by in their respective personal watercrafts. It sat just off the shore of a small inlet on one of the larger lakes of the area, its own private beach loosely roped off preventing curious or photo happy boaters from docking on the beach for a closer look. Where the water met the land on the north side of the beach, a less yielding, eight-foot, white boulder wall, made from the same stock of stone the castle had been made from, rose out of the water and continued into the woods, ultimately encircling the entire four acres of kinship to the castle and reentering the water at the border on the beach's south side where the ropes and buoys took over to complete the rough circle. In addition, for those that failed to observe these obvious efforts for privacy, there were a few dozen discreetly posted notices, both on land and on lake, informing that the law would enforce to its fullest legal potential the penalties for trespassing on private property.

By land, as would be the case with myself and my trusted steed who went by the name of Shadow, the view would have been of a gravel path leading off into the woods. A simple chain spanning the width of the driveway/path connected two 3-foot wooden posts. The ditches on the outer sides of the posts and the forest waiting immediately beyond prevented one from driving around the rustic entrance, but the chain itself was not locked. It was just a polite deterrent. If one were to be criminal enough to ignore the "No Trespassing" signs and lift away the chain and drive down the path into the woods, they would soon encounter a sterner request for privacy in the stone wall and an iron gate with an intercom system and an unhidden camera mounted upon the wall.

By the time Shadow and I crossed the barrier of the initial outer chain link deterrent, the chain had already been laid aside in anticipation of its arriving dinner guests. It was ten after six. I was running a little late. Not because I had had too much to do or got started late or had forgotten or gotten lost or anything. I had in fact been early. It was in fact my third time by the driveway when I finally entered the darker pathway of shadows. It was still bright out, the summer sun willing to stave off the darkness for another three hours yet in a Minnesota August, but the path itself was totally engulfed in the shadows of the forest which was as thick as any jungle as far as I was concerned. I felt vulnerable on my motorcycle as I slowly wound through the trees following the path that had only been marked by a faded "14" painted on each post that held the chain out on Crimson Lane.

My first trip by had been a half an hour earlier. The chain had even then already been removed and there were also already fresh tire tracks in the gravel serving as the driveway for the half-mile path leading to the inner stone and iron gate and ultimately, the castle itself.

It wasn't actually a castle, at least not in the Scottish sense or even the Hearst sense, but certainly qualified in the local sense. Yesterday afternoon, after getting the dessert put together so quickly and leaving myself with twenty-nine long hours to kill, I had gone to the Internet and entered the address to see if I could learn anything.

The "castle," though possessing the look of a structure that had to be centuries old, had in fact been built in 1989 by a slightly eccentric local weatherman who worked for a local news station. A couple of years earlier, he had patented a major improvement to the now standard and universally used Doppler Weather Radar System which had instantly propelled him into the world of the wealthy and he had apparently chosen the more eccentric side of that class to be kin to.

The "castle," which featured five bedrooms and four and half baths, three entertaining parlors, a large library, two dining rooms, an industrial size kitchen, a viewing room with a 120" projection TV and a sound system built into the walls and ceiling, and a large wine cellar in the basement, had no secret passageways hidden in the closets. There were no grand hallways with tapestries portraying the ancestors making all this living in luxury possible. Not even a giant portrait of an evil looking grandmother. It was perfectly modern on the inside. The complete antithesis of its outer appearance. The kitchen was outfitted with every modern appliance necessary to please the pickiest of chefs in preparation for a festive feast despite how natural it would appear from outside the castle to see a servant woman walking from the giant arched, wooden front doorway with a large vase in her arms to fetch some water for the Master's bath.

All this I already knew as I rode my motorcycle right on past the welcome sign of the laid down chain the first time by. For the life of me, I couldn't imagine why Harry had invited me out here, and discovering who actually owned the place rendered the poser even more ridiculously unanswerable. Maybe Harry wanted me to perform for some party here, introduce me as his discovery, stealing the glory from his helpless friend in Benny while he lays dying in the hospital. Maybe he is doing it *for* Benny, because Benny can't. Maybe Harry was responsible for the dessert and couldn't afford it so he got me to bring it. Once in the door, my cookies will be confiscated and I will be quickly escorted back to my bike and out the gate. I figured whatever the real reason would end up being, it would probably seem no less ridiculous.

Once around the lake wasn't enough, but twice would have made me far too late. After passing the drive the second time, I was no closer to figuring out if I should accept the invitation or just go home and eat the other thirty cookies. Ten had already not survived long enough to make this trip. The survivors were in a plastic airtight Tupperware container strapped to my seat behind me by a couple of bungee cords. The aluminum foil had not proven to be strong enough to fend off bored fingers. I got a couple of blocks past, realized the time, decided if I was going it better be now and made a U-turn on the narrow blacktop heading back to the driveway.

From the tracks beneath my feet as I turned onto the gravel, it appeared that quite a few cars had already arrived. At the main entrance, the iron gate was already slowly opening in anticipation of my arrival as I rounded the final dim corner and saw the Castle standing tall in a sunlit, John Deere made clearing. Beyond the gate, the drive became paved and arched into a smooth landing, passing by the front doors before reaching the five-car garage that more closely resembled a peasant's stable off to the left of the miniature castle replica. The drive then swooped past the garage and rejoined its beginning shortly before reaching the same gate in order to exit. Two vehicles traveling in opposite directions down the half-mile driveway outside the gate would result in one backing out the way it came. There was not enough room for two cars to pass, though I would have had no problem leaving in a hurry on a motorcycle if I had to.

Each stall in front of the closed garage doors had a car occupying it. Half a dozen more cars were parked along the side of the drive, past the stable/garage, one pair of tires each in the well-manicured and maintained grassy lawn, probably with the disapproval and a blind eye for one night by the lawn's caretaker. Half of the cars were just as one would expect to find parked in front of a money pit like this, black, fast, expensive looking. I've never been much of a car buff, if it gets you from point A to point B, that's always been good enough for me. But I know an expensive car when I see one. The rest of the cars looked no more distinguishing than those parked outside Bob's place down the street for the big game. A couple of old blue Chevy's, a mini van, a pick-up truck and two SUVs mingled with the Jaguars and Porches and a Lexus. Assuming the weatherman's cars were inside the garage, and that at least half the cars had contained more than one person in them, I estimated that there would be about twenty people here and I felt a knot begin to form in my reclusive stomach.

A man stepped out of nowhere surprising me as I coasted slowly by the front door looking the opposite direction at the strange mélange of cars. He was dressed in a plain black suit with a black bow tie and white shirt. He appeared to be somewhere between 70 and 90 years old and was apparently the valet. I jerked the handlebars instinctively away from him when I become suddenly aware of his close presence and then noticed he was pointing to the far-right hand side of the garage, away from the line of grass-smashing cars, where two more motorcycles I hadn't yet noticed were parked. Again, like the cars, one was a big 1200cc Honda GoldWing loaded to the teeth, the other was a naked Kawasaki 250 dirt bike. I heard both engines still ticking as they cooled, signifying that they were not just more play things belonging to the eccentric weatherman, but rather, they too belonged to a pair of guests at this mysterious dinner party which appeared to be catering to samples of all walks of life, at least according to the tale of the vehicles out front.

I parked the motorcycle next to the other two, pulled the cookies out from under their cords and returned towards the front doors. Mr. Valet had disappeared just as arcanely as he had appeared. I walked up to the massive twin wooden doors alone and rang the bell. I half expected Lurch from the Addams Family, or maybe Vincent Price himself to answer the door, but instead a younger version of Mr. Valet opened the door while a familiar looking excited grin impatiently towered over him from behind, it's owner practically prancing from foot to foot in unrestrained glee.

"Mr. John, I presume?" Mr. Doorman said a bit sarcastically, as he stepped in front of the doorway blocking entry without first properly identifying myself.

"John Johnson," I said. "That would be me."

"Very good," Mr. Doorman replied with a slight bow as he stepped aside allowing me room to enter. Glancing up as I passed by him in the doorway, Mr. Doorman asked in the same slightly sarcastic tone, "May I take your gloves, Mr. John Johnson?"

"No thank you, sir. I will be wearing them, thanks."

Mr. Doorman closed the door behind me without a second glance my way, accepting the fact that I wanted to wear my gloves indoors in late August. It probably hadn't even been all that high on the eccentric meter compared to the things he'd seen in his career as a servant to those that can afford to be lazy.

Meanwhile, Harry, the giant, bald, black Cheshire Cat, was holding out his massive bear paw and smiling down at me broadly enough to leave no doubt that he was, even still at the age of 72, the proud owner of a complete set of pearly white originals. His teeth also matched his white jacket, white shirt, white slacks and white bow tie. In fact, the only color on Harry this evening besides his skin was a red hanky sticking artistically out of his left breast pocket serving as a backdrop for the white rose pinned to his jacket in front of it. I suddenly felt severely underdressed in my red and blue plaid lumberjack shirt, blue jeans and black motorcycle gloves with a red stripe down the side. At least I'd worn the only pair of jeans I had that didn't have a hole in the left knee due to using said knee to drive when I had been a courier.

"Welcome! Welcome, Mr. John!" Harry said, as I took his hand and allowed him to vigorously pump it up and down a few times. He didn't ask about the gloves. "Let me take that for you," he said, releasing my hand and reaching towards the container of cookies which I readily conceded. "Chauncy, take these on over to Katharine and have her put 'em on a platter for us, if you would, please. Have her make 'em pertty," he added with a wink to me as he handed the Tupperware over to Chauncy Doorman.

Chauncy disappeared through an open doorway to our right in search of Katharine while Harry and I took the left option out of the castle's entry room towards the sound of the live piano music overlaying a wordless buzz easily distinguishable as numerous people chatting with drinks in their hands.

"I was to answer the door for you," Harry was saying, "but Chauncy says, 'Oh goodie. Then I can come do your job for you tomorrow.' But I'm retired so I let 'em do it. You ready to meet the gang?"

"Why am I here?" I blatantly asked. I'm not sure I intended to state that out loud, but there it was. Harry just laughed in response as if I had just told him the funniest joke he had ever heard in his life.

Before I had a chance to repeat the question or rephrase it, the noise level doubled and we were standing in a brightly lit, large ballroom. A few chairs were spread out along the walls, none in use. Mr. Piano Player was sitting behind a black Grand Piano in the same black castle-issued suit that Mr. Valet and Mr. Doorman wore, playing happy and bouncy tunes without the aid of a tip jar on the piano's edge. The room itself was large enough to only appear about two thirds full, even with the piano player and his instrument. There were four servants walking around with trays of snack foods or drinks and wearing the female version of the castle-issue uniform, a black dress cut at the knees with a white lace apron and bib. No imagination at all in either version. And as predicted, twenty or so guests chatting amiably, most with a drink in one hand.

I was relieved to see more jeans among the crowd than not. Harry was not the only one dressed in his Sunday Best, although his attire certainly stole the spotlight when he entered a room. Despite the relief in seeing that I wasn't inappropriately dressed for this seemingly unconventional gathering of mutts, half-breeds and thoroughbreds, I felt an instant surety that I had made the wrong decision in coming here. I felt a fine sweat break out on the apex of my bald held and felt self-conscious of not having the hair to hide it anymore and quickly checked the zipper of my jeans with the pinky of my right hand while pretending to adjust the belt I wasn't wearing to make sure it was up.

Too many people. I hadn't been around this many people in the same room since the reception after my parents' funeral. And to make things worse, they were all now looking at us. No, not at us, I quickly discovered. At me. Harry was doing the talking but they were all looking at me. I wanted to run. Harry was still talking and I didn't have a clue what he was saying. The clusters of faces that had ceased talking and turned to look at me all seemed to lose their individual features and began to meld together as one large, threatening face. The piano had either stopped or strayed from music to join the growing buzz inside my head that was preventing me from being able to hear words with any clarity. I closed my eyes. Harry was still speaking. The people still stared. My knees felt weak.

relax john. you are with friends. relax john. be yourself.

I reopened my eyes and they were instantly drawn to a woman who looked to be in her mid to late forties, well dressed in a smart looking, dark blue pant suit. Her shoulder length hair was in transition to gray, still holding stubbornly to a few brunette tresses here and there, her face emitting a caring look of motherly concern.

relax john. you are with friends. in time you will have your answers. relax.

I don't know why I knew it was her. There were more than twenty pairs of eyes looking right at me but I knew she was the one that was trying to calm me down inside my head.

take a deep breath john

I took a deep breath.

let it out nice and slow

I let it out nice and slow.

you're going to be just fine john

I started to feel a little better.

my name is ronnie

The loud buzz started to subside.

good john good

Harry's words began to become distinguishable again.

now relax john. you are with friends.

"I think it would be a good time to move into the dining room," Harry was saying to the room, "and commence with the feasting. After dinner and dessert, after John has had a chance to get comfortable with at least the sight of all yer ugly mugs, you can all start slowly introducing yourselves one at a time so as not to overwhelm the poor young man. Mr. Northrop?"

I recognized the man responding to the name of Northrop as the weatherman on the channel seven local nightly news at six and ten. I briefly wondered who was covering for him at the station. He was at the back of the crowd that had pretty much reacquired their individual personal traits since obtaining Ronnie's help to stave off the panic attack. He waved a friendly welcome to the crowd that had finally taken their eyes off me at the mention of food and were now noisily turning towards the weatherman and his fine dining room through the door at the rear of the ballroom.

Harry laid a gentle hand on my back, reminding me that I had to move my feet in order to walk, and the two of us brought up the rear as we entered the dining room for a feast in obvious celebration of something that I had as yet still been left in the dark about.

The banquet table was huge. It took five servers, filing out of the kitchen and splitting up around the table as if choreographed and well rehearsed, to get everyone's opening appetizers of something that smelled like fish and looked like seaweed which I couldn't readily identify, distributed to all with only a few seconds of time between the first and last to receive. I just rearranged the stuff resembling food on my plate for a while until the second wave of synchronized service delivered the next course, a much more appetizing assortment of breads and cheeses and fruits.

I remained silent, concentrating on my food, wondering how long I was going to have to endure this before I could grab a few more cookies and sneak out the door. As though everyone present could sense my trepidation, no one directed any questions towards me or even made comments in my direction. I had tensed myself from the moment we took our seats. I had expected to be drilled, questioned, probed or something. I had taken the last available seat being the last one into the dining room. The table had been preset with precisely the number of settings needed. To my left was Harry, to my right was Ronnie. I had at least expected *her* to try to start up some sort of conversation. I sat in the center of one of the long sides of the table. Mr. Northrop was at one head of the table on my left and a girl of no more than 17 with a punk-looking, pink and green highlighted, jet black mane of hair that looked totally out of control, long down the back, straight up on the top, flowing towards all points of the compass in between, sat at the other head to my right. There were ten more guests dining down the far side and nine more besides myself on my side of the beautifully prepared banquet table.

Noticing that Harry, Ronnie, and the other nineteen guests had all managed to keep themselves entertained through the first course and into the second without including me, I was able to relax a bit and gain a little comfort in my new crowded environment. I began to make a game out of placing the guests with the vehicles I had seen outside. I only knew the names of Harry, Mr. Northrop and the woman I presumed was Ronnie, so this was the only way I had at the time to define them.

I had already thought Ronnie looked like the Lexus type. More from a process of elimination than anything else. She had the air of enough money to not be driving the old Chevy's and she would have traded in the mini-van when the kids went off to college. The SUVs wouldn't be practical enough for daily use. The two Jaguars and two Porches didn't look like her speed and the image of her on either bike was almost laughable. That left the Lexus.

After our initial meeting of a few days ago, I would have placed Harry in the pick-up truck, but after seeing him in his fancy duds tonight, I decided to get a few more of the obvious ones before coming back to him with what was left.

Mr. Winthrop, the only other one in the room I felt I had any connection to prior to or since my arrival 25 minutes earlier, only because I recognized him from the TV, would have his cars in his garage/stable so I disqualified him from my game.

The next person that quite obviously grabbed my attention was at the opposite head of the table. This girl fell into the previously mentioned category of half-breed. If the stereotypes were to hold true, she had been born of, and subsequently at some point bored of, money and its accompanied codes of conduct. She had rebelled, embarrassed her wealthy, well-to-do-but-haven't-a-clue parents in any way she could think to do so. I put her in one of the old Chevy's. Not because I thought she couldn't afford better, but so as not to be accused of having anything to do with her unappreciated, unwanted and unearned wealth. If not for the pastel flashes of color in her long, raven hair, along with the black jeans and the three or four black shirts and tanks she was wearing, hiding any evidence of her womanly development, I would have guessed her to be Goth. She wore half a dozen earrings in each ear, like snowflakes only in the sense that no two were alike. Several were crosses but I doubted they were due to a devout faith in Christianity. Several appeared to be small cannabis sativa leaves and related miniature paraphernalia that probably more closely represented any version of religion she had ever embraced. She wore rings on each and every finger, including both thumbs. I was sure there was a tattoo or two somewhere, probably around the ankles or on the back and possibly a stud of some kind piercing what had once probably been a cute bellybutton. Her eyes...

...were watching me study her. Lost in my own thoughts and assessments, taking in her entire visage as I put together my own unauthorized version of her history and psyche, her dark eyes stared back boldly, challengingly, not the least bit intimidated by my obvious attempt to undress her being. Caught, embarrassed, losing a little ground that I had recently gained in my cope-ability, I looked at the slice of bread that had been suspended in front of my lips for who knows how long, another telltale sign, her eyes accusing, mine responding with 'guilty as charged.'

take a picture next time. they last longer

I glanced quickly back at the younger, updated version of Elvira. She was already talking to the guy on her right as though our eyes had never met, a younger looking version of Roger Moore in his James Bond days, definitely a Jaguar man. I couldn't hear her voice from where I sat over the steady dinner chatter that twenty-one people inevitably cause, but I knew that last thought had not originated from my own archive of slams and snide remarks. I suddenly had a hunch that my gloves, which I had removed in order to eat and were now sitting on my lap in place of the napkin, would probably not be of much further use on this particular gathering.

For the rest of the excruciatingly long, five course meal that ended in an array of exquisite looking, artery-blocking desserts, my cookies with a fresh layer of mouth-watering cinnamon frosting spread sparsely on top and distributed on a large silver platter among dark and light truffles not excluded, I abandoned my match-the-car-to-the-guest game and made a point of avoiding eye contact with anyone else. Although I had already realized that in neither of these last two "connections" had physical contact been necessary, it hadn't yet occurred to me that I had also not been looking into their eyes when their messages had entered my thoughts. Even so, it wasn't much beyond dinner when this latter realization also came to light. That turned out to be one of the easier revelations of the evening to accept.

17

I had gotten home shortly after three in the morning. I had left Mr. Northrop's anything but humble abode with a near full gas tank at 12:30. I had been traveling farther *away* from home for forty minutes before I even stopped to consider which direction I was going when I noticed I had just over half a tank left. Even after getting back on the right path home, every few minutes I had to confirm where I was with reassuring familiar landmarks as though I had been lost again just moments before identifying each one. If my gas tank had held more than three and a half gallons of gasoline, I might have driven all night. It was a good thing I was still able to use my auto-pilot on the motorcycle as I did while conducting business out of my car for so many years because the wind may have been blowing by the outside of my head at 60 miles per hour, but inside, a regular ol' typhoon was making a real mess of things. The only sense of time I felt when I finally pulled into my own drive was due to the gas tank being right on the empty marker.

After a grand finale of servants had appeared in a swooping graceful attack on the table and replaced each guest's dessert plate with a steaming cup of cappuccino using the speed and precision that would have made any pit crew at the Indy 500 proud, one by one, though I had not heard the instruction to do so, the dinner guests casually picked up their cappuccinos and disappeared through a different door than we had entered from on the opposite side of the table. With half the table empty, which in my mind was better than half the table full, a single black and white clad servant of the female variety came through the kitchen door behind Elvira with a pre-opened 20-ounce bottle of cold, crisp, refreshing Mountain Dew and placed it in front of me with a smile and a wink while picking up my untouched cappuccino.

After Mr. Northrop, or Paul, as he had later asked me to call him, and Elvira had each disappeared in turn through the new door, I caught on to the pattern being employed and the reason why, but I still got the impression this was a sequence of events, piano parlor to dining room to next room, that everyone here, excluding myself of course, had done before.

The first two that had left were the two directly across from me. They looked to be together, probably husband and wife. Both were in their mid to late forties, smartly dressed in formal dinner party attire, his complete with a hand-tied, black bow tie, hers, a long, satin, dark blue, skin tight, perfect cleavage-featuring dinner gown that at the same time complimented his suit. He, with the distinguishing streaks of gray appearing in his perfect dark hair, she, noticeably trying to defy time and its laws of aging, the outfit a little too revealing, the hair a little too red, the facial skin a little too tight...I gave them a Porsche. It appeared to me that I would have absolutely nothing in common with this couple and the idea that they and I would be invited to the same exclusive dinner party only further supported my growing belief that for whatever reason Harry had invited me here for, it had been a mistake.

With the casual air of normality, one by one, the other side of the table emptied up and the two heads stood a moment later in unison as I realized that once again, possibly by design, I would be the last person to enter the new room. I took a long refreshing drink from my bottle of Dew and wondered if we were going to be allowed a smoke break any time soon. As a few more guests left the room in orderly fashion, I presumed in order to avoid spilled drinks in a mad rush to the next activity on tonight's exciting agenda, I tried to calculate my odds of slipping out the opposite direction unnoticed and through the massive doors for an early escape. I figured if I were lucky enough to get passed Mr. Doorman and Mr. Valet, I probably wouldn't be able to get past Mr. Iron Gate, at least not with Shadow still supplying the source for a speedy getaway.

Ronnie gathered in her cappuccino, stood up next to me and without even a glance my direction began walking around the table towards the black hole that had just vacuumed up eighteen of the other strangers I had broken bread with. As she rounded the head of the table in unison with whomever had been sitting unnoticed by me on the other side of Harry's massive body, Harry likewise stood and waited for me to follow suit as though he knew I had been contemplating a jailbreak.

I had no reason to fear moving blindly and trustingly on to the next portion of the night's festivities. The piano music when I entered had been upbeat and the tone of the chatting people had been pleasant. The meal itself, first course forgiven, was better than any I had been party to in longer than I could remember, if ever. It reminded me of three or four of my family's annual Thanksgiving get-togethers with all the relatives when I had been a kid, all put together. More different kinds of delectable food than I had stomach enough to sample. And though I had chosen not to be involved in any of the conversation, it had all sounded comfortable and friendly enough throughout.

Still, I didn't want to follow Harry into the room. Although everyone else appeared to know what was going to come next and had no qualms or misgivings in anticipation of it, I had a feeling that once I went through that door, my whole life was going to drastically change and I wasn't sure if it would be for the better or not. Harry was still smiling broadly but all of a sudden, I was questioning myself as to whether I could truly tell the difference between the innocent smile of an excited child and the malevolent smile of a scheming madman.

"They're a harmless bunch," Harry said, as though he could read my mind, and I was beginning to believe he could. I was beginning to believe they *all* could. "You'll see when you get to know 'em. Now grab your sugar juice there and let's you and me see if we can't find us a couch close to the fire to socialize in."

Harry began to walk around the table to the left. The price for the wonderful meal waited beyond the opposite wall. I stood up, stuffed a glove in each front pocket, grabbed my Dew, started around the table to my right, and then stopped to pull my gloves back out of my pockets to hand them over to an almost but not quite grinning Chauncy Doorman who seemed to have magically appeared by my side holding out his hand. I watched him retreat with my gloves through the door of our initial entry into the dining room before continuing around, catching up with Harry, and following him through the door. I just wanted to get the night over with, although I understood on some level for some unknown reason that going through this door would not get me closer to the end of anything, but would in fact only be the beginning of everything.

It was the library. I had seen a couple pictures of it online earlier that day. It was in one of the four rounded corners of the castle and the ceiling was two floors high giving room for the massive shelves found on two of the walls. The little photos I had seen on my 13" computer screen had not done justice to the size of this room or the sense of open space you felt standing below two stories of books. Each wall of shelves had its own built-in ladder that slid horizontally along the wall to retrieve the books stocked out of reach. A third wall was ninety percent glass and looked out over the beach and lake that extended out past a brief grassy lawn. There was no doorway leading directly outside from the library. It was purely for the lighting and the view.

The fourth wall featured a large circular stone fireplace with three comfortable couches loosely surrounding it and a genuine bearskin rug that lay at its base. Above the stone fireplace, the entire two stories of wall space were covered with a huge painted mural of seven Dragons in a fiery lair. The Dragons appeared to have golden scales, the fire surrounding them, engulfing them, causing a green tinted reflection on the insides of their wings which appeared poised for flight. If Dragons can have facial expressions, these looked determined and dedicated, wise and fearless. Together, the sinister seven looked more like a sentinel, blocking passage to some magical no-man's land. There had been no pictures of this wall on the Internet.

Spread out throughout the rest of the library, scattered among a wide variety of exotic-looking plant life and antique-looking lamps and coffee tables, enough seating and more was available for the entire party to sit in small groups and converse while sipping cappuccinos, although half had decided to remain standing and chatted in small circles while holding their warm cups with two hands close to their hearts.

Two of the three couches in front of the fireplace had indeed been vacant and I followed Harry toward the center one that faced the already steadily blazing six log fire. With the sun beginning to set behind the trees that bordered Northrop's Inlet, reflections of the red and yellow leaping flames began to dance here and there across the massive glass wall. The library was climate controlled, kept on the cooler side year-round for the comfort and preservation of its permanent elderly residents, the books. For this reason, even in late August, even before the sun had pulled up stakes allowing the night to embrace our world with its dark and chilling touch, the heat emitting from the large fire felt a perfect balance.

"This is quite the place," I said to Harry, trying on my voice for the first time since asking him why I was here a little over two hours earlier. It wasn't a confident sounding voice yet but I didn't actually feel the presence of twenty more people in this room. It hardly felt like we were *in* a room at all. To see a bird fly from one bush or plant to the potted tree in the center of the room would not have struck me as odd at the time. The ceiling was too high to be noticed in your peripheral vision giving the affect of open sky. A domed skylight in the center of the massive room added to the a la naturale ambience.

"Yes, it is," said Harry, settling into the couch on the opposite end from me. "I like comin' here when I got me something to think hard about. Things just kinda got a way of makin' sense in here."

"I think it's because of all the books," added the only other person that had opted for sitting around the fire. "Somewhere in all the millions and millions of words, ideas and stories in this room, is written all the questions and all the answers. Even if you can't find the book itself or even know the question you need to be asking, sometimes just meditating in the company and presence of the energy created by all the wisdom and knowledge in all these old books just being together in the same place can somehow put things in proper perspective for you."

need some oil for that jaw or you just waiting to let the flies in

I closed my mouth. I hadn't even noticed Elvira tucked into the corner of the cushiony couch on my right...

...and the name's miranda, kojak.

"Sorry," I said, looking down. The glaring, angry stare coming up at me from the bear's head on the floor wasn't much of an improvement.

"Wha...Randi, you messin' with John here?" Harry asked, looking at me first and then over to Elvira/Miranda/Randi in response to my comment and ensuing look of dejection and embarrassment. "I told you to keep that stuff to yourself tonight." Pause. "I don't care what he called you, you know he ain't in the know yet." Pause. "Sticks and stones."

"Whatever," the girl in black said out loud to Harry. "I'm sorry," she said to me.

I felt seriously left out of the loop.

"Randi is a telepath, John. She reads thoughts and can direct thoughts just as easily as you and I speak."

"Can everyone here read minds?" I asked, suddenly feeling very naked and vulnerable.

"Not everyone. Many can to one degree or another, but none like Randi."

"Can you read minds?" I asked Harry. I figured that would have explained a lot.

Harry laughed. "No. I can't read minds any better than I can read palms like my mamma used to, which I can't. Drive me critters havin' everyone's nasty thoughts runnin' into my head like that. No thank you."

"You know how to shut your mouth when you want to shut up, Harry?" Randi asked, with a little extra emphasis on the word "shut" each time by. "Or close your eyes if you don't want to see. If you concentrate, you can shut out a noise, ignore a smell. Same thing here. If I don't want to hear your nasty, smelly old thoughts, I just don't listen to them. What's so tough."

"She's a real sweetheart if you get to know her," Harry said, smiling at me while giving Randi a nod and a wink.

"What's going on here, anyway?" I asked. Harry had just said I wasn't 'in the know yet.' I thought it was about time I was let in on 'the know.' "What am I doing here?"

"Just wanted to get to know you, John To let you get to know us," Harry said to me. Then to Randi, still smiling like a proud parent, "Which is easier when we all behave."

"Whatever," Randi said again.

"You know, that's not an answer," I said to Harry. "Why am I here getting to know anyone, let alone everyone. I'm not much of a socialite. I only came because..." I was hoping to learn something to help me save Katelynn. But I didn't want to say that. I didn't want to be here. I was just hoping, for Katelynn...

"Who is Katelynn," Randi nonchalantly asked, as though the name had just been brought up in conversation.

flies

I closed my mouth.

"Well?"

Now I couldn't open my mouth. I couldn't think of anything to say. I couldn't even think.

"I think John and I need to talk a spell, Randi. You mind?"

"Whatever," Randi said, and stood up. Walking right up the brown bear's spine in bare feet with black polish on every other toenail, she stepped over his snarling mouth still full of sharp white teeth and slipped between the couches towards the rest of the party.

welcome aboard, kojak

After Shadow got me safely home and I got it tucked away in the garage for what was left of the night, I got undressed and stepped into the shower where I once again completely lost track of time. I didn't break out the soap or the shampoo. I turned on the shower as hot as I thought I could get away with without blistering and stood facing the waterfall, taking short breaths between the individual streams that make up the river. I stood there motionless, hypnotized by the sound and the feel of the water beating against my face and my bald head. I'm not sure how long I stood there trying to decide if I had made the right decision or not, and I probably would have remained wrapped in the comfort of the water's warm embrace a lot longer had her touch not eventually lost its heat and begun to turn cold. I promised Harry that I would return, that I would at least hear him out. I could have still walked away from the whole mess by just not showing up...I think. However, looking back, did I really have a choice? Had someone else already made up my mind for me? Or was I caught like a deer in headlights in front of a crazy string of tumbling dominos?

At any rate, by whatever means of transport time uses to get from one moment to the next, it had delivered me to then, in that spot at that time, faced with a decision to make that may or may not have been my own. I was given a choice. I made a decision. And life goes on...for most.

"This house," Harry started, as soon as Randi had made her gracious exit, "but most importantly, this room, belongs to all of us here right now and some more that couldn't make it tonight. Benny, the old fart you met at the hospital, he also owns this house. Even though Paul Northrop's name appears on the deed and takes care of all the house affairs and upkeep, most of us here tonight are the one's that put our heads together to design it and ol' Benny put up most of the dough. We're like a family, John. We come from all over the country, and even a few from farther than that. But for all of us, this is also our home."

"So why are they all here tonight?" I asked. "Where are you from?"

"I'm from New Orleans, Louisiana," Harry said with pride. "But I've been spendin' more and more time up here at the house. And when Benny took ill, Benny's from Dallas, Texas, he said he wanted be close to here."

Harry paused and for a brief moment, the smile seemed to falter in his eyes as he maybe thought about his friend in the hospital. But it quickly returned and he continued.

"Quite a few members of our little family though have moved near by or bought second homes in the area. We all love it here and come as often as we can."

"This is a normal crowd for a Wednesday night?" I asked sarcastically. I knew it wasn't. That hadn't been a nightly meal we had eaten in the dining room. That had been a special meal, a feast fit for celebrations. Tonight was a special occasion. For whatever reason, Harry was obviously not going to reveal to me what the special occasion was until he had to, or until I figured it out, maybe which ever came first. But he had also said that a few others "hadn't been able to make it tonight."

"No," Harry replied honestly. "I asked everyone to come tonight. I wanted everyone to get a chance to meet you, but I see now that may take a little time. We're a lot to throw at someone in one night," he added with a chuckle.

If he couldn't read minds, his intuitions of my feelings and thoughts had been remarkably accurate all night. The last thing I wanted to do was meet twenty new people tonight. Or any night. If I hadn't met twenty more new people throughout the rest of my life, it would have been fine by me. But as reclusive as I had become over the years, a more embedded nature wouldn't allow me to be rude to these people that had treated me thus far with nothing but considerateness and fine food. I decided I could endure whatever Harry had in mind for one night. I mean, what were the chances I'd ever see any of these people ever again? As fine as this library was, as nice and generous as this weird array of folks appeared to be, I knew that I would be much more apt to spend an evening after work hanging around in my own greasy garage/den with the view of the run-down house across the street reading a Stephen King novel than to hang out here and shoot the shit with people I don't even know...and whom might even be trying to read my mind. I was trying to remember why I had even come to begin with when Harry started up again.

"We want you to join our family."

I still had no clue why I had gone against my nature in accepting a mysterious telepathic invitation to an unfamiliar place from a complete stranger, although I had now developed half a reason for the invitation itself. Randi was a telepath and some others, Ronnie to name one, were as well, "to some degree." But Harry said he wasn't. So then how did I get the invitation?

"Does everyone in this *family* have a special talent like Randi's? What is your talent?"

"Yes, John. They do," he said, and then added, "Just like you."

"All I can do is tell how old people are and I'm not sure I can even do that every time," I dared to lie. If he were lying about reading minds, he would know I was lying. I hoped Randi wasn't within mind-shot but to risk a look around to see if she were would certainly be admitting the lie to the sharp intuition of Harry so I forced myself not to back away from his eyes. I don't think he was fooled anyway.

"I don't know what your gift is," Harry said, his smile back in high gear again. His subtle substitution of my word, talent, with his word, gift, did not slip by unrecognized. "*You* might not even be aware of what your gift is yet. But how do you think you knew to come here tonight?"

"You told me," I answered. "Just like you told me your age."

"But I'm not telepathic, John."

"And I need to be touching skin for it to work for me."

"Do you? I am not telepathic, John. And neither is Benny. It was you. You have the gift. I just thought the invitation real hard and you plucked it out of my mind. Just like I knew you would, too. You weren't too quick on my age. I thought you might not be feelin' me for a second there. I was practically screamin' 'seventy-two' but then at the last second, you must have found it."

"How about Ronnie?"

"Ronnie's got herself a touch. She says she can hear some folks' thoughts and others' she can't. She has a few theories why and she might share if you ask."

"What's *your* gift," I asked again.

"I get premonitions."

"You can see the future?" I challenged, thinking he was possibly senile. I can handle a little ESP among friends. But I don't care who you are, seeing the future never was, isn't now, and never will be possible. Period.

"Not exactly," he said, I thought to his credit. "I don't get cloudy visions or a voice in my head telling me what's going to happen. I get like feelings. Feelings that sometimes form into ideas kind of the way water forms into ice. It was twenty years ago that I got Benny and Pauly together on one of those premonitions and it wasn't three years later before Benny was financing some new weather doohickey Pauly dreamed up which made them both a whole lotta money. Then I had another premonition about a great house and a great library and names would get stuck in my head when I heard them. It took Benny and Pauly and me three more years to figure out the names that were trying to sneak into my head and then to track them down. But we did track them down. And we formed the family. Then we built this great castle around this priceless library and moved the family here. And I still get names sneakin' into my head and gettin' stuck there every now and then. One had been stuck in there for quite some time now, been drivin' me critters. Then Benny calls me the other day and as soon as he said that name, I knew it was the one that been nibblin' on my brain. John Johnson. Can't get more common a name than that. But when he said it, I knew it was the name. Then you walk in and I met you and I knew *you* was the name. I don't know how or why. It's just my gift. I knew it was you."

It was me. I was *it*. Part of me wanted to just stop Harry right there and tell him that whatever *it* was that I was supposed to be, I honestly didn't want to have anything to do with *it*. I appreciated the invite, the meal, the sentiment, but I must respectfully decline. My plan was to take care of some immediate personal business over the next couple of weeks and then try to essentially disappear from organized society, probably up in the West Virginia mountains (easier than trying to find an isolated island in the Pacific to lay claim to) or maybe some small desert town in New Mexico. I hadn't figured out yet how I was going to make a living or even survive, but I didn't have time to worry about that right now. Nor did I have any desire to be joining any new families. Katelynn was all that was important right now. After that, getting out of Dodge. Then staying alive. No mention of new families in the plan. No mention of new friends with different psychic powers. I had my plan. I have freewill. I have good manners. I have legs. I had everything necessary to stand up, politely say thank you but no thank you and proceed to walk out the door, taking full control of my own fate and destiny, sidestepping a falling domino.

But I also had that bothersome curious side of me that looked up words in the dictionary just to finish a crossword puzzle, that couldn't let questions I ask myself go without attempting to answer them or to at least speculate potential answers, that presence in me that needed reasons and answers for everything it encountered. If I were to get up and leave right then, which I was more than capable of doing physically, I might never know what it was that I was supposed to bring to this talented family. The cat-like side of me would forever wonder, if not mind reading, what the hell the rest of the family's special "gifts" could possibly be. Physically, I was ready, willing and able to leave. Mentally, the curious side had too much control. It was confining me to my seat and was already busy trying to formulate the best questions to ask to get the most revealing answers.

And Paul Northrop had just stepped in front of our couch. With the angry bear nipping at his ankles, he extended a hand towards me.

"I'm Paul," he said, with a familiar smile that I had seen used many times on television. "Paul Northrop."

My curious side allowed me to stand to greet him as etiquette would require, but I froze half way up and then fell clumsily back into my seat unsure of what to do. Paul was holding out his hand for me to shake. I wasn't wearing my gloves. I recovered quickly, trying to make the return to the couch appear unintentional, re-stood and looked at Harry the moment before my hand clasped Paul's. A quick single pump and I pulled my hand back and sat down again before looking back at Paul.

"Glad to meet you, Mr. Northrop," I said, as I sat this time with a bit more grace. "I have seen you on the news." He looked like he had just come from the news, still in his clear-sky blue suit jacket and wide dark blue tie and slacks accompanying his white shirt. His dark hair was still perfect, not a one out of place as though permanently molded into shape. And he also had smiling eyes and a friendly, trusting face, one easy to believe when he said the rain would not spoil your weekend this week.

"It's a job," he chuckled. "and call me Paul. This is my true passion here," he said, sweeping his arm in a wide arc encompassing the library behind me. "The books, the people, the stars. The job helps finance the passion, is all."

"Harry has been telling me everyone here has a special gift. What's your special gift?" my curious side asked, quickly dispensing with the small talk going right for the juicy stuff.

Paul gave Harry an amused glance and then returned his attention to me to answer my question. "I am a reader," he said proudly. "I read ancient writings and hieroglyphics as well as the stars and the constellations. I read and study and translate the writings of old prophets and astrologers. And I think I'm pretty good at reading people, too." he added with a wink. "I speak for myself and everyone here when saying that I hope you decide to join our unique little family. Harry has told us much about you and we would welcome the opportunity to work with you."

"Thank you," I said as a conditioned response to this second proposal that I become a member of their odd family.

Paul nodded in simulation of a brief bow and said, "If you have any questions tonight after your chat with Harry here, feel free to ask me or anyone here anything you want, John. I'll let you and

Harry continue your chat now, I was just very anxious to come say hi. Hopefully I'll see you around here a lot more very soon."

"Thank you," I said again.

He gave Harry the same nod/bow before leaving the two of us alone again with the bear and the fireplace before us and the seven fire-breathing serpents looming over us.

"A passion for History and Astrology," I said to Harry after Paul had left. "Doesn't sound much like an unusual *gift* to me. A lot of people go to college for that stuff."

"But Paul was never taught these things in college," Harry said. "When he was five years old, he discovered he could look up at the stars and see the zodiac patterns without ever having been told they were there. He knew which star wasn't a star before he knew what planets were. When he saw hieroglyphics at the age of eleven in his first world history class in school, he read the message as though it were written in English. He hadn't mentioned anything at the time to his teacher because what he was readin' wasn't even close to what the text book reported the hieroglyphics read, so he thought he was the one that was wrong. Studying ancient Greek and Egyptian Cultures on his own time, he discovered that he could read all the hieroglyphics and that much of it pertained to the alignment of the stars, connecting his two talents and beginning to define them as one. He had also discovered that 80% of all accepted translations of the Egyptian hieroglyphics were in fact wrong due to the universally accepted translation of only ten or eleven very common symbols that actually meant something very different, completely changing the true context and meaning of the accepted translation by the world's experts in the field. Now 40 years later, he still works privately with his hieroglyphic and astrologic discoveries. With his *gift*, he knows more about this planet's ancient history than probably anyone else in the world."

"What did he mean when he said he looked forward to 'working' with me?" I asked. I was quite sure he had no intention of getting me a job down at the news room if I joined the family. And then the other most recent question Paul had inspired during his brief interruption moved into its place next in line and I didn't wait for an answer to the first one. "And how could you have told them so much about me when you don't even know me?"

"I told them of the things I *felt* in relation to your name," Harry explained. "It grew stronger over time. Benny and I figured you were a Johnson just before he took sick about two months ago. Every time I heard the name Johnson or John, which we figured was just part of the Johnson, I would feel lighter, happy, warm. This is what I was telling them at first. I came here to be with Benny four weeks ago. There was a Nurse Johnson that tended to Benny in the evenings. When she would come in and Benny would say 'Howdy, Miss Johnson,' the feeling was stronger, more intense, almost inspirational. Benny said he felt inspired too every time Miss Johnson came in the room, but it was for a different reason then me. Then last week, that Doc of Benny's came in and told him a man named John Johnson wanted to do a test with him. Benny didn't feel the vibes the way I did whenever I heard any part of that name, but he knew better than to believe in coincidence. He called me as soon as the Doc left his room and told me the name John Johnson and I knew another piece of the puzzle was about to be filled in. Well, I jumped on my hog and got to Benny so fast I was lucky I didn't spill her. And I wasn't disappointed either when you came walkin' in that door. You had a shine on you I'd never seen before. Made me shine too.

"Randi, she's got a shine to her too, different than yours, also like none I've ever seen before. She joined our family three years ago after both her parents were killed in a drug raid."

Harry leaned in a bit and lowered his voice, the couch creaking under his shifting weight. "Don't ask her about it. Still kind of a touchy subject, a lot of mixed emotions towards her parents' death. She's healing herself though, and she'll tell you when she's ready. She really is a sweetheart. You'll see."

He resettled against the far arm rest again with only a small protest from the couch's skeletal structure. "Everyone here has a certain shine to them that I can feel, but only a few shine like stars." He leaned forward again, "You, John, are one of those few."

18

Only because hot water always eventually becomes cold, I got out of the shower and headed for bed. Exhausted as I was, I didn't think I would be able slow my conscious mind down to sleep speed but seemingly minutes after I laid my head down on the pillow, the sun was slipping through the cracks in my curtains and knocking on my closed eyelids until they opened. The morning brought no new revelations discovered by my ever-working subconscious during a handful of hours of sleep. The reason I had ventured off to the mysterious dinner party in the first place had not been realized. I had learned nothing that might help Katelynn in her plight.

After Harry had revealed to me that I was one of the few that had some sort of special positive effect on his demeanor, the party had started to thin out a bit. A few people had slipped out without my noticing, but most of the rest stopped by the couch on their way out to briefly introduce themselves, repeating Paul Northrop's hope to see me here in the future. All were pleasant and smiling. None held out their hand to shake as they came and went. I imagined that in their little revolving groups they had been standing and chatting in since dinner, my name had probably come up more than a few times. And not knowing who were the mind-readers and who weren't, I felt very self-conscious and guarded despite their friendly faces and words of welcome. Even though I certainly possessed a *gift* of some kind related to the mind-reading phenomenon, I felt very out-of-my-league here and had already decided to politely decline Harry's offer to join his family. Besides, my *gift* was related to death. I still had not been honest with Harry about the true nature of my new talent. He might be a little less exuberant about my membership if he knew that all I could bring to the family would be the news of when each of them will die.

I didn't ask anyone else what their gifts were as they stopped by to confirm their consent in making me the newest family member on their way out. Nor did I try to remember their names or match them up with any of the vehicles I had seen when arriving. As much as they all apparently agreed that they would like to see me here in the future, I had no plans on ever seeing any of them again.

Harry gave me brief bits of info, nothing very revealing, where they're from, how long as a member, kids raising or business running, etc., about the departing people as they passed between the couch and the angry bear on the floor. I wasn't paying too close attention. I was busy trying to figure out the nicest way to decline his offer as soon as the steady, but slow parade of current family members said their good-byes to Harry and me.

Harry waved towards the door. I turned and saw Paul Northrop standing in it, waving also to me. I half-heartedly waved back and he vanished into the dining room. The same woman that had brought me my first Mountain Dew at the banquet table came through the door Paul had just exited carrying a tray with another bottle of Dew and a fresh steamy cup of cappuccino for Harry. Despite the fact that everyone else in the library had just left during the past fifteen minutes, she somehow assumed the two us would still be here for a while. Maybe that was her "gift".

She placed the fresh drinks with fresh coasters on their appropriate lamp tables at each end of the couch and picked up the old ones. "I'll be heading home now for the night, Harry."

"Thank you, Mary," Harry said to the woman. "I'm sure we can find anything else we need. Thanks for all your service and you have yourself a good night, dear."

Then Mary too, turned and faced me as each of the family members that had chosen to stop by when leaving had. "I hope to see you again soon, Mr. Johnson." She gave me a brief curtsy and then she left, leaving Harry and I alone in the huge library.

"I can't really tell how old people are," I said to Harry, as soon as Mary had disappeared through the doorway and I prepared to reveal to him the truth so that he could maybe retract his invitation once he understood my real talent. "I see how old they will be when they are going to die. That's why we were testing it out on people in the hospital. I don't really think I am what you are looking for in a new family member."

Harry's smile never even faltered for a second during my confession. "You belong here maybe even more than I do," Harry said matter-of-factly. "I know because that is *my* gift. I know that you are a part of the answer."

"The answer to what?"

"We're not sure. This is the 'work' Pauly referred to. We believe that we are in a defining period of time for mankind on this earth. Paul, with the help of some others, is studying the transcripts from ancient times that all seem to point to a series of catastrophic events that will occur in our near future. We're not sure when exactly, but it is very near. Janis, one you did not meet tonight, is another of the true shiners. She says our time is short."

Suddenly the *family* was starting to sound like some doomsday cult bent on preventing some wrath of God or Satan that was about to be unleashed upon the world. Should this trend continue, I figured, I could probably justify foregoing good manners and just get up and walk out any time I want with no further explanation.

"Are you all part of some religious cult?" I went ahead and asked. I didn't expect him to say yes, therefore allowing me to stand up, say thanks for the meal, been real, and see ya, but I did want to hear him try to explain how this family was different than your garden variety religious cult, aside from the fact that each member supposedly possessed some unusual *gift* that set them apart from the other six billion humans sharing this planet.

Harry chuckled. "We are not a religious group. No one here goes to church every Sunday or prays to God. Do you believe in God, John?"

"No," I admitted. "I can't believe in a Supreme Being that created Adam and Eve and the Universe and all that. I believe we simply are what we are, a life born to die."

"Do you believe in other life forms and other worlds in our universe?

"Sure," I said. "There's bound to be something else out there somewhere."

"And what do you imagine might be out there?" he asked.

"I wouldn't have a clue. As far as I know, we haven't gone there and none of them have ever come here. Until they do, or the government suddenly decides to tell the truth about things like Roswell, I keep an open mind on who they might be or what they might look like."

"What if I told you that I knew they were out there watching us?" Harry said, still looking as though he hadn't had this much fun in years. "What if I told you I knew what they looked like and how they live and what they like and don't like. What if I told you I had met them?"

The thought of Randi informing me that flies would love to explore mouths left hanging open passed quickly though my mind and I made an effort to shut mine once again. He hadn't actually said he *had* met aliens from another planet, but it sure sounded like he was heading in that direction. I liked Harry. He was a very pleasant old man. His smile was contagious. His eyes were alive and friendly. It pained me to think he might also be delusional or senile. As much as I enjoyed leaving reality behind for a while and accepting a world of fiction as the real world while I read books written by imaginative writers, as soon as the book was closed, the fictional world it brings to life is left within the bindings on the pages from which it had been born. I glanced at the two walls containing more books than I would ever have time to read even if I never left this room again for the rest of my life, and wondered if maybe Harry had lost the ability to differentiate between the fictional world and the real world.

"So, *have* you met them?" I asked, wondering if this was the time to stand and walk, after he said yes.

"Not like I met you and everyone else I know," he said, "not when awake. In a dream."

"Of course," I responded sarcastically.

"It has been in dreams throughout history, John. That is how they talk to us. That is how they talked to Moses and Hadrian and Odysseus, all the way back to the Pharaohs of Egypt. They communicate with us in our dreams."

"And they have chosen you, along with all the pharaohs and Kings of the past, to communicate with," I interrupted, not concealing my doubt.

"They didn't choose me. No." Harry said, shaking his head. "Paul taught me how to make them recognize me. But I've only done it once. And I probably won't be doing it again."

"So how did Paul know," I asked, though I knew the answer before I had finished the question. Paul's gift, of course.

"He read the secret in some old hieroglyphics on the wall of a new chamber discovered just last year inside the Great Pyramid of Giza. The secret was supposed to stay buried there and even after its discovery, it had remained buried in misinterpretations of the hieroglyphics."

Okay, this was all cool and interesting stuff, except for the fact that Harry actually believed it all.

"How do you know your mind wasn't just dreaming what you wanted it to dream, playing out your fantasy while you sleep? How do you know Paul is reading it right since everyone else reads something else in it? What about the Rosetta Stone?" I wasn't bothered so much by the subject as I was by the fact that this intelligent-looking and otherwise delightful older gentleman was apparently slowly losing touch with reality here. "Did Paul see them in his dreams, too?"

"No," Harry replied. "I am the only one in our family that has employed the secret so far."

"What did they look like," I asked. I figured if I asked enough questions, eventually I would ask the right one and be able to officially label Harry as one that has lost touch.

"The one that I met, Gabriel, the messenger for God himself, looked very much like you or I. He had eyes and a nose and a mouth. Two arms, two legs, no wings. And he had long yellow hair that came to rest in curls on his broad shoulders. In my dream, I was on a mountain top and he appeared in the sky before me, floating about thirty feet away from me over a dark valley that looked to be a mile or more below us. The sky was bright all around us even though it was night when I had called for him and I could see the moon sitting full in the sky behind him. He was big, bigger than me, bigger than Benny, bigger than Shaquille O'Neil. Probably ten feet tall, at least. He wore a gray robe that swept the tops of his giant bare feet and it was held closed with a wide, red sash tied around the waist. His eyes were a burning green like I'd never seen before. His lips didn't move when he spoke but his voice boomed inside my head. 'Why have you summoned me, old man? What message have you for God?' he asked me. I was pretty scared at that point. I knew I should have maybe learned a bit more from Pauly before I dove in head first in all my excitement. According to Pauly's reading of the wall in the Great Pyramid, Ra was the one I would be summoning. I looked behind me and saw that I had no where to go. I knew I was sleeping, dreaming, but I also felt if I had taken a step off the top of that mountain, I would never wake up again.

"One thing I learned from living with this family of mine is that it don't pay to lie, so I told the truth to Gabriel too, as best I could. 'I thought I was calling for Ra.' 'I am Gabriel,' he tells me, 'Messenger of God. What message have you for God?'

"I figured if I didn't have a message, Gabriel might just heave me over the side of the mountain for wastin' his time an' summoning him here. 'I am seeking truths,' I told him. 'What is your message for God?' Gabriel asked again, with a little more insistence in the voice inside my head. I couldn't think of any information I could possibly pass on to God but I felt if I ever wanted to wake up again, I better come up with something. 'We are four strong,' I said, thinking of the four members of our family with that special shine. It was the only thing I could think of to pass along that might have meaning to it, though I didn't know what it might mean. I still don't know what that shine is, but when I saw you at the hospital a few weeks later, I knew I had found number five. But 'four strong' was the message that Gabriel supposedly then sent to God."

"Wait a minute," I interrupted. "Are you telling me this just happened? This was like a month ago?"

"July 21st," Harry said without thinking about it. "Or maybe the 22nd. I went to bed on the 21st and woke up after on the 22nd. Somewhere in the middle, I met Gabriel and passed along a message to God."

A little over a month. About a week before my accident. "Did you get a response?" I asked, just humoring him...for now.

"I think so," Harry said. "Gabriel only said one more word to me before I was off that mountain and woke up in my bed again. For a moment after I gave him my message, he just floated out there in front of me boring a hole in my head with his green eyes. I started to think he was waiting for more of the message, or maybe he was thinking about whether or not he might just toss me off that mountain anyway. Then he said that one word and vanished. He didn't fly away or fade away. He was just there, and then he wasn't and it was night time again. But before he disappeared on me, leavin' me to wonder how I was going to get off that mountain in the dark, he said, 'Seven.'"

Seven. I laid in bed, not wanting to leave the warmth and false sense of security one feels when wrapped in their own familiar bed sheets, slowly reviewing everything Harry had unfolded for me the previous night.

God must be a man of few words. Seven. That was all He had supposedly passed along to Harry through His messenger, Gabriel. And according to Harry, I was number five. Had the evening ended then, I would have just considered all I had heard as the ramblings of an old man looking desperately to find some meaning to his life before it ended.

But the evening had not ended there.

"I thought you didn't believe in God," I said, after he had finished his story.

"I didn't say I didn't believe in Him. I said we don't go to church and pray to Him. God is very real, as real as you and I are."

It was a religious cult after all then, only they used books and history for their insights instead of psychedelic drugs. They were probably working on some crusade to save themselves come Judgment Day, which would undoubtedly be right around the corner. Maybe Paul had convinced them all that a certain alignment of the stars predicted in Biblical times had come to fruition and that it was time to act. I wasn't surprised that Harry had picked the number seven for this mission. There were seven Dragons in the giant mural. Seven, throughout history, which this family seemed to have an interest in, has been considered a lucky number.

Luck, however, is just another superstition. There's no such thing as luck. What happens, happens. Good luck, bad luck, Lady Luck, all just excuses, reasons for the things that happen to us during our lives. No different than God and Satan who serve as the excuses and reasons for the good and evil in our world as well as provide us with purpose for our life and our death. God, Ra, Lady Luck, they are all born of the same desperate need for answers that has been evident in every culture during every time period throughout mankind's known history on this planet. We are a needy species. Needy of mind as well as body. Needy of reasons and purposes. Needy of believing that death is not the end.

"God is of the Immortals," Harry continued. "The Egyptians and the Mayans each wrote in great detail about the Immortals. Ra, the Immortal that claimed the Egyptian race as his for more than a hundred centuries, was not shy about his visits to them in their sleep. Nor were his Parliament. Many of the pharaohs were in nightly contact with the Immortals.

"The Immortals are similar to us in appearance, though they have much larger bodies, probably perfect bodies, unflawed like our mortal shells. It is said to be written in the Hall of Records buried in a chamber deep under the left front paw of the Sphinx, as well as buried somewhere in the great tomb of Atlantis on the ocean's floor, a written record of how the Immortals created and instilled a spirit on this earth named Eoa, a unisex being that eventually gave birth to the first man and then the two of them, the son and the Mother/Father, joined to create the first woman.

"The records also explain the secret of the Immortals. They can live forever, but they can also die. Pieces and hints of what The Hall of Records contains are left everywhere ancient Egyptian writings can be found. We, our family, have managed to put together quite a few of the pieces. But there is still a lot of work to do. It's like putting together a giant jigsaw puzzle but with a lot of pieces missing. While some of us are trying to put together the puzzle, others of us are trying to find new pieces to bring to it."

Frankly, it sounded to me like Harry had recently lost a few pieces himself, but even so, he told a great story and was drawing me in like many a good fiction book had done in the past. He seemed to tell it with such pride and emotion. I could almost see the awe in his eyes as he had described his brief meeting with Gabriel on a mountain top. The excitement in his voice was almost youthful as he talked about all the new writings Paul was discovering about the Immortals in hieroglyphics.

Apparently, the Immortals were basically a more perfect and complete version of ourselves. Ra had been the fist to discover this planet. It had been a lush, green, living ball of life. In the billions of years that followed the Ice Age and the fall of the Dinosaur, The Earth had been regenerating Herself, growing, breathing, breeding life from Her Soil and Her Oceans; nurturing it with The Sun and The Rain. The planet was then inhabited for millions upon millions of years only by the abundant life that Mother Earth had spawned. Even the animals lived by the instinct that Mother Nature Herself had implanted into Her creations. Everything had a purpose. Between the plant life and the animal life, the life of The Oceans and The Skies, Mother Earth had created a perfect balance. A perfect paradise. A perfect Eden.

When Ra and his Parliament and his followers found The Earth, they themselves were in awe at the life that She had created. They had come across many planets that had created life of one form or another, as well as many that were dead and dilapidating. But this one, this Earth, was more alive than any ten put together that they had ever come across in their immortal lives traveling the Universe. They bathed in Her life, got drunk on Her spirit, and were inspired by Her creations, so much so that they put their immortal heads together and tried to match Mother Nature by creating their own version of life. And in the end, they had created Eoa.

According to Harry, according to Paul, Eoa was more a spirit, a consciousness containing a subconscious built within, than it was a human. Using themselves as models, they created a smaller version of themselves to house Eoa and then set it upon The Earth to do as it will. Ra and his co-creators watched with great satisfaction in their accomplishment as Eoa grew fertile and The Son grew to be the first Man. They watched as the two became six and the six became twenty and the twenty became four hundred. They had succeeded in creating a life more intelligent than any of the millions of species Mother Earth had been able to create. Their egos were soaring.

As the Human Race evolved and learned and became civilized, Ra and his Parliament, having created the life forms now trying to become a rooted and productive civilization, naturally had opinions on how their *children* should live and of course, their children must always be grateful for the life given unto them by always honoring, worshipping and obeying Ra's every command.

And so it was for tens of thousands of years, which really isn't all that long in the life of the Immortals. Humans grew and expanded and began to spread out around the Earth and venture out on their own.

As it always seems to be, when you think you've discovered the best, most private, most flourishing fishing hole in the state, suddenly next season everyone seems to know about it. And so it was for Ra, for in 3500 B.C., Zeus and his band of rebels and thugs had also discovered this thriving and busy little planet that Ra had been trying to keep a secret for thousands of years. Ra and his faithful had already watched and occasionally guided one chapter of the human race as it grew, evolved, learned, and advanced over a 12,000-year period before it ultimately almost wiped itself out completely due to the greed and a hunger for power by just a handful of the billions of souls that had spawned from the original Eoa they had created almost 18,000 years ago. Ra was busily trying to get the second chapter of humankind off on a the right foot, trying to take a more hands-on approach in their development this time when Zeus and company stubbled into this section of the galaxy and discovered what Ra was up to.

The two Kings of their kind, Ra and Zeus, coexisted on this planet for more than three thousand years, each claiming ownership to their separate areas of The Earth, to rule and command their race of humans and do as they will. Zeus and most of his gang of Immortals were not as sympathetic to the fears and plights of humankind since they had not been here since the beginning to watch it grow and evolve and then start over again. Ra, though still a very demanding and sometimes ruthless ruler, still possessed more of a Father/Child relationship with the human race.

And a couple of thousand years after Zeus had found Ra's perfect little fishing hole isolated off by itself in a remote section of the universe, a galaxy so far from the center that it had only nine planets around its sun, another Immortal quietly settled in and began to spread His word and His will among The People.

For a thousand years, God, digging some roots into The Earth, created a following from a smaller population and spread out from there. While advertising Himself as The Good One, The Righteous One, The Only True Father and God, while performing miracles for the hapless and needy and less fortunate humans roaming the earth, God was building the most powerful Army of Angels the Universe has ever known. And when He was ready, once he had a thousand times the power of Zeus and Ra and all their family put together, God sent His young Son to the Earth to win over the rest of the human race, allowing Him to walk among the humans, to live and then to die among the humans, something never done by the Immortals before, stealing the loyalties of those that had once honored the Two Kings, weakening their power and any remaining hold over mankind.

Their independently made decisions to head off to some other galaxy and find a nice quiet planet to take it easy for a few thousand years or so was not only their wisest choice, it had been their only choice. God had amassed one of the largest and strongest armies in the Universe. And it was led by one of the wisest, craftiest, dirtiest Generals in the Universe. Better to head for Zuritica or Hertiulis or Arfigop. Any other part of the Universe that He wasn't in is better than trying to go up against the wrath of God and his Army of Angels. Even Hades was better than death.

And so it was, The Earth now belonged to God. And because Ra had allowed freewill to be a trait of his creation in order to allow it to rise above all those of Mother Earth's design, God gave the Earth to humankind, freeing them from the tyranny of its creators.

By this time, I was hooked. It didn't matter anymore if Harry was only playing with half a deck. It didn't matter what was real and what wasn't. I was fascinated with his story and the fact that he believed with all of his kind and gracious heart that every word of it was the god's honest truth made it all the more fascinating. At this point, I would have sat there all night and listened to him tell his tales and would have actually been willing to come back tomorrow night for more. The only thing missing was the popcorn.

At least this is what I was telling myself as I let him continue.

The sky had grown black. Hundreds of suns for other worlds appeared through the large skylight and over the dark lake as tiny, silver dots of shimmering light. The seven Dragons stood watch in the glow of the fire beneath them, silently listening to Harry's tale along with me.

"How can you possibly know all this?" I asked.

"Most of this we have only recently put together in the last two or three years," Harry said, after pausing to sip his cappuccino. "The Egyptian government has been making new discoveries difficult. They are trying to restore the monuments left behind by their ancient ancestors and don't appreciate the rest of the world trying to come in and tear them apart with excavations and tests. Janis is over there right now trying to lobby for the right to re-enter some of the older excavations to try to find any information or writings that were missed or left out that might have been more important than those who made the original discovery had understood. So far, she hasn't had much luck with the government but she isn't alone over there. Many universities and scores of ethnologists and historians and theologians are every bit as anxious as we are to learn more of what the ancient Egyptians knew. There is also a lot of pressure being put on the state of Egypt right now to allow the Hall of Records under the Sphinx to be excavated. On this, the government has not budged. Yet at the same time, a university out of Japan who was able to get permission to use some new technology that determines ground density below the surface has determined that there are several large chambers beneath the Sphinx, including one about 35 feet below the front left paw, exactly where many of the writings have placed the Hall of Records."

"Couldn't all this stuff about Eoa and Ra and other worlds just be man's first attempt to give reason for life and death? Or maybe even simply the earliest version of fiction, an imaginative slave trying to please the pharaoh, for example? I mean, what are people going to think of a horror novel of today when it is discovered in ten thousand years? They might assume spirits and the walking dead actually used to roam the world and feed on the brains of the living."

"That would be a possibility," Harry chuckled, seemingly amused with my suggestions. "But then how did they build the pyramids? The answer is in the Hall of Records. Also in the Hall of Records is the explanation of how they knew the distance between the earth and the sun, the diameter of the moon, the cycles of the stars and comets. Even the mere existence of the other planets in our solar system should have been beyond their means, but they knew. They had no telescopes. There are miraculous structures from that era all over the earth that seem impossible for the people of that time to build, yet they *were* built. There are things that would have been impossible to know, yet they wrote in great detail of these very things that weren't *rediscovered* by modern man until the scientists of the last two centuries. This was not early fiction. They *knew* then what we are still trying desperately to know now because they had been told and helped by those who knew. They got their information straight from the horse's mouth."

"Okay, Harry," I said. "I'm not exactly sold on this the way you are. There are far too many holes."

"We are filling more and more of those holes all the time, John. It seems with just about everything Pauly gets his hands on, he discovers another piece to the puzzle. And Egyptian hieroglyphics is not the only source we are using. We also have two people in the Mayan Territories studying the calendars and prophecies of their culture. They date back to 3114 B.C. The Greeks began their history in 3300 B.C. We have a representative of the family over there, too. The Mayans, with the knowledge they took with them when they left, became the Masters of Time and invented many different calendars, including the one that we use today, The Haab, as it was called in their day. They understood time in a much deeper sense than we do even today. In fact, the Mayans accurately predicted the beginning of a shift in the magnetic pull of the earth's poles. This shift began in 1992. The Mayans say that when the shift is complete, in December of 2025, the Earth will enter into a fourth dimension of time where it doesn't always move in the same direction.

"Even the Native Americans, it has recently been discovered, had a much deeper knowledge of time and astrology than the Europeans had in 1400's A.D. Keep in mind that at that time, the Europeans that discovered the American Indians and thought of them as savages and barbarians, had only just discovered that earth was not flat, something the American Indians had already been aware of...or maybe more aptly put, they had never forgotten. And these European ancestors of ours that had forgotten that the Earth is round are the same folks that write our history text books. Throughout mankind's more recent 'civilized' history, it seems the more civilized that we become, the more of our own history we forget.

"But all that is getting ahead of ourselves. Originally our main concern was trying to dig up information on 2025. Every where we look, the Egyptians, The Mayans and their calendars, even later predictions that are cryptically written in Revelations in the Bible and the even more cryptic Nostradamus and his Quatrains, all point to 2025, specifically December, at the time of a global shift in energy, as a natural cycle of the Earth completes and begins anew.

"But lately we are learning of something else that might happen much sooner. Janis thinks maybe even as soon as this year or next. It may be something that has already begun and we simply aren't reading the signs properly. Although, here we are dealing more in prophecy than in fact. But from what little we have been able to piece together of this possibly more urgent matter for mankind, is that Lucifer may be involved. We think he may try to take control of this world before it enters into its new dimension of time."

"Lucifer? As in the Devil? Satan?" I asked, making sure he meant who I thought he meant. I had to admit, he had done his homework, but Lucifer? I had previously seen documentaries on Nostradamus and I was aware of the Mayan Calendar. Atlantis had always been a myth in my mind but I must admit, the pyramids were as mysterious and unexplainable as that single miracle bullet that had killed JFK. Okay, so maybe the latter of those is more fiction than miracle, but the pyramids are very real. I have yet to see a satisfying explanation of how they were built and I had simply accepted the fact that we, modern man, may never know. But of course, not believing in God, Lucifer was even more a fairy tale in my mind than God had been. Harry had been close to roping me in with all his historical facts, but at the mention of Lucifer coming to take over the world, he was about to lose me again.

"Yes," Harry said, seemingly unconcerned with my skepticism. "When God had quietly built his army to run off Zeus and Ra, Lucifer was his General, his strategist, the leader and the strength of the Army of Angels.

"Then somewhere along the way, shortly after God had left His only son to spread His Word in person to humankind, Lucifer apparently took a liking to this particular busy, lush world and decided he would kinda like to maybe have it for his own."

"Harry, stop right there," I said. It was after eleven and getting late. I was getting tired. Talking of history and related discoveries and listening to theories on the beginning of man could hold my interest deep into the night. But discussing a modern-day clash that was to take place in the near future here on earth between old rivals such as Lucifer and God, which appeared to be where this last bit of dialogue seemed to be heading, got old really quick. "Unless you have something concrete to show me, to prove to me that there is anything other than an overactive imagination at work here, I should probably be heading home." More than anything, I wanted a cigarette. "I enjoyed your stories, I appreciate your offer to become a member of your little club of *gifted* people, but I am really not much of a people person to begin with and don't think I really belong here. I can't say that I share your beliefs, not without some proof that I can sink my teeth into. It's just all too far out there for me."

Harry smiled. It was a slightly different smile than I had grown accustomed to on his boyishly friendly, old face. He leaned forward, lowered his voice even though we had been alone in the library now for almost an hour and a half, "Oh, I got something I can show you, John. I was savin' it for when you said just what you just said because I knew eventually you would. Give me thirty more minutes of your time and then you can make up your mind. Deal?"

As I lay in bed, preparing to review the final thirty minutes of my meeting with Harry on that previous evening, I started to tremble in the daylight that filtered into my room as I wondered once again how I had gotten myself mixed up in all this.

I was given a choice. I made a decision. And life goes on... hopefully.

19

Harry stood and stretched his old muscles before turning toward one of the walls containing thousands and thousands of books. Sighing, I tapped my left breast pocket to assure myself the necessary tools were still there to satisfy the nic-fit I was enduring as soon as I made my escape in thirty minutes. I decided I could make it another half-hour, but no longer. I stood and followed Harry around the potted tree in the room's center to the opposite wall.

"The first one is easy," Harry was saying, as I caught up with him at the base of one of the massive walls of words.

He reached out and pulled a newer looking, oversized book on astrology off the shelf from shoulder height. It had a bright, colorful, glossy cover displaying Jupiter and its moons. Reaching back to the frame of the bookshelf, he pressed a blue button and I saw the attached ladder at the other end of the wall start to slowly and silently slide our direction. Pressing the black button that sat below the green and blue buttons on the same small panel a moment later brought the ladder to a stop in front of us.

"But I'll need your legs to get the other one we want," Harry said when the ladder had come to rest. "The blue button is left, the green one is right and the black one is stop. There's a panel every four feet up the ladder if you need to get closer, but I think I got you right where you need to be."

Harry reached up and pulled a strap I hadn't noticed yet that hung on the side just above eye level. It turned out to be a belt attached to both sides of the ladder.

"Step under this and pull it down to your waist. Tighten it up. It works like a seat belt. You can move up and down the ladder slowly, but if you fall, it locks and holds you in place. You ain't 'fraid a heights or nothin', are ya?"

I assured him I wasn't as he pulled the belt over my head and I tightened it snuggly around my waist. I was only doing it for him. Had I been alone, I probably wouldn't bother with the belt. "What am I looking for?" I asked.

"The yellow one on the second shelf from the top," he said, looking straight up. "There's no words on the spine but it's the only yellow one in that row. You'll know it when you see it. Just place it in the basket." He pointed up. I spotted the basket about halfway up, attached to the right side of the ladder on some type of pulley system. "I'll bring the book down in the basket while you climb back down the ladder."

Glancing at the books as I made my way up the ladder towards the library's high ceiling, they didn't appear to be in alphabetical order, but rather, in chronological order. The higher I got, the older the books appeared to become. The lower shelves all contained brighter, newer looking spines. The book's titles and authors or illustrators were prominently marked for easy identification. This was clearly the 'Astrology' section of the library as the titles I read all pertained to the heavens, the stars, the planets, the galaxy and such. The higher I got, however, the fewer dust jackets I saw and the paler the spines' colors became and then farther up, more frayed and dog-eared. The titles grew harder to read, some had no information at all on the spine. In the second row from the top, none of the books had words on the spines and the only yellow one, which Harry had managed to park the ladder directly next to, had no indication whatsoever anywhere on the outside of the book pertaining to what might be found on the inside.

I pulled on one of the thin cords on my right and the basket responded in the proper direction. I placed the book in the basket once it had reached my height and it started descending right away with Harry pulling the opposite cord from below. I thought about pushing the green button and taking a cruise down the length of wall just out of curiosity but my desire to get this over with so I could escape to some fresh air and pollute my lungs with some tasty chemicals got me down the ladder by the same time Harry was pulling the book out of the basket.

"That's the one," he said triumphantly, while I slid out of the safety harness.

I couldn't imagine this taking thirty minutes. There was absolutely nothing I could think of that Harry could show me in a book that would suddenly enlighten me to the truth in his stories. Man has always possessed a fascination with stories. Stories of the past. Stories of the future. Fact and fiction. Once upon a time we used natural paints and stone, now we use printing presses and trees. They used pictures and hieroglyphics. We use letters and words. But we have always told our stories. It's just another one of those abilities that apparently Mother Nature hadn't instilled into any of Her own life creations. The ability to imagine. The ability to ask, "What if...?" But maybe She had a reason for not instilling that particular talent, too.

I knew that whatever might be found in his oldest books of this impressive library, whether intended to be fact or fiction by its author, would most likely be a mixture of both at best. And there was no real way to truly draw the line between which was which.

I was being as polite as I knew how, riding out the evening, but the timer was on. My patience would expire soon, but the next twenty-six or seven minutes, I didn't think would be a problem.

Harry turned left, leaving the basket and ladder where they were, both books tucked under his left arm, and walked towards the adjoining wall of shelves. We were only ten feet from the corner where the two walls met and I hadn't noticed the dark brown door nestled directly in the corner until Harry stopped in front of it and turned to see that I was following.

The book shelves framed the doorway on the hinged left side and directly above. The wall we had retrieved our books from met the right side of the doorway at a 90-degree angle such that the door must swing towards the new room or it would knock some books off the shelf swinging in our direction. Picturing the layout of the house that I had traversed thus far, this had to be a tiny room behind the dining room we had eaten in, but there hadn't been a door to enter from that side. This door wasn't exactly hidden, but it did appear to be less conspicuous by design.

Harry reached into his pocket with his right hand and pulled out a small key chain. He selected a key from the few options available and inserted it into the door's lock. Harry's bulky body filled most of the doorway. As he turned the knob and opened it just a crack before facing me once again, a stale musty smell, faint but obvious, slipped through the open space and lingered in the doorway with us.

With gleaming eyes and a mischievous smile, Harry turned to me before opening the door more than a few inches and asked, "Are you ready for your first lesson?"

I didn't actually have an immediate response to that question and Harry turned and entered the dark room as if he hadn't expected one.

I shrugged and followed. Twenty-five minutes and counting.

THE MASTER PLAN

Harry flicked on the light switch beside the door and it took a moment for my eyes to adjust as I walked in behind him. The lighting in here was three times as bright as the library had been all evening, twice as bright as the dining room for dinner. In here it was high noon. The ceiling was low once again in here though still a couple feet higher than normal. There were no windows and no doorways other than the one we had just entered through. The room itself was quite a bit larger than I had imagined on the other side of the door, about half the size of the piano parlor next to the entry, but it felt much smaller as it was crammed full of what looked at first like old junk. As my eyes adjusted to the bright lights of the room, the old junk began to take on the air of old *valuable* junk. After looking around for another thirty seconds from the doorway, the room became a storage room for a museum. Here were all the exhibits that were either awaiting their turn on the floor or had been replaced but not yet displaced. Many of the items looked Egyptian, probably artifacts sent back by Janis and Co. Although most looked from origins that I would not be able to distinguish so readily. In here were more books, too. A very small book case compared to any in the other room, but at least a hundred more very old looking books filled all five of its shelves.

Each wall was very busy. One was covered with maps. Large maps, small maps, old cracked and yellowed maps. I couldn't see from the doorway what areas they were covering, but I figured I could probably guess a few correctly. The only two couches in the room were beneath the maps, away from the wall to allow closer inspection of any map without moving anything out of the way. The wall next to that, straight ahead as we entered the room, had the small book case and was covered with ancient-looking masks hanging from hooks, each, I was sure, with its own intriguing story behind it. The wall housing the door we had entered had large items leaning against it as well as three life-size stone statues that must have weighed a ton a piece. They looked like those old wooden Indian statues you'd see by the front door of the old general store, except these weren't wooden and they weren't Indians. Two of them had human heads atop their human bodies, one did not.

The final wall to our right was lined with wide shelves filled with small statues and goblets and tools. It looked like something you might find in the main tent of an excavation site, minus the dirt.

Speaking of dirt, however, there were also several barrels mingling among the statues to our left that appeared to be filled to the brim with dirt and the center of the room looked like a giant sandbox. Actually, it was more like a sand*bowl*. It was about two feet high and ten feet in diameter. The sides sloped inward in bowl fashion. It was made of the same thick, white stone as the three statues and looked to weigh twice their weight all put together. How they got it into this room could have been a mystery rivaling the construction of the pyramids themselves. It was five times the size of the only door in this room. And it was heaping full with dirt. Yellowish, off-white dirt.

"What do ya think?" Harry was asking, obviously proud of this room's collection of history.

"What *is* all this stuff?" I finally asked, knowing full well there could not be one simple answer. Then more specifically, "How did you get that thing in here?" I pointed to the bowl of sand, the room's center piece.

"Shkarbala," Harry said, ever smiling. "Benny found that one himself two years ago in the ancient city of Tulum. It is right off the Caribbean Sea in The Yucatan, the old Mayan Territories. He and his money got it shipped out of the country before they ever knew he had found what he had found. Maybe they never did know. He told them it was a giant bird bath he had custom made from local stone for his front lawn in Texas because in Texas they liked to have the biggest of everything and now he had himself the biggest damn bird bath in the U.S. of A. Benny has a way of making people believe any ol' thing he says. It's kinda like his gift, though I've never seen a shine on ol' Benny. But he does have a way about him. He had it flown out of the country with three helicopters within minutes of approval, before they had a chance to investigate or change their minds. Then in Havana, Cuba he got it aboard a freight liner to the States, paid off a couple people, supplied his own cranes and transportation immediately upon the ship docking back home, and suspended it here next to the house with a crane until the floor was laid underneath it. Once the floor was done, the crane lowered it to where it now sits and the room was added to the house around Shkarbala."

"What is it?"

"Shkarbala was like a primitive satellite dish linking mortals and immortals. It was used for rituals and sacrifices, intended to communicate with and to please the gods. Only the royal recipients and their closest advisors were allowed near it and they were kept under close guard at all times. Legend was that the Immortals had personally hand crafted seven of these Shkarbala and had given them to the seven most powerful mortal leaders on the earth of that era. They did not come without a price however, and several were soon destroyed by the same Immortals that had made them when payment had not been fulfilled. Only three were said to have survived. Benny knew what he had found the moment he had laid eyes on it. He's been reading up on that kind of stuff his whole life. He put on his best poker face and played out his story, and here it is. The only known Shkarbala in captivity, though only truly known by a handful of people."

"Not if you keep showing it to everyone you invite over for dinner," I said sarcastically.

"No one outside the family had seen it once it got crated up in Tulum. It was in the crate the entire journey. We removed the crate after the room had been completed around it. Benny did a real good job of keeping a tight lid on his find, mostly thanks to arranging its transport in record time."

"You showed it to me and I'm not in the family," I pointed out.

Benny's smile broadened a hair. "You will be."

So. How about magic? Do you believe in magic? I never believed in magic. Ask me then if I believed in magic and I'd say no. Deception, trickery, double-joints, advantageous physical defects, all a yes. Magic, no.

Ask me now if I believe in magic. I guess I'd have to ask you to define magic first.

Harry moved over to the couches beneath the wall of maps and I obediently followed as I had all evening long. The floor had no carpeting or bear skin rugs. There were no lamps, all the brightness came from some track lighting near the tops of the walls. The ceiling was bare.

Harry sat and motioned for me to join him. I sat next to him as he opened the larger book with Jupiter on its cover and started leafing through it looking for a particular page.

"Ever been into astrology?" he asked me.

"Not particularly," I confessed. "I can recognize Orion and the Dippers but that's about the extent of my knowledge of the universe."

"Oh, I almost forgot. We need one more book. Do you mind, John?" Harry pointed towards the small bookshelf.

I stood and headed towards it. "Which one?"

"Top shelf. From the right. Third book."

I slid the third book from the right off the shelf and carefully walked it back to Harry. It was a thin book, and like the other one I had retrieved for Harry, it looked ancient and had no markings on its stained and dirty, dark red, cloth cover. It looked more like a journal than a book. The pages were yellowed and slightly warped. The cover was chipped, peeling and falling apart. It hardly weighed a thing. I imagined if I were to drop this book to the ground, it would disintegrate on impact into a puff of dust. I felt a sense of relief when Harry assumed control of this book's fate from me.

Harry discarded the journal/book to the couch on his left for the time being and we returned our attention to the page he had settled on in the Jupiter book while I was retrieving the latest edition for my 'first lesson'.

"You recognize our galaxy, right?" he was asking me.

"Yes, of course."

He moved the book more between us so I could easily see as he explained. "This is what our Galaxy looked like in May of 2002. See how the planets line up. Saturn, Jupiter, Mars is just a hair off line, then Venus and Mercury are on one side of the Sun. The Earth and Pluto are on the other. Only Uranus and Neptune are out of line on the Earth/Pluto side of the Sun.

"Now look at Orion. You see it?" He pointed it out in case I didn't. It was directly aligned with Neptune and Uranus but on the opposite side of the Sun. "The three stars in Orion's belt are often used as a directional home in ancient astrology. When the three pyramids were built around the Sphinx, they were aligned directly beneath the stars of the belt. In this shot, the belt's angle is off about ten degrees from the line formed by seven of the nine planets."

It was easy to see what Harry was pointing out.

"This book is about the planets," Harry continued. "It doesn't mention Orion or the stars. It does look at the future alignments of the planets and predicts that in 2040, all nine planets will come as close as they ever have to forming a single fairly straight line through the Sun."

Harry flipped ahead two pages. "The next time, however, that these same seven line up again is sometime late December of this year. Mars, in this picture, you can see has tucked itself more neatly in line. And look at Orion."

I looked at what would be northwest of the sun on a regular map and found Orion. The three stars of its belt seemed to now line up perfectly parallel with the planetary line.

"So they line up. Looks like the year to worry about is 2040 though which is still a long way off."

Harry smiled. "Just remember what I've showed you here. This is part one."

He closed the Jupiter book and placed it on the couch next to the journal book. The yellow book had remained in his lap and he now opened that one and carefully began leafing through the old, delicate pages. He stopped on a page about halfway through that looked like a hand drawing of Shkarbala.

"This is the only book we've ever been able to find that has a picture of Shkarbala," Harry said. "Only a few of the ancient scripts have ever even mentioned them, they are considered to be myth by most historians. Only we know different. They were only for the eyes of the royal owners. The common folk were never allowed to be near them. We have used this picture as a model." He closed the book and stood, placing the book down where he had been seated. "The picture showed four sticks," Harry was saying, as he walked around Shkarbala towards the shelves on the opposite wall, "attached to the sides. They look like torches. Like these." Harry pulled four stumps of wood off the shelf that looked like prop torches from the Indiana Jones movies. He started inserting them one by one into slots on the outer edge of Shkarbala, explaining as he went.

"When we dropped Shkarbala in here, we didn't think about anything other than trying to center it in the room that hadn't yet been built." He slipped a second stake into a second small stone ringlet built into the outer rim. "Later we discovered that we needed these *corners* of the circle to align with north, south, east, west and we had to have the crane come back out and turn it a little for us."

"How did you manage that?" I asked. "There's no way a crane could reach it in here."

Harry placed the fourth and final stake in place and turned towards the door. Below the light switch, he turned a large white knob and the track lighting began to dim closer to library level. Below that knob, he flicked a second switch and I could faintly hear a motor somewhere kick into gear. The ceiling began to roll back into the wall. A few moments later, the sky peered in on us with hundreds of tiny, twinkling eyes through a glass ceiling.

"We just had to take the glass out," he said. Stepping back to Shkarbala, he reached into his jacket pocket and pulled out a lighter. He held it up to the first stake and it immediately flared up becoming a living torch. As he moved towards the next stake, he looked at me over Shkarbala and asked, "You ready for part two?"

With all four stakes transformed into torches, Harry dimmed the track lighting to a faint glow. Most of the room's lighting and growing heat was coming from the four torches placed in the compass points of Shkarbala. Harry returned to the couch, removed his white jacket laying it neatly over the arm of the couch and picked up the final book, the dirty red one. He walked back to Shkarbala with the book and motioned for me to follow with a nod of the head. The glow cast out by the flames of the torches gave his smile a slightly mad looking quality. The reflections of the flames dancing in his eyes only enhanced the unsettling impression.

I stepped up next to Harry facing Shkarbala as he was. We were standing at what would have been between the east and south points of the compass. He held the book still closed in his left hand while he rolled up the left sleeve of his white shirt. Shifting the book to his right hand, he rolled the other sleeve up and then looked at me, grinning.

I wasn't grinning but I returned the look and waited for his next move or instruction. I felt like an audience member that had been singled out and asked to assist the magician on stage with his next trick without having a clue of what it was going to be. I wasn't sure whether or not I hoped his trick to be successful.

Harry opened the book. The pages were handwritten. It was a journal, or at least something along that nature. I couldn't recognize the writing. It wasn't English. He slowly and carefully turned each page, one at a time, gently pressing each page down before going for the next page. There were no more than 30 pages or so in the entire book. The lighting was set very dim but the torches provided plenty of light by themselves to still read the pages of the book, assuming you could read the language of symbols and pictures.

Apparently Harry could.

About ten pages into the book, he stopped. He looked at the sand filling Shkarbala and then to the stars shining through the glass ceiling for a long moment before returning to the book to begin reading. Somewhere in route, his smile had disappeared.

"Shkarbala shkarbo jukombo farmas som. Touher poitome. Touher singgoma. Touher Shkarbala farmas."

Harry closed the book after repeating the mantra three or four times. It was hard for me to tell where it ended and began each time through, but I could tell he was repeating himself. There was a rhythm to his chant as he carefully enunciated each word and his voice grew stronger as he went.

With the book closed and in his left hand, he raised both arms and his eyes towards the glass ceiling and the watching stars. Sweat was forming on his bald head and beginning to slide down between his eyes and the bridge of his nose. He closed his eyes and called to the stars in a voice only a notch or two below a yell, "Show me the time of Lucifer's plan! Show me the time of His revenge!" Raised hands noticeably shaking now, the track lighting suddenly went dark on its own. The torches around Shkarbala just as suddenly doubled in size and I had to force myself not to take a step backward when the heat also seemed to double causing a fresh sweat to break out on the top of my own bald head. Harry said one more time, this time in an all-out-no-doubt-about-it full fledged baritone scream, "SHOW ME!"

I sensed movement in the room and brought my attention back to Shkarbala. Harry lowered his arms, opened his eyes and also watched Shkarbala as the sand was definitely beginning to shift and sink in the center on its own. Two of the torches flared even brighter and a column of sand suddenly rose out of Shkarbala from the east and the west points. It rose straight into the air, the sand in constant motion, my brain trying to convince me that the motion was downward, the sand being dropped instead of levitated, but there was nothing above the millions of moving grains to be dispersing them. Seven feet above the level of the sand in Shkarbala, just before it would have reached the glass ceiling, both columns took a shape ninety degree turn towards each other and joined in the middle creating a large frame of busily moving grains of yellow sand. Grains and clumps of sand began to break away from the frame though the frame itself never lost its density, constantly replacing the pieces that break away with new racing grains of sand. Harry slid towards me, edging me south until we stood on either side of the lower burning south torch, facing the sandy frame squarely.

As smaller clumps of sand ran frantically around the inside of the frame, I noticed shapes beginning to form. The shapes became small balls of different sizes and started to fall into a line diagonally across the center of the frame from the lower left to the upper right. One small ball broke out from the pack in the center and positioned itself on the edge of the lower left corner. That would be Pluto, I realized. Two of the balls remained out of the forming line, off by themselves in the middle-right quadrant. These would be Neptune and Uranus. The rest of them were all within a couple feet from the center, slowly orbiting one sand-ball directly in the center that had already stopped moving. That one would be the Sun. As the five I took for Saturn, Jupiter, Mars, Venus and Mercury moved into line on one side of the Sun, the Earth and Pluto took their places on the other side. Then came the final touch. Orion suddenly came into view. The grains of sand not participating in any of the clumped groups forming images suddenly dropped back into Shkarbala and the picture was crystal clear like someone had just blown a layer of eraser droppings off the page. It was an exact duplicate of the page Harry had last shown me, the alignment that was supposed to come to fruition sometime in December of this year. If this was a trick, I didn't think it was one that David Copperfield was familiar with.

Harry turned away from Shkarbala and quickly retrieved the shiny Jupiter book. He leafed through to the page in question and handed the book to me. I didn't need to look to know that it was identical but I confirmed it anyway.

Two seconds later, the sand suddenly collapsed in a massive sand-fall. Not a grain of sand landed outside Shkarbala. The tracking lights came back on and the torches suddenly winked out completely on their own. Harry stepped back and turned the lights back up to library level. I stood staring at the dormant sand, inviting flies to come explore the inside of my mouth.

20

The decision whether or not to accept membership into this odd family did not come instantly after witnessing the giant, mystical Etch-A-Sketch map out an accurate near-future Milky Way blueprint. At that moment in time, I could have gone either way on a different day. The decision, or I should say, the decision not to make a decision, had come about an hour later while I was still trying to find my way home on the motorcycle.

"You probably have a million questions about now," Harry had said.

"Just one right this minute," I had replied. "Where can I smoke a cigarette?"

Outside, while I pulled hard with my lungs and relished the feeling of the nicotine being transported to my blood system while walking silently in small circles at the base of the steps, Harry sat on the top step of six leading up to the front entrance of the mini-castle enjoying a fat cigar with the air of someone who had just hit the jackpot on Wall St. He remained very patient, appearing to savor his cigar and allowing me to inhale my first Winston in record time and quickly light up another, while waiting for me to sort things out first in my own head.

Out here away from the big city lights, in a clearing of the woods next to a lake, the sky was filled with more twinkling stars than I had ever seen in my life. Or maybe I was just looking at them with new eyes, a new respect, a new awe. I picked out Orion in the southwest sky. The stars that made up the belt appeared to wink at me.

After lighting up my second dose of nicotine, I turned to Harry. "What was that stuff you were reading?"

"I was summoning Touher. He is the Immortal, according to the second book we looked at, that is the master of time. Touher was said to have taken the Mayans under his wing, so to speak, teaching them all of their insights into understanding time and making calendars. The sand in Shkarbala and the barrels is also native to the Yucatan."

"What about that stuff about Lucifer?"

"I don't mean to leave you hanging, John, but that will have to be part of our next lesson. I don't have the energy left to get into that tonight." Harry took in a long pull from his cigar and slowly released the smoke into the night without inhaling it. "I think we should get some rest and continue tomorrow. We have room for you if you would like to stay the night."

"No," I said, without needing to think about it. "Thanks, but I would like to sleep on my own pillow tonight...especially tonight," I added.

"We need you, John. You are one of us," Harry calmly said. "I have so much to tell you to get you up to date and prepared."

"Prepared for what?"

"I don't know yet what your role will be. But you are definitely one of us. Of this, I am sure. You carry the shine. You are part of the plan."

"Part of what plan? Who's plan?" I asked.

"His plan." Harry casually pointed towards the stars. "The Master Plan."

I didn't try to pull any more information out of Harry. He was obviously very tired. I was very overwhelmed and equally as tired. As we said our good-byes and I promised to stop by again for the "rest of the story" tomorrow afternoon after lunch, I proceeded to turn out of the driveway onto Crimson Lane heading the opposite way I had been going when coming in, forgetting that I had entered after a u-turn, and proceeded to travel the wrong direction for forty minutes before turning around.

It was during this drive home that I decided not to accept Harry's offer, but at the same time, not to say no, at least not yet. It's not like I had a job to go to. It's not like I had anyone to explain myself or whereabouts to. It's not like I had anything better to do. I wasn't expecting a call from Katelynn for almost a week still so I allowed my curious side to win the argument. I wanted to hear the end of the story. I decided to honor my promise and return for 'lesson two.'

By the time I had found home, just before running out of gas, the questions running amok in my head were feeding off one another, expanding to areas they shouldn't have even been considering, yet refusing to be ignored. *Was it really my decision to return or were things already beyond my control, the events to come foretold by ancient prophets or foreseen by the Immortals? Was it coincidence that Dr. James had chosen Benny as one of the test subjects? That Benny had been sick and in that very hospital despite the fact that his home was in Texas? If Dr. Getz had not died when he did, I would not have worried about Katelynn, would not have met Dr. James, Benny, Harry.* And of course, the biggest unsettling brain buster of them all, *Was my accident really an accident?* I had no answers, of course, leaving me suddenly unsure of anything, past, present or future. My life had become an open book and I was no longer sure that I was its only author.

I got out of bed shortly before noon. Hiding out under the covers and looking for answers to the questions brought forth from the previous evening's activities was only introducing new unanswerable questions.

In the bathroom, preparing to trim the beard of the stranger in the mirror, I found myself in a brief moment of self-pity and despair, wishing none of this had ever happened, beginning with my stupid decision leading to the accident. The trim turned into a clean shave as I tried to dig down far enough to find a familiar me, the old me. But even with a smooth chin again, I didn't even look like a bald version of me.

Whether from the stress surrounding Katelynn and the emotions she had awakened in me or from Harry's performance the previous night, my new face appeared harder than it had been, older, more experienced. I imagined walking back into Al's office and applying for a courier job again, him handing me an application oblivious to who I was. I wouldn't have recognized me myself if there had been more than one image in the mirror.

Obviously, I was unable to go back in time while standing in front of the mirror so I directed my thoughts more towards the future and the upcoming 'lesson' with Harry. As much as I wished none of this was being dumped on my doorstep, as much as I wanted to wash and scrub away whatever shine Harry could see embracing me, as much as I had now accepted and even slightly looked forward to just getting this business with Katelynn successfully over with and starting a new life in a new place, I also desperately wanted to see how many of these other mind-bending questions Harry could answer before I left.

I briefly considered not returning to the castle just to prove that I was absolutely in control of my own future and destiny. Harry was so sure that I was going to return, so sure that I was going to be a member of his family, part of me wanted to simply forget the entire day ever happened and stick with plan 'A' in regards to Katelynn just to spite him. Just to let him know that no one controlled me but me. Or maybe just to let *me* know. Who knows? I don't know.

But I did know I had to go back. I *had* to. I was at least able to convince myself that I *had* to go back because I wanted to hear the whole story out of genuine curiosity. I couldn't stay away any more than I could put away a good book half read and never open it again. I convinced myself that I was returning because I wanted to. It was far better than thinking about the alternative.

After refueling myself with a quick brunch of cereal and warmed up left-over pizza, washed down with lots of orange juice, I hopped on Shadow and took it down for its turn to refuel at the Kwik Trip.

Once again, after purposely passing the drive for number 14 off Crimson Lane, I took the 25-minute scenic route around the lake to re-collect my thoughts and steady the nerves, to settle my stomach. And once again, the iron gate had already begun to slowly swing open as I rounded the final curve out of the woods and I didn't even need to slow my speed as I passed under its threshold. Mr. Valet was once again stepping into the drive to point me in the proper direction as I arrived and Chauncy Doorman was waiting in the open front door this time as I returned to the castle after parking Shadow.

"Good afternoon, Mr. Johnson," he said, all business, no smile, as I approached the top step.

"Hi there," I said, removing my gloves and holding them out for him. I think I almost saw a smile in those dark eyes as he accepted my gloves, but I could have been just being paranoid. Still, I could tell he would have been a tough opponent at the poker table.

"Harry is expecting you, sir. He awaits in the library. He has instructed me to ask if you have eaten."

I liked Chauncy. I don't know that he would have liked it if he knew that I liked him, but I got the impression that he was probably a pretty funny guy when not in uniform, when among friends. "Thank you," I said. "But I'm fine. I just ate before I came."

"Very well, sir. Would you like for me to escort you to the library?"

Stifling back the urge to chuckle at the slightly sarcastic tone in his voice, I told him I could find my own way, thanks. He went one way, I went the other, through the piano parlor, around the dining room table, and found Harry sitting in the couch before the fireplace reading from a thin, newer looking journal.

"John, good to see you," Harry said, looking up from his reading as I stepped into the circle of couches. He closed the book without saving his place, set it on the couch next to him and struggled a quick moment to stand and shake my hand before sitting back down again. I glanced at my feet when our hands clasped and turned and sat in the couch Randi had been in the night before to better face him while we talked.

This afternoon the fire had been extinguished. The sunny day made the room bright and comfortably warm. The bushes and shrubbery gave the air of the library a feeling of freshness. Harry was much more sensibly dressed in a white T-shirt, an open denim jacket and blue jeans. The Dragons still watched and listened from the wall directly over us and the bear at my feet still snarled up in anger, but this time not directed at me from where I sat.

"So how ya feeling this morning? Manage to get any sleep last night?" Harry asked me after I had settled into the overstuffed, extremely comfortable corner of the couch.

"Surprisingly enough, I did," I confessed. I may have been thoroughly overwhelmed with stimuli and still feeling slightly numb from all the information and revelations that had been hurled at me the day before, and today might even only make things worse, but I was going into it well rested and alert.

Harry repeated Chauncy's offer for food which I again declined.

"What is today's lesson?" I had asked him, anxious to get started after we got through the opening pleasantries.

"More history," Harry said, picking up the journal he had laid next to him when I had come in. "This is one of the journal's that Pauly is putting together. Since much of what historians commonly accept as proper translations of old scripts and hieroglyphics is actually wrong, Paul has been keeping journals on what he discovers through his own translations."

"And you are convinced that Paul's interpretations are right and the rest of the world is wrong," I interrupted. This was still a fact I was having a hard time accepting.

"I am," Harry said without hesitation. "It is more like an alteration in the wording of the translation that Paul uses. The accepted versions are not far off, but that slight alteration changes the entire meaning of most writings. Now take into the fact that Pauly was never taught to translate the stuff. He just knew what it said even as a kid, as though he had been taught it maybe from a previous life."

Uh-oh. Already another warning alarm went off in my head as his words made themselves at home and our lesson hadn't even begun yet. My brain quickly replayed his last statement and judged yes, it was true, Harry had just mentioned the phrase, "...a previous life."

There are a lot of things I believe in that I have never seen or experienced in my life. There are also things that I have never seen that I am *willing* to believe in if ever given even a smidgen of solid proof. Then there are basically three things that I would have a hard time believing even if the proof were right in front of my stubborn nose.

History had always been part of that first group. I hadn't been there to witness it, but I believed most of what the text books had taught me growing up.

The second group contained what I had always considered "the fun stuff." UFO's and aliens, ESP, Big Foot, Loch Ness, etc. Some I believed more possible than others, but things like this I was certainly *willing* to believe if anyone could ever come up with one concrete bit of proof. The mystical sandbox from the previous night had been that proof for something, I just wasn't sure yet what it was that it had proved.

The final group, the Big Three, the concepts that I can not even slightly accept as real or even give a hint of plausibility to are Time Travel, One Supreme Being, and Reincarnation.

I had already allowed Harry to get away with bringing God into his story. Sorting things out while laying in bed, I had already moved Harry's version of God out of the third group, as the one supreme being who created the universe and everything in it in six days and then rested on the seventh. Harry's version of God fell into the second group, as an alien who happens to go by the name of, or at least our translation of the name, God. The immortal stuff was a little far-fetched, of course, but it could possibly squeeze into group two. There's a whole universe of the unknown out there.

But now Harry had just brought reincarnation into his story. One of the major no-can-do's.

"I don't believe in reincarnation?" I tossed out there, not really caring if he responded to the comment or not, just to let him know where I stand on that particular subject.

"I didn't say he learned it *in* a previous life. I said *from* a previous life."

"What's the difference?" I asked.

"It's just a theory, but it might explain Pauly's gift. It's kind of like inherited memory. Like deja vu. We inherit all sorts of stuff from our parents and ancestors. Baldness, hair and skin color, eye color, body types, weaknesses or strengths against certain diseases, even fears and certain moods and emotions can be passed along within the gene pool...the list is endless. Some genes skip generations like giving birth to twins or being left-handed. Others may lay dormant for several generations, rarely, if ever, resurfacing on down their bloodline and many may never get the chance to be discovered. But memory can also be passed along. When you feel like you have been somewhere before when you know you never have, maybe your parents were. Or their parents.

"Someone in Pauly's bloodline probably learned to read hieroglyphics and ancient scripts. Possibly someone in Pauly's bloodline used to *write* hieroglyphics and stuff some three thousand years ago. The knowledge always there ever since but laying dormant or undiscovered until resurfacing in Paul."

"Why Paul?" I asked. "Why not Paul's father or son or brother or all of them?"

"That's a good question," Harry said, clearly enjoying his current teaching job. "I confess I don't have all the answers. For now, for our purpose, we'll consider it good fortune or luck of the draw. But there is another possibility that I am sure we will be discussing at a later time and in a larger group for more opinions.

"But if it matters, John, I don't believe in reincarnation either. But I do believe in inherited memory."

That'll work, for now, I convinced myself. I could safely move that into the second group. Reincarnation and God as the one supreme being, two of the three big no-way-no-how's, had managed to remain where they belonged through Harry's interpretations of events. I was sure time travel would not even come into play so I was now ready to give Harry's story a chance. I only interrupted once more a moment later when I asked if he knew if there was still any Mountain Dew left over. He led me to the kitchen, through the door that had been behind Randi during dinner, and to the walk-in refrigerator where several cases of twenty-ounce bottles of Dew were being kept chilled. No other soft drinks, just Dew. Harry snapped one off a plastic ring and handed it to me. I decided not to ask why they happen to have so much Dew in their walk-in refrigerator. I wasn't sure I'd like the answer.

I silently followed Harry back to the library and for the next two hours, obediently paid attention to the history lesson Harry wanted to teach.

Neither Harry nor Chauncy Doorman had even mentioned that my full beard had disappeared.

21

arry flipped through the first few pages, speaking as he scanned the neatly penned handwriting in the journal. "We've already covered some of this stuff in the beginning here about Ra and Eoa. I suppose we should start with the arrival of God and Lucifer."

According to Harry, according to Paul, according to those who had supposedly heard it from the Immortals themselves...now here, a condensed version according to me for you...

...The Immortals are very similar to us, like the human race. Their appearance was as Harry had described Gabriel, a larger, more perfect body. Their people on the whole were also much like us. Some wealthy, some poor. Some strong, some weak. Some good and some bad. Most somewhere in the middle.

The Immortals were not truly immortal. A few stories told of Immortals turning on each other, fighting amongst themselves, and every once in a great while, one dies from the hand of another. But death, and especially murder, is very rare. The penalty for murder, if ever in your immortal life you are caught, is a life of imprisonment with just enough space to breath and enough nourishment to stay alive...forever. This sentence, to an immortal, is far worse than even death. For us, a 'life sentence' may be fifty to sixty years, yours given up for those you stole from the victim. No big deal. Not very long compared to the hundreds of thousands of years of complete solitude, the penalty for stealing as many years from an immortal. Spending hundreds of thousands of years alone, unable to move, forced to stay alive, for eternity...one could only look forward to death.

The taking of an immortal life was the greatest wrong that could ever be committed, held the greatest penalty, and was therefore very rare. The consequences were far too high to ever warrant the risk. The death of a human being, well, that's a different story all together. What have we got? A hundred years tops. Compared to hundreds of thousands of years, what's our life worth? What could we possibly accomplish in such little time? How could any one life be important? Sound familiar? Ever stepped on an ant? Swatted a fly? It's okay, they only live a couple of days anyway. What's one day less? Half their life, that's what! You want a just penalty for swatting a fly? Try fifty years in solitary confinement. Half your life for half the life you took.

Silly, right? To the Immortals, we have the life span of a housefly.

Although we may not have a life span worth worrying about, we are capable of communicating better with the Immortals than can houseflies with us. This makes us at least a bit more interesting, or maybe entertaining. I suppose if a fly was to suddenly stop buzzing around your food and offer up a sacrifice and create a miniature statue in your honor and kneel before this statue and pray to you to allow it and its family to live another day, you might think twice about squashing it flat with the classified section of the newspaper.

And maybe you might not. The Immortals are not that different than us.

Just like we have those among our race who wouldn't hurt a fly, who have a strong respect for all forms of life and their right to live out that life as they choose or by natural instinct, so do the Immortals. And the Immortal we call God falls into this category.

When He discovered this world of life being used and abused, toyed with and tortured by others of His own race, He made it His mission to free us from this injustice.

If you were walking down the street and saw a couple of bullies terrorizing a smaller boy, you would step in and put a stop to it, right? So would God.

Living forever, one can only stay in one place for so long before getting bored and needing to move on anyway, so when God had recruited Lucifer and His Army of Angels to free the earth's race of people from the "inhumane" treatment often inflicted upon us by Ra and Zeus and their cronies, the old rulers hadn't put up too much of a fight. Besides, God's army was a hundred times stronger. Most of the Immortals use about 80% of their brains, compared to the 6% we humans use, but even with our limited thought capacity, it would have been easy to predict the outcome of standing against Lucifer and God and the power He had in His Word.

God, like many humans, does not have a huge ego to feed. He is fine with who He is. He has nothing to prove. He is not interested in sacrifices and statues or even churches. He doesn't really care if we worship him or not. That is our choice. Everything is supposed to be our choice. That's why He chased off the bullies, so we could live as we choose. If we want to erect Churches as a means of spreading His Word, that is our choice. If we want to live our short lives not believing in Him or Them or that the world is flat or that Elvis still lives, that too is our choice. God really doesn't care. Do you care what an ant does when it punches out on the time clock after a full day of work transporting a bread crumb home to the hill?

But God is also very wise. He has lived a long time. He has seen many worlds. He understands our need to believe in something, in someone, that can give purpose to our short and meaningless lives. He delivered to us through Moses the Ten Commandments, knowing like children, we needed to have direction. He gave us that direction and told us what we needed to hear in a way in which we were used to hearing it. After sharing his basic personal morality system with us through Moses, he instructed us to listen to only Him, to obey none others but Him. He tells us this in the same vein a parent would tell his children not to talk to strangers. God simply doesn't want us to get thrown of track by others of His own race with lesser values or respect for all life that might tell us something different or make promises with hidden agendas.

Once God was sure that Ra and Zeus were gone and that the human race was at least pointed in the right direction, towards independence and free will, God's mission had been accomplished. It was His desire to move on, to find more wrongs to right, more wills to free. He is like the Lone Ranger of the Universe. Roaming the solar systems and galaxies, seeking out the bad and making it good. It is His purpose. It is what makes Him tick.

Because the Earth was so rich with life, and such cognizant life at that, God decided he could not leave this world unprotected from the wanderers of His own race that don't give life and free will the same regard that He does. For the same reason, He chose His only Son, Jesus, to provide that watchful eye. And to give His Son the ability to stave off any vindictive or defiant threats against His Will for the human race on Earth, He also chose to leave Lucifer and half His Army of Angels under Jesus' leadership.

Very shortly after Ra and Zeus were run out of Dodge, while Jesus was still doing his thing "in person" on earth, God moved on, confident His Son and Lucifer could handle things, anxious to free some more depraved souls.

This is probably God's only true fault, a case of over-confidence. He has never believed in failure. He holds this same confidence in His Son's desire and ability to maintain His goals and intentions for the luscious, green planet and its inhabitants. He is equally as confident in Lucifer's abilities and loyalties towards the cause.

Apparently even God occasionally makes a mistake in character judgment. Or maybe it wasn't a mistake at all. Maybe He is just testing His Son. Confident that His Son will succeed. Maybe even while gone, He is still keeping an eye on what's going on.

I figured if Harry knows the answer, I will too before too long. I quickly took a sip from my Dew and snuggled back into the cushions so as not to miss a word when he resumed after sipping his tea.

Lucifer had then of course betrayed God. He desired the earth and control of the life roaming its surface in the way that Ra and Zeus had enjoyed it. He began to recruit his own army from the ranks of Angels that had served under Him in the name of God and His Son, Jesus. Once his own numbers began to climb too large to remain unnoticed, Lucifer approached Jesus and tried to tempt him with power and potential. But of course, Jesus was a chip off the old block and could not be swayed by Lucifer. Jesus declared Lucifer an outcast, an enemy to God and His Word.

Though his army of Fallen Angels, or his Demons, as he called them, was only a quarter of the size of that which God had left in His Son's service, Lucifer had plucked out the most ruthless and merciless Angels to serve his own cause of chaos, turmoil and bedlam. There was a battle that lasted three hundred years in which many of Lucifer's recruits were killed. Lucifer and his surviving collection of mendacious Demons were finally forced to retreat.

At the time of Lucifer's withdrawal, just as all the villainous humans who survive a losing battle tend to do, he vowed to Jesus that he would return, that he would have his revenge, "...when the seven planets align and The Archer points the way."

In the meantime, for almost two thousand years now, Lucifer has remained near, rebuilding his own Army, planning his revenge. Even with Angels stationed all over the world keeping an eye out for interference with God's Will, the free will of Humankind, spiteful Demons have continued to sneak in and stir up some Immortal-made trouble. They talk to Humans and lie to them, make them promises. They use them and deceive them. Every now and then they get lucky and cause an assassination or a Holy War. Humans are very easy to manipulate.

Harry closed Paul's journal and looked up at me. The smile that I had assumed the previous night was glued to his face had vanished. He said nothing, waiting for me to reveal my first impression of Paul's revelations. I wondered if he could handle my true feelings. The last line he had just spoken said it all, didn't it? *Humans are very easy to manipulate.* Once the manipulat*ee,* now the manipulat*or,* sat in the next couch, possibly unaware that any manipulat*ing* was even taking place. I decided that in the long run, it couldn't matter. The truth is always best, right?

"Sounds about as real as Star Wars to me," I finally said. "I know you believe all this, Harry, but I just can't. It's all just too much. It sounds like something Steven Spielberg might have fun with though." I stood with the intention of thanking him for his time and escaping. "I have enough to deal with right now, Harry. A woman I know might be dying soon and I need to try to prevent it. I don't know why I thought coming here might help me do that, but I did and that was the only reason why I accepted your strange invitation to begin with. I thank you for your hospitality. You and everyone here have been very kind and friendly, but I think it is time for me to get back to what I need to do. My friend and her daughter need me thinking about them, not about what Lucifer may or may not be supposedly planning on doing to Jesus or mankind soon because he promised he would some two thousand years ago." I stepped in front of him to shake his hand. "Sorry, but thanks anyway and good luck with your quest."

Harry slowly stood and accepted my hand. With his story still running around loose in my mind and Katelynn pushing her way back into the already overcrowded picture, I didn't think to avert my eyes when our hands touched.

we can help you help katelynn, john. just give us the chance.

I quickly let go of Harry's hand as though it had burned me and took a step back, looking down at my own hand as I reeled it in. But the sensation I was getting wasn't pain and the source was not my hand.

The sensation was a numbness of the brain. The source had once again been the mind of Harry. He alone seemed to be sending me messages other than the date of his death whenever we touched and I peered into his eyes. I shook my head back and forth a couple of times as though I were trying to shake free the thoughts and rid myself of them once and for all as I sat back down on the couch. Unaware that I was again seated, I stared at Harry. He was smiling again. I shut my fly hole again.

"Tell me about Katelynn," Harry said.

"How do you even know who Katelynn is?" I asked suspiciously. "You told me you couldn't read minds."

"I don't know who she is," Harry replied, confusing me even more. "Randi mentioned her name yesterday when she was sitting where you are now. Then you just now mentioned a woman who needs you. I put one and one together, is all."

"Then how do you know you can help me help her? You don't even know what kind of help she needs," I reasoned.

"I would assume," Harry said slowly, "that you touched her and saw she was going to die soon because you told me that is what you do, and you want to change her destiny."

"I don't believe it is her destiny," I said.

"And what does she believe?"

"Well obviously she doesn't want to die," I snapped back, probably a little too sardonically. Knowing what he meant, I added, "She believes she will end up doing whatever God wants her to do. She figures if she dies, God has a good reason. I convinced her that God sent me to save her."

"But you don't believe in God, John."

"What I don't *believe* is that Katelynn has to die. There's nothing wrong with her. And besides, according to you, God isn't even in our galaxy at the moment and even if He were, He wouldn't care. All she's got is me. And I plan on being there for her. So don't be using her to rope me into your family because it would be dirty pool and I think you are a better person than that, Harry. If you can help me, tell me how. If not, then I hope you will understand why I must go."

Before the accident, I would never speak my mind as boldly as I had with Harry just then, or as I had during the last visit with Dr. James. Maybe it was because my feelings for Katelynn had possibly grown a little more than I would have admitted and her ever nearing d-day was affecting me more than I knew. Or maybe the events of the past few weeks had simply hardened me somewhat. I wouldn't have dreamed of taking off to who-knows-where with just the cash in my pocket a couple of months ago. Even though that was going to be a fairly healthy wad of cash, there was a reason why I was still living in the same house I had been born in. Yet I *was* looking a little bit forward to going, to starting fresh, as soon as I had seen Katelynn into the 30th day of her twenty-ninth year. It's not like I was going to be a wanted criminal on the lam. I would just be trying to avoid the Medical and Science communities, as well as any physical contact with other people for the rest of my life. If I ran low on money before establishing a half-decent income, I could always sell the house. For now, I just planned on preparing it to sit empty for a while. Let them wonder.

At any rate, whether it be Dr. James for the advancement in brain-ology or Harry for some psychic war against the Immortals to save mankind, I couldn't imagine either one having a place in my world.

"Tell me about Katelynn, John. Tell me your story. When did you start seeing into people's minds? If what I feel is true about you," he said, and I could see in his eyes that he believed what he was telling me, "then yes, I believe we can help you."

"I don't see inside minds. I just suddenly know when they are supposed to die when I touch them and look into their eyes," I explained. "It's like I've always known and just suddenly remembered."

"You've been inside my mind," he reminded me. "You are here, aren't you?"

True. I was there. I didn't feel like I had been inside anybody's mind. Both Randi and Ronnie had been inside my head but that was their doing, not mine. I wasn't really anxious to go over the whole story again, but he had said he thought he could help. I wasn't as confident as he was about that, but if there was the slightest chance he *could* help me help Katelynn, I couldn't leave without exploring that possibility.

By 4:30, I had caught Harry up to the point where we had met in Benny's room at the hospital, and Mary walked in to see if we needed anything.

"Will you be staying for dinner with us tonight, Mr. Johnson?" Mary asked me, after Harry had requested two Mountain Dews.

I looked at Harry. He saw the reluctance in my eyes and said, "Small group tonight, John. Nothing like last night. If you don't have any place else to be, I think we've still got a lot to talk about."

"If I stay," I said, "we need to start taking more smoke breaks."

Randi and I sat across from each other at the table. Everyone else, Paul, Harry, Ronnie and Steven had adjourned to the library after dinner. We had eaten in the smaller of the two dining rooms this time, on the opposite side of the kitchen, but the meal had been just as grand on a smaller scale. Mary and two others dressed in castle employee attire whose names I didn't know cleared away the final dishes. I had a fresh bottle of Dew in front of me, Randi was blowing on a fresh coffee.

Harry had explained to me what he had in mind before dinner. I was a little bothered by the fact that he had apparently already talked to Randi about working with me before he even knew whether or not I would agree. Randi had been the last to arrive for dinner. It had not been talked about during dinner yet there she was, the last one at the table with me. *I* knew that had been the plan...but she shouldn't have.

Then it dawned on me. I was possibly sitting at a table of mind readers. Randi was a pro. Ronnie had a touch to some degree. Steven was new to me but appeared to be probably Ronnie's husband. He hadn't been at last night's dinner table. For all I knew, there could have been a completely separate conversation going on at the table that I hadn't even been aware of. While I thought I was listening to talk about trivial things like the weather and the price of gas, Randi could have also been reading the thoughts of others and sending thoughts all around. Or more likely, she and Harry had had a long silent discussion between them. What he was asking of her was not something one could take lightly. But there we were, just as Harry had hoped, facing each other from across the table. I felt naked when her eyes met mine.

She put down her coffee cup in front of her. She was no longer the essence of black. Today she was green. She wore a short lime green skirt and green hose covered her legs. Her long-sleeved shirt with the ends that snap together between two of the fingers on each hand was a deeper emerald green. Over that was a sharper, darker green sleeveless tank top. She had a green jewel in her belly that had revealed itself when she had pulled the chair out to take a seat at the table. Her finger nails were all painted green and if I could have seen her feet under the table, I was sure that her toenails were now green as well. Her hair was raven black and still seemed to be trying to escape her head in all directions, but the pink was gone. Now there were streaks of lime green running around amidst her black mane. And of course, she wore a shade of green on her lips that I don't think I had ever seen before, certainly never on a pair of lips.

Our eyes met, I waited for her to break the ice, which she thankfully did right away. I couldn't have held her eyes more than a few seconds. Even though she was probably half my age, she had a confident, knowing look in her eye that was more than a little intimidating.

"So. Harry thinks you need some training with that gift you got."

"Did you two talk about it during dinner?" I asked. "I mean, in your minds?"

She nodded.

"Are you reading my mind right now?"

She shook her head no. But who would know?

"Do you know the specifics about my thing?" I still refused to call it a gift.

"You can see when people are supposed to die."

"Basically, yes."

"But you have no idea how you get the information," she continued.

"Other than the touch and the eyes, correct."

"Yet you have read thoughts from Harry's mind twice."

I realized Harry had managed to tell her quite a bit over dinner. "Apparently, I guess I have," I said. "But I don't know why it was different those times with him."

"It's because he was concentrating so hard on the messages. He was waiting for you to come." Then she said, inside my head, *and you don't need to be touching them, john. eventually, you won't even need to be looking at them.*

22

H ere," Randi said, extending one of her arms across the table. "Take my hand."

"But then I will know when you are going to die and if you happen to peak into my mind, you will also know. I'm not sure that is a good idea."

"You haven't seen Harry's time yet, have you?"

"No," I confessed. "Twice no."

"And you won't see mine either," she said, as though she already knew this for fact.

Hesitantly, I reached across the table and our hands met in the middle.

Welcome. Welcome. Welcome.

I instinctively tried to jerk my hand away as the word suddenly repeated itself a few times in my head. Randi's grip tightened slightly, just enough to prevent my hand's escape. Before, when Randi had infiltrated my mind with her thoughts, the thoughts had actually been in her voice. The "welcome" message I had just received wasn't in any voice. It sat in my mind the way the numbers always had, like a fresh memory.

relax your mind, john. follow these thoughts. let your mind float with the words.

This was in her voice again. She had sent that thought. I let my mind wrap around the imagined sound I heard as her voice. I was peering deeply into the black pupil in the center of one of her green eyes. Had her eyes been green yesterday? I couldn't remember and tried to ignore that part of my brain again. I imagined myself floating into her head, through her dark pupils, down the narrow optical nerve and into her brain, seeking her mind.

I began to feel a little lightheaded and dizzy and wondered what the inside of someone's brain would look like when my eyes blinked and I was once again simply looking at the green eyes of the girl across the table. I blinked a few times as though I had just awakened from a quick nap and this time when I heard Randi speak, I saw her lips moving in sync.

"You can't *see* anything in there," she was telling me. "That would just be gross. Try again, but this time, imagine your mind and mine linked together by a phone line." She still held my hand, still locking my eyes with hers. Still no numbers had come to mind. *now listen to your mind, john. listen to the part that is connected to the phone line. pick up the receiver, john. open your mind. listen to what it tells you but not with your ears. see but not with your eyes.*

This was again in her voice in my head and I tried to concentrate hard and relax at the same time, tried to ride her voice, tried to feel the voice's source through the imagined line and I was suddenly bombarded with so many thoughts of no voice that I couldn't get a grasp on any single one. I felt confused and disoriented and this time when I reflexively pulled my hand away from hers, it slid free and I broke her hold on my eyes. The confusion and swarming thoughts dissipated just as suddenly as they had arrived and I expelled a deep breath.

I looked back up at Randi, a hundred new questions running through my head. I grabbed the question I was looking for and opened my mouth to verbalize it but got no farther than that.

"Yes, I do," Randi was saying, pushing her chair away from the table. "And I could probably use one about now, too." She stood up, the jewel in her belly made another brief appearance, and she pulled a green pack of Salem's out of a front pocket in her skirt. "We'll go out the back by the lake. I have a coffee can for the butts out there."

Randi silently sat cross-legged on the beach smoking her Salem and staring out over the water. I sat next to her, using my elbows on my knees as a perch for my chin while savoring my Winston, still having trouble holding on to any one thought for more than a second. Finally, she said, "Harry was right about you."

"How so?" I asked, blowing a white plume of exhaled smoke towards the darkening sky. With summer solstice over a month behind us, the days were noticeably growing a little shorter each evening, the darkness a little more eager to swallow up the light.

"He said you had a shine on you. A big shine. Like mine."

"You can see it, too?" I asked.

"No, of course not," she said, still looking out at the lake. "But I saw my thoughts in your head for a second before you closed them out. It was kinda weird."

"Before *I* closed them out?"

"Yep. You kind of *turned off.* I've seen some people take thoughts from me without knowing it. I've seen my thought in their mind, just a word or a phrase and even sometimes confusion on their faces as to how the thought had come to them as they walk by me. If Harry saw them, he might see a little bit of that shine squeezing out of them. I think everyone has the mechanics to do what I do, but most don't know how or don't have access to that part of the brain. Maybe all those drugs my Mom took while I was in her belly made my brain defective or more sensitive. And maybe the injuries of your accident had a similar effect on your brain. But in there, with you," she said, nodding back at the house with her great mane of hair, "it was like you had taken a hundred thoughts at once. Your mind was at once filled with my thoughts and then suddenly they were gone. You disconnected."

"All I was doing was trying to *feel* your voice. Then I felt like I had walked into a crowded room where everyone was talking over each other. But at the same time, there was no noise, no sound at all."

She looked at me with a half smile, amusement in her eyes. "You bit off more than you could chew. When you open a book and look at a page, you can see the whole page in front of you. But if you try to read the whole page at once, none of it will make any sense. In order to make sense of it, you need to read a word at a time. Only in this case, it isn't words you are reading or pictures you are seeing. It is thoughts you are thinking.

"When you think of water, you don't *see* water, you don't *taste* water, you don't see it spelled out in your mind. You *sense* it. It is a thought. Thought is the sixth sense. Not ESP like everyone says. There's taste, sight, touch, smell, hearing, and *thought*. Everyone has the sixth sense. Everyone has thoughts. You can't taste, see, touch, smell or hear a thought, but it still plays a part in your evaluation of an object or situation making it just as valid and equally important as the other five senses. I would say the ability to reach out and *experience* someone *else's* thoughts would be the *seventh* sense. I believe everyone has that capability too, but only a few, like you and me, have tapped into it."

I had no response. I had always lived in my own little world, comfortable with my meaningless role in life, satisfied with my belief systems. In the last two days, I had discovered the world outside the personal one which I had been constructing for most of my life to hide out in, was a lot larger and more mysterious than I had ever imagined. In fact, over the last month I seemed to have lost sight of my own little world. And it was looking more and more like I would never be able to find my way back.

"Why am I not seeing your numbers like I do with everyone else?" I asked when we had gotten back inside after our break on the beach.

We were now in the smallest of the three downstairs parlors. This was a cozy wood paneled den suitable for about a dozen people to sit in the assorted couches and chairs spread out about the room. There was a self-serve mini-bar in one corner along the far wall. The other three walls featured two or three paintings each that all appeared to be from the same hand, probably a collection of someone's works. The theme seemed to be strange landscapes and figures that didn't quite look human, but everything was purposely painted slightly out of focus making you not quite sure. It occurred to me that the artist of this collection might even be a member of the family here. If not that, someone here was certainly obsessed with this particular artist.

Randi and I had faced two of the La-Z-Boys a couple of feet apart before we sat, preparing for another attempt at this mind stuff. Sitting forward, we would easily be able to hold each other's hand with a comfortably short reach. For now, we were both sitting back with our arms on the over-stuffed armrests.

"I'm not sure," Randi replied. "It could be like depth perception or different levels of thought. I have never seen anyone's death the way you say you have. But I have no doubt you are plucking that information out of their minds from somewhere. As I said before, I have seen my thoughts in others, thoughts I had not sent them. They had unknowingly read my mind, and many times they had never even looked my way. They just *sensed* it, soaked it in. Maybe our brain waves, our thought *patterns*, had been on the same channel as we neared or something. Maybe a lot of things. You could be unknowingly looking even deeper, probably into a subconscious that I can't even reach. You're slipping right past the conscious mind. You just need to figure out how to refocus your *sight* to a closer point. Maybe once we figure that part out, you can show *me* where that subconscious is."

"Or maybe you can show me how to block it off and shut it down so I never have to go there again," I said.

"Yeah," she agreed, quickly considering the advantages versus the disadvantages. "You're probably right. A lot in there I probably don't want to know. Still, an intriguing thought."

The remainder of our session only lasted for another hour. Initially, we had clasped both hands in front of us, sitting forward in our seats. I relaxed my physical and mental state as best I could, but I still felt a tenseness in my neck and could hear my heart thumping a little too quickly in anticipation of our purpose. I took a deep breath as though I was getting ready to take a plunge underwater, then released it slowly and evenly, trying to relax a little more. I looked into her right eye...

...she was singing. I couldn't hear her voice but the lyrics went racing through my mind and I found my own imagination adding in the music and a version of my own voice for the lyrics. I was familiar with the song, but had only heard it a couple times on the radio. "One Of Us," by Joan Osborne, and I didn't even know what the song was about, let alone all the words making up the lyrics. Yet I sang the entire song in my head, word for word, with Randi in her head.

When the final line had played out, when God had found his way home on the bus to wait for a call from the Pope that would never come and Joan had revealed her version of the meaning of life in a three-and-a-half-minute song, I noticed that sometime during the song, Randi had let go of both my hands. This fact then stole enough of my attention to break any connection I had held with her mind and I slumped back into my padded chair trying to remember the lyrics to the song...and there they were. I knew them now. Not just the repeated chorus. I *knew* the lyrics. All of them.

"Wow," was all I could say.

Randi smiled. "She is my favorite."

"When did you let go of my hands? I didn't even notice."

"As soon as I saw the smile spread across your face," she said. "It looked good on you. You should wear it more often."

I smile plenty, I wanted to say, but she was right from her perspective. Here, it hadn't been too often. Usually just in greetings and when socially necessary. My most common expressions within these walls had been awe, confusion, concern, disbelieve...not a lot of smiley opportunities. But I guess if I were to be honest, there really hadn't yet been very many smiles at all under my new bald cap, and those that had surfaced had been drawn out by Katelynn just before she left for home. Randi would not have seen any before.

"Interesting song," I said.

"Now relax again," she said. "Look me in the eyes here." I was still leaning back in my chair, as was she. *you can hear me can't you.*

I nodded.

you have permission to join me here. reach out. but softly, gently, look into my eyes...

...suddenly she was singing about Ray Charles and some spider web except Ray Charles could see now and was warning her about the webs. It was another Osborne song, I figured, just one I'd never heard. The lyrics a bit more cryptic and harder to follow for the first time with no music to relate to for accompaniment, but when it was over, it had been an equally thrilling experience and I felt that the lyrics to each of these songs would forever be readily retrievable.

One more, I heard her say in my mind. The lyrics had all been in my own voice. My gaze remained calm and relaxed. I was looking into her eye but focusing somewhere ten or fifteen feet behind her. I reached for her with my mind, she wondered what I might know and then what I might not, in my voice. Then I started singing, more like chanting since there was no music. But I knew the words. I knew them for the first time just moments before reciting them in our heads but once they had been revealed, they would not be forgotten. I gathered this one was called either Crazy Baby or The Light. It appeared to be about someone slowly going insane. About half way through she closed her eyes and lost me.

"Okay," she said, offering up the first live sound for our ears in almost ten minutes. "You don't need my eyes. You don't need your eyes. All you need is the frequency. You can find that frequency. You have access. You were using touch and sight because those are senses that you understood. You weren't listening to the real source. You can't touch my thoughts. You can't see my thoughts in my eyes. They just helped explain what you couldn't. Now sit back." Her voice softened like a trained hypnotist. "Relax. Breath." She spoke the word slowly, enacting it out with her hands slowly spreading up and out, away from her chest. "Now close your eyes." Her voice, soft to my ear. I relaxed. Closed my eyes. *Now take my hand with your mind, sing with me, over here...*

And we sang. We sang the entire Joan Osborne album together in her head. All eleven songs. To someone peaking in from the doorway, it would appear that we had each fallen asleep in our respective chairs or were each in some form of deep meditation with silly looking grins on our faces when in reality (or some version of reality, I suppose) we were havin' a party of the minds. Forty minutes later, I knew the entire album's lyrics by heart. I fully understood why Joan was Randi's favorite, having also sensed her emotions that accompanied each song.

When our eyes did finally open, Randi was smiling so hard she looked like she was about to burst.

"What?" I asked, suddenly feeling self-conscious.

She couldn't hold it in and speak at that same time. As she opened her mouth to explain, laughter first spilled out before she could say, "Don't quit your day job." and then giggled a little more.

It suddenly occurred to me. If she had been singing along with me, sending her thoughts, I would have heard the lyrics in her voice. But as it was, I was the guest in her mind, plucking them from her mind. If I had been unknowingly sending my thoughts back to her, singing to her, as opposed to her plucking them from me, then she would have heard me singing along with her. I had only heard myself, not her. I had assumed she had only heard herself. Now I realized I had assumed wrong. She had been singing along with me in her own voice of course, but could also hear me shamelessly displaying my lack of any musical talent or ear, inner or outer. I'm sure my face turned beat red if it was in relation to how embarrassed I suddenly felt just then.

"Relax," she said, still giggling a bit. "You weren't *that* bad. Look, I got some homework I need to do..."

"Oh, I'm sorry. Sure."

"No, it's okay. I got plenty of time. But what I was going to say is that I want to do some more tomorrow. You really do got it. You got it strong, too. I've been working with Ronnie for almost a year and she will probably never be able to do what we just did but she has come a long way. But we need to give you some practice. Let you figure this stuff out. For me, I was born with it. I learned in a natural way how to find my potentials and reach for my boundaries. Now it's as second nature as sleepin' and shittin'. Pardon my French. For you though, it might be more like learning to ride a skate board for the first time in your forties."

"I'm in my thirties," I said.

"Thirties, forties...you're gonna fall off a few times before getting the hang of it. I wanna make sure we get you past that part. And I really do think you got a *lot* more potential than you know. I get out of school tomorrow at 3:30. Pick me up?"

"I drive a motorcycle."

"Perfect!"

Part Two

23

I sat by the phone waiting for Katelynn's call. I had no idea what time it was going to come. Her appointment with Dr. James wasn't until three that afternoon, yet it was still eight in the morning when I had started making sure the phone was never more than a single ring away from my grasp.

I had picked up Randi on my motorcycle the day after our first meeting of the minds. School, though she was only seventeen, had turned out to be the University of Minnesota. She was already preparing to be a Junior next month, in the process of completing her Sophomore year during the summer. She was majoring in history with a minor in astrology. I wondered how much she had used her gift on her teachers and professors to accelerate her way through the educational system, though I'm not so sure she would have needed to use it at all. She appeared to be a very bright and motivated young woman, despite her constantly changing appearance that seemed to want to beg to differ.

We held two more two-hour sessions over the next two days. We didn't do any more singing, however, and I noticed that once I had left her company, I could no longer recall *every* word on the Joan Osborne album, but the next morning I certainly remembered enough to assure myself that it had indeed really happened, just in case I was having my doubts.

By the time we were done, we were able to hold conversations within our minds while sitting with our backs to one another. I discovered all I needed to do was think of her to receive the dominant thoughts that were in her mind. Facing her, I found that I could read a lot more.

On the third day, near the end of our last two-hour session, she had purposely tried to empty her mind. Our eyes had locked, I briefly heard a mantra, a steady hum she was using to still her thoughts. I looked deeper within her mind. Suddenly *(24/289)* flashed in my mind and I immediately tried to tuck it away, hide it behind loud thoughts. As much as I tried not to react to the sudden knowledge of what I could only assume was to be the day of her death, I must have failed. In my mind, she said, *What?* I shook my head, saying nothing, and looked away from her for a quick instant, apparently successfully hiding this new knowledge before she had been able to react to my reaction. I felt suspicion and curiosity when I looked back at her.

Letting it go, she had then instructed me to try to pull a childhood memory out of her mind. I got passed the hum that had begun once again in her mind and this time felt a mixture of emotions, love, hate, disgust, fear. A door. Locked. Voices turning to shouts. Gunfire. Panic. I had closed my eyes and looked immediately at my own feet. This time she was able to see what was on my mind.

Out loud, she said softly, "Sorry about that. That was the day my parents died. I guess it is still lingering in my mind more than I knew. It was three years ago, when I was fourteen."

"I'm sorry," I had said.

"You lost your parents, too," she said, looking into my eyes. "A car accident."

"Yes, sixteen years ago for me."

Something else we have in common, then, I heard her think.

The next two days, up until the day Katelynn was supposed to return for her physical, I didn't leave the house. I was afraid of what might happen. Visions of stepping into a crowd and being overwhelmed by hundreds of thoughts had kept me at home. I had asked Randi before I had left the castle after our final session if that's what would happen when I went out. Her response had been, "Only if you let it. Only if you open up and try to read the whole page at once again. As you get used to the *feel*, you should be able to turn it on and off like a light switch. Occasionally thoughts may leak in without your initiating it, but it will become second nature eventually for you to recognize them for what they are and ignore them the same way you would ignore a conversation within ear shot between two people you don't know as you walk past them."

I believed her, but still didn't feel quite ready to test out her theory until I had to. That time came when the phone finally rang shortly past noon.

I hopped on Shadow right after the call had come in. She was a half an hour from town and I was fifteen minutes from her home. I had time for two Winstons while sitting on my bike in her drive before she and her mother pulled into the driveway next to me.

Katelynn had the car door open even as I watched her mother throw the gear shift on the steering wheel into park and I was climbing off the motorcycle. I took one step towards the car, she had already taken five and was flinging her arms around my neck though it was only a hug, not a kiss, that I received. I felt very self-conscious not knowing what she had told her mother about me, who was now getting out of the car herself and looking my way as she walked around from the other side towards us, not smiling as Katelynn had.

Katelynn released me taking a step back. "Hi John. You shaved off your beard. You look a little younger without it," she said smiling. Then turning away from me towards her mother, "This is my mother, Abby. Mom, this is John Johnson."

"Hi John," she said with a strong steady voice, an octave lower than I would have expected coming from her thin frame. She was probably in her early sixties. She had a pleasant looking face, though it had a leathery appearance of one that had worked outside much of her life. Her eyes looked dark and confident. Her hair, though a solid gray, was still long reaching the middle of her back and held together in a single ponytail. She reached out to shake my hand and her grip was firm. Still not sure of myself, I averted my eyes and glanced at Katelynn when our hands briefly clasped. I had given up on the gloves. Randi had told me I shouldn't need them. Looking back at Abby, trying not to 'turn on the light switch,' I said, "Glad to meet you, Mrs...." I paused, looking at her, then suddenly finished my sentence after only a second had passed, "Brogan." It occurred to me once again then that I still didn't even know what Katelynn's last name was yet.

"So, you're the one that thinks my daughter is going to die soon," she said boldly, getting right to the point.

"No," I corrected her. "I'm the one that thinks she doesn't *have* to die soon."

She studied me. I remained 'turned off' as best I could, but I couldn't help feeling her emotions which were tainted with an anger that she was concealing well on her face. "I hope we can get to the bottom of this today," she said to me, then looked at

Katelynn who was standing by my side. "Shall we go in and grab some lunch before we go to the Hospital?"

We went inside Katelynn's house and her mother and I sat in the living room while Katelynn threw a frozen pizza in the oven. Once the timer had been set, Katelynn joined us, sitting on the couch next to her mother, I was on the La-Z-Boy on the right.

For the next twenty minutes, her mother asked me questions, confirming the story her daughter had conveyed to her when she had returned to the farm. I wanted to add to the story, tell Katelynn all about my experience with Harry and Randi and all the things I had learned, but I still wasn't sure how any of it was going to help us with her situation and I assumed if I were to spill all that happened over the six days she had been gone, I might lose all credibility with Mrs. Brogan.I decided to wait and tell Katelynn about it later if we were ever left alone for a little while.

Abby Brogan fell silent after she had confirmed all she felt she could, but her eyes remained fixed on me, still trying to evaluate. A moment later, the timer went off and we all went to the kitchen. Mrs. Brogan pulled out a chair and sat as Katelynn went to a cabinet and pulled out some plates and I went to a drawer and pulled out three knives and three forks. I turned towards the table. Mrs. Brogan was staring at me. *He knows where the silverware is,* was in the front of her mind and I had to consciously 'turn off' again.

"Will you get some glasses, too?" Katelynn asked as she placed the plates on the table and turned to retrieve the pizza from the oven. I briefly thought of asking which cabinet, for her mother's sake, then just decided what the hell and went straight to the correct door next to the refrigerator and pulled out three glasses.

"Did you have a good week?" I asked, trying to ignore her mother's eyes that felt like they were borrowing into my head. I wanted to turn on and find out exactly what she thought of me but not only was I still not confident in my control of this ability to read minds yet, I also wasn't sure I really wanted to know what she was thinking of me at that point.

"Yes," Katelynn replied. "Faith took to the water like a fish. She always loves being at the farm."

By two-thirty, we had cleaned up the lunch dishes and Katelynn and her mother climbed back into the car to head for the hospital while I followed on my motorcycle. The day was clear and warm and the slight chill in the wind from the north felt good as I sped up on the highway leading to the hospital.

After parking in the employee lot, we walked across the street and checked in with a nurse that Katelynn knew before sitting down in a large waiting room. Dr. James appeared a few moments later to greet us.

Dr. James shook hands with Katelynn, asking her how her week had been and then turned towards Mrs. Brogan as Katelynn introduced him to her mother. He shook her hand and greeted her and then turned to me and said 'hi, how ya doin', John,' without shaking my hand.

"I assume they have told you everything that has led us to this point," Dr. James said, addressing Mrs. Brogan. She nodded and he turned again to me. "Have you checked to see if Katelynn's number is still the same?" he asked.

"I haven't checked, but I assume it hasn't changed," I said, knowing he intended to have me do it again to be sure before we began.

"I think the prudent thing to do here would be to make sure it hasn't changed. Do you mind?"

I looked at Katelynn, her hand was already reaching towards me as she took a step my direction.

I looked into her eyes and tried to clear my mind of the surroundings and focus on Katelynn. Before, the numbers had always just appeared on contact. There was no effort involved in retrieving them. This time however, as I tried to consciously 'turn on', Katelynn's emotions flooded my mind. Fear was dominant though you wouldn't have known it looking at her face. Our hands touched. *Be different,* she was thinking, pleading. I concentrated harder. Tried to get past her thoughts. I saw Faith, whom I recognized from many pictures in her home the night I had stayed. I saw her father. I saw her husband who had passed away five years ago. And the numbers *(29:29)* suddenly lingered on my brain and I knew it had not been my own memory producing the numbers. They hadn't changed.

I shook my head slowly and let go of her hand. "They haven't changed," I said, looking down.

"Okay, then. Why don't you and Mrs. Brogan try to make yourself comfortable in the waiting room. Katelynn, you can follow me and we'll get the physical started. After that, I have ordered a CAT scan and want to take some skin and blood samples to send to the lab. The whole thing should only take a couple of hours but we probably won't know a whole lot until the results are in from the lab tomorrow morning. I have already let the lab know that I want quick and thorough results by morning."

Katelynn glanced at the two of us, a look of helplessness on her face.

"It'll be okay," I said. "I promise."

She gave me a weak smile and followed Dr. James out of sight on the other side of the nurse's station. Mrs. Brogan and I went back to our seats in the waiting room.

"Katelynn tells me you are a courier," Mrs. Brogan said when we had sat down once again. I hadn't any idea how we were going to fill two hours with conversation and had been hoping she wasn't going to try.

"*Was* a courier," I responded. "I am between careers right now."

"Any idea what you are going to do?"

"Right now, I just want to get Katelynn to September 19th. After that, I really haven't given it a whole lot of thought."

"You know she really likes you," Abby said. "I'm still trying to figure out why, myself, considering you were the bearer of this awful news to begin with, but you were about all she talked about this past week."

"I like her, too," I confessed. "But right now, like I said, I just want to help her get through this."

She looked at me a moment longer. I waited for her next question, trying to decide whether or not I should 'turn on' and get a head start coming up with the answer to her next probing question but our attention was diverted and the questions forgotten as we heard a commotion at the main door.

A man ran in holding a young boy of four or five years old in his arms. A distraught looking woman, presumably the mother, following close behind, her face covered in tears. The boy was unconscious and a nurse hurried around the counter towards them.

"He fell and hit his head," the man was saying. A purple lump the size of a plumb was growing out of the boy's forehead. The nurse called for a stretcher and a doctor and within moments both came around the corner. The man laid the boy down and the doctor and nurse moved to his side, edging away the mother and father.

The doctor asked a couple of quick questions to the parents while inspecting the head injury and the eyes and the pulse and then wheeled the boy quickly away. The nurse stopped the parents from following, assured them that their boy was going to be fine and explained that they needed to remain here and start filling out some paperwork while the doctors did what they do best. She took them to the nurse's counter and handed the man some papers and a pen, and the two of them, both looking very worried for their son, sat down a few yards away to begin with the history and info on their son.

The woman's emotions of fear and worry were so strong, I had to work at blocking them out of my head when I looked at her. Successfully done, I looked at the man and tried to open up just a little bit. Rage was the emotion felt. I opened up a little more and saw him swatting his son. His son spinning on his feet, going down hard, his head bouncing off a kitchen table as he fell.

I closed down immediately, feeling like I had been trespassing, not really confident enough in my new talent to trust that all I had just sensed had been real.

I looked back at the mother again, this time just trying to crack open the doorway to her mind a little at a time. She was looking at her husband. Hate joined the other emotions as he began filling in the blanks on the pages attached to a clipboard. Hate and fear. *How could you!* was running over and over in her mind. Looking a little beyond that, I had an image of other times, words being yelled in anger, other falls the boy had taken due to less damaging swats from his father's hand. *I'll take him away when he gets well...if he gets well. I won't let him do this again.* And the woman broke out in fresh tears as she watched her abusive husband calmly fill out the paperwork.

Why not just call the police? I thought to myself. Then I had an idea. Randi had said she had seen her own thoughts in other people's minds from time to time, even though the recipients of the thought had no idea how it got there. I sent an idea to the woman.

Why should I leave? feeding her the thought as if it were her own. *Call the police right now.* He's *the one that needs to leave, not us.* He's *the monster that needs to be stopped. Call them now while he is filling out the paperwork. Call them now and tell them the truth. Right now!*

The woman stood up.

"Where you goin'?" the man asked, looking up from his papers.

"The bathroom," she said, without looking his direction.

A few minutes later she returned and sat next to her husband again. Abby had picked up a National Geographic and was flipping through the pages looking for something that was interesting enough to pass a little time with. I was the only one in the waiting room besides the mother that knew she had been no where near the bathroom.

Ten minutes later, the husband was standing at the nurse's station turning in the completed paperwork when two uniformed policemen walked into the waiting room. They looked at the man at the counter, then at the mother who was still seated. I followed their gaze. She nodded. They stepped up on either side of the father at the counter.

"Mr. Williams?"

"Yes," the man said hesitantly. Realization of what was going on suddenly hit him and he sent his wife a particularly ugly and nasty glare.

"We would like to ask you some questions about your son's accident," the one on his right said, drawing Mr. Williams' gaze away from his wife who was trying to keep her focus on the floor in front of her.

"I haven't done anything wrong," he said feebly. Not only was he a horrible father, he was an equally bad liar.

"Would you come with us, please," the officer said, coming to the same conclusion I had about his ability to lie. The man turned and started to run, the second officer that hadn't yet spoken stuck out his hand and grabbed the father's left arm before he had taken two steps. The man swung a fist balled at the end of his right arm, missing the officer, exposing the same lack of self-control he had used with his son and he was immediately taken to the floor and cuffed in seconds by the two policemen.

A minute later, the waiting room was quiet again as if none of it had actually happened at all. Abby, myself and the mother, the only three people in the waiting room, the nurse had vanished behind the counter presumably to inform someone of what had just transpired.

"Wow," Abby said quietly. "Life in the big city never ceases to amaze me."

"It's not the city's fault," I said. "It's the people." I've never been a fan of people.

The mother raised her attention from the floor as I spoke and stared directly at me.

"It was you," she said softly.

Abby looked to the woman, saw her looking at me, then looked suspiciously at me herself.

"You told me to call the police, didn't you," she said. "It was your voice I heard in my head."

In my sudden desire to help this woman, I forgot that if I plant the idea, the idea is in my voice. In my brief comment to Abby about the city versus people, she had recognized my voice.

She stood and walked over to me, stopping in front of me. I was almost more aware of Abby's intense eyes on me than I was of the woman standing before me.

"Thank you so much," the mother said, holding out her hand. "I'm not sure how you did it, but it was you, wasn't it? You gave me the strength to call the police."

I stood and shook her hand. I wasn't sure what to say. I looked at Abby. Her eyes were glued to me, waiting for my response even more than the woman holding my hand was.

I said nothing. Just nodded to the woman once.

"Thank you so much," the woman said again. Then she turned and went looking for the nurse.

I sat back down. Abbey's eyes never left me as I watched the woman round the corner.

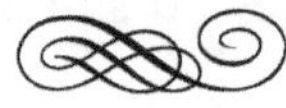

"You want to tell me what just happened there?" Abby Brogan finally asked after the woman had disappeared around the corner.

I wasn't ready to start this discussion, at least not with Mrs. Brogan, but she was awaiting an answer. "I'm not sure," I said.

"You see more than just when people are supposedly going to die, don't you."

"Sometimes," I said, then added, "just recently, anyway."

Abby studied me a moment longer. Her National Geographic forgotten in her lap. I continued to look at the abandoned nurse's station in front of me.

"Does Katelynn know that you can see inside people's minds?" she finally asked.

"No," I replied, seeing no way of escaping her questions and wishing I'd chosen a more subtle way of getting the woman to turn in her abusive husband. "I've only just figured it out myself in the last few days."

"So you *did* tell her to call the police, didn't you," she said.

"I was certainly thinking she should, yes."

"What am I thinking right now?" she asked me.

"I don't know," I told her honestly enough, still looking straight ahead.

"Well look at me and try," she said firmly. It was obvious that she was not going to let it go until I at least tried, so I looked at her and tried to open up just a hair to her mind.

"You're thinking your daughter has fallen for a freak," I told her. "You are worried that I might break her heart."

"And is that what you are going to do?" she asked, not even denying or trying to change the wording of what I had read.

"First we have to get her past her date," I answered. "After that, I don't have any idea what's going to happen."

"My daughter is putting a lot of faith in you," she said. "She told me that you told her that God sent you to save her, but God has nothing to do with this, does He?"

Busted.

"No, He doesn't. But that was the only way I could convince her to return for the physical. She was planning on just staying at the farm and dying there if it was going to happen. I couldn't let her do that. I couldn't let her die without trying to figure out why and whether or not it can be prevented."

"Do you believe in God?" Mrs. Brogan then asked me.

I thought for a second, this being the first time in my life I had ever paused before answering that particular question. To be honest, I wasn't quite sure what I believed anymore. Finally, I answered, "I guess that depends on your definition of God."

"I didn't realize there was more than one definition," she said. "But I guess I am glad you convinced her to return. You obviously care about her."

"Of course, I do."

Just then Katelynn thankfully came walking around from the back of the nurse's station putting an end to our conversation, at least for now. She was still wearing the baby blue hospital gown tied shut in the rear and matching hospital issued slippers. She sat in a row of chairs facing us. "He said it'll be a few minutes before they are ready to do the CAT scan and that I could come out here and wait with you."

"How'd the physical go?" I asked, grateful for the interruption.

"He said he couldn't find anything unusual, that I appear to be as healthy as I should be. He also made me pee in a cup and took some blood but said those results won't be known until tomorrow morning."

Abby Brogan had said nothing. She was still paying more attention to me than she had been to her daughter. As though she had suddenly made her mind up about something, she stood and went to the nurse's station tapping the bell that sat on the desk. A nurse was in front of her within seconds.

"Is there an empty room we can use for a few minutes to discuss a few things privately?" she asked the nurse.

"I'm not sure," the nurse replied, "just a moment." She disappeared again, returning a moment later with Dr. James.

"What is it you need, Mrs. Brogan?" Dr. James asked.

"I just wanted to have a little pow-wow with the three of us. Somewhere private where we won't get interrupted."

Dr. James immediately looked passed Mrs. Brogan at me suspiciously. I refrained from opening up to see what he was thinking. I was still very uncomfortable with peaking into people's private thoughts. I looked at the floor instead, avoiding his questioning eyes.

"I suppose we can let you wait in the room where Katelynn had her physical," he said, looking back to Mrs. Brogan. "Is there something I can help you all with?"

"No, but thank you. This is family business," she replied. "We just need a few minutes."

"You can wait in there until the specialist is ready to do the CAT scan."

"Thank you," Abby said and turned to us, waving for us to follow her.

Katelynn jumped up on the examination table to sit. Mrs. Brogan and I took the two chairs that Dr. James had brought into the small cubicle of a room for us, facing Katelynn on the table.It was Abby's show right now and we waited patiently for her to begin once Dr. James had finally, but still hesitantly, left us alone in the room.

"I was born and raised on the farm," she began. "I have always attributed my understanding of animals to that."

"She always knows when animals are sick or scared," Katelynn interjected. "She's really good at that."

"But I was never guessing," Abby continued. "I knew. I never knew how I knew, but if the horses were spooked or the pigs wouldn't eat or even if the cows were feeling depressed, as silly as that sounds, I have always been able to look into the animal's eyes and *sense* what the problem was. It's always felt like I could relate to the animals, sometimes even better than I related to people." She looked directly at me. "I want you to look into Katelynn's eyes, John. Tell me what you feel, not what you see. Don't read her thoughts. Try to feel what she feels. The animals can't tell me what they feel. They don't speak our language and I can't speak theirs. But they still seem to always let me know what isn't right. I want you to look into Katelynn's eyes and try to see what might not be right."

I looked at Katelynn. She was looking at me, wide-eyed and inviting. She began to hold out her hand for me but I waved her off, letting her know it wasn't necessary. I had no idea what I was looking for. I opened up. I saw what I felt was an undeserved admiration for myself in her mind and wondered briefly if I would ever be able to live up to her expectations and trust in me. I narrowed my mind and dug deeper. *(29:29)* entered my mind and I shut down, breaking our gaze and looking at the floor.

"I only see the numbers again," I said.

"That's just the door," Mrs. Brogan said. "Try looking inside it for the cause."

It occurred to me that every time someone's number had entered my mind, I had instinctively shut down. Randi had taught me to see the conscious mind. The numbers were obviously a part of the sub-conscious mind which apparently even Randi had never been able to enter. Yet the only thing I had ever plucked from anyone's sub-conscious mind had been the numbers. And every time that had occurred, I had shut down immediately.

I looked back up at Katelynn. With the link still fresh in my mind, I was thinking of her numbers instantly again. I didn't shut down this time but instead concentrated harder. I extended my imaginary phone line deeper into her mind, past the numbers. And a new thought came instantly to the front of my mind. Appendix. It was her appendix. Her appendix! Simple as that. Her appendix was weak or faltering. I suddenly knew this just as sure as I knew when I was hungry or tired. It was like I should have known all along but just hadn't thought of it. Not only that, I knew I was right. I had no doubt that on the 29th day of her 29th year, her appendix was going to burst. Most people, in this day of modern medicine, survive a burst appendix. But had Katelynn been out on the farm, maybe out teaching her daughter to swim in the pond out on the edge of her property line as she had been planning to do about that time, maybe they wouldn't have been able to get her to a hospital in time to prevent that burst appendix from killing her.

Or maybe they would have. Her death was no longer the point.

A new thought, more like a revelation, suddenly dawned on me. The numbers *DID NOT* represent one's death, but rather a failure within the body, probably predicted by the brain in much the same manner that Dr. James had suggested it might with his original theory on how I could predict a death. It hadn't been Dr. Getz's and Mr. Crawley's *deaths* I had seen; it had merely been when their hearts were going to fail. If I hadn't shut down immediately after seeing their numbers, and everyone else's for that matter, I would have probably seen the reasons for those numbers as well, but I hadn't ever stayed long enough or known enough to look for it. If Dr. Getz had been at the hospital, maybe he *wouldn't* have died. And though I had voiced my *opinion* that I didn't think Katelynn needed to die several times, now I *knew*. I KNEW!

"Her appendix is going to burst," I said, barely able to hold back the excitement, as though a burst appendix was something to look forward to. My own words severed the connection and brought me back to the room. I was smiling. "It's her appendix!"

24

It turned out to be a periappendiceal abscess within her appendix. Though Dr. James had refused to even entertain the idea that I had figured out what Katelynn's problem had been by merely looking into her eyes, he got his confirmation when the urine sample results had come in the next morning. Having gone untreated, her appendix would have likely ruptured soon, possibly, he admitted to Mrs. Brogan, on the eighteenth, twelve days away.

The surgery performed later that afternoon further proved that her appendix, despite the lack of pain in her abdomen, was indeed degenerating but the fact that it had been discovered when it had been meant she had been able to keep her appendix instead of needing to have it removed. The one-and-a-half-hour surgery went smoothly and her appendix was given a clean bill of health. Katelynn would need to be in the hospital for two more days in case any unexpected complications arose from the surgery or anesthetics but would be allowed to return to the farm to finish the week-long recovery period after that. She was given an additional week off by the hospital to get things put back together but was expected back to work in two weeks and a few days.

Katelynn had received the news that the test results had confirmed my unprofessional diagnosis over the phone the morning after the physical. She had then called me to tell me of the news. She asked if I would come with her to the hospital when she had her surgery. I told her I couldn't make it and was answered with silence.

"Why not?" she had finally asked, sounding a little dejected.

"Your mom will be there with you, right?"

"Yes, of course. And I wanted you there, too."

"How long do you have to stay there?"

"Dr. James said for just a couple of days. Then I will be going back to the farm for a couple of weeks before returning to work."

"I would like to see you before you go back to the farm," I said. "But I won't be staying at my home."

"Where are you going, John? What's going on?"

"I have a lot to tell you about the week you were out at the farm. I want to tell you everything but I need to avoid Dr. James. He is going to want to know how I knew what I knew and maybe a lot more. When he asks, please tell him I couldn't make it but will be by to see how you are doing later."

"But you won't be, will you," she almost whispered.

"I can't, Katelynn. But I will explain everything to you when I see you before you go back to the farm."

"You want to come to the farm with us?" she asked, sounding suddenly optimistic again.

"I can't. Please trust me. I'll tell you all about it in a few days. I will call you at the hospital after the surgery to make sure everything went as planned and to find out when exactly you will be able to go, but please don't let Dr. James know that I am avoiding him."

"Okay, John. I promise. Call me though. You promise?"

"I promise."

<h1 style="text-align:center">25</h1>

Her surgery was at four in the afternoon. I spent most of the morning packing the clothes I wanted to take with me and throwing away everything that was in the refrigerator and freezer. I took the garbage out to the curb even though the city would not be by to pick it up for three days yet, but I wasn't planning on being around to take it out to the street at the proper time.

By three in the afternoon, the phone had rung at least a dozen times. Every time, looking at the caller ID, Park Nicollet Hospital appeared as the source of the call. I knew it was Dr. James and I refrained from answering. At six pm, the calls had begun again. At eight pm, I ignored the knock at my door and quickly hit the mute button on the remote for the TV. The car I saw driving away when I finally felt it was safe enough to peak through the curtains of the living room had not been Mrs. Brogan's.

The next morning, kicking myself a little for buying a motorcycle instead of a car, I strapped a pair of small suitcases to the rear passenger seat of the bike and headed for the bank to wait for it to open. I pulled out $75,000 and change, closing my account, taking cash against the advice of the bank president. He asked for an explanation. I told him it wasn't his business as politely as I could and checked into a Motel 6 a few miles from Katelynn's home in Richfield. I still had no idea where I was going to go. I hadn't planned on having to leave so soon and hadn't really given it any serious thought yet.

After a few hours of mindless TV, I couldn't wait any longer and dialed up the Hospital. When someone answered the phone asking where I wanted my call directed, I realized once again that I had no idea what Katelynn's last name was.

"I'm trying to reach Katelynn Brogan," I said, on the off chance that she had assumed her old name, though she hadn't gotten divorced and I wasn't surprised when the receptionist informed me that they had no patients by that name.

"She's a nurse there herself and was in surgery yesterday for her appendix," I said, hoping she could connect me based on that information.

"Oh! Um, just a moment, please," she had replied, sounding like she knew who I had meant.

I waited for a few minutes while listening to a Musak version of some Beatle's song without the lyrics when it was interrupted by a couple of clicks and a voice cut in. "John?"

I hung up the phone. It had been Dr. James.

Worried that the Hospital might also have caller ID and the receptionist would be able to tell Dr. James where the call had come in from, I packed up and was checked out of the motel less than ten minutes later.

Having no where to go, my chosen life style not providing me with any friends close enough to barge in on with my current dilemma, I headed for the only other place I could think of to hide out for a little while, 14 Crimson Lane.

Although Katelynn's surgery had been routine and successful, though at that point, that was only an assumption, I still wanted to see her again, and not just because that was what I had promised her. I wanted to see if her numbers had indeed changed since the operation. I was now of the opinion that the numbers I had been seeing were *not* representative of the sender's death, but merely a bodily malfunction, yet it *was* still just a theory. I needed to see Katelynn's numbers to prove that my new theory was correct. But I was equally as adamant about not going to the hospital to find out.

When I arrived at the stone gate outside the castle, this time not being expected, I had to ring the buzzer on the intercom to gain entrance. Chauncy had answered and opened the gate without hesitation after I had identified myself. He was waiting at the oversized front doors for me after I parked the bike and walked up the steps to its entrance.

"Good afternoon, Mr. Johnson. I'm afraid no one is here right now except myself and Mary. Harry is not expected back for a couple of hours but he did leave this for you in case you should arrive when he wasn't here."

"Thank you, Chauncy," I said, taking the shoebox he was holding out for me. "And please, call me John."

"Very well, sir," he replied, maintaining his usual stoic face. "May I show you to your room?"

"My room?"

"If you will inspect the contents of your box, I believe you will understand, sir."

Still standing in the doorway, I lifted the lid off the shoebox and peered inside. There was a key, a note, and what looked like a garage door opener. I looked up at Chauncy who was waiting patiently to shut the door behind me as soon as I got out of the entryway.

"I believe the note should explain, sir."

The note was from Harry.

'Welcome, John. The items accompanying this note are the gate opener and a key to the house. Have Chauncy show you to your room. I am at the hospital with Benny right now and will be home by 4 PM. Make yourself at home and don't be afraid to ask for anything you might need. I will see you later. Harry'

I looked up at Chauncy. "Would you like to get your bags and see your room at this time, sir?"

Upstairs, Chauncy led the way to 'my room'. He pointed out Harry's room and Randi's room as we walked down a long hallway towards my own. Before entering, he stopped to point out farther down the hallway which doors belonged to Paul, one being his study, the other his bedroom. There were two more doors down at the far end of the hallway that he didn't mention.

"Will there be anything else you need at the moment, sir?" he asked, still yet to call me John.

"No thank you, Chauncy. I'm fine."

"Very well, sir. Mary and I are in the kitchen should you require anything at all."

I thanked him and laid my bags down inside the door as he turned and left me alone. The room was quite large and had its own bathroom. The bed was huge, complete with a dark blue canopy that matched the dark blue curtains on the north wall that overlooked the back yard and the lake. The walls had two more seemingly fuzzy paintings from the same artist that had decorated the small parlor Randi had fine tuned my new talents in. There was a couch and a coffee table under one of the paintings and a dresser next to a walk-in closet under the other. A bedside table had a phone and a remote control for the TV and there was a small TV on a swivel stand in one corner. Beyond that the room was empty. I placed my suitcases on the coffee table, opened them up but left them packed. I didn't know how long I'd be staying. I had only planned on staying until I could make contact with Katelynn.

I skipped dinner that evening, staying in my room trying to devise a plan on how to reach Katelynn. Chauncy had been the one that knocked on my door around 5 PM to ask if I was going to eat with the others. I didn't ask who the others were and he didn't question my refusal. I waited for Harry to arrive at my door next, once hearing him talking to someone out in the hallway, but then I heard a door shut that I assumed was his own and only quietness followed for the rest of the evening. I went to bed early, deciding to let my subconscious work on the problem while I slept.

When I awoke the next morning, no solutions had come to mind.

By 9 AM, hunger and a raging nic-fit finally drew me out of the room and down stairs to the kitchen. Harry was sitting in a chair next to the walk-in refrigerator, his face hidden behind the morning paper.

"Good Morning, John," Harry said, looking around the paper with his usual pleasant smile and cheery disposition when he heard me enter the kitchen. "Is your room okay?"

"Yes, thank you," I told him. "It's fine. I would like to know how you knew I was coming, though."

"I didn't know *when* you were coming, but as I had told you before, you are one of us, John. I was pretty sure you'd be along before too long."

"I am not sure how long I will be staying," I told him honestly. "I have a couple of things I need to figure out and then I plan on leaving this area for good."

"Where ya gonna go? Whatcha ya runnin' from?"

I told him all about the last few days, emphasizing my desire not to allow Dr. James to have his way with me. Dr. James, I knew, would never understand my selfish desire not to use my talent to benefit the sick or the advancement of medical science. I didn't think he could actually force me to do anything I didn't want to, but I wasn't sure to what extent he would try and had no intentions of giving him the chance. I just wanted to be left alone, to get back to my eventless, reclusive life. Despite my deeper feelings towards Katelynn, a bigger part of me didn't consider myself even worthy of her and I felt she would be better off, too, if I were to silently take my leave before we traveled any farther down the path we had discovered on that eve before she had gone to the farm. I guess her mother had been right about me after all. I was only going to break her heart, but at least if done sooner, maybe it wouldn't break as much and might mend all the quicker.

"How 'bout I stop in and pay a visit to Katelynn to see how she's doing when I go to see Benny today?" he suggested.

"That might work," I said. At least then I would know for sure that the operation had gone as planned "But you can't tell her where I am. It'll be better if she doesn't have to lie when Dr. James questions her about me. But I still want to see her before she leaves again for the farm so that I know her numbers have changed. And there's something else," I suddenly remembered while we were on the subject, looking down at my feet. If I was going to leave, I felt at least *someone* should know this other fact. I figured Harry would know what to do about this information better than anyone else. "I saw Randi's numbers the other day too, though she doesn't know it."

"And?"

"Something will happen to her in seven years."

"Let's just take one step at a time here, John. Seven years in a long time away. A lot will happen between now and then." Harry folded up the paper. "Let's get us some breakfast and see if we can't figure out what we can do about your first d'limma for now."

Over breakfast, Harry and I discussed what we might do about getting me in touch with Katelynn. He ended up leaving me with his cell phone. He was going to drop in on Katelynn when he went to visit Benny and give her the number to call. That way I could find out what time she was planning on leaving for the farm and maybe I could meet her at her home before she left and get a chance to confirm that her numbers had indeed changed since the surgery.

Outside, after breakfast, while I was enjoying my first cigarette since the previous afternoon and Harry was tinkering with his Honda GoldWing before he left for the hospital, he asked me what I was going to do about my house.

"I'm not sure," I said. "I figured it would be a safety net in case I ran out of money. I also figured that I could probably return in a year or so. If Dr. James was still looking for me, I could simply tell him that my ability to see inside people's minds had vanished over time. Maybe that my hiding out and its lack of use had caused the ability to be forgotten in some manner, like forgetting a learned foreign language after not using it over time. I don't think he'd believe me if I said that right now, but in a year he might."

"What if someone in our family bought it from you. It could belong to us, our group. Then if you wanted to buy it back sometime, you'd know you could get it back. Those of us from out of town could stay there instead of hotels when this house is full, which seems to be happening more and more these days. As I said before, those that can afford it have already bought second homes in the area. But not all of them can afford to do that."

I really hadn't wanted to sell the house that I had been born in. Even though I was planning on leaving the area and was going to tell the few people that I knew that I was leaving for good, I had always assumed in the back of my mind that I would return to it some day.

Harry saw my hesitation and continued. "Benny would be happy to pay whatever price you are asking and we'd put it in the name of someone that Dr. James hasn't met which would avoid suspicion if he went so far as to look into who bought it. Personally, I think Dr. James will forget about you a lot quicker than you apparently do, but this way, he won't make the connection to Benny or myself if he is persistent."

"What about all my stuff, my furniture? I don't have anyplace to put it or store it."

"Leave it there. No one would actually be moving in there. It'll be our extra space when we over flow here."

"I guess we could do that," I said, still not really sure I wanted to sell it at all, but that would pretty much tell Dr. James that I had really left. Even if he was determined to try to follow or find out where I had gone, he may just give up and consider me gone for good if he knew I sold my home.

"Very good," Harry said, before I could change my mind. "I will talk to Benny about it today and we'll figure out whose name to put it under. And it'll still be your house, too."

It was almost annoying the way he kept assuming I was going to be a member of this family but I was tired of telling him I wasn't planning on sticking around and I tried to change the subject. "What's wrong with Benny anyway?" I asked.

"He has a brain tumor that won't stop growing. It's still very small but it's in a particular spot that they can't operate on without a major risk of likely doing some other type of damage to the brain in the process. Benny told them he'd rather die keeping his wits about him than possibly living a few more years as an invalid. It's a matter of stubborn pride on his part. I'd rather see him take his chances on the operation, but he doesn't want to be anybody's burden. So instead, he consented to all kinds of new experimental drugs and procedures to reduce or stop the tumor without surgery. They haven't done any good at all so far."

"I'm sorry," I said, seeing that Harry was somewhat unsuccessfully trying to conceal his sadness at the thought of losing his best friend.

"Happens to us all eventually," Harry said, standing up. "I better get going. Benny's gonna want to win his money back from yesterday's round of poker. You keep that phone with you. I imagine your lady friend will be calling you as soon as she can."

"I will. Thanks, Harry."

26

"D r. James said he thought you called once but that you hung up when he answered," Katelynn said over the phone. "He keeps asking me if I've heard from you yet and if I know where you are. What's going on, John?"

"I need to disappear for a while is all," I told her. "I don't want to become his guinea pig with this talent I seem to have acquired."

"You can disappear at the farm with me and Faith. I can get a job at the hospital in Duluth. It's only an hour's drive away from there."

"I'm sure your parents would be thrilled about that," I said. "Besides, Dr. James would certainly check that possibility out if he were looking for me."

Katelynn fell silent. I thought briefly about asking her to come with me but I knew that wouldn't be a good idea. What if it didn't work out? I couldn't ask her to uproot her life based on one emotional night in which she wasn't even sure at that time that she had much time left on this earth. And there was Faith, too. Running away to who knows where was not a good idea with a five-year-old. She would need a more stable life than I would probably be able to provide.

"Do you know when you plan on leaving the hospital?" I asked.

"My parents are picking me up tomorrow at noon. They are all staying at my house tonight. We'll be going back to my place for lunch before heading back to the farm."

"Okay. I'm glad everything went smoothly there. I will plan on being at you home around twelve-thirty then," I told her. "I want to make sure your numbers have changed."

"And what if they haven't?" she asked.

"I'm sure they have. I'm not worried about it and you shouldn't be either. I just need to make sure."

"Okay."

"And please don't tell Dr. James that you talked to me."

"I'll eat the scrap of paper I wrote the number down on," she said sarcastically. Once again, this time along with a pang in my gut, I wished for a moment I could take her with me. "Where are you staying? Harry wouldn't tell me."

"Probably better you don't know, at least for now," I said. "Then you don't need to lie. But I will see you tomorrow before you go, Katelynn. I promise."

"Okay, John. But we'll talk more then. Okay?"

"I'll tell you what I can."

"I thought you were going to eat the number," I said. It was just after five of the same afternoon I had talked to Katelynn earlier. I had heard Randi come home and drop off some things in her room next door to mine before returning back downstairs and a little while later, I heard Harry go in and out of his room across the hall. I had remained in my room all day watching TV and trying not to think about too much of anything. I took occasional smoke breaks between shows that I really hadn't paid any attention to. I was just waiting to see Katelynn tomorrow, then make arrangements with Harry on the sale of my house. I was hoping I could sign a few things and then the rest could be completed after I had already left.

"I memorized it," Katelynn said. "I couldn't wait until tomorrow to talk to you and I didn't know how much time or privacy we would have then. Who is Harry? How do you know him?"

I explained to her that he had been a friend of Benny's, the third patient that I had met the day we had been testing my talents with Dr. James.

"Is that where you are staying? How did you end up with his phone?"

I had wanted to tell her all about my experience here at Paul's place but not over the phone. Yet like she had pointed out, I might not get a better chance, so breaking my promise to Harry (...*tell no one, john*) I told her about my visit to Benny's room and the message Harry had left waiting for me in his head instead of numbers. I told her all about Randi and her training me to use my newly found talent to read minds. I didn't tell her about the rest of the family or what I knew of their true mission, their belief that Lucifer was planning to take control of the world when the seven planets aligned in December. I left out the history Harry believed to be true, the sand show Harry had summoned from Shkarbala, and the fact that they thought I was number five of seven that God had told Harry he needed to do whatever it was that they were supposed to do, if that was indeed the significance of the number Gabriel had presumably passed on to him. As far as I was concerned, even if I accepted all that Harry had told me as fact, the number seven could have represented any number of things.

"Dr. James really wants to see you," she said. ''I guess the other person you saw died yesterday and he told me you had been right on her number, too. I hope you are right about my numbers changing."

"I'm sure I am, Katelynn, but we'll both know for sure tomorrow."

"Well, thank Harry for me for giving me a number to reach you with. He seemed like a very nice man."

"He is," I replied, "and I will. I feel very badly for Benny, though. He is Harry's best friend and seems to also be a really good guy. I guess he has a brain tumor, but that's just what Harry has told me. He visits him every day there at the hospital."

"I rarely work on the terminal floor," Katelynn said, "but I think I know who he is. He's been here for a couple months. I think he is one that Dr. Getz had wanted to operate on but couldn't get his permission to do so. I seem to remember him talking about that a couple of times shortly before he had his heart attack."

"That sounds like him, according to what Harry and Dr. James have told me."

"Maybe I'll stop by and meet him before I leave," she said.

"Just make sure Dr. James doesn't know it if you do. He may be helping me with my escape."

"I can't believe you are leaving because of this, John. I thought we might, you know, get to know each other a little better now that I know I'll have the time to do it."

"It doesn't have to be forever," I said, hoping she would accept that and let it go, let me go. "But I do have to go, at least for a while."

"How long?"

"I don't know."

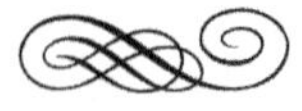

"You still planning on being at my home tomorrow at one?"

It was a little after 9 PM, I had just been getting ready to go to sleep when Harry's cell phone had rung for the third time that day, but otherwise I had successfully managed to avoid contact with anyone else but Chauncy since having breakfast with Harry early in the day. Chauncy had knocked on my door after I hadn't come down for dinner and delivered to me a couple of grilled cheese sandwiches and a bowl filled with five different kinds of fruits cut into little squares, and a Mountain Dew.

"I'll be there," I assured Katelynn.

"Okay. Just checking. Good night then."

"Good night, Katelynn."

27

Hi John! Where's your bike? I thought you hadn't come as we drove up."

"I parked it in the back," I said as I came around the corner of the house. I had waited until they had pulled into the driveway and were already getting out of the car before I showed myself. Maybe I was just being paranoid, but I wanted to make sure Dr. James hadn't followed them here.

"This is my father, Ted. Dad, this is John, the one that saved my life."

"Glad to meet you, Mr. Brogan," I said, holding out my hand to shake. I was fairly confident by then that if I didn't want to see any numbers, I didn't have to. I wasn't wrong. I simply didn't open up. It was becoming as easy as Randi had said it should be.

"I guess we owe you some sincere thanks for what you did for our daughter," he said in a gravelly voice. "And call me Dusty. Everyone does."

"Thank you, Dusty," I said, releasing his strong grip.

Ted "Dusty" Brogan was a tall man, well rounded in the middle. His skin had a permanent tan from working the land all his life. His face was etched with more lines than one could count but he still had a pleasant look about him and smiling blue eyes that made him instantly likable. His silver hair was thinning on the top but he still stood straight and used every inch of his 6'3" frame. Looking at him and Abby Brogan side by side, both in old worn blue jeans and different colored lumberjack shirts, you knew it was a match made in heaven.

"And this is Faith," Katelynn said, pointing to the little girl with long blonde curls staring up at me from behind her grandmother's leg with the bluest eyes I had ever seen. She was wearing blue jean overalls with a red apple on the bib, over a red blouse with white polka dots and a little ruffle around the neck. Her tiny arms were wrapped around her grandmother's left leg as she bashfully took in the stranger standing before her.

"Hi, Faith," I said, bending over just a hair in her direction.

She slid a little farther behind the protection of the leg.

"She's a little shy with new people," Abby said, looking down at her granddaughter.

"She sure wasn't shy when meeting Benny," Katelynn said. "You guys didn't see it because you were waiting in the hallway, but as soon as those two met, she hopped right up on the side of his bed and said hi. I couldn't believe it."

"Was Harry there?" I asked.

"No. Benny said he had gone out to get a pizza to smuggle in for lunch. I wanted him to meet Faith, too, and to thank him for the phone number to reach you with, but I had to ask Benny to thank him for me." Katelynn paused and looked to be running something over again in her mind. I looked down not wanting to be tempted to take a peek at what was obviously puzzling her.

"But it was weird," she finally continued. "Benny asked me to get his water from the window sill and when I turned around, Faith was standing on his bed, facing him. She was giggling like he had just told her a joke but I was right there. He hadn't said a word. And both her hands were on his head. Benny was laughing, too. It was really weird," she said, looking down at her daughter. "Are you going to say hi to John, Faith?"

Faith returned to her original position, only partially protected by her grandmother's leg and smiled bashfully. "Hi, John."

She was the definition of cute.

"Hi, Faith," I said again, putting on the smile we reserve for small children. "I'm happy to meet you."

"Me, too," she said, and then scurried back behind the leg with a smile.

"You going to stay for lunch with us?" Abby asked me.

"Sure, I can do that," I replied.

"So, have my daughter's numbers changed?" Dusty asked out of the blue before we had even started for the front door. Straight to the point. No beating around the bush. I was sure he had probably spoken whatever was on his mind all his life and he wasn't about to change in his autumn years.

"I haven't looked yet," I confessed.

"I am sure everyone of us is very anxious for you to do your thing and put all this behind us," he said, essentially giving me no choice but to do it right then and there. So, I did.

I looked at Katelynn. She again started to hold out her hand for me out of habit and I again waved her off. "I don't need the touch anymore I've discovered," I told her. "But I think I do still need the eyes to reach the subconscious."

She took a step to better face me squarely and I looked into her blue eyes, wishing silently that it wouldn't be the last time I got the opportunity. She smiled and I wondered if I had accidentally sent that thought. Or maybe it wasn't an accident. I'm not sure. At any rate, I narrowed my focus and instantly the numbers appeared. This time, finally, Katelynn read the relief in my eyes instead of the disappointment and before I was able to inform her family that, at least as far as my talents could tell, Katelynn had a long life to live in front of her, she threw her arms around me kissing my cheek and squeezing hard. I returned the hug, not wanting to let go. When she backed away, she was crying again, but this time they were tears of joy.

"Your daughter is fine," I told them, not taking my eyes off the happy vision in front of me, never wanting to forget that face. "The numbers have changed to something any of us would be pleased with, though that is all I am going to say so don't ask me to be more specific than that."

Her father again stepped forward, this time shaking my hand much more vigorously than before. "Glad to hear it," he said with a smile. "Now let's go inside and eat."

Despite the celebratory mood that Abby and Dusty Brogan had been in through the lunch made up of cold ham and cheese sandwiches and chips, Katelynn's mood was more sullen. She had barely touched her food. She kept catching my eye, inviting me to peak into her head, but I refrained. I knew what she was trying to convey to me without opening up. She wanted to know where I was going, how long I was going to be gone, and if we would ever see each other again. I couldn't answer any of those questions for her and tried to focus on my food.

Finally, Abby picking up on the mood of her daughter, who should have been the happiest person at the table knowing she would now live to see her own daughter grow up, had also noticed that Katelynn had been eyeing me, the questions written plainly on her face.

"What are you going to do now?" Abby asked me for her daughter.

"I'm not sure," I confessed. I had no idea how much Katelynn had told them of my plans to leave. Abby answered that much for me as she continued.

"Katelynn says you are going to try to disappear for a while. Any idea where you are going to go?"

"Come with us to the farm," Katelynn again suggested.

"You are welcome to stay with us until you figure things out," Abby said, confirming her approval should I agree. "We've got plenty of room."

"Thank you," I said. "I really do appreciate the offer but I think I need to get away for a little while, alone. I need to figure out what I am going to do about this new ability I have acquired. And I need to be somewhere that Dr. James won't find me. He's tried to call quite a few times and I think he even came to my house once."

"Why don't you just tell him to leave you alone?" Katelynn asked.

"Because he wouldn't do it," I said. I hadn't gotten into his head to confirm that, but I hadn't needed to. His professional curiosity had obviously gotten the best of him. It had been all over his face when I had informed him of what his physical on Katelynn had confirmed the next morning. He hadn't wanted to believe me when I had told him about her appendix, and I hadn't yet actually seen him since, but even the constant ringing of the phone on the day of Katelynn's surgery had an obsessive sound to it. The answering machine had been turned off.

Thankfully, Faith had then spilled her milk on the table and the subject had been changed.

As I told everyone good bye when they were climbing into their car, while I was sitting on my bike waiting to follow them out of the driveway, Katelynn got back out of the car, still walking a bit gingerly from the surgery, and gave me a slip of paper with a few phone numbers on it.

"Call me when you can," she said, knowing my mind was made up to go. "Let me know where you are and how you're doing. I won't tell anyone, John."

I nodded, wished her well, and then watched the only person I had dared to have any truly strong feelings for since the death of my parents drive off before starting my bike and heading back to 14 Crimson Lane.

28

I didn't drive straight back to Crimson Lane. When I had gotten to Minnetonka, I didn't feel ready to speak to anyone yet and rode aimlessly through the winding wooded neighborhoods of expensive looking homes and lost myself in thought with the sound of the wind whipping past my ears and the steady drone of the engine between my legs. My depleting gas level once again forced me to finally turn towards my destination.

By 4 PM, I was back in my room at Paul Northrop's home. It was Saturday and more than the usual number of cars were parked in the drive. I parked my bike next to Harry's GoldWing, noting that he had probably returned from his daily visit to the hospital a little earlier than usual. The motor wasn't still ticking as it should have been had he just returned at his usual time, in the last ten minutes or so. I went straight upstairs, staying clear of the library where I assumed most of the visitors would be. I figured Harry and I wouldn't be able to start drawing up papers on the sale of my house until Monday so I had a couple days yet to pick a place to go vanish, to start over.

Mostly I was just feeling relieved that Katelynn was safe, that her ordeal was over and we had successfully defeated fate. I laid down on the bed and had just started trying to think about which part of the country I might want to start out with when Chauncy knocked at my door.

"Harry was wondering if you were feeling up to joining him in the library, sir," he said.

Hesitantly, I told him I would be down in a few minutes. They had given me a place to stay when I needed it. They were going to buy my home and even let me buy it back later if I decided I wanted to. They had fed me, allowed me to take care of my business without interfering and had even been happy to help whenever possible. As much as I *wasn't* feeling up to it at the moment, I knew I couldn't refuse Harry. I owed him big time. I laid there a few more minutes, simply stalling, and then headed down to the library.

There were about a dozen mostly familiar faces in the large room. A couple of couches had been turned around and quite a few chairs had been moved such that everyone was seated as a large discussion group. They all turned to look at me as I entered the doorway and stopped to take in the scene before becoming a part of it. One whose back had been to me as I entered stood and approached me, all smiles, holding out his hand as he neared. I returned his infectious smile with a genuine one of my own and shook his hand, my face full of questions and confusion overlaying the smile as Benny exuberantly pumped my hand up and down a few times.

"Welcome home," Benny said, as he finally released my hand. "Come join us, please."

I followed Benny back to the group and took the last available seat on a small couch next to Randi.

"Well," Benny said, after I had settled into my seat and quickly surveyed all the happy faces, most of which had returned their attention back to Benny. "Now that we are all present, I would like to announce that I am witness to a true miracle. And all I had needed was a little faith."

Instantly, recalling what Katelynn had said before we had gone in for lunch, I made the connection. I didn't understand how it could be possible, but I knew the 'little faith' he was referring to began with a capital 'F', not a small one.

Benny turned towards me as he continued. "As soon as that little girl put her hands on my head, a funny sensation came over my brain, as though she were tickling my mind, and I knew she had taken the tumor out of my head. And John is the one that brought her to me. Thank you, John. What's mine is now yours," he said, raising the cup in his hand in my direction. "You have allowed me the opportunity to spend yet a few more years on the old Earth."

That was the second time today someone had accused me of saving a life yet I had been directly responsible for neither one. It had been the results of the physical that had led to Dr. James operating on Katelynn and I hadn't even seen Benny since the day I had met him and Harry with the doctor. Yet everyone in the room then turned to me and applauded as though I had just been introduced to speak at their function. But at that moment, my voice was unavailable.

Benny continued as the clapping quickly died down. "In fact, after Dr. James retook the x-rays I was demanding, he asked if you had been in to visit me, John. I told him no one but Harry had been to see me, but Harry was as surprised as Dr. James had been with the new results."

"I didn't want you to have the x-ray and be disappointed," Harry interjected. "You seemed so sure the tumor was going to be gone and I thought you were out of your mind. It really is a miracle."

"That it is, that it is," Benny said. "And Harry had even been the one telling me all along just to keep the faith."

"But until you had told me her *name* was Faith, that hadn't been what I meant," Harry said, barely able to speak through his emotional smile. "But now I have a feeling, a *strong* feeling. I would like to know her last name. I'll bet if I hear it, we will have found number six. I just know it." He turned to me. "What's Katelynn and Faith's last name, John?"

I still didn't know. I still hadn't asked. I felt like an idiot. Everyone was looking at me, waiting for me to reveal something as simple as the last name of the woman whose life I had been trying to save for the past few weeks, the woman whom I had fallen in love with, despite my unwillingness to admit the fact to even myself, though I knew in my heart that it was true. And yet I didn't know the answer. Maybe I had never asked because I knew I was going to be leaving as soon as her ordeal was over, or maybe because I never actually believed she would live long enough for it to matter. But for whatever reason, I simply hadn't asked yet.

"I, um, haven't ever asked her," I admitted, feeling a little embarrassed with the confession.

"That's okay," Harry said, noticing my discomfort at the situation. "If she *is* number six, we'll find out soon enough. We have all been delivered here for a reason and we are almost complete. But today, we celebrate the return of our friend. Today we celebrate Benny's life." He held up a drink, "To Benny," he said, and everyone but myself followed suit, repeating the toast, raising their varying cups, glasses and mugs in Benny's honor before taking a sip. Mary entered precisely at that moment and handed me a pre-opened bottle of dew and I joined in the toast, "To Benny," I said.

I smiled with the others and took a long refreshing drink from the tall bottle. For the very first time, I thought maybe it was just as Benny had said. Maybe I was home after all. Maybe I *was* one of them. And maybe everything Harry had been telling me was the truth. It was a lot to swallow, but I couldn't get those 'maybes' out of my mind. Maybe, I thought, just maybe, I had finally found where I belonged.

"You should have seen the look on Dr. James' face when he came back into my room with the results of the x-rays," Benny was saying. "It was priceless!"

"I'm surprised he let you out so quickly," I said.

"He didn't want to," Benny said. "He wanted to run tests and find out how it had disappeared. He wasn't too happy that I up and left on him. I told him it was simply a miracle and he'd just have to accept that. I told him that I had checked myself into that hospital of my own free will and now that I was cured, I was checkin' myself *out* of the hospital of that same free will and there weren't nothin' he could do to stop me. I thanked him for all his help and concern and me and Harry got out of there as fast as we could. I was hopin' to meet that little girl again and thank her. *She* is the real miracle!"

"She's going to be on a farm with her mother and her grandparents for a couple weeks while her mother recuperates," I informed him. "But I have their phone number if you want to get a hold of them."

Benny said he could wait to do it in person, but Harry was still looking at me when everyone else's attention had gone back to Benny and I knew exactly what he was thinking without the use of any special talents. He wanted to know their last name. He wanted to know if Faith was number six. I think he already had an idea, but he wanted to make sure. He wanted to feel the vibes that would make his innards smile at the sound of her name. But most of all, he wanted to see her shine. She was apparently a healer. She must have had a shine to her like none he had ever seen before.

A thought occurred to me and I waited for Benny to stop talking before directing my question to Harry. "Why do you suppose Faith healed Benny and not her own mother?"

A silence fell on the group. It was Ronnie that finally spoke.

"She probably didn't know her mother had been sick. And I'm sure she probably hadn't even discovered yet that she even had the ability to do what she did. She may still not know exactly what she's done."

Another woman I didn't know supported Ronnie's thought. "I'm sure they hadn't discussed her mother's condition around her daughter. I certainly wouldn't have," she said. "They wouldn't have wanted to scare her. But when she met Benny, he was in a hospital bed. Of course, she knew that *something* was wrong with him."

"But how'd she know where and what?" Benny asked. "I certainly didn't tell her. She just sat on my bed and was lookin' at me. I made a funny face at her and next thing I knew, she stood up on the bed in front of me and laid both her hands on the ol' cue ball up there. She started to laugh and I couldn't help but to laugh with her and then a funny sensation started in my head. It felt like someone had lifted a blanket off my brain that had been tightly wrapped around it. And all of a sudden, I knew she had done what she had done but I won't even begin to pretend I know how she done it."

"It's her gift," Harry said. "She probably doesn't know either, but it's why she was put on this earth. I wish I had been there, but more than anything," he looked back to Benny, "I'm glad you are here with us."

It wasn't long after that when Chauncy came in and announced that dinner would be ready in a few minutes and the group slowly started moving into the large dining room, picking up the chairs that they had been seated in and putting them back in their original places before they left the room. Randi and I, each taking an end, turned our couch around as we got up and joined the others.

Casual, happy chatter once again never ceased throughout the exquisitely prepared and equally tasty meal. This time, however, many questions and comments came my way from several different people and I even asked a few myself, feeling quite comfortable with the semi-large group of people that surrounded me. I was beginning to think I could get used to this. Everyone was so happy and nice. It was such a pleasant atmosphere, so very different than the rest of the world I had been basically hiding from the past fifteen years or so. I was actually beginning to *feel* like one of the family.

Once again, I guess Harry hadn't been wrong.

29

I slept better that night than I had in what felt like weeks, certainly at least since the accident that had ultimately landed me where I was.

Where I was...how I got there...the thought lingered on my mind as I lay in bed awake but not wanting to get up quite yet. It was Sunday morning and the house was very quiet.

Half the guests had gone back to where ever they had come from after last night's dinner, the rest of us moving into the smaller parlor with the bar where Randi had fine tuned my mind reading abilities. The talk had been light hearted and happy, mostly about Benny's two month stay at the hospital and how great he felt to be among the living once again. Benny, Harry, Ronnie, Steven and Paul were all slowly getting buzzed from mixed drinks made by Randi from the bar, while she and I both drank Mountain Dews. She had asked Harry if she could make herself one to celebrate Benny's recovery with them, but Harry, playing the role of a caring and concerned father, reminded her that she still had a few more years before she could drink the hard stuff. She wasn't happy with his disciplinary decision, but she only pouted for a few moments before the issue was accepted and forgotten like an obedient daughter and she had as good a time as the rest of us while she mixed drinks for the others and sipped her Dew. I had simply never been much of a drinker. I didn't see the point in feeling fuzzy in the head all night just to have it pound you awake in the morning as you swear never to do it again...so I had never really started.

Sometime shortly after ten, we had called it a night and everyone congratulated Benny one more time on his amazing recovery as we all adjourned to our separate rooms.

So, there I was, in a strange bed looking at some strange paintings on the walls in a strange looking house that was trying to look like an ancient castle owned by a slightly eccentric weatherman I had only seen on TV before the last couple of weeks. Also living here was a very strange teenaged girl genius who could read minds (and whom had taught me to do the same) and who's parents had also died as mine had, suddenly and without warning and both at the same time. There was a very wealthy old Texan that had moved into one of the rooms at the end of the hall after having a brain tumor miraculously removed from his head by a five-year-old girl. And there was Harry, an incessantly happy old, bald, black man from Louisiana that claimed we were all here for a reason, that we had been brought together for a purpose, that we were family.

Three months ago, when I had been living by myself, working by myself, content with my daily crossword puzzles and a routine existence where each day was predictable and so similar to the previous day it was sometimes hard to tell them apart, now seemed more like three years ago.

Now I lived in a world of mind readers, of shiners and gut feelings that were trusted and accurate more often than not, of sand boxes that magically sent messages into the air with floating grains of sand, of miraculous healers. And of God and Lucifer and some incredible immortal race that I never fathomed could even exist...though I still had a few doubts about that one. But then, how much more far-fetched was that possibility from a five-year-old girl removing brain tumors with the touch of her hands? Benny's mere presence at the house and the supposed bafflement of Dr. James was proof enough that it had really happened.

My world had changed. It felt as though it had changed for the better, but the jury was still out on that one. It wasn't until that very moment, laying in the strange bed, thinking about what Katelynn's daughter had done for Benny, that I finally decided to verbally accept Harry's offer to be considered one of their own, to become a part of this strange family. I figured my new ability brought about from my accident (and briefly wondered again for the first time in a while, if it had indeed even been an accident at all) made me no stranger than the rest of them. I belonged here. I'd commit myself to sticking around. I wasn't yet committed to believing everything Harry had told me of Paul's discoveries about the creation and history of mankind, but decided to officially let Harry know of my acceptance of his offer to join his eclectic family over breakfast this morning.

With that decision made, I felt a weight lift from my being that I hadn't even known was there. I got out of bed with a self-assuring smile and headed for the bathroom to prepare for the new day, and the new me.

I found Harry already up and poring over the morning paper. He had a strong look of concern on his face and this time, unlike the previous day, didn't even notice I had entered the kitchen. Next to his feet on the floor were more newspapers, a stack of papers a foot and a half high. Granted it was Sunday, but not even the annual Thanksgiving edition of the Star Tribune was that thick. He must have had ten different Sunday papers at his feet, unless they weren't all Sundays, but that would have meant they numbered better than two dozen.

"I've heard of keeping up with the news, but that looks a little obsessive, don't you think?" I said jokingly, as I moved towards the pantry to see what kind of cereals Paul kept stocked.

Harry didn't even look up, still engrossed in whatever story he was reading.

I shrugged it off and found a box of Chex and a banana and grabbed some milk out of the refrigerator and took them to the small table that Harry was seated at where the staff probably usually ate. After looking through a couple of drawers and cupboards, I found the appropriate silverware and a bowl and took a seat across from Harry. He still hadn't looked up from his paper.

I sliced up my banana, added some milk and was already half way through the bowl before Harry finally put down the story that had required his full attention and acknowledged my presence.

"Mornin', John," He said as he dropped the paper to the floor on one side of him and picked up another from the stack on the other side. He had a worried look on his face that seemed totally out of character, at least from the short time I had known him.

"Bad news?" I asked.

"I'm 'fraid so," he replied.

He opened the paper he had just picked up and flipped through it a moment until he found the story he was looking for. Creasing the page open, he slid the paper across the table towards me. "Read this."

As I began to read the story he had previously circled with a red marker while continuing to eat my cereal, he picked up different paper and started flipping through it looking for another article.

The paper he had given me, I noticed, was the Canadian Press. The circled story was entitled "Exploding Toads in Hamburg Pond Baffle Scientists."

BERLIN (AP) - More than 1,000 toads have puffed up and exploded in a Hamburg pond in recent weeks, and German scientists still have noexplanation for what's causing the combustion, an official said Wednesday.

Both the pond water and body parts of the toads have been tested, but scientists have been unable to find a bacteria or virus that would have caused the toads to swell up and pop, said Janne Kloepper, of the Hamburg based Institute for Hygiene and the Environment.

"It's absolutely strange," she said. "We have a really unique story here in Hamburg. This phenomenon really doesn't seem to have appeared anywhere before."

The toads at a pond in the upscale neighborhood of Altona have been blowing up since the beginning of the month, filling up like balloons until their stomachs suddenly burst.

"It looks like a scene from a science-fiction movie," Werner Schmolnik, the head of a local environment group, told the Hamburg Abendblatt daily. "The bloated animals suffer for several minutes before they die."

Biologists have come up with several theories, but Kloepper said that most have been ruled out.

The pond's water quality is no better or worse than other bodies of water in Hamburg, the toads did not appear to have a disease, and a laboratory in Berlin has ruled out the possibility that it is a fungus that made its way from South America, she said.

She said tests will continue. In the meantime, city residents have been warned to stay away from the pond.

By the time I had finished reading the article, Harry had two more lined up for me to look at next, each circled in the same red marker. I pushed the one about the exploding toads back across the table towards Harry and read the next one without comment on the first.

The next story was in a British paper. It had nothing to do with exploding toads but was equally strange. This one reported that hundreds of birds had been falling out of the sky over the past week, already dead by the time they hit the ground, in the small town of Tarporley, about forty miles southeast of Manchester. Scientists, environmentalists and ecologists were again completely baffled by the phenomenon and could find nothing wrong with the birds or the atmosphere in the area.

Finishing up my cereal, pushing aside the British paper and the empty bowl, I looked at the next article Harry had circled, this one in the Richmond Times out of Virginia. This article was even accompanied with a picture of the oddity it was describing. Just two days ago, a farmer had discovered a group of trees in his orchard had all been somehow "bent." The article was entitled "The Bowing Trees." Eighteen trees, forming a rough but obvious circle, had mysteriously bent over towards the circle's center as though bowing, though none had cracked or broken trunks. They had simply bent over like iron that had been heated up and shaped, their branches leaning over and gracefully scraping the earth out in front of their roots. Again, no explanation could be decided upon by the experts in related fields of science on how this impossible phenomenon could have possibly occurred. They were simply stumped.

I looked up at Harry. He had three more articles in front of him waiting for me to read if I wanted to see more.

"What's all this about?" I asked him, pushing the one about the bowing trees back across the table. "What's it mean?"

Harry gave me a grave look, hesitated, then in a sullen voice with a slight tremor in it, he said, "It's starting."

30

Over the next few days, I saw a side of Harry that I wouldn't have guessed even existed based on what I had known of him up to that point. He was all business, very quiet, and rarely smiled. Monday morning, Harry, Benny, Gerald Spritzer and I sat down with a realtor and all but closed the cash deal on the sale of my house. I was glad we were able to get it done so quickly, but I knew Harry wasn't rushing the deal for me. He was going to need that space and more by the end of the week.

Gerald Spritzer was someone I hadn't seen before and had flown in from Florida Monday morning for the signatures and then returned to Florida that same afternoon. I heard him promise Harry as he left for the airport that he would be back by Thursday after making sure the employees of his pet store were prepared to keep the business running in his absence for a while.

During most of the next few days, Harry and Benny spent a lot of time on the phone. Ronnie, I discovered, was a travel agent by trade and was in close contact with Harry every day collecting names and making arrangements for 'family members' to be flown in from all over the world. Each evening at the castle, I saw a few more new faces milling around the library. They generally didn't stay too long, some of them picking out a few books from the library and then returning home or to where ever it was they had been set up by Ronnie to stay while in town. Even though I had not yet been directly told as much, it was quite obvious to me what was going on. Harry and Benny were calling in the troops.

I had some of my own chores to take care of. I spent Monday afternoon canceling all the services I had in my name, phone, gas, water, garbage, electric, Internet, newspaper subscription, and collected all the information I needed to get my final payments sent to them in the form of money orders without waiting for final bills to arrive and leaving no reason for the Post Office to need a forwarding address. Tuesday, I called my Aunt out in Seattle and explained to her that I would be unavailable for a while as I had sold my home and planned on starting a new life somewhere in the southwestern part of the country. I told her I was tired of the long winter months of Minnesota, a reason I knew she would understand having once been a resident of Minnesota herself in her younger days, and assured her that I would be in touch once I had settled into my new area. By Wednesday afternoon, had anyone been looking for me, namely Dr. James, it would appear that I had simply vanished.

Thursday afternoon, the larger party room that Harry had originally introduced me to some of the family in, the piano rolled off into a corner, was set up with several large banquet tables forming a square leaving gaps at the corners, preparing to seat as many as 40 people on the outside of the square as the staff served the guests from the inside. Apparently, this family I had agreed to become a part of was quite a bit larger than I had imagined. But the very sober and almost dour mood that seemed to envelope the castle during the week left no doubt that the gathering was not going to be a party. Also set up in the parlor was a large tack board on one of the walls that displayed some twenty articles similar to and including the three Harry had shown me Sunday morning.

Harry had never actually explained to me what he thought had been "starting" when he had said as much that Sunday morning, but I'm sure he knew he hadn't needed to. I had been standing right next to him when Shkarbala had answered his call for when Lucifer was supposedly going to make his move on the Earth. The answer had been December of 2005. It was the middle of September. If I were to believe everything that Harry had told me as fact, as apparently all the people who were willing to put their lives on hold at the drop of a hat in answer to Harry's call did, then mankind had two and a half months left before it became the playpen of a ruthless and evil Immortal. How Harry had planned to stop this Immortal from keeping His two-thousand-year-old promise from coming to fruition, I had no idea, but then I didn't think Harry did either.

Friday morning, battling a small case of cabin fever, I decided to put on my helmet for the first time and take a ride on Shadow just to get out of the house for a while. The whole scene and atmosphere had taken on a surreal feeling and the feel of the crisp, chilly autumn wind pressing against me had a taste of reality that I had been missing while cooped up in the castle since going out to buy money orders on Tuesday morning. I found myself riding by the house I had grown up in and the sense of things just not being quite right returned as I saw parked in the driveway two cars I didn't recognize and two more parked on the street out front.

When I returned to 14 Crimson Lane a couple of hours later, there were only a few cars parked along side the drive, but I knew by evening, the entire driveway was going to be lined with vehicles.

I took a deep breath as I met Chauncy at the front door. This was my family now. Granted most of them were still strangers to me, but I promised myself I wasn't going to let the claustrophobic feeling that usually came over me in large crowds overcome me tonight. I was, after all, number five. Even though I had not volunteered for the role, I was apparently going to be playing an important one in whatever the coming weeks and months were going to unfold, and for Harry, for all he had done for me, I didn't want to let him down.

The library began to fill up by 5 PM. I had to search for any familiar faces when I left my room shortly after five and joined the collection of people assembling in the large room. I found Randi sitting by herself on the same couch we had shared when celebrating Benny's return from the hospital earlier that week, solemnly watching the fire burning in the hearth and sat down next to her. Like me, she seemed to shy away from the crowds. We sat in silence for a long moment watching the dancing flames of the fire, paying no attention to the subdued chatter coming from all the people that had begun to fill the room.

"Do you believe all this stuff about Lucifer coming back to claim the Earth as his own?" I finally asked her.

"He tried once before," she said, without looking up from the fire. "I don't see why He wouldn't try again."

"But how can you know that everything Harry says is true?" I asked her. " How do you know Paul's translations are right? How can *any* of this be real? And why are we the only ones that know about it?"

I had a hundred more questions I wanted to ask her, too.

Without looking away from the fire, she said softly, "I can see inside their minds, remember? What I *know* is that they both believe everything they have told us and I trust Harry. If he or Paul were lying or had any doubts at all about what they believe, I would know it. Harry hasn't lied and he has no doubts. It's all very real."

Suddenly the rest of the questions that had been lining up in my head didn't seem to matter. I stared at the fire with her trying to absorb what she had just said and all the implications that came with it. It only stood to reason that if Harry and the rest of the family believed all this to be true, that Lucifer was indeed coming to assume control of the Earth and its people, then this family's purpose was to try to stop Him from succeeding. And I was expected to help. Both Randi and I, in fact, being strong shiners according to Harry, were supposedly going to be playing key roles in this attempt to prevent Lucifer and his band of Immortals from having their way with us. I may not have known Randi all that well yet and I still hadn't met the other three shiners Harry had apparently recruited into our family, but I did know myself pretty well and I was fairly certain that there was absolutely nothing I could do to prevent this all from happening, if indeed it was happening at all. What chance could I possibly have, or any of us mortals have, against a giant Immortal race that used 80% of their brains and plotted to take over entire planets?

Not sure that I really wanted to know her answer, I asked anyway. "Do you think we have a chance?"

The pensive look on her face didn't even flinch as she answered my question without hesitation. "Not a chance in Hell."

...which, it occurred to me, would be precisely where we'd be if we failed.

At 6 PM Chauncy came in and announced that we could begin moving to the parlor where dinner would be served shortly and the crowded room slowly began filing out of the library a few at a time. When Randi got up to follow suit, I did the same.

We hadn't spoken another word during the half-hour that had followed her hopeless response to my question, each of us lost in our own thoughts about what may or may not lie in our near future. I had indeed shared in her belief, that we didn't have a chance in the battle that apparently awaited us in the next couple of months, but I was also very anxious to see how Harry was going to approach this "defining time in mankind's history," as he had put it in one of our earlier talks. I knew he wasn't about to give up, and I didn't believe Randi had actually 'given up' either. But I had a feeling that Harry didn't share our belief in our chances and that idea alone gave me at least a little hope. I barely knew him, when I thought about it, but for some reason that I couldn't readily explain even to myself, I had faith in Harry. I trusted him. It might not have been visible to the naked eye, but Harry seemed to have his own little shine that I think everyone there was aware of even if they couldn't see it. And as I followed Randi through the main dining room and then took a seat at one of the long tables in the parlor, I decided I would follow him to the end and do whatever I could to help him help us. The decision wasn't actually all that tough. If he were right, the other options were far worse.

The conversation had understandably not been the happy, light hearted chatter of the previous dinners I had experienced in Paul's home. Every single chair had been filled with family members and most, a few at a time as we ate, had gotten out of their seats to scan the stories tacked up on the board on the wall. The voices were not whispered by any means, but the sound of silverware clinking against the plates and bowls could still easily be heard above the chatter as people talked quietly mostly to those seated next to them instead of to the group or across the tables as had been the case before.

I took my turn as well at the board, reading about several other totally unexplainable phenomena that had left the scientific experts of the area completely in the dark. The articles came from all of over the world. I assumed that it had been one or more of the family members' job to scan news reports worldwide looking for just such things and had sent them to Harry once so many had begun to accumulate within such a small span of time. Throughout my life, I had every now and then read or heard somewhere about things that had occurred that appeared mysterious and could not be explained with traditional logic or scientific study. Many were just shrugged off as exaggerations or masterful frauds by publicity hounds. But looking at the dates of these articles, every single one of them had begun within the past thirty days, and most of them within the past couple of weeks. Individually, they may have meant nothing. Together, one could only conclude that something sinister had certainly begun. And I guess the forty of us present at that meal were the only ones that thought we knew exactly what it was that had begun.

After the staff had cleared everyone's place in front of them, taken and filled everyone's after dinner drink requests, Harry stood from his chair, faced the group and all were instantly quiet without him having to utter a word. He took the time to look slowly around the tables at each face before he began to talk. He had everyone's attention, all eyes and ears waiting nervously to hear his take on the recent events and what his first plan of action could possibly be. I noticed I was holding my breath and let it out slowly, wondering how many others were doing the same.

"I see everyone of us has managed to make it here tonight and I want to thank you all, first of all, for your recognition of the importance in the task that lays before us, and also for the sacrifices many of you must have had to make in order to be here. I can assure you that it is of a worthy cause and hopefully, in the end, we can all return to our lives just as we have left them." He was talking slowly and precisely, choosing his words carefully as he went.

"I think you've all seen the board on the wall and understand the implications it carries with it," he continued. "I believe you are all also quite aware of what it is we are up against and I don't need to remind you that there is a lot more at stake here than just you and your family's personal safety. Lucifer and his Demons have arrived."

Looking around the room, no one appeared to be as shocked by that statement as I would have thought any would be a few weeks ago, including myself.

"Not all of the locations indicated by these articles are necessarily points of entry, but I do believe that most, if not all, are exactly that. Benny and I have paired each of you up to go visit each of these sites in search of anything that might give us an idea of how he plans to do what it is he has come to do. With any luck, we will be able to prevent him from succeeding.

"I must confess that I haven't a clue what it is we are looking for, but trust your instincts. Check in with Paul every day. Report anything that seems not right, no matter how trivial it may appear. Paul will remain here looking for patterns in your reports and I will be checking in with him every day to find out if anyone has discovered anything or needs more assistance in their area. We are all working together on this. Do not be afraid to ask for help should you feel you need it.

"Keep in mind that the Immortals are not that different than us. They are bound to most of the same laws of physics that we are though they are capable of manipulating our minds, making us see things that may not be as they are. If they are aware of your presence, they may also implant ideas in your head that you will believe to be your own. If you do think you have found one of Lucifer's army, let Paul know and wait for help. Do not take any action alone.

"They can not travel without transportation. Many will more than likely still be in the same areas that they have arrived. But also keep in mind that we have no idea of their numbers or how many may have arrived at each of these points of entry. Although the Immortals are not truly immortal and can be killed, I don't want any of you to try to do so on your own. You will not succeed and will only end up getting yourselves killed instead.

"I don't believe we need to be hunting down his Demons and killing them off as we find them. Ultimately, we are looking for Lucifer himself. He is the one we must stop…or kill, if it comes to that. We don't believe his Army will continue without him. The only way we know of at this point that they can be killed is by decapitation. But again, don't try to do this alone. We will need all the help we can get once we have located Lucifer.

"Are there any questions?"

I had a couple of hundred questions myself, as I am sure most everyone else in the room did as well, but no one spoke up.

Harry continued after a short pause. "Benny will hand out your assigned areas at this time. Some of you have more than one area but they will be relatively close together in those cases. You can pick up your airline tickets and on-site accommodations from Ronnie tonight before you go. Everything has already been arranged. Benny will also supply each of you with $25,000 cash for expenses before you leave. That money is yours and what is left will not need to be returned once our job is done. But spare no expense on your mission.

If you need more, just let Paul know. Benny has also informed me that he has another $100,000 waiting in each and every one of your names should we succeed.

"If there are no questions at this time then, Benny will begin handing out the assignments. I encourage all of you to spend the evening here discussing whatever is on your mind and asking any questions that come to mind. I believe the earliest departure times are noon tomorrow. That's about all I can tell you for now, except thank you all and good luck."

31

Just as Harry took a seat after his short speech, Benny stood and carried a sheet of paper with him over to the tack board containing all the articles. He reached out and removed two of the clippings from the board and then turned to face the group.

"As I call out your names, come on up and get the articles that pertain to your area and then head on into the library where Paul will help you find maps and literature that you can use to start getting familiar with and take with you when you go."

He paused for a moment as Paul rose from his chair and silently headed for the library to prepare for his part in the evening's program.

"Marcus Blythe and John Wellerton."

Two men looking to be in their mid to late fifties got up from their seats and soberly walked over to Benny.

"You two will be going to England," Benny said, handing the clippings he had pulled off the wall to the first of the two men that approached him. He shook each of their hands and wished them good luck as they proceeded to follow Paul towards the library.

Benny looked back down at the list of names and locations on the sheet in his hand and called out two more names then turned to the board and removed another of the articles as they approached him to receive their destination. Again, shaking their hand and wishing them luck, it almost appeared to be a graduation ceremony of sorts, but without the gowns and caps. And without the happy faces.

I watched as pairs of people were sent to Mexico, South America, Japan, Germany, Israel. Two pairs had been assigned to

Africa. Then another to India and another pair to California. As the pairs of names were systematically called out and the articles slowly disappeared from the board, I began to wonder if perhaps I wasn't going to be assigned an area, maybe because I was so new to the group. Randi too, was still seated a few chairs down to my right, busily fidgeting with a napkin, her eyes riveted to her fingers as they folded and unfolded and ripped and folded again, working the napkin down to nothing but wrinkled slivers of paper. She was by far the youngest member of the family and I wondered if maybe Harry might be thinking a little too young to be sending off into the world in search of immortal demons.

Two more pairs were assigned to China, and then a pair to Turkey, one of which had been Mr. Spritzer who now owned my home. Another was off to Canada while the next pair was assigned to Russia. Three articles remained on the board. The next two were assigned to South America again and then one more to Saudi Arabia. One article remained yet there were still five of us seated in the parlor besides Harry and Benny. I recognized Ronnie and Steven seated across the room from me, the only other person being a woman about my own age that I had never seen before.

Benny removed the last article from the wall and walked back over to Harry handing it directly to him without calling out the final names and retook his seat next to him. Harry looked at the article a moment as though he were re-reading it before looking up at those of us left in the room.

Without standing up, with a bit of angst yet still sounding fully committed, he said, "The rest of us will be going to Virginia. Although I think it is essential that all the locations be investigated in hopes of finding some sort of lead or information that will help us accomplish what we need to do, I have a strong feeling that this is where Lucifer himself has arrived. If any of you want to back out, I will certainly understand and now is the time to do so. I won't make you walk into what I believe to be the heart of the fire with me, but if you are willing to come, you are the ones I feel should be there with me. But it must be your choice."

He made eye contact with each one of us, one at a time. No one spoke up.

"Very good," Harry then continued. "I'll see you all in the morning then at nine in the library."

He handed Benny back the article about the bowing trees and headed out the opposite door towards the stairway and his room upstairs.

"Why don't we move into the bar where it'll be a little quieter and let everyone get another look at this article," Benny said after a moment. "Maybe we can toss around a few ideas to sleep on tonight."

"Sounds good to me," Ronnie said. "I think I'd like to add something a little stronger to my tea about now anyway."

Benny smiled and walked over to Ronnie, handing her the article. "I'll meet you in there then. I want to go let Paul know where we are in case anyone decides to leave soon."

As Benny went off towards the library, Randi, the woman I hadn't seen before tonight, and I followed Ronnie and Steven the other direction towards the smallest parlor. I pointed to the woman with the loosely tied blond ponytail swishing back and forth as she walked a few paces ahead of Randi and I and quietly asked who she was.

"That's Janis," Randi told me. "She just came back from Egypt this morning. She's been trying to convince the Egyptian government that the world's future beyond 2025 may depend on whether or not they ever decide to let us excavate the Hall of Records beneath the Sphinx."

Benny joined us in the smaller room a few minutes later while Ronnie was still behind the bar lightly spiking her tea. "Is everyone familiar with the Virginia story?" he asked, taking a seat in one of the La-Z-Boys the rest of us had moved to form a small circle with.

I had just finished re-reading the short article for the first time since Harry had shown it to me Sunday morning and handed it to Randi sitting in the next over-stuffed chair to my left. "Why does Harry think this is where Lucifer is?" I asked him as Ronnie returned from the bar and took a seat next to her husband.

"Mostly because it is the nearest location to the Capital. Harry thinks it only makes sense that Lucifer would want to first contaminate the most powerful government in the world. He thinks he will try to gain some kind of control over the President and then those that make the laws."

"Any idea what we might be looking for?" Janis asked.

"To start with," Benny replied, "how they got here. As Harry pointed out, they would need transportation to go anywhere. They are physical beings just as we are and don't have any more control over time and space than we do. They didn't fly down to earth through space like birds. They breathe with lungs just like we do, though theirs may be larger and more efficient than ours. Yet they would still be no more capable of surviving travel through the galaxy without a ship of some kind than we would. If we can find their ship or whatever they may have used to land in these areas around the earth, then maybe we can find some logs or records or maps or something that might give us a clue as to what we might be up against or what their plans may be."

"But Harry told me when he met Gabriel in his dream, he had been floating in the air in front of him atop some mountain," I reminded him.

"It wasn't a dream," Steven said, fielding this one for Benny. "The human conscious mind gets in the way of communication with the Immortals for some reason. That is why they have always communicated with us in our sleep, just as they did to the pharaohs and kings in the days of Ra and Zeus. That is when the conscious mind lays dormant and the subconscious takes over. But they not only send their thoughts, or implant their messages into our subconscious minds, as Harry reminded everyone this evening. They can also make the subconscious perceive things as they want us to perceive them. They can manipulate what we believe we are seeing. Harry never left his bed when talking to Gabriel. And Paul never left his side. Gabriel responded to Harry's call just as Ra used to respond to the calls of the pharaohs of Egypt. And once Harry had fallen asleep and his subconscious had become dominant, he was then better capable of receiving Gabriel's telepathic message, which included the images Harry perceived as well as the message he was passing along."

"But we don't have to be asleep for them to make us perceive what they want us to," Ronnie added. "Remember that Jesus walked among us for thirty-six years. We all saw him, or perceived him, as he willed us to, not as he actually was. It was really just a form of masking, of mass hypnosis, if you will. My personal theory is that if they are physically here, they can reach into our subconscious and conscious minds at will even when the conscious mind is fully awake. But to communicate with us from long distance, for whatever reason, they need the conscious mind to be asleep. But it is only my theory. Of course, there is no way of knowing for sure without asking them, which as far as I know, no one has ever done."

"They could actually be walking among us right now and we wouldn't even know it?" I asked, the trepidation obvious in my voice despite my efforts at trying not to sound as uneasy as I was beginning to feel. The more I learned of this race of immortals, it seemed the less of a chance I thought we had against them.

"Yes," Ronnie replied. "And I am sure that a few have been doing so ever since Jesus had done so himself. I believe he was the first, but there's no way of knowing if he had also been the last. I tend to think not."

Suddenly Randi looked up from the article she had been staring at since the talk had begun and spoke for the first time. "Harry's right," she said softly. "This is where Lucifer arrived."

Everyone turned their attention to the youngest member of the family and waited for her to elaborate. She got up and pulled an end table to the center of the circle we had formed with the chairs and kneeled down on the floor in front of it, placing the article on the table. "Has anyone got a pen or a pencil?" she asked.

Janis pulled a pen out of the purse she had laying on the floor next to her chair and handed it to Randi. Randi pushed the table with the article centered on top of it closer to Janis.

"Look at the picture of the bowing trees," she said, handing the pen back to Janis. "If you were to section them off, go ahead and draw a circle around each section that appears to be slightly more clumped together."

Janis studied the picture for a moment and then slowly drew three circles around sets of trees that seemed to have a slightly larger gap between them and the next set.

"Now draw a line extending from the right side of each circle, between the gaps, and bring it towards the center of the circle formed by the trees, but don't connect the lines in the center." Randi instructed her.

Janis did as Randi said and then dropped the pen instantly as though she had been suddenly startled the moment she was done. Raising a hand to her mouth in disbelief, she backed into her seat as though trying to bury herself in the soft cushions. I leaned forward with the others and peered at the results of her circles and lines and we all saw it at the same time. She had circled six trees within each of the three sections that had formed a clump of trees. With the lines extending from the sides of the circles, slightly arched in order to reach towards the larger circle's center formed by all eighteen trees, the results formed three sixes arranged in the traditional trademark pattern that everyone readily recognized as belonging to Satan. It was quite obvious now looking at the bowing trees that Randi was right. Lucifer had left his mark here. This was all most certainly where he himself had arrived.

Any reservations I still held as to the validity of the stories and lessons I had been told over the last few weeks evaporated completely at that moment. For the first time, I realized that what we were preparing for was truly 100% real. It was actually going to happen. And we were actually going to try to stop it from happening. And for the first time, the consequences of failure on our part suddenly hit home. I had never believed in Heaven and Hell, but I now realized that Hell was only a couple of months from becoming more real than anyone could have ever imagined, at which time all we would have to do to find it would be to look out the windows of our homes. And worst of all, even knowing what we now knew, I still didn't believe we had a chance at stopping any of it from happening. But I knew we had to try and I had no doubt that each one of us there staring at the three sixes Janis had drawn over the picture accompanying the article were thinking the same thing. We'd die trying, but in the end, we will probably succeed in doing only just that...die trying.

32

I went down stairs to the kitchen at 8:30 AM after showering and shaving to grab some breakfast before we were to meet Harry in the library at nine. Our meeting the previous night hadn't lasted more than a few more minutes beyond Randi's discovery. Both Benny and Ronnie were going to be needed very soon to start handing out their travel packages to the members that were ready to leave and no one really had much to say after the discovery anyway. It was one thing to have heard Harry say he *thought* Lucifer had arrived at that point. It was another thing all together once we all agreed with him.

I had the kitchen to myself though there were a couple of newspapers on the table and I knew Harry had been down there earlier and was probably already in the library preparing for our trip to Virginia. We were to be leaving at three that afternoon.

After the meeting, before going to bed, I had repacked one of my two bags with a week's worth of clothes and the money Benny had given me for the trip. The rest of my money, both from the bank and from the sale of my house, were now being kept in a safe in Paul's study. I was very surprised when Paul had actually given me the combination of the safe so that I could get at it any time I needed to, but when he had opened it, it had been empty. Now my cash was all that it contained.

Paul's office had been an impressive bank of computers along one wall and a massive mahogany desk in front of the only window with several large metal filing cabinets along another wall. A few weatherman related awards and certificates were hung on the wall above the filing cabinets. It looked like he did most of his daily weather-related homework here as opposed to at the TV station. Most of the computer equipment and accompanying gadgets I didn't recognize. There was also a small bookcase that looked to have another forty or so of his journals in it, his own collection of personal translations of ancient writings, I assumed, since they were identical to the one Harry had read to me from before. I almost laughed out loud as I thought for a moment about what the "experts" in ancient world history and hieroglyphics would think if they discovered this room and his journals, to say nothing of the heads of every religious sect in the world. And with that thought, I was suddenly surprised the room itself didn't have a steel door and a combination to get inside. But then I guess the stone and iron gate out front and the cameras and Chauncy made that unnecessary. And at least since I had been here, the only people that had been allowed past the gate and into the house were those that were already in the know anyway.

Finishing up my cereal, I washed the bowl and silverware I had used and replaced them in the cupboards before heading to the library to join the others. I was ten minutes early and was still the last one to arrive, the others already there sipping coffees, seated in the couches surrounding the bear skin rug in front of the fireplace.

The article about the trees with the three sixes Janis had drawn on it was sitting on the end table next to Harry so I knew they had already shown him what Randi had discovered the previous night. I took a seat in my usual corner of the small couch next to Randi. Across from us sat Ronnie and Steven, both looking sensibly dressed for travel in jeans and comfortable cotton shirts. Facing the fireplace and the massive wall of Dragons were Benny and Harry with Janis in between them on the long couch. I returned their pleasant greetings as I sat down with my morning Dew I had pulled out of the walk-in refrigerator as I had left the kitchen.

"I had hoped that I would have found a few more members before this trip we are going to make was to be made," Harry began after I had settled in. He looked at Randi. "I hadn't initially planned on taking you along Randi. I think your schooling is still very important and I want you to know that you do not have to go with us if you don't want to."

"I want to go," she said firmly without hesitation, almost sounding offended by his suggestion that she might not.

"Okay," Harry said with a smile. "Then you shall come. I am pleased that you are as devoted as you are, but I would never forgive myself if anything happened to you." Then adding to the rest of us as well, "As would also be the case if anything happened to *any* of you. Now that we are more aware of what we are walking into, I want to stress to all of you not to take on anything on your own. While we are out there, should you discover anything that seems unusual or out of place, do not act alone. We are a team and I expect each of you to remember that on this trip."

"What about Faith?" Benny asked. "You had said you thought she was number six."

"I still believe Katelynn's daughter has her place in our family and our future," Harry replied, "though I will not know that for sure until I know her last name. But even so, I can't imagine this mission has any place for a five-year-old. This simply becomes another reason for me to believe that the seven of us is simply a coincidence as far as Gabriel's message goes. I still believe that Faith might be one of those seven and I have no doubt that her meeting with you was no accident. Whether or not she has already played her role by healing you or if she has more to contribute later, time will tell. But I am sure she was not meant to be with us at this time. We are seven here with young Randi joining us. Maybe that is the significance of the number Gabriel related to me…but I think probably not."

I looked at the wall above the fireplace, which I had always thought ever since I had first stepped foot in this room, was just as impressive as the thousands of books making up most of the other two walls, and a thought came to me.

"There are seven Dragons on the wall," I said, almost to myself as much as to the group. And then a question I had briefly wondered about on more than one occasion, "Where did this come from, anyway?"

"Steven painted it," Harry said, and I noticed Steven across from me suddenly smiling with obvious pride as Harry continued. "The scene appeared to me in a very vivid dream during the time this house was being constructed. I knew Steven was an artist, he is the one that painted most of the paintings you see hanging on the walls in the other rooms, too. I described to him the scene and he duplicated it as precisely as it could have been done, certainly more so that I would have imagined anyone was capable of. It took him six months to paint it, and I'd swear, it is exactly as I remember it from the dream."

"You were very precise in your descriptions," Steven added. "You made it easy. And if you remember, during those six months, you were in here almost as much as I was, always looking over my shoulder and feeding me little details as I went."

"Still, it was an amazing job. You are a gifted artist, Steven. I have never understood why you refuse to sell any of your work."

"But then I would never be able to see them again myself. It's just a personal hobby," he said, looking a little flustered by the compliment.

"But that is something to be considered as we move on here," Harry said, looking back at me with another of his rare smiles over the past week. "An observation worth keeping in mind."

The subject as to the significance of the number seven being dropped for now, the conversation turned towards the trip itself, where we would be staying, and our initial plan of action. The plan started with going to the site of the bowing trees of course, after getting settled into our rooms at the Holiday Inn Ronnie had made reservations for us at, and looking for clues or less obvious signs of Lucifer's arrival. At shortly past eleven, Ronnie, Steven and Janis left to get their things together and promised to meet us at the airport. Benny and Harry went upstairs to start packing, and Randi and I, already packed, went out towards the small beach for a smoke.

By 2 PM, the seven of us were once again united at the airport while slowly making our way through security to wait for our departure time. There wasn't much talk among us as we sat waiting in the settee area to board. I had never even been on a plane before, to say nothing of traveling so far from where I had spent my entire life, but it was obvious that I was not the only one feeling more than a little bit nervous about the trip which we were about to embark on.

33

B y the time we had finally arrived in Richmond, Virginia, rented three cars and settled in to our rooms, it was already past 9 PM having also lost an hour to the time change somewhere during the flight. We had a late meal together in the hotel's restaurant and made plans to meet in the lobby the next morning at ten. I didn't sleep that well and what little sleep I had gotten had been filled with terrifying dreams like I had never had before. Fortunately, they dissipated rapidly each time I had awakened, but a sheen of nervous sweat had dampened my pillow. But despite Harry's assurance that Lucifer most certainly looked nothing like the red, horned villain which traditional folklore had assigned to him, and that even if we *did* find him, we probably wouldn't know it because he would appear just as we did, it seemed his traditional appearance was an ever-present figure in my mind whenever my eyes had shut.

Finally, once the sun began peaking through the curtains, I gave up on trying for any solid rest and watched several versions of the morning news while trying to do a crossword puzzle out of a paper I picked up in the lobby. Nothing appeared to be out of the ordinary locally, but then if Harry had been correct as to why Lucifer had chosen this particular spot to arrive, it only stood to reason that he had been in Washington DC for more than a week already.

Over breakfast, Harry didn't speak much. He appeared to be lost in his own thoughts, often frowning suddenly even at times when nothing had been said. The rest of us tried tossing around ideas on what we might be looking for at the site of the bowing trees. We decided that today we'd try to scour the entire orchard, see if any trees other than those in the picture had been affected in any way, talk to the owner of the field as well as his neighbors to see if they had heard or seen anything peculiar the night the phenomenon had occurred. We all agreed that Lucifer himself had long since left the area so our nerves had noticeably settled down though several of the others looked as though they hadn't slept any better than I had that night.

Ultimately, we all decided that Ronnie and Steven would go to the office of the Richmond Times and look for any follow up stories the paper might have written and possibly even try to talk to the reporters that had written them while the rest of us went out to the farm a few miles north of the city limits.

Finding out where it was had been no trouble at all. When Janis had asked the desk clerk if she was familiar with the story and knew where it was, she had given us the information without even thinking about it. It was fairly obvious that it hadn't been the first time. She rattled off the directions to Bob Bailey's farm from memory and even suggested we get there early before the lines got too long.

Asked if she had seen it herself yet, she said no, she hadn't had the time with work and all. I got the impression that she maybe thought it was all just a publicity stunt put on by Mr. Bailey somehow.

When we got out there ourselves, it was easy to understand why the desk clerk might have believed that it was all an elaborate hoax cooked up by Mr. Bailey. There was a $5 admission charge to gaze at the bowing trees and he had quickly built a seven-foot-high fence around the area to keep people from trying to cut through the orchard from a different direction for a free peek.

The country road was already lined with cars when we arrived a little before noon. I half expected Mrs. Bailey to be in the driveway selling apples at outrageous prices, claiming they were from the bowing trees themselves. But all we found was a sign pointing to the roped off pathway that said, "Bowing Trees This Way!" Maybe they simply hadn't thought of the apple angle yet.

The hike out to the site itself was about a half mile through his orchard, the $5 charge coming *after* the short walk to the opposite end of his field. Mr. Bailey probably figured people would be more apt to pay his fee once they had already made the trek out there. He was only allowing a single group at a time to enter. It didn't matter how many were in the group, as long as they had come to see the spectacle together. "That way," he explained to each group as he took their money and shoved it into the bib of his permanently dirty overalls while making them wait for the previous group to exit back through the gate, "it don't get too crowded on the inside an' you kin better 'preciate God's miracle."

I'm sure he had no idea how close to the truth that statement actually was.

There were about two dozen people in line ahead of us but the wait was only about fifteen minutes as people tended to walk in, examine the unbroken trunks and then exit only a couple of minutes later through the same gate which blocked any view to those that hadn't yet paid their fee. There really wasn't anything else to do inside the fence once you had seen the phenomenon first hand.

When it came to be our turn to enter, Harry spoke to Bob a moment and then paid the man $50 instead of the posted $25. This was to get permission to take a walk around outside the roped off area so we could inspect the supposedly unaffected trees as well. Bob grinned a big toothless grin as he shoved the money into his overalls with the rest of his bounty.

The circle made by the trees was much less obvious than it had been from the over head shot from the newspaper's helicopter.

The five of us walked silently around the outside of the circle as the many people before us had, feeling the bends in the trunks for any stress cracks and marveling at the seemingly impossibly still smooth bark that lined them. Randi even went so far as to give a hard tug downward on some of the branches that had reached out to sweep the ground. There was no give. It was just as though the trees had been grown that way.

Hesitantly, I was the first to venture out into the center of the circle made by the bowing trees and scraped with my feet at the soil beneath them. "You think we should get a metal detector out here?" I asked Harry as he joined me at the center following my attention to ground.

"That's not a bad idea," he said, "but I don't think we are going to find anything here anyway. The ground doesn't look like it's been dug up. If anything were down there, the dirt it displaced would have to have gone somewhere and there would probably be a slight bulge over the ground or some slightly off colored topsoil. This area looks natural and undisturbed."

Janis, who was an archeologist by trade, also heard my question and walked over for a closer look at the ground herself before agreeing with Harry. "There's nothing down there that was put there in the last couple weeks anyway," she said. "But I still want to get a good look at the rest of the field around here."

Looking up, I saw nothing but a few puffy clouds floating by on a nice early fall Virginia afternoon. Randi, standing by and looking bored as though waiting for us all to make up our minds to go, bent over and casually picked up a pebble, heaving it into the air above the circle's center. The resulting pang that sounded as the pebble deflected of the air itself and almost hit me in the head froze everyone of us instantly. No one said a word. All of us staring up at the empty sky.

Randi picked up another pebble, a larger one this time and Harry quickly stopped her from throwing it. "We all saw it," he said. "No need to let everyone know what we've found here."

Randi dropped the rock. If I'd had my wits about me at the time, I would have reminded her that flies love to explore open mouths, but just then I was sending out my own invitation to the flies as well.

Before anyone else could speak, Harry headed for the gate, the rest of us still rooted to the ground with our necks cocked back as we stared at absolutely nothing.

At the gate I heard Harry call Bob inside to join us. "Would $500 get you to close up shop for the day?" he asked.

Bob played coy for a moment even though he was already practically salivating at the thought. "I don know. We git a whole lotta folks comin' down e'ery day, y'know. Some a dem travel quite a spell to git here, too"

"Make it a thousand and you hold 'em all off at the drive back at the house for the day," Harry said.

Bob Bailey's smile vanished and his brows drew closer together. It was easy to read the gear or two still working in his mind. "You fin' sometin' in here I should know 'bout?" he asked. Suddenly he was thinking maybe if this man was willing to pay a thousand bucks just to keep people away for a day, there must be something even more valuable in there than he knew. He might just want to close up and chase everybody away, including us, and have another peek himself for what he had apparently missed.

Harry could also see what was going through ol' Bob's mind and tried to settle his worries. "We're from the Department of Conservation out of DC. We just need some time to take some soil samples and maybe a little sap from a couple of the trees, but we'll make sure we don't damage anything for you. We can get the sap from some of the branches and maybe a few leaves and a sample of the bark, but we won't touch the bends. Tomorrow you can open up again and no one will be able to even tell we were here. Your little business can keep right on going as it was. But I would like to have it for the day and we might need to go get a few pieces of equipment, you know, cameras, spades, and stuff. Tomorrow you wouldn't even know we were here yourself. You think you can keep people away from here the rest of the day?"

Bob paused and for a minute I didn't think he was going to fall for it. We didn't look much like the Department of Conservation out of DC. Two large, older bald men, one younger bald man, one good looking young lady and another wild looking one that was dressed in all black and looked more like she belonged in a back alley in New York City with fellow gang members of misfits and rebellious teens instead of working for the government.

"Make it two gran' an' ya got yerseff a deal," he said, still looking at us like we might be trying to pull something over on him.

"You drive a hard bargain," Harry said, pulling his wallet out of his pocket. He counted out two thousand dollars in hundreds and then held it out in front of Bob, but pulled it back a bit as Bob started to grab at it. "You sure you can keep folks from trying to sneak back here now? And you don't want to go tellin' everyone that it's government folks out here either 'cause that'll just make your job even harder, if you know what I mean. Everybody always wants to see what the government is doing, but we really won't be doing too much. We just need a little privacy so we can do our job proper." Harry said, not yet turning over the cash.

"Oh, I'm sure," Bob said, his eyes never leaving the wad in Harry's hand. "I make real sure. You jus' make sure you leave dis place jus' da way ya found her an' I'll keep 'em 'way fer ya."

"Then I guess we have a deal," Harry said, finally handing over the money.

Bob stuffed the cash into his overalls and went back out the gate leaving us inside again by ourselves. "Sorry, folks," we heard him holler to the people that had already lined up behind us to get a peek at 'God's miracle.' "We gotta shut 'er down fer today but we'll be open t'morra at eight. Gimme yer name for ya go an' I'll git ya in for half price t'morra."

We heard a few moans and complaints about how far they'd come but Bob, making good on his word, was herding them off. "Let's go folks. No more today. Come back t'morra. Closed up for reason outta my control today, but y'all come back t'morra an' I take good care of ya. Let's go folks."

Once the voices had died away, as though she'd had a tough time waiting it out, Randi immediately picked up another rock and hurled it in the same direction as the first one she had thrown. And just as the first time, there was a loud clink as the rock appeared to bounce off a metal sky about twenty feet above our heads.

"Now what?" I asked, breaking the stunned silence. We all looked at Harry as if he would know what to do, but obviously he was just as paralyzed as the rest of us, still staring up at the nothing that was apparently something.

"We call in," he finally said. "I will call Paul and let him know what we have found. He can let everyone else know what they might be looking for when they call in." He tossed the car keys to Janis. "Janis, why don't you and Benny take the car and go get a camera, a thirty-foot ladder, a bunch of highlighters, some industrial strength soap, and a blanket and some lunch so we can have a picnic. We're going to be here a while it looks like. Don't want anyone complaining of an empty stomach. John, you and Randi go see if Mr. Bailey has a tub we can fill with water and bring back out here. Then when Janis and Benny get back, we'll think about what to do over lunch."

Harry pulled out his cell phone, the rest of us headed back down the path, still too stunned to talk.

An hour later, the five of us were sitting on a blanket in the center of the trees below the something that looked like nothing, eating from a bucket of KFC. Lined up on the ground beside us were the supplies Harry had requested. All he had said since we had returned was that it was easier to think when you weren't hungry, so in silence, we ate.

After we had cleaned up our lunch and folded up the blanket, standing near the gate on the perimeter of the circle, Harry finally told us about his phone call to Paul.

"This morning, Tim Ang and Kyle Harnish found the same thing over a small pond in China. Since then, knowing what we are looking for, four others have also located an invisible mass about twenty feet off the ground. Ours makes six. Everyone has been instructed to try to isolate the area so that no one discovers what we have found until we decide what to do about it."

"What *are* we going to do about it?" Randi asked.

"We should try to figure out how big it is and if we can get inside it," Harry said. "I am sure it is a transport machine of some kind, but I doubt very much we will be able to get inside easily, if at all."

Randi bent over and picked up a handful of rocks and moved back into the circle's center. "Watch your heads," she called out and started lofting rocks straight up. The first one thrown straight up from the center ricocheted right back at her. She took two steps forward and tossed the next one. This time it ricocheted off at a slight angle. Two more steps and the next one took a broader angle, almost hitting us by the gate. Two more steps and the rock sailed up into the air unobstructed. Repeating the experiment in the opposite direction, she had the same results.

"Okay," Harry said, "it doesn't appear to be too big and it is apparently round. Janis, see if you and John can get the ladder to lean up against it."

Extending the ladder to near its fullest height by the gate, we then slowly walked towards the center waiting for the ladder to bump into the suspended invisible orb. Once we bumped it, we pulled the bottom of the ladder back and laid it at a climbable angle against the object. Janis pushed on the ladder and it slid off and crashed to the ground as I leaped out of the way just before it came down on top of me.

"It's obviously round," she said. "Sorry about that, John."

"No problem," I said. "Let's try again."

Using the original spot as a guide, we leaned the ladder against the unseen orb again and adjusted the angle of the ladder a hair in the opposite direction it had slid off the first time. This time it didn't crash to the ground when Janis pushed lightly against the ladder. She climbed up the first three rungs and the ladder remained in place, eerily seeming to lean on nothing but thin air. She didn't go up any more than that.

"I think it is safe here," she said, waiting to see if Harry wanted her to continue on up.

He picked up one of the highlighters and walked it over to her. "Take it real slow," he cautioned her. "See if you can mark a few X's on it so we can get a better idea of it's shape."

Slowly she ascended the ladder. Two thirds of the way up, she paused and groped at the air with her hand out in front of the ladder.

Nothing. She climbed two more rungs and this time as she stuck out her hand, there was a sudden zapping sound and Janis instinctively jumped back retracting her hand and went flying off the ladder backwards as the ladder slid once again in the opposite direction off the invisible orb and both came crashing hard to the ground.

Janis got up slowly as we rushed to see if she was okay.

"I'm fine," she said, brushing the dirt from here jeans. "It was like a mild shock, but it scared me more than it hurt." She took a tentative step and then paused. "I think I might have sprained a knee, though."

Harry was already on the cell phone to Paul.

After telling Paul what had happened and instructing him to make sure he informs all the others not to try to touch it, he disconnected and joined the rest of us around Janis.

Randi went and got the blanket back out and laid it on the ground next to the gate as Benny and I helped Janis limp over to it and then proceeded to gently lower her onto the blanket to get her off her injured leg. Leaving the ladder where it lay on the ground, we all took a seat next to her to try and figure out what to do next.

"Okay," Harry said once again. "No more blind experiments. We know he was here. We can assume that he is not here now and has already begun whatever it is he hopes to accomplish over the next couple of months. And our job is to stop him. We need to talk about how we are going to do that."

Randi finally voiced the question that I am sure everyone of us had been thinking from the moment our mission had been unveiled at the dinner back at Paul's castle but had been afraid to ask. "Do you really think we even *can* stop him?"

Harry at least gave an honest answer. "I don't know," he said slowly. "But you know we have to try."

Benny asked the next question. "What if we alert the government?"

"They'd never believe us," I said.

"They'd have to if we brought them here," Benny replied.

"But then Lucifer will know we are on to him," I told Benny. "I think the only thing we've got going for us is the element of surprise."

"No. Benny's right," Harry said, looking at me. "We can't surprise him. Even if we find him and figure out who he is and what he is trying to do, he will know who we are at the same time and probably take care of the problem right then and there and then the whole mission is lost." Harry thought for a moment before continuing.

"I think we need to let people know that we have found something, but not tell them that we know what it is. Let them find the rest of them around the world. Let the government do their tests and try to get inside, though I still don't think they'll be able to. But at least they will know that something is going on. That will make them aware and their guards will be up, if nothing else. In the meantime," He hesitated, trying to decide if what he was about to say next was really the smart way to go or not, then finally said, "I think we need to make him come looking for us. But we need to all be together if we are going to try to stop him. We need to give him reason to change or delay his plans...at least until he tries to get us out of the way. We need to make him believe we are a threat. What do you think?" he asked us as a group.

No one disagreed, but no one agreed. I knew Harry was right about a couple of things. The seven of us had no chance of tracking him down and preventing him from doing whatever he had planned on our own. Nor did we have the manpower or the type of equipment to bring down the ship and study it. But at the same time, we couldn't go running to the government, even with the proof of invisible ships all over the world, and claim that Lucifer had arrived to take over the world. We didn't think they would lock us up or anything with the evidence we would be bringing them, unless they wanted to keep us quiet, which also suddenly seemed a distinct possibility. It would most certainly be obvious even to them that *some* sort of alien race had begun some sort of sinister plot against the world with camouflaged ships already possibly strategically in place, but there's no way they'd believe the true story we brought with it. Lucifer may even have already established some influence among those making the decisions where the discovery was concerned. Lucifer would probably be able to just carry on knowing if he needed to, he could always reclaim his ship later. And who knows how many were down here already. We had gone in search of twenty. Some may have been wild goose chases while at the same time, there could be a hundred more that didn't disturb the surrounding environment enough to warrant a news story.

Harry was right. The only chance we had was to make Lucifer come after us, to make him think that we were a threat, and we had to be together when he came. All forty of us. I still didn't think we stood much of any chance, but it might be the only chance we had.

One by one, we slowly all agreed that we should call in the troops and head home. The only questions that remained were who and how to inform of our discovery and how to get Lucifer pissed off enough to come looking for us.

We sat on the blanket amidst the bowing trees for another hour trying to come up with some answers. We finally decided that if we went straight to the government, the first thing they would do is cover it all up so as not to cause a public panic. We didn't want to cause a panic, but we felt we did need the whole world to be aware in order for Lucifer to feel any kind of threat. If it got covered up, not only would Lucifer never know to come after us, he would also be able to go about his merry way unobstructed no matter how alert or wary the people in Washington were. And those were surely the ones he'd be after. He may have, in fact, already begun to manipulate the minds of those in power on Capital Hill. Ultimately, we decided it was the media that we needed to let in on what we had found. Let the media have a short-lived field day with them all over the world before the government has time to react and take over. Then, through the media, we'd send Lucifer a message that only he will understand, something that let's him know that we are on to him, that we plan on stopping him. And then wait for him to come after us.

It sounded to me like mass panic for the world and suicide for us, but logically, I agreed with the others that it was the best way to go. The only thing left to decide on now was how to get Lucifer to come after us...a sobering thought indeed.

34

It was two-thirty when Harry called Ronnie and Steven and told them to drop whatever they were doing, grab a reporter and join us out at Mr. Bailey's farm as soon as possible. At three I was sent to go out and wait for them to arrive in order to get them past Bob who I found sincerely trying to earn his money turning a slow but steady flow of people away as they arrived. I also got a couple of cans of red spray paint off of him that he had used to make his signs with.

"Whatch y'all doin' out dare, anyway?" he asked suspiciously.

"I don't know that I am at liberty to say right now," I told him. "But you might want to think about raising your admission price for tomorrow."

Bob's eyes suddenly doubled in size. "Y'all fin' sometin out dare y'know its' mine if'n it be on my property!"

"We won't be taking anything off your property," I assured him.

"Y'all *did* fin' sometin, dintchya!" he exclaimed.

Just then Steven drove into the driveway with a Richmond Times news van following right behind him. Bob Bailey saw the van and turned back to me. "You call dem out here?"

"Yeah," I told him. "They're all with us."

Ronnie and Steven got out and we waited for the reporter to gather his equipment and join us by the roped off pathway. Bob was standing by watching, barely able to contain his new excitement. Finally, as we turned down the path, Bob could stand it no longer. "Betty!" he yelled at the house. "Git out here an' tell the folk we closed up for today!" Then he turned and started jogging to catch up with us. "I'm comin' wit y'all!" he called after us. "It's mine after all! It's on my property!"

When we got back to the site, Benny and Harry had reset up the ladder so it appeared to be leaning against the air again at what looked like an impossible angle. I showed Harry the cans of paint and he nodded. "You remember how far up she was? I don't want you coming down as fast as she did."

"I remember," I said, as I started up the ladder while the reporter, Jerry Cross was his name, and Bob watched in stunned amazement. Harry had already let Ronnie and Steven know what it was we had found but had asked them to keep it under their hats until they got out there.

"Dis some kinda trick?" Bob was asking, and then I reached the point where Janis had made contact and sprayed the red paint through the rungs of the ladder trying not to get close enough to touch the ship.

The paint held and seeing where the ship was now, I was able to stretch out a bit and make a huge 'X' that appeared to float in the air and then started back down the ladder. As the paint began to drip and run down the curve of the side of the ship, it became obvious that something not visible to the eye was indeed there propping up the ladder.

"Holy crap!" Bob yelled. "I'm gonna need me a bigger fence!"

Jerry Cross had been the one to write the original story that we had read about the bowing trees and immediately started taking pictures of the dripping 'X' in the sky and asking questions at the same time. "What have we got here?

It's invisible? How'd you find it? How big is it? Where'd it come from?"

I'm sure Harry would have enjoyed just leaving them there to do as they will at that moment without any explanation, but he still needed to make sure we got our message off to Lucifer and let him know that we knew what he was up to and that we planned on stopping him. While I had been waiting for Ronnie and Steven to arrive, Benny and Randi had dug out a message in the dirt on the far side away from the gate. Harry figured the reporter would find it okay, but needed to ensure that it was found before it got trampled by careless gawkers. All that remained was a group picture, which I had asked not to be a part of, and then for Lucifer to use his new connections in DC to find us. With a multi-millionaire in the shot who had recently been in the hospital for two months, he didn't think Lucifer would have much trouble tracking us down.

"It's some kind of spaceship," Harry said. "It has an electrical field around it so I wouldn't advise getting up there and checking it out yourselves. But I don't want the government coming in and covering it all up like they have in the past. That's why we got you in here. We also found this over here," he said, pointing along the far fence where the message had been dug into the ground.

"Don't you worry about that," Jerry said, "I just want to try to keep it under wraps until the morning paper comes out. This is going to be the biggest story of the century! What else you know about this thing?"

"Not a thing. We only found it a couple of hours ago."

Harry walked over to Bob who was already outside the fence pulling his $5 sign down so he could raise the price. "It's real important that you don't let anyone in here until tomorrow now, Mr. Bailey. You sure you can handle that? You're gonna have to keep tight lipped about it until the paper can get your advertising done right."

"Ain't no problem here," Bob said, looking for one of the spray paint cans I had dropped just inside the gate.

Smiling once again, looking like the old Harry I had come to know and love, he turned back towards Jerry who was already snapping pictures of the message in the dirt. "I'd like you to get a picture of us saying we were the ones discovering the ship, but I need you to write into your article that we requested to have our names left out of it, if you would please. We don't need the phone ringing off the hook, but we might want to prove to the folks back home that already know us that we were the ones that discovered it. That okay with you?"

"You're the boss," Jerry said. "What do you suppose this message means?"

"Your guess is as good as mine," Harry said. "I suppose they wanted to let us know why they were here. You think you can get that shot now? We have to catch a flight back home yet this evening."

"One more question," Jerry said, laying the camera back on his chest for the first time since entering the enclosed area. "And I want the God's honest truth. Is this some kind of hoax that you set up that's going to end up making me look like fool?"

"I can assure you, Mr. Cross, this is the real McCoy. Now how about that shot so we can get out of here and leave you to do your thing."

"You're the boss," he repeated.

Harry, Benny and Randi were posing for their picture while Ronnie and Steven helped Janis limp towards the path.

As I was following them out the gate with the remains from our picnic while Jerry was setting up his shot with the proper background, I saw Bob had already crossed out the new $15 charge and had turned the sign over starting fresh with a $25 admission.

35

We got back to Paul's castle on Crimson Lane shortly after midnight. Ronnie and Steven had gone back to their own home for the night from the airport and said they'd come out to Paul's in the morning. Janis, who was walking on her own now with only a slight limp, said she was going back to the new house to clean up and would also see us first thing in the morning. I figured the 'new house' was probably my 'old house' but didn't ask.

Paul was waiting for us as the rest of us got home. Before boarding the flight in Richmond, Harry had called him to let him know we were on our way back and to keep telling anyone that called in to keep their area isolated until 7 AM our time if they found what they now knew they were looking for. Paul had informed him then that five more invisible ships had been located, bringing the total to eleven at that time, and were being kept under wraps without any problems. As he met us at the door, having seen us arriving from one of the security monitors in his office, he told us the new updated total was fourteen.

"In about seven hours," Harry told him, "we're going to have each of the others alert the local medias in their areas and return here as soon as they can get here. They are to say nothing of anything we know about the ships. In fact, if they can let them know of their finds with anonymous phone calls and then leave without having to even speak to the media in person, that would be best. The rest can stop looking and also return on the next available flight. I'm sure we've uncovered enough of them all of a sudden in one night to give Lucifer good reason to be more than a little concerned."

"Isn't that going to cause some kind of mass panic?" Paul had asked.

"It might, but I don't think it will be near as bad as the government has always believed it would be," Harry told him. "But we're hoping to maybe cause one immortal in particular to feel at least a little panic."

"The phone has been quiet the last couple of hours. I think we've probably found about all we're going to."

"Then why don't you go get some sleep, Paul. I think I'm going to start calling everyone right now and let them know when and how to let the media in on their discoveries and tell the others to start heading back now."

"What are we going to do about Lucifer? You still think he's the one that landed in Virginia?"

"I'm pretty sure of it. We left him a message and a photo. I suspect he'll come looking for us before too long here. That's why I want to get everyone back here as soon as possible. We're going to need all the help and ideas we can get. I don't know how much time we're going to have to prepare for him and I still have no idea what we're going to do when he does come."

I got up at 7 AM and hurried down to the kitchen to see the paper, just throwing on a pair of cut-off shorts before leaving my room. Both the Star Tribune and the Pioneer Press were laying on the table still untouched and it occurred to me that there was only one paper that would have the news of our discovery and that one probably wouldn't arrive here until the mail came on the following day. But the news would certainly already be all over the world by then so I headed to the TV room that I hadn't even been in yet during my stay at the castle.

Harry, Benny, Paul and Randi were already in there glued to the big screen, sipping coffee and watching footage of the field we had all been in the day before. Bob Bailey could be seen every now and then with a very worried look on his face as he helplessly watched the news crews and specialists invading his private gold mine, undoubtedly without paying any admission fees, with tons of complex and sophisticated equipment as they tried to learn more about the invisible ship that was hovering over his land.

I got there just in time to hear the TV reporter saying, "But just as disturbing as the presence of what appears to be some kind of UFO suspended twenty feet above the ground here is a message discovered," the picture on the TV screen cut to another that was zooming in on Benny and Randi's work in the dirt, "etched into the ground on the perimeter of the circle, presumably from the occupants of the ship which simply states, 'We know what you are doing and we won't let you do it.'"

"I hope that's enough," Harry was saying, shaking his head slightly.

"Well, you can bet Lucifer is watching this stuff right now as we speak and despite what the news guy just said," Benny assured him, "he'll know *he* didn't put that message there."

"Earlier we interviewed the owner of the orchard," the reporter was saying, "and here's what he had to say."

They went to a taped clip of the conversation held earlier that morning as Bob Bailey was saying, "These folks come in an' fin' it right off de bat an' tell me to close up fer the day. I been in dare fer two weeks an' never known it was up dare, but dey act like dey knew it was dare all along. Paid me a pretty penny to shoo folks off for de rest o' the day, too." The picture then switched to the shot of Harry, Benny and Randi that Jerry Cross had taken while the conversation continued, the reporter asking Bob if he knew who we were. "Dey neber gave me no names. N' fact, dat struck me as kinda odd, if you as' me. Weren't no family and weren't no gober'ment agents like dey say dey was. Fer all I know, dey may a been de aliens demselves."

The news reporter came back live, cutting away from Bob's moment in the spot light. "Jerry Cross, the news reporter that broke this story for the Richmond Times this morning, has assured us in an earlier interview that the people that discovered this and brought him in on it were most certainly *not* aliens and had simply requested to have their names left out to avoid the publicity that would have inevitably invaded their lives after a find of this magnitude. In fact, he said they never even told him their names so he would be unable to reveal them even if he had wanted to. All he got from them was the one picture that we just showed you on your screen."

Harry hit the remote control switching over to the CNN news station. There was another shot there of Bob's fenced in area from a different angle. The reporter here had some new news he was unsuccessfully trying to report with a steady voice. "We have also just learned that ten more of these UFO's have also just been reported found in..." he looked down at a sheet of paper that had just been handed to him by a member of his crew, the paper noticeably shaking in his slightly trembling hand, "in Mexico, South America, England, Canada, Africa, China, Germany, Israel, Turkey as well as another in the U.S. in southern California. All we ask is that everyone remain calm. We don't know why they are here or what their message to us left here in Virginia means so it is important that we don't over react as a society until we do know. President Bush is preparing to address the nation about these discoveries in fifteen minutes at eight-thirty, Eastern Standard Time.

"This is Jim Bellows, CNN reporting from Richmond, Virginia. Back to you Bill."

Back in New York, "The President has indeed just released word that he will be addressing this issue to the nation at eight-thirty and we will carry his news conference live and in full right here. I would like to reiterate what Jim said in the fact that it is important that we not draw any conclusions from these discoveries until we know more about them. We encourage you all to remain here for the latest updates that we will bring to you just as soon as they are made known. We'll be right back."

The news cut away to a commercial.

Flipping from station to station, it was all more of the same. The world was probably holding its collective breath awaiting the President's statement. We were holding ours for another reason entirely. I was sure Lucifer would be worried, if he was capable of such an emotion. Even worse, I figured he was probably pretty pissed off about now, and we were the ones he'd be pissed at. Suddenly Dr. James' microscope didn't seem like much of a threat at all any more.

While Harry was roaming from station to station with the remote control finding nothing new, Randi looked at me and I nodded. No need for any messages sent between our minds. We both got up at the same time and headed out to the beach for a quick cigarette before the President was to begin his speech.

"How'd it feel to know that just about everybody in the country was looking at your face in there?" I asked her.

She just shrugged. "The only ones that would know me are the ones I go to school with and most of them probably haven't even gotten up yet. For that matter, it's not even five-thirty on the west coast yet."

"I'm sure by the end of the day, practically everyone in the *world* that owns a TV is going to know what you look like. You're a regular celebrity now. Speaking of school though, I suppose you won't be going back for a little while anyway."

"I called in on Friday and told them I was sick and would probably be out a week or more."

"I guess they'll figure out pretty soon that you were lying. But under the circumstances, I think they'll probably forgive you."

"Assuming they ever get the chance to. I mean, what are we going to do," she said sardonically, "start lopping the heads off everyone that comes to the gate and hope green blood comes spurting out?"

"I'm sure their blood is just as red as ours," I said, with a lighthearted chuckle. "We *are* created in their image, after all."

"How can you joke about this, John," Randi suddenly snapped back. "There's a good chance none of us are going to survive and even if we do, we'll probably wish we hadn't!"

"Sorry," I said. "I guess that's just my way of coping. I'm just as scared as you are right now, but I believe in Harry. And Benny. And even you. Who do you think found that ship, anyway?"

"Yeah. I believe in them, too. I just wish I had been in a green mood for that picture instead of black," she said, cracking a small smile of her own. "I really looked like crap."

I couldn't help but let a little laugh spill out again. "You looked fine," I told her. "I bet half the teenagers in the country will be wearing all black today in your honor. Come on, let's go see what the President has to say."

When we got back inside the TV room with the others, the President was just beginning his press conference.

"As I am sure most of you watching this morning are aware, it has been reported that several possible UFO's have been discovered this morning in several countries around the world, including two here in the U.S. Obviously the first thing I have to stress to every American out there is that there is no need to over react. We may even still discover that this is some kind of elaborate prank. We're trying to locate the individuals that claim to have found the ship in Virginia who refused to leave their names and find out how they discovered them. The rest of the presumed UFO's that were discovered around the world were phoned in to the media anonymously. The fact that they were all revealed at once and everyone of them with the exception of the one found in Virginia was disclosed to the media within the same time frame, about a half an hour ago, makes us lean towards the idea that it is very likely all a well performed hoax."

"That's hogwash!" Benny yelled at the TV. "George knows who the hell I am. He'd've recognized me as soon as he saw my picture."

"He meets a lot of people as President," I said. "You can't expect him to remember everyone he meets."

"He'd sure as hell remember everyone that donated half a million dollars to his election campaign! Hell, I helped his daddy get elected, too!"

"Shhh!" Harry said loudly. "Let's hear what the man has to say."

"At the same time, we can't go ahead and assume it is a hoax and get caught with our pants down, so to speak," President Bush was saying. "We will have all of our top scientists working around the clock until we figure out exactly what these spheres are. We are currently trying to get the first one down in Virginia so we can find out what's inside them. Aside from that, we really don't know anything else yet because it is just too soon. But you can rest assured that we will let the public know just as soon as we learn anything at all.

"Finally, I just need to say that I feel it was very irresponsible of the people that found these things to let the media know in the manner that they did. We almost have to believe that what they were trying to do was cause a massive worldwide panic for reasons of their own that we are not yet aware of, but we will find out. You can trust that if this is a hoax, they will be brought up on charges and will face the consequences for this kind of outrageous stunt.

"We have time for just a couple questions but keep in mind, we have only just begun our research and I have already told you about everything we know at this time.

"Yes, Mr. Jacobs."

"Thank you, Mr. President. What about the message that was found in the dirt at the Virginia site and were there any messages found at any of the other sites?"

"First of all, there have been no messages found at any of the other sites. And the message found here in Virginia by the same folks that found the sphere is another reason we believe it is a hoax. The proprietor of the orchard has been allowing the public in to see his bent trees for two weeks now and neither he nor any of the hundreds of people that have been there previous to yesterday had discovered either the message or the sphere. We believe the three people in the photograph are probably behind the message as well.

"Yes, Ms. McNally."

"Um, thank you, Mr. President. Isn't it true that one of the people in that photo is the multi-millionaire Benjamin Randall who has been in the hospital for a brain tumor and was also a major contributor to your campaign?"

"Alright!" Benny hollered out. "Finally, someone who does their homework!"

"That has yet to be determined," President Bush replied. "We are working on that too right now.

"I'm sorry but that's all the time we have right now. As I said, we will pass along any and all information we receive to you just as soon as anything is confirmed. But I must say once again to the American people, please, please, do not over react to these discoveries until we know more about them. Chances are better than not that it is just a well thought out hoax. Thank you."

Despite the fact that everyone in the conference room was on there feet yelling questions at the President, he turned his back and walked quickly out the same way he had come in.

"Well, there you have it," Bill Warner for CNN News was saying as the picture on the TV cut back to him in New York. "Most likely an elaborate hoax. Please stay with us. When we come back after a quick break, we will have our discussion panel give *their* views on what the President has just said."

"It was bullshit," Benny said. "He knows it ain't no hoax and he knows it was me in that picture. He's already trying to cover it up."

Harry had a slightly different view of what the President had said. "Of course, he's trying to cover it up," he told Benny. "He can't afford to have the country running around on an alien bounty hunt or trying to dig themselves holes to hide in, either. And of course, he knows it was you in that picture and he probably picked that woman reporter 'cause he *knew* what question she was going to ask. Both of those questions were probably staged, for that matter. He's trying to make you come forward and tell him what you know. He's not going to throw you in jail and he probably knows it ain't a hoax, too. He's probably scared to death right now."

"He ain't the only one scared to death right now," Benny said, calming down a bit.

"Let's just hope the one we're meaning to scare is also feeling a little scared this morning," Harry said. "And he's already got a name to start lookin' into so we are gonna have to do some quick thinking as soon as everybody gets back. We start tonight."

36

Throughout the day, the house slowly began to fill up again as the family members returned from their assigned sites from all over the world. By the time dinner was served in the larger piano parlor, however, there were still sixteen empty seats around the banquet tables as many were coming back from half way around the globe and not all were able to find immediate departing flights or connections, but all had at least reported in that they were on their way.

Harry spent most of the day with Benny and Paul in the library reading and studying everything they could find related to the Immortal race, looking for anything that might give them a clue as to how to deal with Lucifer if and when he came looking for the people in the photograph taken by Jerry Cross. Paul, for the most part, had his nose buried in hieroglyphic writings by the Egyptians from Ra's era, while Harry and Benny studied all the journals Paul himself had put together and translated through the years. A few of the others, probably simply trying to at least appear productive, were browsing through different old looking books they found that they thought might have something useful hidden within their pages. But for the most part, the rest of us, feeling a bit helpless and useless, milled around in small groups discussing the trips we had just returned from and tossing around theories and ideas about what might happen in the near future.

Harry was not convinced that the message we had left for Lucifer was going to be enough to sidetrack him from whatever his original plans had been. Despite the continual news coverage on the supposed UFO's, which numbered fourteen by that time with no additional ones to date found by people outside our family, President Bush had done a pretty good job of making it all appear to the American people that it had been a hoax. More than once on TV throughout the day, I had heard David Copperfield's name come up in reference to the 747 Boeing jet airplane he had made disappear before the nation's eyes some years earlier during a nationally televised magic trick, so people were even already finding ways to try to explain away the invisibility of the ships without actually coming up with an explanation. In the end, what it came down to was simply that the human race will believe whatever it is that they want to believe. If they can't find a way to explain it, they'll find a way to accept it and that was pretty much what the American people seemed to be in the process of doing with the UFO's. Until some strange looking creatures that matched the image of the aliens Hollywood had been churning out over the years came forward and addressed or threatened the earth and its people, the concept was just more than the human mind allowed for us to accept. And if Lucifer were to make this same observation, he would probably decide to just continue as planned and ignore us. What it came down to was the message left in the dirt? If he thought we might actually know more than we did and could truly be a threat in trying to foil his efforts, then he might feel the need to seek us out and strike first. If he saw the message in the dirt as the empty threat that it really was, then we would have to come up with some other way to draw him to us. And that was what Harry, with the assistance of Benny and Paul, was so desperately trying to find.

Randi and I spent most of the day out on the beach away from the crowd, occasionally joined by others in short spurts as they came outside for a quick smoke, discussing our own ideas without the aid of history or legend. Though Randi had been born with her mind reading talents, I met two others that had achieved similar abilities, although no where near as strong as Randi's and my own, after suffering head injuries from different accidents in their lives just as I had. The topic of whether or not any of them had truly been accidents at all was something Randi and I began to feel should possibly be at least considered.

"Harry says we have all been *drawn* together, that we are here because we are supposed to be here, that this family has some purpose for coming together, as though it is part of some master plan," Michael Ross reminded us at one point. He was a bit younger than me, late twenties I guessed, and had developed an ability to read minds similar to Ronnie's, when the emotions were high in the subject's mind. His had begun after falling from a house he had been constructing. He was in a coma for a month and when he awoke with his mother standing over him, he had been able to read her every thought. At first, he had thought it was just a blood thing, like a strong case of mother's intuition reversed. But after getting released from the hospital, he soon discovered that whenever emotions were high within any individual, yet only under those circumstances, he could easily see the cause for their stress.

While recovering from having been in a coma for a month, not having the strength or the will to return to his construction company, he had been bagging groceries in a Minneapolis Safeway to make ends meet when he met Harry. Harry had caught a glimpse of his shine and asked him his name. A month later he was a member of Harry's family and has been a councilor for troubled children over the past two years. He'd always felt his meeting Harry and finding his new career, and possibly even the accident itself, had not been merely coincidence. Over time, he had come to believe as wholeheartedly as Harry did, that we all had a purpose and that, in the case of this family in particular, we had all been brought together for a reason.

Melissa Finch had a similar experience. She hadn't been in a coma, but she had spent some time in the hospital after hitting her head in a fall from a ladder while hanging Christmas decorations when she was a teenager. She couldn't read thoughts, but she had very vivid dreams and visions of people that were under great duress, and on a few occasions over the last ten years had actually assisted the police in locating lost or missing children that were still alive. She had met Harry in a KFC, adding that she rarely went there because she didn't even care for chicken that much, but was feeling even more tired of fast-food burgers that particular day.

"It does make you wonder," I said to Randi when we had once again been left alone on the beach.

"But if that were true, does it even matter what we think or do?" she asked. "I mean, if we are all being manipulated and used for some unknown purpose, it means we don't have any of the free will we've always thought we've had. And who's the one writing the script?"

"Well, *if* it were true, and I am no where near as convinced as Michael is that it is true," I told her, still kind of thinking the concept through as I spoke, "it doesn't mean it is true for everyone and it also doesn't mean that we still don't have choices. I can't believe that accidents don't exist and there is some master plan for everyone. Maybe some of us are singled out, selected or unknowingly recruited for a cause. But I still feel like it had been ultimately my choice to stay here or not. I had options and chose to stick around and see what happened. I have a lot of trouble believing anyone made me try to slow down that truck so that I would have a rod go through my head so that I would obtain this particular talent so that I could try to stop Lucifer from sending mankind back to the ages of human sacrifice and fearful worship of the Gods. That's just too far out there. But maybe *because* I had the accident, *because* I developed this ability within my mind, maybe Harry was *steered* my direction as a possible recruit. But by whom, you're guess is as good as mine and I'm still not even sure I can accept that any *plan* exists at all. Despite my recent acceptance of the Immortal race, of the roles God and Jesus and Lucifer and Ra and all of them supposedly play within that race, I still believe in chance and coincidence. The future can not be written. Our destinies are what we make them. I don't think I'd want to even continue living if I believed anything different.

"How did you meet Harry, anyway?" I asked her. "I don't think you've ever mentioned it."

"He read my name in the paper when my folks were killed. The article had also mentioned that even though I was only fourteen at the time, I had just graduated from High School. But he said he knew I was meant to be in this family as soon as he read my name. I had no where else to go and Paul was willing to adopt me and let me keep my last name. So here I am."

"You are actually Paul's daughter?"

"Legally, yeah. I used to call Harry, Uncle Harry," she said with a little smile. "But now he's just Harry. I think he considers himself my father though more than Paul does, which is fine with me. I think of him more as a dad anyway than an uncle."

"He's a good man," I agreed. "I just hope we can figure out what we need to do."

Left for a moment with our own thoughts, I remembered something else that had been tugging at my mind for several days now, even more so since I had discovered its origin. Unable to shake the thought, I tested it out on Randi. "I tell you what though," I said, "I can't help but feel there's more to those Dragons on that wall in there than just decoration. They look too real."

"I know what you mean," Randi agreed. "I have trouble looking them in the eye. It feels like they know I am looking at them. That's why I always sit right next to the fireplace. It makes me feel like they can't see me as well when I am sitting right below them."

"Maybe we should talk to Harry a little more about them," I suggested. "Maybe his seeing the Dragons in his dream is related to his seeing the shine in us. I don't know. It sounds stupid when said out loud. They can't be real or anything. But that painting isn't like the rest of the stuff Steven has around the house at all. It just seems weird is all, you know? But then, everything in my life the past couple of months has felt weird. I just don't know what to believe any more."

"Welcome to my world," Randi said, the smile of a moment ago no longer apparent.

Chauncy had come out to let us know dinner would be served soon at that moment and we headed towards the parlor, the subject dropped, but not forgotten.

Before anyone left the parlor, after dinner had been served and eaten, Harry stood and briefly addressed those that had made it back. He thanked everyone for their continued efforts and devotion to the cause (as if, knowing the alternative, any of us really had any choice) and presented us with the current dilemma that was worrying him most, how to get Lucifer concerned enough with us to drop what he was doing and come after us. He asked that everyone give this problem some serious thought tonight and that we were to all meet again tomorrow at noon when the entire group should be back so we could try to come up with a solid plan with our collective minds.

Shortly before dinner, being who he was and knowing how to do so, Benny had managed to reach President Bush on the phone and related to all of us their conversation while we ate. As we had suspected, he told us that President Bush was indeed very angry with him for not letting him know about this before letting the media in on it. Benny was able to calm him down however, and assured him that it had to be done this way while at the same time complimenting him on how he had handled the situation to help prevent the mass panic neither of them had wanted to see happen. Without revealing too much information, he told the President that the only reason why he was calling now was to warn him to be on his guard for people possibly acting out of character, that the aliens (not Lucifer or the Immortals) were probably going to try to influence those in power, not excluding the President himself. Then before hanging up, as Randi and I were walking in from the beach through the den's entrance where the conversation had taken place, I heard him saying "I know you've probably had this call traced already, George, but you need to trust me here. Please don't let that information get out and don't send anyone here looking for us. We knew where all those ships were because we are on top of this thing. We left that message in the dirt in Virginia ourselves for the owner of that ship in particular. We are trying to draw him away from there and make him come looking for us because we don't know who he may appear to be, but we still need a little time. He'll find us if he wants to, but we can't make it too easy for him. Just remember, we're on your side, George. You know me. You have to trust me. But trust no one else out there for a while but yourself." Pause. "You bet. I'll buy you a beer when it's all over with and tell you what I can." Pause. "Thank you, George. You're a good man."

Benny turned and winked at Randi and I as he hung up the phone. With a smile, he patted his ample belly and said, "Let's eat!"

About an hour after dinner, Harry, Benny, Randi and myself were finally left alone sitting around a low burning fire in the library lost in our own thoughts. Everyone else had returned to their homes or hotels for the night. I finally broke the tension filled silence with another question that had been gnawing at me throughout the day.

"When you were telling me about the history of the Immortals," I said to Harry, "you said that God had left Jesus and half the Army of Angels here to watch over the Earth for specifically this reason, to protect it and us from others of His race that might come along to do us harm. Why aren't they trying to prevent Lucifer from doing whatever it is he is trying to do now? Even if Lucifer and his Demons had snuck in unnoticed, if the Angels are doing their job, they must certainly know they are here by now. Why is it our job to stop him at all? Where's the cavalry?"

"Well first of all, John, that was two thousand years ago. A lot has happened down here since that time, and probably up there, too. We have no idea what is going on between the Immortals out there," Harry said. "But we do know Lucifer has arrived as he promised he would when his first attempt failed and he was exiled some seventeen hundred years ago. Maybe the Angels are out there right now and maybe they aren't. Maybe Lucifer has already taken care of that problem or maybe he has something in mind if the problem comes up. Either way, I don't think we can afford to sit around and wait to find out.

"When God ran Ra and Zeus off," he continued, "He did it by first gaining the trust and faith of as many of our race as He could. He even sent His Son down to live with us and to spread His Word, to give us reason to believe. It may be that for them to help, we need to believe in them. These days, however, with the world's population growing as fast as it has been, maybe there just aren't enough believers left for the Angels to have the power that they once had. Just look at our history as a race over the last century," he explained. "We've had two world wars, murder and crime has more than quadrupled as the population has grown at an incredibly accelerated rate, and whole races of people have turned on other races trying to annihilate them completely. Maybe Lucifer and His Demons have actually been slowly working their plan for more than a hundred years already, slowly causing the Human race to lose their faith in God and His Angels, weakening the power they have to protect us. Maybe they can only help us if our belief in them is still strong and dominant, which if you read the paper and watch the news these days, may no longer be the case. Or maybe not. I don't know the real answer to that question, John. But like I said, I don't think we can afford to sit around and wait. I think we have to take our future into our own hands."

"Or maybe this is something they feel needs to happen," Benny added, "in order for us, as a race, to regain our faith. Maybe we are being punished for our growing lack of faith. They may feel we've already turned our backs on God's Word. Could be that *after* Lucifer has had a little fun and wiped out half the population, that is when Jesus and His Army will try to save those of us left that want to be saved. It may simply come down to who they feel we believe in more. But the bottom line is, we don't know. Yet knowing what we *do* know, we have to act on it and try to prevent Lucifer from getting the control he is after."

"Can't you go back to that mountain top and make a plea for mankind?" I asked. "Tell Gabriel what's going on and ask for help?"

"I am but one man," Harry replied. "I could beg all I want, but if either what Benny or I just theorized is correct or even close, they wouldn't listen. We can only assume that they have reasons for their actions or lack of action. I would not be able to change their minds. I'm afraid if Lucifer is going to be stopped, it is going to be up to us to do it."

"So where do they come into the picture?" I asked, pointing up at the wall and the seven Dragons that almost appeared to be silently listening in on our conversation.

"I'm not sure they do," Harry said, "But ever since you mentioned it the other day, that's one of the things I've been looking for in Paul's journals, any reference to them in history. It might be nothing more than simply the vivid dream I've always believed it was. But recently I've been trying to recall anything else I can about that dream. So far, I've come up with nothing and the dream *was* sixteen years ago. Without Steven's mural there, I probably would have forgotten it entirely a long time ago."

I had nothing else to contribute having exhausted my questions and not really getting the answers I had wanted, not that I had expected to. I excused myself from the group and headed out to the beach alone for a quick worry stick before heading up stairs to try to get some sleep. I wasn't actually expecting too much success there either that night.

<h1 style="text-align:center">37</h1>

The more I thought about it, as I lay in the darkness unable to sleep, the more I was convinced that the seven Dragons on the wall were more than just a vivid dream of Harry's. And if that were the case, it only made sense that he had also been wrong about the significance of the number seven that Gabriel had passed on to him. Of course, I had never believed in Dragons, but then I hadn't believed in a lot of things that I now accepted as very real. In fact, the one we were supposedly preparing to do battle with had once been near the top of that particular list. But like Lucifer, if they did really exist, I was sure they weren't of this world which made it even harder to understand how they could possibly play a role in what we were trying to accomplish. At any rate, I hadn't been that surprised when they had dominated my dreams that night.

Ever present in my conscious mind as I lay in bed trying to find sleep, they had remained the focus of my subconscious mind when sleep finally did come over me. But it wasn't the nightmare I would have expected when looking up at the menacing faces that Steven had resurrected from Harry's dream.

In my dream, they loomed over me, forty feet tall at least, surrounded by brilliant yellow and red flames of fire that also rose well above my head. But as I cautiously approached them, they didn't seem to notice me as I felt they did when staring at the wall in the library. Their green and golden wings were fully extended, constantly in motion and churning the air around me, although they remained grounded at their posts, their eyes never sleeping, ever searching the landscape before them, fire occasionally spewing forth from their scaly snouts. To both sides were rocky cliffs that rose straight up, the peaks lost in a dark, star filled sky as the Dragons appeared to be guarding the passage between the mountainous towers.

I continued to slowly draw closer to the giant serpents, surprisingly void of any fear. The heat from the fire enveloped me, but for a reason I couldn't explain, I knew the fire would not leap out and sear my mortal skin as I drew nearer and stepped around the initial flames at my feet. Sweat spilling from my pores from the intense heat filling the air. I began to step through the gaps in the flames, and still the Dragons seemed unaware of my presence.

There was something beyond them, I could sense it, something I needed to retrieve, something important to our cause. Something within that passage that they had been guarding for a long time. And still, they seemed not to notice me approaching beneath them. But just as I was drawing near enough to the Dragons to reach out and touch a scaly leg, I awoke, my pillow and sheets drenched in the sweat from the heat of the flames of my dream.

I didn't feel like I had been asleep very long at all, but looking at the red numerals of the digital clock on the nightstand next to the bed, it was just after five in the morning. Still feeling exhausted, however, I knew there was no way I was going to sleep any more that morning. I laid in bed awake for another hour, unwilling to move, trying to hold on to the dream in my conscious mind, wondering what it was they could have been guarding. The sun eventually rose as it does every morning and began to fill the room with light so I finally got up for a much-needed rejuvenating shower.

When I got downstairs, I went straight to the library and studied the mural again. The painting was indeed amazingly detailed and duplicated the visions of my dream. But then why wouldn't it, I thought, as I tried to convince myself that my dream had merely been a product of the mural and my own frame of mind as I had drifted off to sleep. This was easier to do standing in the reality of the morning sun light coming through the massive eastern glass wall. The passage they were guarding, the sense that something lay beyond and my need to retrieve it, was all simply my own imagination expanding on the image that Steven had painted.

That had to be it.

Then I noticed Randi, not sitting in her usual place directly beneath the Dragons, but out in front, watching me stare at the two-story high wall of fiery serpents.

"You dreamed it too, didn't you?" she asked when she saw that I had finally noticed her huddled in the corner of the couch clutching one of the large cushions against her chest. "They're real, aren't they."

I couldn't answer her, at least not out loud. I had thought they were real when I had awakened, but I had just gotten done convincing myself in the last few minutes that they hadn't been. Even knowing then that she had somehow shared the same dream, I still couldn't bring myself to agree with her out loud.

"There's something in there," she said softly, looking back up at the wall, ignoring my unwillingness to admit that they might be real. "There's something we need. I don't know what it is but I don't think they can stop us from getting it."

I still refused to respond, but I had felt the same thing when I had been approaching them in my dream. It was like they couldn't see me at all, couldn't even sense my presence. I felt like I could have continued right on past them had I actually been there. But I hadn't been there. And wherever *there* was, it certainly wasn't any place that existed on this earth, so it seemed to be a mute point to me.

But Randi persisted.

"How do you think we had the same dream?" she asked.

Not only had we had the same dream, but it suddenly occurred to me that it had probably been the same dream that Harry had sixteen years earlier. And once accepting that thought, I had to accept the fact that it was obviously more than mere coincidence or the product of an overly active imagination.

The idea I had the day before returned, that although I didn't think anyone was out there writing scripts for us to play out, maybe we *were* being steered in a certain direction, as Harry had been steered towards those he had recruited into his family. And despite my questioning who could be doing the steering yesterday, there was only one possible answer. Maybe the Army of Angels left to protect us, or even the Prodigious Son himself, hadn't turned their backs on us entirely. Maybe this was how they were trying to help, through dreams and intuitions and subtle shoves in the right direction.

Reading my thoughts that I refused to utter aloud, Randi looked back at me and sent one of her own into my mind. It was her voice that I heard in my head confirming the thought I had just had. *I agree. They're still out there. They're going to help us, John. They have to.*

Randi and I had not been the only ones to share this vision in our sleep. Very soon we were joined by both Harry and Benny who had also had the same dream. Harry later confirmed that it had been the exact same dream that led to the painting, sixteen years earlier, but at that time, all he had remembered from it when waking were the Dragons themselves, and the fact that he had been sweating.

At seven-thirty, Janis arrived very early, a little distressed about a dream she had, only to discover that we were already discussing the same dream. And half an hour later, Ronnie and Steven arrived, but it had only been Ronnie that had awakened in a pool of sweat after experiencing the dream. Steven actually seemed a bit disappointed that he had been left out of the experience for whatever reason after discovering that the rest of us had all been through the same thing that night.

"I wish I'd been invited to the party," he half jokingly complained.

By nine o'clock, while the seven of us sat in the library trying to hash out the significance of this odd and unexplainable new twist, Paul was busy trying to reach everyone by phone, to find out if any others had experienced the mysterious dream during the night. Paul, like Steven, had not. He also found that none of the rest of the members had either. Harry then had Paul call everyone back, canceling our scheduled meeting for the day at noon.

"In light of this dream that we apparently shared last night," Harry said, "at this point, I believe it is going to be just us that are going to need to do whatever it is that is going to need to be done. And I also think that someone *is* trying to tell us what it is we need to do through this dream."

"But how are we supposed to find these Dragons?" I asked. "I doubt they are even on this planet, if they exist at all."

"You found them last night," he said. "What makes you think you can't find them again?"

"That was a dream."

"Yet you remember the heat and woke up sweating. Do you remember hearing their wings as they slapped at the air? Feeling the breeze they made? It may have been more real than you think."

"Well, if you're trying to sell me on the idea that I went traveling in space last night like a galactic sleepwalker to another planet, I'm not buying it."

"I'm not saying you did that," Harry said, being patient with my role as devil's advocate. "And I'm not saying last night *wasn't* just a very vivid dream, the very same one I had sixteen years ago, by the way. And I don't think we will be traveling to another planet to find this place and whatever the Dragons are guarding. At least not in the sense you are talking about. But maybe our subconscious minds will. If last night *was* just a dream, it might have been one of the Immortals trying to show us what we are capable of so that we can save our own race of people.

"When I met Gabriel on that mountain, it was real. It really happened. I was there. Yet at the same time, I never left my room, either. Paul was at my side watching me the whole time. But while I was with Gabriel, I believed that if I had died there, I would never have woken up again here. At least that was how I perceived it. This is how I believe we must find the Dragons. And I agree with Randi. I don't think they can stop us. I think they are guarding against their own kind, the Immortals. They may not see us because we *aren't* really there. We feel like we are there in person because that is the only way we can understand being there, accompanied by our physical bodies. When in fact, it is only our subconscious that is there, which is why the Dragons can *not* see us. They can't see our thoughts. Yet if an Immortal tried to sneak by them in spirit, they may still be sending off some kind of a signal that the Dragons *can* pick up on. Maybe this is why someone is trying to send us. This could be why we are the ones that need to stop Lucifer.

"That would also explain why you felt like you wouldn't get burned by the fire. But we can imagine the heat because we know that fire is hot. We see the wings flapping and imagine the sound and the wind that it must cause and perceive it as blowing against us. Perception is ninety per cent of reality. If you believe it is real, if you perceive it as real, then to you, it is very real."

I had never opted for the philosophy classes offered in High School, and Harry had just reminded me why. In my mind, everything was either real or not real. There was no in between. No gray areas. And Dragons weren't real. But then a month ago, neither was an Immortal race of people that used eighty per cent of their brain. Once again, I had to remind myself that I was in a different world now, a world Harry knew a lot more about than I did. If I wanted to survive in this world, I figured I had better just pay attention to what Harry had to say and learn.

"You think we're going to be going back there again?" Randi asked Harry.

"Yes, but I think we need to go together, and we need to get beyond the Dragons."

"How are we going to go together?" I asked.

This time Steven spoke up. "Sounds to me like you were all there together last night, but since you didn't know it, no one realized the presence of the others. How close to the dragons did each of you get? Ronnie told me this morning she awoke just as she began to walk towards the Dragons, when she realized they didn't seem to know she was there."

"Pretty much the same here," I said. "I had just gotten beyond the initial patches of fire on the ground and even though I could feel the heat, it was like I told Harry earlier, I felt pretty sure the fire wasn't going to burn me. I was almost to where I could have touched the leg of the one out front and was thinking about actually trying to get to something beyond them that I felt sure was there. And then I woke up."

"You were braver than I was," Benny said. "I never moved from where I stood. But I did get the same feeling, that I was safer than I should have been."

The others said they had done pretty much the same thing I had but hadn't drawn quite as close to the fire-breathing creatures as I had apparently dared.

"So why didn't any of us get past them?" I asked. "We all felt like there was something back there we needed to reach, yet all of us awoke before getting past the guards."

"We weren't ready," Janis said. "We weren't aware yet that each of us was also there and whatever it is we are supposed to do, we need to do it together. Whatever is back there, it may take all of us to bring it back."

"Or most likely, it *was* just a dream," Harry said, "And whomever is feeding us the dream has never been beyond the Dragons themselves because they are an Immortal. They would not be allowed to pass. But they needed to show us where we must go and what we will see when we get there. I think we need to figure out how to get there ourselves, probably using the same method I had used to find Gabriel. But this time, I think we need to all go together."

It made sense. I didn't like it. I wasn't looking forward to it. But I had to admit, considering the nature of this new world I had been unwillingly introduced and inducted into, it made sense.

"When do we go?" I asked.

"As soon as we can figure out how, I suppose," Harry said. "I don't think they would be showing us the site in the dream if they didn't also believe we already have the means to get there. And I sense that time may be running short. So probably the sooner the better."

38

I may have something here," Paul said.

We were in the room behind the west wall of books in the library that contained Shkarbala and the book case of journals Paul had put together and collected over the years. A few chairs had been brought in so that the eight of us all had a place to sit. The ceiling had been rolled back to allow the sun light in. Each of us had a journal in our laps, looking for a reference of any kind to Dragons or serpents or anything that we thought might pertain to something we had seen or felt in our shared dream.

The book I had in my lap contained all the pieces of the puzzle pertaining to the Sphinx and the Hall of Records that Paul had found thus far. I hadn't found anything related to what we were looking for yet, but much of the history of the Immortals that Harry had related to me in our initial meetings I could see had come from this book. The book Harry had been studying I recognized as the same book that he had used to reach Touher, the Immortal that we had summoned when Shkarbala had come to life the last time I had been in this room.

We had been in the room for more than two hours and Paul's words were the first that had been spoken since we had settled into our seats and begun our search.

"It's a piece I had forgotten about," Paul said, as everyone turned their attention to him. "It's about an eternally dark land where the sentinels stand guard over God's treasures. It's the only time I ever found mention of this place, but it came from ancient Greek scripts dating a thousand years before Jesus and Lucifer had their confrontation so it may not be what we are looking for. But here's the interesting part. It says that 'No Immortal can pass the Sentinel, including God himself, His treasures and powers laid upon this land are never to be used again.' It doesn't say who or what the sentinels are or what it is specifically that they are guarding, but it sounds like it might hold the type of power you are going to need if you plan on coming face to face with Lucifer."

"Is there any reference as to how to get there?" Harry asked.

"Not that I can see. But it does name the land. It's called 'Aιώvious ttou Xάvetai' which is Greek for 'The Eternal Lost.' Maybe Janis could do her thing and try to go there since she has seen it, if it's the same place, anyway."

"What's Janis' thing?" I asked, looking at Janis. I vaguely remembered Harry telling me she had been one of the true shiners when he had first mentioned her name on my first night here at the house, but had never even thought of it again since I had met her. Especially looking at her now sitting next to Randi on the couch, she appeared perfectly normal to me, though I really hadn't talked to her much and she had generally remained fairly quiet when we had met in groups.

"I can sort of mentally go places with my mind and see them, but I've never tried to retrieve anything, which is what I thought our intentions were here. I'm not sure that would even be possible. At the Sphinx, I was hoping to mentally enter the Hall of Records, which is why I was there. But that chamber must be surrounded by some kind of barrier that I can't get past. But we have still been able to piece together quite a bit from chambers inside the pyramids that have not yet even been uncovered. I've been able to see the walls inside and some of it I have been able to reproduce while some I simply recognize symbols that Paul has shown me and then he tries to translate what I saw. Also, Paul, you know every time I've done it, the places I '*visit*' with my mind have never been far away. In fact, they have always been relatively nearby. It doesn't sound like what we are looking for here is going to be very near at all."

"But you won't be alone this time," Harry said. "We will be with you, our minds linking with yours, following your lead. I think we should try. What do you think?"

"I've never tried anything like that," she said, looking doubtful. "But I suppose it's worth a shot."

Harry stood up and faced Janis. "Just think about the place in your dream last night and Randi and John will get inside your head and pass on what they see to the rest of us. I know we were all there last night, but if it is to work, I think we all have to be seeing the same thing, exactly as Janis does." He walked over to the switches on the wall and began closing up the roof. "Paul, you and Steven can monitor us. The rest of us will form a circle, holding hands. We are going to try to travel with Janis' mind as one. You must be able to clear your minds of everything else if we are to have a chance. Everyone think you can do that?"

We all agreed, though I was still not quite sure what we were agreeing to other than clearing our minds.

With the ceiling closed back up, Harry dimmed the track lighting down to where we could barely see each others' faces while Steven and Paul moved aside the chairs and couches and end tables in front of the wall of maps, giving us all room to form a circle linked with our hands in the crowded small room. He put Randi and I on either side of Janis. Harry, Benny and

Ronnie completed the circle, Ronnie between the two of them and facing Janis, while Paul and Steven stood back to watch. It looked and felt like we were beginning some kind of séance.

I closed my eyes and heard a collective deep breath inhaled and released. I did the same while trying to clear my mind of all thoughts. I reached out for Janis with my mind and all of a sudden, I could see the Dragons and their fire, but could also tell that all I was seeing was what was in Janis' mind. It didn't have the same realism as the dream had when I had experienced it inside my own head. We all stood there silently for a few minutes and I tried to send the image as well as continuing to hang on to Janis' mind, through the links of our hands. I had no idea if I was succeeding or not.

Then I heard Paul's voice slowly chanting the name of the place he had read in his journal. "Aιώvious ttou Xάvetai, Aιώvious ttou Xάvetai, Aιώvious ttou Xάvetai." Steven joined Paul, softly chanting the same name along with him. I began chanting the name I could barely pronounce silently in my mind, accompanying the vision that was coming from Janis, sending it out again through the link forming the circle, my eyes still held shut.

Suddenly I began to feel dizzy and concentrated harder, refusing to give in to the imbalance I felt in my head. It was as though I had lost the feeling in my legs. I couldn't have told you if I was standing up or lying down. I could no longer feel Janis' or Benny's hands which I had been holding onto. The image slowly seemed to evolve, became more vivid and suddenly I could feel the familiar heat from my dream and could hear the wings as they whooshed against the air. I could no longer hear Paul and Steven. I opened my eyes, the eyes in my mind, and the image became real. I was no longer holding anyone's hand, but they were there. *We* were there. All of us, still standing in a circle but no longer holding hands.

No one spoke as we slowly turned to face the Dragons and began walking towards them. As before, their searching gaze drifted over our heads as though they were unaware of our presence. The sky was still as dark as before, darker than any night I had ever seen, but the way was well lit by the flames that spewed from the Dragons and left the ground burning all around us. Once again, sweat began to spill from my every pore as I made my way past the patches of fire surrounding us.

It took several minutes, but we managed to get past the wall of fire breathers and the air instantly cooled and the night became blacker yet, even the stars were no longer visible with the towering cliffs at our sides. Barely able to see my own hand in front of my face, I continued to walk cautiously straight ahead. I felt a hand clasp mine and I reached my other one out, finding Benny's again and held on as we continued forward like Dorothy and her friends skipping down the Yellow Brick Road on their way to Oz. Only we weren't skipping and this certainly wasn't Oz.

Then we all saw the faint glow ahead of us and we quickened our pace a little. It wasn't far, twenty more paces and we were standing in front of what appeared to be a crude stone altar. The alter only stood about three feet off the ground was about ten feet long. It appeared to be glowing in a low light that had no source. Upon the alter lay at first what looked like a stick. A simple crooked walking stick about seven feet long that one might find on the ground while on a hike. At one end it had a little branch extending out about four inches.

"A staff," Harry said softly, daring to speak.

"It looks like the Staff of Moses," Benny said. "Joshua lost it after Moses had given it to him to lead their people to the land of Milk and Honey after they had escaped the bonds of Egypt. Once he got them there, the staff had simply vanished and was never found again. They thought God Himself had retrieved it, taking the power back so as not to be misused, its purpose fulfilled having demonstrated His true powers and His existence to the Hebrews."

"This is what we are here for, to bring back with us. This is what we need to defeat Lucifer," Harry said.

"But how are we going to get it past the Dragons," I asked. "They may not be able to see us, but I'm sure they can certainly see the object they were sent here to guard."

"Can we pick it up?" Randi asked.

Harry approached the altar. Slowly, cautiously, he reached out and touched it. Nothing happened. He closed his hand around it and slowly picked it up, the glow enveloped his hand as well when he raised it off the altar and turned towards the rest of us, all watching him, our breath collectively held.

"Come," he said. "Hold the Staff as I am, all of us together."

With three of us on each side, we all reached out and grasped the Staff with both hands as Harry held it horizontally chest high, the glow enveloping each of us entirely as we wrapped our hands around the ancient stick.

It almost felt like an electrical charge was sent through my body. The Staff seemed to hum and vibrate with a life of its own in my hands.

Then after all of us had a firm grip on the Staff, Harry said, "Take us home, Janis."

Again, I felt tingly and numb at the same time, off balance, and closed my eyes, searching for Janis' mind. The feeling slowly returned to my legs, and I felt the hands of Benny and Janis again clasping my own. I opened my eyes and we were all back in the room at Paul's castle, still holding hands in the same circle, as if we had never left. Paul was at the light switches as I released Benny's hand and then Janis'. As the lights went up, I saw Harry directly across from me, his old familiar smile spreading across his broad face once again as his gaze was towards the floor. Following his gaze, in the middle of our circle on the floor, where nothing had been when I had closed my eyes, now lay a long stick.

The Staff of Moses.

39

We all stared at the ancient piece of wood that lay on the floor before us, each of us accepting its presence there in our own way even though we all knew exactly how it came to be there. Though it didn't seem possible, its mere existence, its presence here, its presumed powers, there it was, the Staff of Moses, the Power of God, returned to the Earth after more than 3400 hundred years of guarded imprisonment. Returned by the six of us still standing in a circle around it. It was almost more than my mind could accept. If I hadn't been there myself, if I hadn't seen the Dragons and felt the heat of their fire, and seen the glow it held on its stone altar with my own senses, I don't think I even *could* have accepted the significance of the old stick that now lay at my feet. It was all too much...yet there it was.

Steven finally broke the awe inspired silence as none of us seemed capable of moving from our place in the circle.

"We were beginning to worry about you guys," he said.

"We were only there for about thirty minutes," Ronnie replied to her husband.

"No," Paul said. "Steven and I didn't want to speak or make any noise at all for fear of disrupting your concentration. We had no idea what would have happened if one of you awoke before you were ready. At one point I even carefully held a small mirror up in front of each of your faces just to make sure you were all still breathing. But we've been watching you all stand there motionless for more than five hours. We were beginning to worry that you might not be *able* to return."

"You formed your circle at one this afternoon," Steven confirmed, looking at his watch. "It's now ten after six."

Harry finally broke the circle and stooped to pick up the item we had brought back with us.

"That stick just all of a sudden appeared there on the floor out of no where just seconds before you opened your eyes a few moments ago," Paul said. "What is it?"

"It is the Staff of Moses," Harry said, turning it around in his hands as he studied it. "It is what we are going to use to defeat Lucifer. Now we just need to get him to find us."

Harry walked over to the stone statues against the wall and leaned the Staff up against one of them, standing it up on end. At a glance, among the statues and barrels of white sand, it just appeared to be a tall stick. Nothing special. Just an old, long, solid piece of wood. The odd glow that it had held in the strange land that we had taken it from was gone. It was hard to believe that it held any more power than any other branch broken off from its mother tree would have held. Yet I had no doubt that it had powers beyond any of our mortal imaginations.

I stepped away from the circle and immediately realized Steven and Paul were correct about the time. My muscles ached from stiffness as I moved for the first time in hours, though I would have agreed with Ronnie that it had only been but minutes.

"I guess we should first see about getting some dinner," Harry said.

"You're just going to leave the Staff in here?" I asked. It didn't seem right. It had been guarded for 3400 years by seven forty-foot-tall fire-breathing Dragons and we were just leaning it up against an old statue and walking away?

"Benny, Paul and myself are the only ones that have a key to this room which always remains locked and there are no windows," Harry said. "It should be safer in here than anywhere else in the house. Besides," he added, "Lucifer hasn't found us yet and I don't know about you, but I'm hungry."

I had already learned not to argue with Harry, but it still didn't feel right, not that I had any better ideas. So far, he'd been right about everything else. And I was also very hungry. He was right about that, too.

Outside the room, Harry locked the door and turned around. Chauncy was standing in the library as if he had been waiting for us. "Are you all ready for dinner?" he asked as we filed out.

"Quite ready, thank you, Chauncy," Harry said. "Thanks for keeping it waiting."

"Not a problem, sir. It will be served as soon as you are seated and ready," Chauncy replied, and he turned to inform the staff that we would be eating shortly.

"Who says you can't find good help anymore," Benny said jokingly, trying to ease the tension we were probably all feeling from the significance of what we had just done, of what we now possessed, and of what we knew we had to do in the very near future.

Sitting around the dinner table in the smaller of the two dining rooms, we talked about different ways to try to let Lucifer know that we planned on putting an end to his plans before they came to fruition. Not knowing who he could be or what he would look like, we all agreed that we had to draw him to us.

"What if Benny were to tell the President to go ahead and release your names to the press," Janis had suggested. "Or where we are."

"That would cause too many people to flock this way," Harry said. "The media would be all over us and that's the last thing we need. The only reason they aren't already is because no one knows of Benny's connection to Paul. I'm sure they are out there looking for him right now. But as far as he and Paul are concerned, Benny was a silent partner with both the building of this house and whatever that thingamajig was Paul dreamed up for the weather folks. Better that we remain hidden here and find a way to draw just him."

"If he's been in Washington for more than two weeks already, how come we haven't already seen signs of his being there?" I asked. "Seems to me, he'd already be trying to influence the Senate or House, or something. Benny said he certainly hasn't gotten to the President himself yet. But he's got to be out there doing something."

"*If* he is there," Harry said. "That is still only a presumption on our part. Also, I don't believe his *powers* extend much beyond mind control and manipulation. I think his race is truly not all that different from our own with the exception of their perfect immortal bodies and their far superior knowledge and use of their brains. But at the same time, we can ill afford to underestimate him."

"Then maybe we could have Benny ask the President to address his own staff with no media," Ronnie suggested. "He could let it slip out during his briefing where we are while at the same time telling them that this is no hoax, if he hasn't already, and that he has spoken to Benny and believes we will be able to take care of the problem which is why he isn't bringing us in or having us arrested. If Lucifer is already among them or has spies in there, he would be the only one to use that information to seek us out."

"It would still be a shot in the dark," Harry said, vetoing the idea all together. "We wouldn't know if he were coming or when. I think we need to be sure. And we are definitely going to need to be ready."

Chauncy appeared at the doorway as everyone seemed to have finished with their meals. "How many desserts should I have Mary prepare?"

A few hands went up but as I started to raise my own, I heard Randi in my head, *no dessert, smoke, beach, now* so I left it idle in my lap. She had been very silent ever since we entered the dining room and had hardly touched her dinner. Now she was staring straight at me from across the table, a concerned look on her face.

"I think I'm going to have a smoke for dessert," I said standing up. "It may not have felt like we had been in that room for so long, but my body's need for nicotine seems to be confirming that it had been longer than I realized."

"Me too," Randi said casually and stood to follow me out the door.

"I'll pass on both the nicotine and the dessert," Ronnie said with a chuckle. "I'm trying to quit both of those vices."

"Five desserts then," Chauncy said and turned back into the kitchen.

"You've been awfully quiet," I said as Randi and I took our usual seats in the sand on either side of the coffee can ashtray. "What's on your mind?"

"You don't use your talent much, do you?" she asked.

"Not if I can help it. I feel like I'm invading people's privacy when I do."

"Well, I do it all the time," she said matter-of-factly. "I don't think it's wrong unless I use the information against them or something, which I don't. It just makes me feel less weird when I see all the absurd and strange thoughts people have all the time."

"I suppose that wouldn't be *mis*using it," I agreed, but I still figured I'd rather not know what most people thought in the privacy of their own minds.

"I like Chauncy," she continued. "He's always thinking funny things about all of us and the things we do and say. I look into his mind a lot, especially when I'm not feeling good about myself or things in general. His thoughts always seem to remind me that I'm not so weird."

She had a very serious tone to her voice. I could tell there was a point to all this, but she seemed to be having trouble voicing it.

"Did you see some thoughts in someone's head tonight about you this time that you didn't like?" I asked. That was another reason why I didn't browse people's minds. I didn't think I'd actually want to know what people thought of me sometimes. Besides, I was comfortable with myself. Let them think what they want.

"No," she said, "It's not that. Chauncy really is a funny guy if you get to know him. He always makes me laugh. But...well...I didn't see *any* thoughts tonight in his head when I peaked. None at all. Twice. I've always seen his thoughts so clearly. It was like he was blocking them or something. Maybe he just didn't have anything on his mind, but it seemed weird. Everyone has thoughts all the time, as far as I know. And I'm not sure he would know how to block his thoughts like you or I could."

"I'm not sure what you are trying to say, Randi."

"I'm not either. But...but what if *he* has been influenced already or something? What if he were a spy? I don't know," she said, shaking her head. "Maybe I'm just being paranoid."

"We should probably all be feeling a little paranoid right now, I mean, considering the circumstances. But he still seems like the same old Chauncy to me, though I haven't known him as long as you have."

"I wanted to ask you to try to get inside his mind, John. His subconscious mind. I can't seem to do that like you can. If he's blocking his conscious thoughts for any reason, maybe you can see why by getting into his subconscious mind."

"I suppose I can try," I said. "But I'll need to be looking directly into his eyes."

"Maybe that's why I can't do it. I haven't been looking directly into people's eyes when I have tried."

She had apparently not been deterred by my earlier voiced desire to eventually lose the talent.

We sat in silence a few more minutes while finishing our smokes, watching the occasional slow-moving ripples in the calm lake. It had gotten dark outside during dinner and the lights of the docks and lit windows of the houses across the lake looked like little stars that had become earthbound, hovering slightly over the water. I honestly didn't think anything sinister was going on in the mind of Chauncy, but I reminded myself of what we had in the little room behind the library and figured we couldn't be too careful.

Dropping my butt into the coffee can, I stood up. While wiping the sand off the seat of my pants, I said, "We should probably get back inside and see if we can help the others figure out what we are going to do about all this."

"I think I'm going to stay here and have one more," she replied. "I'll be in pretty soon." She looked up at me, obviously still worried about Chauncy. "Don't forget to look, okay?"

"I won't forget," I assured here.

I walked back inside through the den and went left towards the dining room that we had eaten in. It was empty so I headed through the kitchen instead of the parlors to make my way to the library. Chauncy was in there, as I had figured he would be, helping Mary and another woman clean up. There had been just the three of them there tonight since a large crowd had not been expected for dinner.

"Where'd everyone go?" I asked, knowing they had all moved to library but just wanting to get Chauncy to turn and look at me. He did, yet in the brief moment our eyes met, I wasn't able to penetrate his subconscious mind but I was able to read his thoughts the instant before he spoke the very same words I had seen in his mind.

"You'll find them in the library. Can I get you anything to drink, John?"

"No thank you," I said, holding up the bottle of Dew I had been carrying down at my side. "I grabbed one on the way out to the beach, thanks."

Apparently, Randi had been wrong. I had known what he was going to ask before he was done asking, so maybe he could block his thoughts if he wanted to. It was hard to imagine, as Randi had pointed out, that anyone could *completely* empty their mind of all thought. Or maybe, more likely, Randi just had so much on her mind that she hadn't actually gotten through to his.

As I was entering the library to join the others, another thought occurred to me. Chauncy had just called me 'John.' Despite my asking him to do so once before, he had still always called me 'sir' or 'Mr. Johnson.' It was almost as if he didn't think he was allowed to use first names because of his position as a staff member. I had gotten the impression, in the little time that I had known him, that he might have considered it disrespectful on his part, due to his position, to call me or anyone in the family by their first name.

Or maybe now I was the one being paranoid. As I entered the library, I glanced over at the little door in the corner. It still appeared just as we had left it, barely noticeable surrounded by all the books. I told myself to relax as I approached the group in front of the fireplace busily chatting away, but I still felt tense. I promised myself to make another stab at Chauncy's subconscious before the night was over, even if it meant walking right up to him and asking him to look into my eyes. Surely he would understand my rudeness if it was nothing. I had no idea how much he may have been told or had overheard during the last couple of weeks. He may or may not know exactly what it was we were trying to accomplish here, but he was certainly aware that something important was going on. If Randi were wrong, I told myself, he'd get over it.

"I'm sure we are all familiar with the Biblical powers the Staff possesses," Harry was saying, "but I think it might be prudent for us to refresh our memories tomorrow and see if there are any clues as to how it works, how to control it."

"Excuse me," I said, settling into one of the couches. "I was wondering how much the house staff knows of what we are doing here."

"I'm sure they've picked up on most of it," Harry said, seemingly unconcerned by the fact. "All of them have been with us for more than ten years now and I trust them like I do each of the family members. They know the importance of what we do here and would never talk about what they have overheard or ever speak to anyone of what we are up to outside the family. In many ways, I consider them just as much a part of the family as the rest of us. Why do you ask?"

"I'm not sure. Maybe nothing," I told him. "Chauncy just called me 'John.' Even though I had told him he could a couple of weeks ago, this was the first time I can remember him actually doing so. Maybe I'm just being paranoid, but..." I left my statement hanging there. I didn't want to mention what Randi had said, that she frequently looked into everyone's minds for no reason and tonight had twice seen nothing at all in Chauncy's. That felt like tattling and I didn't know how Harry would feel about that. I didn't want to get her in any trouble. She said she never misused the talent and I believed her.

"Chauncy has been with us longer than any of the others," Harry said. "He's as loyal as they come. I'm sure it was just a slip. But I don't think that's being paranoid and we should all be keeping our guards up from here on out. I will talk to Chauncy later and see if I feel anything unusual. But he is probably the *last* one that I would ever worry about. Where's Randi?"

"She'll be joining us soon. She wanted to be alone a little bit."

Harry's brow lowered just a little and he looked concerned for a moment at the thought, just like a father concerned for his daughter, but it quickly passed. He opened his mouth and a long yawn escaped. "I may turn in early tonight. I guess our journey took more out of me this afternoon than I realized."

They say that yawns are contagious, and though I didn't yawn myself, I did notice a couple of others fighting back the urge to yawn just as big as they raised a hand to cover their mouths. Benny even looked about to nod off right where he sat. Of course, he'd only just gotten back from a two month long stay at the hospital where most of his time had been spent laying in bed. Yet, looking around the group, Janis' eyes also seemed to be getting heavy.

"I think we're all probably a little pooped after our trip today," she said. "I know I'll be sleeping well tonight."

At that moment, Benny's head did suddenly droop to his chest as sleep overcame him. Harry started to look at his friend next to him and half way there, he too dropped his head and appeared to instantly be asleep. Then Paul was next. He hadn't even been with us on the trip, so that couldn't have been what was going on. I felt a panic begin to build in my stomach as Janis' head suddenly dropped as well. This definitely wasn't right.

"The dessert!" Ronnie suddenly said, looking across at me. "You and I didn't have any!"

And no sooner had she said that when Steven also nodded off. In a matter of a few seconds, Ronnie and I were the only two left awake. I saw the same panic I was feeling surface in her eyes.

"Oh shit!" she suddenly said, looking over my shoulder.

I turned to follow her gaze and saw Chauncy standing in the doorway to the large dining room, his eyes glossed over with a blank look in them, even more completely void of any emotion than usual. But that hadn't been what had alarmed Ronnie. Chauncy took another step through the doorway and a taller man I'd never seen before appeared behind him and started slowly walking towards us as Chauncy collapsed on the floor in a heap.

The man was as tall as Benny, looked to be in his mid forties, dark, perfectly combed hair with a few streaks of gray around the ears, smartly dressed in a blue suit and tie, smiling broadly. At first glance, he looked like a well-dressed businessman just arriving to a meeting. But what got me on my feet and moving were his eyes. They were red. Not bloodshot whites like he'd been drinking or was overly tired. The irises were a fiery red.

Instantly, I knew who it was.

Looking at Ronnie as I practically leaped over the bear skin rug towards Harry, she appeared to be hypnotized by the slowly approaching new comer. Her eyes held the same glossy expression that I had seen in Chauncy's a moment ago. I tried to close off my mind just as it felt like something was tugging at it. I reached the sleeping Harry and started going through his pockets, searching for his keys. Finding them, I sprinted towards the small door. Risking a look back over my shoulder as I approached it. The new comer was still slowly approaching the couch, still holding on to Ronnie's mind, ignoring me completely as I frantically tried to find the right key.

This was it. The time had come. Lucifer had found us.

I continued to imagine the iron box surrounding my mind, fighting off the fingers that I felt trying to find a way past it. A finally found a key that fit into the keyhole and I threw open the door and ran to the statue where The Staff awaited its resurrection. Only then did it occur to me, as I wrapped my hand around it and turned back towards the door, I didn't have a clue how this miracle stick worked. Obviously, there was no trigger or buttons to push. I knew of no secret incantations to set it off or to call on its powers. It looked and felt just like the ordinary stick it appeared to be. It didn't glow or vibrate when I picked it up like I would have imagined it would. I couldn't feel any power surging through it as I hoped I would. But I didn't have time to think about it. It was just going to have to work. Maybe the mere sight of it would scare him enough to give me some time to regroup figure it out.

After only the slightest hesitation, time enough for a quick, deep breath, I came out of the room and stopped, standing just outside the doorway, looking for my foe, the Staff of Moses and the Power of God gripped tightly in my hands. Lucifer was standing in front of Ronnie now, Steven still sitting at her side, fast asleep, as unaware of his presence as the rest of my new family was, slumped in their seats on the couches beneath the Dragons.

Lucifer turned and looked at me and I saw Ronnie's eyes blink and awareness returned within them. I noticed another movement to my right and saw Randi peering in through the doorway next to where Chauncy lay unconscious on the floor at the other end of the wall from where I stood. As Lucifer followed my gaze, Ronnie scampered from her seat and towards the glass wall that had been at her back. Lucifer didn't seem to care as he turned back to me, looking at the item I held in my hand. But instead of fear, his smile only seemed to grow bigger. And then suddenly, the rest of his body also began to grow.

"You have brought it to me, just as I knew you would when I showed you all where to get it from," he said, obviously pleased with himself and our success. "You have delivered to me the last thing I needed to fulfill my promise. And despite your weaknesses and gullibility, I will show your family mercy and maybe I will allow you all to live and witness what becomes of your silly little human race."

In a matter of a second or two as he spoke, he was no longer the smartly dressed businessman that he had wanted us to perceive him as. Now we saw him as he truly was. Nearly ten feet tall. His hair was red, now long and flowing over his shoulders. His eyes the same burning red as before. His robe was also a duller red, tied with a black band around his waist. He took a step towards me, ignoring Ronnie on one side of him and Randi on the other and stopped between the sleeping Steven on one couch and Benny on the next, His fiery red eyes trying to burrow into my head.

I raised the Staff, pointed it at Lucifer, and not having a clue what to do with it, said in a shaky voice the first thing that came to my mind, "Go back to the Hell you were born from!"

Nothing happened.

Lucifer laughed a booming laugh that seemed to shake the foundation of the entire house, and at that moment, despite what he had just said, I knew I was about to die. I was in over my head. I had been able to keep him from taking over my mind so far, but I had no idea how long I could hold him out. And now he obviously recognized my ignorance of the weapon I held in my hand.

Looking first at Randi and then over at Ronnie, hoping for some help, some knowledge or understanding of how to use the power I held in my hand, I saw some more movement in the shadows outside the glass wall behind Ronnie. The shadow moved a little into the light from the library and I suddenly recognized Katelynn.

Totally confused as to what she would be doing here, how she could be there, scared to death for her life as well as my own, the panic racing through my blood found an even more intense level than it had already reached and I let my guard down for just an instant to try to tell her with my mind to run.

But that was all the time that Lucifer had needed to get into my head.

My arms flew out and I helplessly watched as I threw the Staff across the room right into Lucifer's hands. His laugh booming inside my head increased and my hands instinctively went to my ears trying to shut out the sound even though I knew it was coming as much from inside my head as it was from outside.

"Now you shall see what the Power of God can do!" He yelled. "Now you shall be witness to the Power of Lucifer!"

He raised both hands reaching towards the high ceiling, the Staff gripped in his right hand high over his head. He said nothing more, but I could still hear his laughter seemingly ripping at my mind, tearing it apart piece at a time. The whole castle began to shake as hundreds of books began to fly off their shelves in every direction. The tree in the center of the room toppled over smashing a table as it fell. Several of the bushes around the room suddenly ignited and began to burn, the flames instantly strong and reaching high.

Harry would know what to do, I thought, barely able to still hold a thought at all. But looking at the couch, he was still out cold, oblivious to the destruction going on all around him. But Steven, I noticed, had his eyes wide open and was looking up at Lucifer with an almost calculated calm, unnoticed by the Demon himself as he continued to reek havoc on the castle. And then another thrash of pain swept through my mind and I closed my eyes against the feel of his fingers and his laughter digging deeper into my brain.

"FAITH!" Lucifer boomed. "YOU HAVE NO FAITH, JOHN! THAT IS THE POWER OF THE STAFF! YOU ARE JUST LIKE ALL THE OTHERS OF THIS PUTRID LITTLE PLANET! YOU'VE ALL LOST YOUR FAITH!"

Thunder boomed and flashes of lightening exploded out of the dark sky as it opened to a flood of rain dropping from the Heavens and pounding heavily against the glass dome in the ceiling. Just as I opened my eyes and looked towards the glass wall again where I had thought I had seen Katelynn, a blinding bolt of lightning came crashing through the glass. The massive wall exploded out into millions of pieces of glass and I heard Ronnie let loose a blood curdling scream.

Still standing where she had escaped Lucifer's hold on her mind, her eyes wide open in shock and her mouth still gaping as if continuing a silent scream, she was looking at her chest where a large shard of glass had entered from her back and was now sticking out her chest dripping blood from its pointed end. She looked back up at me with confused eyes for only a second and then collapsed to the floor.

"NOOOOO!" Steven suddenly screamed in anger as he leaped from the couch and swiped at the Staff in Lucifer's hand. I wouldn't have thought he'd even be able to reach it but in the second that it took him to rise from the couch, he too had suddenly grown and changed. He was one of them. He was an Immortal. His hair the same blond it had been when I knew him as Steven, but longer, hanging to the center of his back. He was suddenly in a robe similar to Lucifer's but of a light sky blue in color and lined in gold at the edges with a white band tied at his waste.

I barely had time to register what I was seeing as I saw him strike the Staff from Lucifer's grip and it flew across the room falling to the floor next to his dead wife.

The thunder died away as the two of them struggled for control with their hands gripping each others' throats, though I could tell the true battle was not at their fingertips, but rather inside their heads. The rain continued to pour in where the glass wall had been just a moment ago.

I took a step towards the Staff, knowing I still didn't know what to do with it once I had it but stopped dead in my tracks. Faith was running into the library through the broken wall in bare feet leaving little bloody footprints trailing behind her. Katelynn immediately followed, screaming the name of her daughter, terror in her eyes as she tried to call her back. As Faith approached Ronnie and the Staff, she stopped and solemnly looked down at Ronnie for a moment.

Just as Katelynn caught up to her, Faith bent down and picked up the Staff. Katelynn froze, staring at her daughter as Faith turned to her mother holding the Staff out for her to take it. Suddenly Katelynn's panic caused by her daughter breaking away from her and running right into the heat of the battle instantly dissolved and was replaced by a look of understanding and resolve.

She took the Staff from her daughter's outstretched hands and looked at it for a moment in awe. A look of anger and determination covered her face and her eyes became wide and hateful. She looked like a stranger to me, still in Katelynn's body, but the look on her face was completely alien to anything I would have ever imagined her capable of.

She pointed the Staff at the two Immortals trying to squeeze the life out of each others' minds and screamed, "LUCIFER! DAMNED AND BANISHED ANGEL OF GOD! FORSAKEN BY YOUR MASTER! *I* HAVE THE FAITH! AND IT IS EVEN STRONGER THAN YOUR OWN! *I* HAVE THE POWER *AND* THE LOVE OF GOD, THE ALMIGHTY AND KING OF YOUR RACE! IN THE NAME OF GOD, THE ALL POWERFUL, YOU ARE BANISHED FROM NOW TO ETERNITY TO Ἔδαφος καταδικασμένη, LAND OF THE DAMNED!"

Steven backed away from Lucifer as His face became twisted and distorted. He lunged toward Katelynn who held her ground without even flinching, still pointing the Staff of Moses straight at him. But Lucifer, screaming at her words in some ancient language I couldn't understand, only made it two steps in her direction before he disappeared into the thin air, his screams of rage cut off instantly as he vanished. All that remained was the sound of the rain.

Katelynn dropped the Staff and stood there dazed, her arms dangling lifelessly at her side. She appeared unaware of her surroundings until little Faith suddenly walked to her and hugged her knees. Katelynn, her eyes taking on their old familiar shine but at the same time still appearing confused as though she had no idea what had just happened in the last few moments, bent over and picked Faith up into her arms, the Staff laying at her feet, and stood there, tears flowing down her cheek.

I couldn't move, unable to fully comprehend what I had just witnessed. Randi was sitting huddled on the floor next to Chauncy, her legs drawn up to her chest, still noticeably trembling.

Faith pointed to the couch. "Benny," she said.

Katelynn walked over to the couches as Randi, the Immortal Steven and I silently watched. Putting Faith down, the little five-year old walked over to Benny and placed her tiny hand on his cheek. His eyes came open and he smiled.

"Hi, Faith" he said, totally unaware of what had just taken place as he had slept.

"Hi," Faith giggled back at him. Then she turned and touched the faces of Harry and Janis and Paul, removing whatever disease or spell Lucifer had made Chauncy infect them with in the desert.

Steven the Immortal, went to his mortal wife, tears of a different kind flowing silently in abundance down his large face. He knelt beside her and lifted her off the ground, carrying her towards Faith still standing in the middle of the couches. He knelt down to her, holding Ronnie out towards the little girl.

Faith looked into his giant sad eyes and softly said, "I can't. I'm sorry. It's too late."

Steven pulled Ronnie back towards himself and wrapped her lifeless body in his massive arms, his tears flowing freely, yet he still made not a sound.

Epilogue

The President's address to the nation the next day, after a reassuring phone call from Benny, explained that the UFO sightings had indeed been a hoax and that the perpetrators had since been caught and were being questioned in a maximum-security facility. What had actually happened after Lucifer had lost his control that night, within a few hours, all fourteen ships had once again vanished, this time not to be found. We assumed without a leader, they had gone back to where ever they had come from, just as Harry had suggested they might.

Steven, allowing us to see the form we were more used to in his earthly disguise, had insisted that we return The Staff of Moses to where we had taken it. No one argued with him, knowing it possessed far too much power to remain on earth. He also confessed that he too had received the same dream the rest of us had, but knew he could not go with us. His precise duplication of the Dragons had not been purely his ability to paint from instruction. Though he had never seen them in person, he had seen pictures before in his long life and knew what he was to be painting the moment Harry had begun to describe his dream to him.

He told us that he had been on this planet for more than two hundred years and had been married to many wives during that time, but that Ronnie had been the one that he had loved most of all. He was not part of the Army of Angels, which he knew of, but had never met. He had merely been passing by. His ship, which he said was nothing like those that we had discovered hovering invisibly, was waiting in the Pacific Ocean for the time when he decided to move on again. He told us that time had now come.

It didn't take us long to return the Staff. This time we were able to think of the stone altar itself and bypass the Dragons and the hike that was apparently longer than we had realized. The entire trip took the five of us only thirty minutes the second time, though even then it felt like we had been gone but only a handful at most.

When we returned, Steven was already gone, saying his good-byes and wishing us luck before we had left for the land of the Dragons.

Katelynn had told us that she had been aware of what she was doing when she had stood down Lucifer and banished him to the Land of the Damned, where ever that was. We could only hope he could never return. But she said the words that had come out of her mouth had not been hers. She said they were given to her by God. She couldn't have known that He was presumably off in some other corner of the universe turning bad to good, but no one tried to tell her any different than what she believed. Admittedly, we couldn't have known any better ourselves. Harry told me later that Steven had quietly confessed to him that he had put the words Katelynn had spoken into her head as she spoke them. She owned the faith that had brought the power of the Staff to life, but it had been Steven, not God, that had used her faith and her voice to banish Lucifer. At least for now, we had no plans of letting Katelynn know of this. It would serve no purpose to tell her.

I did ask her how she happened along at just the right time. She explained that she had seen Benny and Harry's picture, along with Randi, on the news. Since she had reached me through Harry's cell phone number before, she put two and two together and assumed I had never actually left town. She hadn't called first, knowing from the circumstances under which the picture had been taken that I would have told her not to come, and she would have been right. She had taken Faith and was heading back to town, planning on trying to start figuring out where I was the next day. But as soon as they had hit the city limits, Faith had mentioned Benny's name and told Katelynn that he needed her. After first trying to convince Faith that they would be looking for him the next morning, Faith continued to insist that he needed her *now* and proceeded to give her directions, telling her where to turn until they had finally arrived at the castle. The gate had been left open. Probably Lucifer's only mistake.

When no one answered the front door, she and Faith started quickly walking around the house until they could see what was going on through the glass wall. She said she also had no problem hearing what Lucifer had been saying. His words had been inside her head just as they had been inside mine.

Harry never said that he was sorry he missed getting a chance to see Lucifer himself go down, but I have always believed that he had secretly wanted to be the one to end it. It was soon forgotten though. He fell in love with Faith and Katelynn Rose. They went back to their home after all was said and done, but they visited often and Harry began to think of them as his new daughter and grandchild. His smile was never bigger than when Faith started calling him Uncle Harry.

I never bought my home back. Harry asked me to stay, to make my residence with Paul permanent and I agreed without having to be asked twice. Yet even as nice as the dinners were at 14 Crimson Lane, I began spending more and more of my evenings with Katelynn and Faith.

Harry sold his home as well and moved into the castle with Paul and Randi and I. And although Benny had a couple of corporations to run and a multi-million-dollar enterprise that needed his attention back in Texas, he was not a stranger and came to visit for a couple of weeks every two or three months.

It wasn't long before Chauncy was calling me John whenever we talked.

Janis went back to Egypt to pick up where she had left off. We still had a lot of work to do. Lucifer may have been foiled once again, but it felt like only the beginning; the beginning of what, we weren't sure. There was an aboding feeling that the future of mankind still hung in the balance. The feeling of having won a battle, but not the war, sat quietly on the back of our collective minds. We weren't sure yet what exactly we were looking for, but we all knew there was still work to be done.

About the Author

Born in Boston, MA and raised in the Carolinas and the midwest, David M. Brooks now lives in Florida where he has retired after 36 years in the newspaper business. It was his personal library, a collection of first editions and signed special editions by Stephen King, Dean Koontz, Bentley Little, John Saul, Chrisopher Moore, Clive Barker, Neil Gaiman and many more that inspired him to take to the keyboard and start writing his own stories. His second novel, *As Fate Would Have It*, won an Honorable Mention in the 2022 Writer's Digest competition among more than 6,000 entries.

When not writing new stories, David enjoys playing competitive pool, web design, and reading new horror and dark fiction. A novella and a collection of short stories, including *It's Only a Dream*, *Billy*, *The Ear*, *A Night at Scruffy's Bar*, and more, is next on the agenda and scheduled to come out late 2023 or early 2024.

David can be contacted through his website,
www.DavidMBrooks.us